8774142

The Sempinski Affair

THE

Sempinski Affair

W. S. KUNICZAK

1969

Doubleday & Company, Inc., Garden City, N.Y.

FOR ARDMORE, PENELOPE AND ULYSSES
WHO STAYED ON THE ISLAND

Contents

The Sempinski Affair

PART ONE:

Assignment and Departure

one

THERE WERE only four envelopes on the mail tray that day. I looked without particular interest at the first three letters: a quarterly statement from my club, where we were having lunch, an alumni bulletin (I passed it to Tommy), and a bookstore bill. But the fourth letter, in a coarse blue-gray envelope plastered with unfamiliar stamps, brought an odd excitement. It looked alien and out of place beside the opulent gloss of bulletins and statements; it seemed to intrude. The unfamiliar green-ink scrawl was perplexing; thin angular letters like a straining insect caught in the thick web of the coarsegrained paper.

I didn't reach for it right away. I didn't feel like reading letters or even like leafing through the new *Archeologie Moderne* that Zungfest, my favorite waiter, laid beside my plate. There had been just enough truth in Tommy's gentle jibes to give this day an extra dimension. We had been talking about mutual schooldays, dreams and aspirations; he had been wondering aloud what had happened to them.

I must have had a hundred lunches with Tommy in the last two years and sooner or later the subject of what we had been and where we had been heading and where we finally found ourselves came up, but it hadn't bothered me until recently. Tommy was something hush-hush with the government and pretended to work for the IRS. He was also, I suppose, my closest friend in town, the only fellow graduate of our obscure denominational college I had run into anywhere. Everyone else I saw with any frequency, other than my elegant Francesca, was a business acquaintance.

Outside our corner window I saw snow and people. The people struggled through the snow, heads down, their eyes on the gray slush underfoot and not on the snowflakes coming down around them. In a few minutes I would be among them, on my way to the unpretentious set of cubicles I shared with a literary agent. There I was Dr. O. H. Shippe, forty-two, antiquities consultant, a man who was becoming a stranger to myself. Then: work that might eventually lead to a bestowal of a gallery's *imprimatur* on an illuminated scroll or piece of statuary or an icon. Once in a while there was the discovery of a rare treasure that took my breath away . . . until I thought of the Neanderthal in whose art-littered mansion the treasure would lie. Then, home: the morning trip reversed. Dinner was at eight. A book and sherry, Mahler or Vivaldi. On Sunday nights chess with Tommy Mackin. Once in a while a gathering of people on whom I could depend to entertain each other. I saw few women other than Francesca Grey who had become something of an institution. Each Wednesday for the past four years she had come up from Greenwich to have lunch in town with her preoccupied Albert and spent the afternoons with me. It was an almost marital arrangement. And every Friday night there was the journey to satisfy a secret vice, my one incurable addiction, practiced in a Lower Eastside store converted to a *salle d'armes* where an elderly former captain of Central European lancers panted *En Garde!*

It didn't seem believable that life would never contain more than this: order without shock, adventure or alarm—and, of course, the scrolls and icons, an occasional book review for the *Sunday Times* (whenever anyone published anything dealing with the Eastern Roman Empire, Byzantium or Trebizond), occasional lectures and another book or two of my own as the years went by. Money had never seemed a worthy stimulus and there had been no need to run after it; my father had also been a practical historian. And if, at times, I wondered why turbulence, excitement and exuberance had passed me by, ignored me, and left me no more than illusions of motion and adventure, I put it down to the traditional Gauguin Syndrome of the businessman. Not everyone could have a South Sea Island and, perhaps, that was just as well.

There had been a time when life seemed painted in more violent colors, but that had been almost twenty years ago. And since I still couldn't bring myself to think of that time without a sense of loss it was probably better not to think about it.

Tommy was teasing Zungfest about the alcohol content of his Chicken Marengo. I picked up the drab, alien envelope and slit it carefully and took out the letter.

I read the stilted paragraphs with astonishment, then with delight, smoothing the cheap gray sheets of gritty paper as carefully as if they were a rare and precious manuscript painted with reeds on papyrus.

I couldn't visualize the author although I had seen him often enough in frontispiece photographs of my favorite translations: the Shelf of Old Friends, the perennial favorites. The portraits never seemed sufficient. Julian Sempinski always seemed to wear the mantle of his heroes: larger than life but infinitely human. It was impossible to imagine him in his eighties, removed by so many generations from the time of his productivity and greatness. Not much of his had been translated into English, but I had read everything I could get my hands on in German or French. Novels and letters, early poetry, articles from long-suppressed liberal newspapers and revolutionary pamphlets, lectures and rare speeches. The man was a giant. Until last autumn I had thought him dead. But he had apparently survived the wars, uprisings and social upheavals that had turned Central and Eastern Europe upside down. I had read in the *Times* that he had been appointed to an honorary chair of Slavonic history at his country's oldest university. And it seemed as if the long arm of coincidence could be stretched still further because, that same week, the *Times* paragraph still fresh in my mind, I had set in motion certain other events which had now brought the unexpected letter.

I had gone to lunch with a young woman editor from a magazine which I no longer remembered, but I remembered the girl uncomfortably well. Beautiful young women have always made me feel uncomfortable, aware of qualities I do not possess. A few years ago Francesca still teased me about that, dissecting my attitudes with that easy carelessness that had become so much a part of our relationship.

It didn't take much effort on my part to feel dull, unwitty and ridiculous in front of young women, well aware that my only worthwhile currency was intelligence which never seemed enough to offer in exchange for beauty. Beautiful young women made it easy for me to remain a bachelor.

I sat through that agonizing lunch, scattering green peas, dropping silverware, and wishing that I had been anywhere but where I was then. But she had been attentive and perceptive and very well informed, so that in time I could start making sense and the lunch was not quite as disastrous as it might have been.

Her name was Kristin Napoji. I had asked her what kind of name that was, having once done a monograph on name origins. Kristin was Scandinavian; one set of grandparents had been born in Sweden. Her other name was something Eastern European. It was her husband's name. I remembered the odd touch of disappointment when I heard that there had been a husband.

We had talked about Eastern Europe and the lost treasures of the great estates—the libraries and statuary and age-old tapestries vanished in the smoke of wars and revolutions. I had wondered how many priceless objects were now doorstoppers in some cattle barn. She said that she was going to take a long vacation—a sort of unpaid sabbatical—in Europe, something to do with gathering material for a book. She was particularly curious about Eastern Europe and its ancient nationalisms, so reviled in the United States except when they helped to strain a fabric which was both socialist and international, and in the pseudo-libertarian gropings behind the Iron Curtain. Recent resurgence of official Nazism in West Germany had set everybody's teeth on edge and Eastern Europe was the place to see. Did I know anyone there, some point of reference where she could begin?

I regretted that I couldn't help her. Then I remembered that paragraph in the *Times.* Why, yes, I said; she could see Sempinski. No, I didn't know him. But if there was one mind worth exploring in the East, it would be his. And she could even do me a small service . . . No, nothing terribly important . . . more sentimental than professional. If she could get Sempinski to autograph a book . . .

She had been less than enthusiastic, I remembered. She thought that, as a leftover from the *ancien régime,* Sempinski would be hardly likely to represent new thought. Germany's new Nazis would soon be trying to put Europe to the torch again, and only Eastern Europe seemed aware of it. She wanted contact with new men, not ancient leftovers.

(But look, I said. This is Sempinski. That kind of mind never deteriorates. Nobel Prize winner. Spokesman for three generations. Granted, he's probably at odds with the system over there; he's one of the most militant liberals of our time. But won't he give you an insight unclouded by Party politics and factional bickering? He's above all that. Seeing him would be like having lunch with Dostoevsky if you wanted to look at Soviet Russia in perspective. It would be like a weekend with Cervantes for a review of modern Spanish thought. Invaluable, I'd think.)

When she agreed, still not particularly enthusiastic but willing to humor me, I rushed her to a taxi and to my apartment and handed her my English edition of Sempinski's *Chaos* and scribbled a quick, apologetic note to the old novelist.

I didn't think that Mrs. Napoji would go to see Sempinski or, if she did, that the old writer would bother to autograph the book. But here was the gray letter with the spidery handwriting and it meant more than any autographs.

Sempinski apologized for not writing sooner. But there were

certain difficulties that, he hoped, his kind American correspondent would understand in time. A new kind of project. He had been touched by the unexpected and encouraging gesture from America; so few people cared, after all, so few remembered the trusted old values. He only hoped that his new American friend would not be disappointed in his next and, he was sure, final work; a fitting epitaph.

He had been shocked, he wrote, by the accident to his charming new American acquaintance, and wished to share my natural grief, and hoped that such tragedies would cease once the aftermath of the last world war was finally erased. He would autograph the book and send it just as soon as he could get a license to export printed matter to a Western country. He hoped that when I got it I would want to read it again, often and with care. Sometimes, the true meaning of a book was never apparent the first few times around.

The angular, green scrawl seemed to leap out of the shoddy paper. It puzzled me with odd undertones I didn't understand. I realized that Tommy had been staring at me curiously for some time.

"Nothing bad, I hope?"

"A voice out of the past, you might say."

It almost seemed as though there had been two letters in one and I had understood only the surface message. My imagination was obviously playing tricks on me. Sempinski's troubles with English had not been a help.

I asked Tommy, who knew about a hundred thousand girls, if he could tell me anything about Kristin Napoji. He treated me to the sleepy stare I had long recognized as his camouflage for attention.

"Sure. Very beautiful but too independent for me. I prefer my girls slightly more frivolous. She was not in my orbit."

"Whose orbit was she in?"

"Her own. As I said, this was one independent girl. But, if you pardon a touch of the classic, *de mortuis nil nisi bonum.*"

"Did something happen to her?"

"Something did. She took a little trip to a Worker State and drove into a minefield left over from the war. Now, that is very odd, don't you think? Don't people mark old minefields? But that's what happened."

"A minefield! Was she hurt?"

"That's kind of the line I was pursuing here, but, perhaps, it didn't sink in. She was hurt dead, like my Latin said."

I said: "A minefield! Dead! Why didn't I hear about it?"

"That's what I was wondering. The papers exercised discretion, by firm request from the State Department, but it made page one here and there in October."

"I was in Turkey in October . . ."

"It was a very sad thing. Was Kristin a friend?"

"I met her once. I thought she was . . . very nice."

"Coming from you, O.H., that's a passionate statement. Did you know Per Lindstrom is her uncle?"

"Senator Lindstrom?"

"Do you know any other Per Lindstrom? Personally, being very prejudiced about the far right, like I'm very prejudiced about the far left, I think that one Per Lindstrom, former senator of his arid and humorless state, seventh richest man in the land of the free, founder and Führer of the Loyal Legion of American Riflemen and twice candidate for President on the Lunatic Ticket, is enough."

"I didn't know Per Lindstrom had a family."

"Did you think, like about three million other people, that he stepped down, ready-made, from heaven? Kristin was all the family the senator had. He doesn't advertise his mortal origins. She didn't like his ideas or his friends, and he went berserk about hers, but blood is blood and dynasty is dynasty, and the senator really blew his cool when Kristin was killed. Called her death an assassination, not an accident. Wanted us to go to war about it. Vowed all kinds of revenge. Got everybody extremely up-tight in Washington. The State Department got the news media to keep more or less quiet but, even so, enough got shouted by the Lindstrom people to make things sticky for a while. Didn't the Turks have it in their papers?"

"Where I was in Turkey there weren't any papers. There weren't even any people."

"You knew she had a husband? A very cool, European gentleman with very curious habits. A charming man but a most unbeautiful person. Some of my business associates, in a department that shall remain nameless, had a professional interest in his activities. He was killed in a hit-and-run in Saigon last spring. Kristin was a widow for only about as long as she had been a wife, but I think she had lost a few illusions about life, marriage, decency, the pursuit of happiness and similar trivia, by the time she became a widow. She was an impassioned sort of girl about causes but her husband, although very charming, wasn't a good cause. Hence, all the people who thought that Kristin was herself a good cause, weren't particularly down about the European gentleman's demise."

"What were her causes? Surely not her uncle's?"

"She was for all the causes that people like her uncle think are un-Godly and un-American. But it was never anything organized with her. If she carried signs it was because she believed what the signs proclaimed. As I said, this was a very independent girl, a beautiful person, and a lot of people are going to miss her."

I thought a moment before asking: "It *was* an accident, wasn't it?"

Tommy looked startled. Despite our easy friendship it wasn't often that I caught him off his guard.

"Why shouldn't it be an accident? Our embassy people said it was. Her car burned right down to the hubcaps, so it was hard to tell exactly what happened, but with Per Lindstrom on their necks you can believe the diplomats looked hard."

"What about her body? Couldn't they tell from that?"

"There was no body. The story was that she was blown to bits. It's possible, you know. Certainly, our embassy people accepted the story, and they were right on the spot to ask all the questions."

"But there was no body?"

Tommy said: with unconvincing patience: "There was the burned car, some pieces of clothing, a part of her passport and other odds and ends identified as hers. I can't explain away the absence of a body; I'm not the State Department."

"I have a good idea of what you are, for all your cover stories about internal revenue. That's why it interests me that you don't buy that accident story yourself."

"How do you know I don't?"

"You have that inscrutable look on your face again. I've put you in check often enough to know it."

Tommy smiled, shrugged, laughed and relaxed, dismissing the subject.

"I wasn't there. I didn't ask the questions. All I know is what I read in the papers, as someone once said."

The Carter clock in the corner shifted cogs and gears and struck its first quavering note. I looked up, astonished. I had been too engrossed in Tommy's story to pay attention to the time. In a moment, the last of the morning would be over. That meant that I would be late for a meeting with Hubertus Pohl, my most important and unpleasant client, and that meant that he'd feel free to make outrageous demands.

I swore softly, not being used to swearing with conviction. Tommy said: "What's up?"

"It's Pohl," I said. "I'm late for a meeting. Now I'm in for it."

Tommy said (shaking his head, his round black face concerned): "Poor old O.H. . . . I wonder how you make it in the business jungle."

I laughed uneasily because lately I had begun to wonder about it myself and didn't want to talk about it or even think of it. There really was no reason for this odd, recurring dissatisfaction with myself; life was extraordinarily comfortable, uninvolved and safe, and only lunatics aspired to trouble.

I said: "Well, beards and poetry are gone for both of us. It's a long way from romantic dreams."

Tommy said: "Whatever happened to that swordstick you carried on campus?"

I hadn't thought about that silly stick for years. It had been part of a life I no longer cared to remember: a life of flourishes and gestures and declamation, and all the possible varieties of angers and loves.

My old briefcase brought home this gradual erosion of the spirit very suddenly. It was old, threadbare, colorless with age, although it had been a bright pigskin yellow when my father gave it to me to start the college adventure, with a variety of straps and buckles that reflected sunlight, handsome white stitching and a big brass lock. Now it was shapeless as well as colorless and reflected nothing. I couldn't understand why I hadn't noticed how weary it looked.

two

WALKING INTO Pohl's establishment I had my usual flare of
wry-faced admiration for his histrionic talents. The bronze doors
studded with silver-headed bosses, the saluting guards, the marble
lobby with its sole display—a simple, ebony box under glass, on
a catafalque draped in purple velvet—combined a sense of the
religious and the profitable; a moneychangers' temple. The private
gendarmerie, the hollow boom of footsteps under the vaulted ceiling,
the single treasure on the immense floor, added up to stage
management at its best, designed to breach the defenses of the
helpless rich at a single stroke.

I took the long circular staircase to the musicians' gallery, past
concealed doors that muffled the clatter of teletypes from branch
offices in London, Ankara, Lima, and Tokyo-Singapore. An electric
eye dissolved a section of Pohl's outer works before me, the
imitation masonry slid open, and I entered the brightly lighted,
modern anteroom.

Miss Gruber, Pohl's private Cerberus, took my coat and hat
and indicated the *Times* and *The Wall Street Journal*. Pohl never
distracted his callers with magazines that might show them treasures
he didn't have for sale. I wondered what he'd have for me this
time; I could think of nothing reported recently by the archae-
ologists.

I leafed through the papers.

They were devoid of stridency that morning, as if the whole world had suddenly declared a moratorium on unpleasantness.

In Europe, the Chairman of the Soviet Union was getting ready to make a speech in a satellite capital where the heads of the assorted Peoples' Governments had been meeting for a month. This was a comparatively recent chairman who had made few speeches; no one quite knew what to expect from him. The *Times* refused to speculate about the coming speech, but *The Wall Street Journal* editorialized a forecast. It would be a conciliatory speech, placating the West, possibly dangling carrots before influential satellites, promising to relax controls, pointedly ignoring Red China, and extending the Khrushchev-like hand of coexistence (minus thumping shoe).

Moscow was mending fences all over the world for the inevitable showdown with Red China, made all the more imperative by the recent military clashes on the Ussuri River. But, all in all, the *Journal* didn't anticipate new problems . . . unless the Chinese chose this sensitive moment for their long-expected stroke. Sooner or later, they'd have to make their try for the hegemony of the Communist world. Pieces would fall, then; probably on the West.

With Eastern Europe in the news, I thought about Sempinski's letter which seemed to have been written with one eye on censors. I made a mental note to find out more about Kristin Napoji's minefield accident.

My vague ruminations about Sempinski's homeland, where the Chairman was to speak, were crudely shattered by the opening of Pohl's inner door, Miss Gruber's simpering smile and a flash of brown.

The man who stepped out of Pohl's office was astonishing: lean as a stalk of celery and immensely tall. My first thought was of the Raymond Massey version of John Brown, he of the moldering body and marching soul, but this was a John Brown who, except for white shirt and a black string tie, had been dipped in chocolate from the low crown of the stiff-brimmed plainsman's hat he carried to the sloping heels of stovepipe boots. His hair was wiry, close-cropped like a scouring pad, and rapidly graying. His face was like bleached parchment with flat, colorless eyes that glanced at me with absolute indifference. In that white face, the pale, unseeing eyes were electrifying. I thought them reptilian. There was the barest flicker in the narrow pupils that made me think of telescopic rifle sights and then the man was gone.

Miss Gruber whinnied and I was stupefied.

"Who or what was that?"

Miss Gruber's maiden eyes focused unkindly on my nose.

"That was Mr. Brown. From Kansas. He's an interior decorator."

"Oh, for God's sake!"

The exclamation was involuntary but the surprise was great. If ever a man failed to match job and looks it was the man in brown. Even Miss Gruber seemed to get the point.

"He doesn't look like one, does he? I mean, I always think of slim young men with odd ways being decorators. But Mr. Brown looks, well, so very much like a *man!* He looks like a fighter!"

Miss Gruber's antique lust was totally unnerving. I said: "What kind of fighter?"

"Well, he's too tall and lean to be a wrestler and not scarred enough to be a boxer. That sort of rules out fighters, doesn't it. But there is something about him that makes me think of fighters."

"Does he come here often?"

"This," she said with a Sabine intonation, "has been the first time. My first thought, when I saw him, was cowboy, of course. I mean the clothes he wears, the way he holds himself. So very still, so lithe. But he's so terribly pale. He looks as if he hasn't seen the sun for a very long time."

The buzzer on Miss Gruber's desk cut short further revelations of her secret longings and speculation about Mr. Brown. I went in to see my most difficult client.

I was prepared for almost anything with Pohl but, to my surprise, he proved to be cordiality itself on that confusing and contradictory day.

He rustled like a giant landcrab in the shadows behind his desk; the bald dome of his head caught stray beams of light supplied by a timid and uncertain sun. His face had the blue-gray tinge of a man with a heart condition and uneasy conscience, and, that day, he wore the round green spectacles of the kind favored by lady missionaries fifty years ago. They turned his eyes into opaque pools, masking all expression: the first sign that he was up to something. His smile, meant to be disarming, couldn't have alarmed me more.

"Come in, dear Doctor," he said in his throaty whisper, and I knew at once that I was in for it. Having no academic titles, Pohl despised them.

I pulled up a chair.

He said: "How long have we been working together, Doctor? When did our happy association begin?"

"It will be five years in March. You asked me to look into the Knossos controversy."

"Ah, yes . . . the Knossos scrolls. Every other expert pronounced them the find of the century. I was about to make those damned Greeks rich, until you came along. You made those expert colleagues of yours look like bumbling schoolboys. How could they make such a mistake?"

"It's easy to be wrong when you're dealing with something that might not have existed. I wasn't sure myself that the scrolls were forged until we got our hands on them and made the tests. The Greeks' aging process was magnificent."

Pohl's dry hands, protruding from the deep shadows of his wing chair, made short scampering motions about the polished desktop and made him look more like a crab than ever.

"But they didn't fool you, Doctor. You knew what to look for. That Greek wanted two hundred thousand dollars for the scrolls. He settled for fifty, when you were done with him, and was glad to get it. I sold the scrolls to the Lowenhaupt Museum for . . . well, that doesn't matter. They were glad to have such perfect reproductions."

"It wasn't any reproduction. It was a complete fraud. You can't make copies without originals to copy, and anything from that period could only have survived in a known collection."

"Hmm . . . a known collection?"

"And that's also out. The only possible collection for that particular material would have been the Romanowski Library. There are no Trebizond illuminations anywhere else. And the Library was completely destroyed during the war in Europe."

"You are, of course, quite sure of that, dear Doctor, are you not?"

"No one would admit setting that kind of fire. But we are all morally sure that the Romanowski Library was burned in 1944."

"The Lowenhaupt people were willing to take the Knossos scrolls for reproductions."

"I have no high opinion of the Lowenhaupt Museum. When we broke down the Greeks' aging process, we pinned the time of manufacture of the Knossos scrolls to about fifteen years ago. That's long after the war. So, if we accept the fact that the originals were lost in the war, the Knossos find was a complete hoax."

"And you are sure the Romanowski Library was lost?"

"As sure as anyone can be. There's been no legal hearing, no investigation; no one has testified that he watched the Library going up in smoke. But we know that the material was intact in 1942. The Germans didn't steal it during the occupation because the Counts Romanowski were distantly related to the King of Sweden. Count Bernadotte visited them in 1942 and mentions the collection in his diaries. Two years later the whole region was laid waste by the Russians. The Romanowski estate was a battlefield for more than a month. If any portion of the Library survived, it can only be fragments. Some peasant has probably lined his winter boots with them."

"Hmm . . . Boots, you say."

Pohl seemed to shrink and recede behind his desk, and I assumed that whatever he was up to wouldn't be as bad as I had thought. He simply wanted information. But I was wondering when he'd get to the point of the meeting.

He said: "Tell me more about this Romanowski Library. Oh, nothing specific; just whatever you happen to know about it. Have you ever seen it? If you saw anything that claimed to be part of that collection you'd know if it was genuine?"

"It's all been catalogued. I wrote my doctoral thesis on a part of it. But what with wars, and Nazi occupations, and now the Iron Curtain, no one in this country has actually seen it since 1938."

Pohl had now all but disappeared in his chair.

"So a piece could turn up somewhere," he said softly.

"That's ridiculous. Some of these works were more than two thousand years old. You know how fragile that makes them. How could they survive a twentieth-century battle, then years of exposure and neglect or outright abuse? They probably blew up in a cloud of dust when the first shell landed in the Romanowski manor."

Pohl nodded gravely and took off his glasses and fixed his little agate eyes on me in an odd mixture of curiosity and secret amusement. Then, just as quickly as they had appeared, his eyes vanished behind the impenetrable lenses.

Talking about the Romanowski Library was a waste of time and I had never known Pohl to waste anything. All this was leading somewhere. But where? It could even be a cat-and-mouse preamble to the cancellation of my contract.

Largely to dispel my rising uneasiness, I began to describe the origins of the Romanowski Library, as if by offering this gratuitous information I could deflect the blow.

The Library had been spirited away from Constantinople in 1204 to save it from rampaging Crusaders, who had found Saracen fierceness not much to their liking and massacred the Byzantines instead. Its next home was the Trebizondian Empire, until the Ottoman Turks put Trebizond to the torch in 1461. The surviving Comneni of Trebizond took the Library across the Black Sea to the mouth of the Dnieper, then westward across the Steppes to what is now a western part of Russia. Part of the Library was lost in the various Eastern European wars of the sixteenth

and seventeenth centuries but most of it had survived through
1942.

Two spots of light reflecting on Pohl's glasses moved up and
down as I talked, but whether they moved because he was nodding
in agreement, or in boredom, or (for that matter) because he
was asleep, I had no idea.

I felt like a man groping in the darkness of an unfamiliar
cellar.

Pohl said: "Has anyone responsible ever tried to buy it?"

"Responsible?"

"One of the great museums. A wealthy collector."

"The British Museum raised a subscription of a million pounds
sterling in 1936 for a part of the Library."

"And those counts wouldn't sell?"

"Of course not. Anyway, their government got wind of the
offer and declared the Library a national treasure. No country
which has anything like that would ever let it go."

"What did the Library consist of?"

"There were four hundred separate manuscripts. And that's
something of a miracle in itself. Byzantine literature is negligible
and it did no better under Constantine's successors than it did
under him. But when he founded Constantinople in A.D. 332, he
wanted to make it the center of world learning. So he began
amassing whatever he could find in older civilizations. His library
included the known records of the Academy of the Immortals . . .
the commentaries of Herodotus . . . Sophocles, Plato . . . the intellectual loot of an age. There were pre-Byzantine works in plenty.
Hellenic manuscripts, Mythratic, Nicean and early Christian writing. Constantine's successors increased the collection after his death
in A.D. 337. And then there were, of course, the Pontic Tribunals."

Pohl sighed and moved out of shadow then, leaning forward.
His dry hands were clasped under his chin as if without their
support his head would roll down upon his chest.

He said: "Tell me about them, Doctor."

"What's there to tell? They were scraps of papyrus and crumbling wax tablets. They represented the penance of Constantine for all the years before he became a Christian. The collection was begun between A.D. 320 and 330 and continued through centuries afterward. It consisted of one hundred and twenty-seven pieces; not one of them had been lost in all the voyages of the Trebizondian princes or in all the wars. They were a sort of Holy Grail, I suppose; no one would lift a hand against them. Until, of course, the civilized twentieth century came along.

"What were they . . . exactly?"

"The complete record of the trial of Christ."

"Everything? It doesn't seem possible they'd have everything."

"Why not? Rome was a bureaucracy. Bureaucracies love papers. It was all there, from the original complaint by the Temple to the disappearance of the body from the tomb. There is the order for Christ's arrest, the deposition of the witnesses, the transcript of Christ's interrogation under torture—verbatim, with direct quotations—and Christ's *proces verbal* itself, with the famous questions and His answers; and Pilate's decision finding Christ innocent and his reversal of his own decision; and there are the proceedings of the viceregal inquiry into Christianity—as a subversive, antisocial and unpatriotic organization, aimed at the overthrow of the established system—and the report to Rome. The whole story behind the Barrabas episode is there. Would you like to know how much it cost to prosecute Christ? There are eleven scrolls with a minute fiscal accounting that even includes the payoff to Judas. There is the equivalent of a medical death certificate, the report of the officer commanding the execution escort and police reports on Judas' suicide and the theft of Christ's body. It's a complete, bureaucratic rendering of the Passion, all the more unnerving because it's dispassionate. It's Christ's police dossier. What more can I say?"

Pohl sighed again, and leaned back in his chair where the shadows hid him.

I said: "They even had a part of the sign that had been fixed over Christ's head on the cross."

Pohl said, with immense satisfaction: "Iesus Nasarensis Rex Juditorum."

"That's the one. Hangmen are given to peculiar humor."

"What a loss," Pohl said. "What a loss."

For a moment I thought I heard him chuckle. But that would have been impossible, even for him.

Still softly, gently, he said: "Think what it would mean if somehow, miraculously, the Pontic Tribunals were found, recovered and taken to safety. You had said something about peasant boots?"

I nodded, feeling tired. I heard Pohl saying, "Curious, curious," his hands darting about the papers on his desk. He moved aside some papers to reveal the corner of a flat, rectangular box made of heavy metal.

"If you saw such material," he said finally. "And if your first impression suggested authenticity, how long would it take you to be dead sure? I'm talking about one hundred and twenty-seven pieces of papyrus, wax tablets and leather scrolls."

"I don't know. You can't set up arbitrary schedules for that kind of thing. It could take a month or ten years. It would depend on what you had to work with. You know what's involved. But if you think the Pontic Tribunals still exist you're out of your mind."

He was offhand, quite careless as he said: "You're wrong, dear Doctor; they exist. I'm going to buy them."

"I have a client," he said. "A most distinguished and distinctive man. He was in London recently. There, if you'll exercise your imagination, opportunity came knocking at his hotel door. He was approached by a man who told him a story. The man claimed to represent the heirs of an estate in Eastern Europe who have a treasure of historical value that they want to sell to an American. They want this treasure to defect to the West, you might say. Unfortunately our distinguished client detests all foreigners, particularly Eastern Europeans. The story sounded to him like a confidence trick so he had his visitor thrown out.

"Luckily, the visitor left a sample of his treasure—an inscription preserved under glass. The story could have ended right there because our client is a man of action, in the finest American tradition, not an intellectual bookworm, and he had never heard of this particular treasure. But we were again in luck. Because, next day, our client saw his visitor's picture in the morning papers; he had been run over by a car outside our client's hotel.

"I must explain that our distinguished client is not only rich, powerful and distinctive, but is known for his hate of Communism. The dead man, according to the papers, had been associated with anti-Communist emigrée groups in London; thus the story of defecting treasures acquired a possible validity. Our client has little sympathy for run-over Slavs, but he began to regret his suspicious nature. The dead man's story still sounded like flim-flam but our man is a realist. He knows enough about Red terror methods to recognize the gambit of the hit-and-run. He thought the dead man's story worth checking. If it was true, he thought, he'd have a chance to strike a blow at a Communist state, inflict a hurt on its national pride that could shake it apart. So he called me. I had Hamish Potter, my London manager, put his best men on checking the sample."

"And?"

"They said it was authentic. Have a look, O.H."

He brushed concealing papers off the metal case I had noticed earlier. I took it, opened it. Inside the casket were two panes of glass, their primitive quality unmistakable. Between them lay a brown, leaflike strip of papyrus, the fibers bared, the powdery texture undisturbed. One glance could date it within two centuries of the age it claimed.

The touch of antique glass and ancient fibers were irrelevant to the certainty that seemed to come, like a current, from the papyrus itself. I had seen reproductions of this simple sign. The immemorial jeer had been made almost illegible by the centuries.

Pohl spelled it out.

I couldn't make myself believe it, despite my certainty, and said so. Pohl laughed.

"But I know you think it's the real thing. Your face betrays you. It took Potter's people three months to be sure and even then they tried to hedge. Amateurs! You know instinctively. That is expertise!"

I muttered that it was only an impression. I would still have to test.

"Of course! It's as much your reputation as mine, after all. But only you could do the work in reasonable time. Time is our greatest enemy. Each day is a threat. Who knows who's finding out about this? Too many know now. But I was the first to know, so I can move first. And I have you, the foremost authority on Trebizond illuminations, to authenticate my treasure. Well, what do you say? Is that a good assignment?"

It was a magnificent assignment and I said so, whether or not I believed that the Pontic Tribunals still existed. The restoration of any part of this priceless treasure would be its own reward. I felt immensely grateful to Hubertus Pohl. I had misjudged him; this was a good man.

He went on laughing for some time, moving around his office. I also laughed, but for a different reason. I knew that this was probably the most significant day of my life. Work on the Pontic Tribunals would make me the best-known Eastern antiquarian in the world.

"When can you start?" Pohl asked.

"When can I have the rest?"

"As soon as we can get you to Europe."

"You know how I feel about traveling but for this I'd go to China."

Pohl said: "Imagine, Doctor! You'll be the first scholar in the Free World to see the Pontic Tribunals in their original."

"In the Free World? I understood the collection was already in London."

"Did you? I don't see how you could have. I thought I made it clear that everything was still on the Continent. Still, that's not much farther, is it? Hardly as far as China, eh?"

Pohl's voice and manner clamored for attention but I knew that the sudden warning had come too late. I knew he had me;

he had done it again. I didn't want to ask the next question but there was no way to avoid it.

"Where are the Pontic Tribunals, then?"

"In Russia. Wasn't that made clear? Still, our fellow conspirators will get them out for you. You'll only have to go a few hundred miles beyond the Iron Curtain."

three

I DIDN'T KNOW which angered me more: Hubertus Pohl's masterly puppeteering or Miss Gruber's ironic eyes as she brought in the visa application forms (all filled-out and ready for signing), currency coupons, and the supplementary papers. They had forgotten nothing, including even a pocket dictionary and a book of useful conversational phrases.

Hark, I read, opening it at random. My postilion has been struck by lightning.

Pohl had given one of his best performances. The rapid shifts from unexpected kindness to flattering attention, then to quick generosity and disarming candor, made a refusal impossible. The prize itself, and my own enthusiasm, had been used against me. Indignation would have made me look even a bigger fool than I felt.

I had no wish to play art thief, cloak and dagger plotter, currency violator and smuggler of national treasures behind the Iron Curtain where justice tends to be a little abrupt.

On the other hand Pohl's plans, as he explained them, had been laid with care. He had made provision for just about every eventuality.

First I would get a week's briefing in London, which was another way of saying that I'd have seven days to get used to the idea of doing something a lot more dangerous than anything I had ever done before. Then I would fly east, to Sempinski's country, which I had always wanted to visit anyway. There I would go about my "cultural researches"—the official reason for my trip to a land few American tourists ever enter. That much had been left, as if to flatter me, to my own ingenuity. In due time someone would contact me on behalf of the Romanowski heirs. In the meantime, money would have been deposited in ten British banks that had Swedish branches. How the deposits were to be made, in view of dwindling American gold reserves, was none of my business. The purchase price of the Pontic Tribunals would be staggering; as far as I was concerned that was a job for professional financiers.

My job would start once I was taken to wherever the Pontic Tribunals were hidden. I was glad this wouldn't be actual Soviet territory; like every other American, I suppose, I had been taught to dread Soviet security policemen—an unlikely but enduring image of superintelligence mixed with inhumanity. Satellite territory didn't seem as dreadful.

It didn't seem likely that I would be able to authenticate the materials on the spot. All I could hope to do at that stage, all that Pohl expected, would be to satisfy myself as best I could that the material could be genuine. It was a risk but, as Pohl explained, the risk was worth taking in view of the probability and, he was quick to add with an insufferable smile, in view of my expertise. Once I was satisfied that the supposed Tribunals looked sufficiently authentic to warrant the necessary laboratory tests, I would send a holiday postcard to Pohl's London manager. The text would be a prearranged message. Pohl's London office would advance one hundred thousand dollars to cover the conspirators' expenses. The payment would be made in Sweden. The smugglers could, then, go about the business of bribing and suborning and the Pontic Tribunals would begin yet another journey, this time across the Baltic. I'd meet them in Sweden where a full-scale investigation could be undertaken at the Royal Institute. Time would no longer be so much of a problem once we had the treasure in our hands in Sweden, although security was another matter. Pohl was arranging a suitable cover for me with the Institute. At any rate, in Stockholm I would be able to proceed with comparative leisure. Once I was sure of authenticity I would telegraph Pohl, the balance of the purchase price would be paid to the smugglers, and that would be that. Transporting the treasure to America would be gallery business.

It was a simple and efficient plan. If there was any slip up, I was free to act as I thought best. Pohl warned me to expect no help from U.S. consuls if I got in trouble; they would be hardly sympathetic toward anyone who muddied their waters.

"But," he said with candor that would have been disarming if I didn't know him, "what could go wrong? Everything has been perfectly arranged."

Seen in this light, the adventure didn't seem particularly dangerous. The acquisition of true antiquities had always included an element of smuggling, and this assignment had just enough foreign intrigue about it to make it exciting. The secret meetings, coded telegrams and the vicarious smuggling of a treasure would flavor the job. Hindsight would make it memorable indeed.

I suppose I was a fool about it all; I frequently am. But only that morning I had wondered why adventure had passed me by, and whether anything exciting, memorable, would ever happen to me, and here was an adventure with a deep personal as well as professional meaning. To have the Romanowski Library once more available for scholars, to be instrumental in saving that treasure, was a psychological bonus beyond calculable worth. I couldn't believe that I was part of a conspiracy to rescue the Library. Dangers and difficulties didn't seem to matter; I couldn't visualize the dangers, anyway.

Only my injured pride of being manipulated remained but Pohl seemed to have made provision even for that.

He had Miss Gruber bring in a decanter of a venerable brandy and drank a toast to the success of my mission. He even went so far as to give me a present—ostensibly to commemorate the nearing fifth anniversary of our association—but, in reality, to make amends for the dirty trick.

The present was a briefcase, a black, shining rectangle of expensive leather, with my name and address embossed in discreet gold under the handle. My old, battered bag was like a derelict beside it.

The next few days were difficult and rushed. I had work to finish for clients other than Hubertus Pohl. Most of them didn't believe that I was merely taking a winter vacation, but Pohl had bound me to secrecy and I had to lie. They knew Pohl as well as I knew him and they worried about what Pohl could have been putting over on them.

I did what seemed most pressing and put off the rest. I had several more meetings with Hubertus Pohl whose distinguished client and backer had so much pull in Washington that all my papers were back in a week. I wondered about the man's identity. There weren't many men who would put up such enormous sums as would be involved here just to do an injury to a Communist state. Pohl didn't say any more about him and I didn't ask; a client's customers were a client's business; if Pohl wished to keep his backer out of sight that was his privilege.

I sent a cable to Julian Sempinski asking if I might visit him. This was my contribution to Pohl's excellent arrangements: the official reason for my trip to Sempinski's country. I was pleased to have been able to come up with something. The old writer cabled back an immediate invitation. Almost before I knew it, the preliminary arrangements were complete. I flew to London before the end of the month.

four

THE LONDON streets were dreary; gray in early evening with the rain quite heavy. We drove through a broad boulevard where trees and grass median-strips would have blazed a brilliant flowered green in summer or spring but now, in my least favorite season, there were no flowers and no grass and the leaves were dead.

The trip had tired me. The flight had been uneventful but nervous excitement had taken its toll. I couldn't get the melodrama of foreign intrigue out of my mind.

There was a time when I had enjoyed travel; now I dreaded it. I never doubted that my aircraft would get to where it was supposed to without accident, but traveling upset my sense of routine. There was always some stupid emergency about lost luggage, taxis, and hotels. And foreign air carried unfamiliar rhythms. And, more prosaically, there were cheating guides, greedy porters, confusing streets, unkept appointments and, all too often, a language like the honking of wild geese. I tried to keep my foreign travel to a minimum but, frequently, I was unable to convince a client that I could do my work easily enough in New York.

In ten years I had been five times in Turkey, twice in Greece, once each in Lebanon and Iraq and twice in Yugoslavia. As a student, I had hitchhiked across France, northern Italy and Austria—the last a mildly sentimental journey to the university town where a certain beautiful but unkind young woman had been studying. I had never been in England, never wished to go there. I admitted ruefully to myself that in this grim age of prejudices I was prejudiced against the English without any reason. I was also ill at ease with Germans, but there I could find reason. Germans set my teeth on edge to such an extent that I could hardly bear to hear German spoken without irritation and, all too often, German was the only language in which I could make myself understood. As for the English, they had their own bland way of getting under my skin. I had hoped that Hamish Potter, Pohl's man in London, wouldn't be too professionally English.

Potter turned out to be a quiet, helpful man with kind eyes and a pale mustache. He met me at the airport, and drove me to London. We said little at first but I revived enough at mid-city to thank him for coming out to get me.

"Least I could do," he mumbled with genuine shyness. "Just thought the customs, and all that, might be a bit much for you under the circumstances. They're a decent enough bunch of chaps, normally, but they can bother you a bit if you have something on your mind."

It was unusual to see a grown man blushing. I said: "You mean the assignment?"

Potter laughed a little.

"It hasn't helped my insomnia. But I'd rather do my small bit than the job you have. You could transfer all of Mr. Pohl's secret millions to my account and I still wouldn't go where you're going. Incidentally, are you up to having some dinner tonight?"

I realized suddenly that I was hungry.

"I certainly am."

"Are you sure? As you Americans say, it must have been quite a day."

"The excitement seems to have given me an appetite. If you let me invite you to dinner I can break in my expense account."

"Done," Potter said.

We drove to the Culloden in Marble Arch, a modernistic pile of glass and concrete where Potter had reserved a small suite for me. He said apologetically that it wasn't the most exclusive hotel in London; I would find fewer coronets among the guests than I could find elsewhere. But, as a compensation, the toilets were faultless and bathroom pipes were guaranteed not to bellow at night.

Potter stayed with a scotch and water in the American Bar while I followed a clerk in perfect evening clothes and was, in turn, followed by a small procession of bellboys carrying my luggage, the suite waiter with a menu and winelist, the housekeeper, a maid, and some other functionaries of indefinite title. The clerk was affable, the bellboys were swift. The rooms were not only comfortable but handsome. The view was fine despite the rain and rapidly falling darkness: Hyde Park (brown but airy), Soap Box Corner (quiet in inclement weather), Park Row with beautiful houses converted into offices but still retaining the well-bred look of old-money-rich men's homes, and the Arch itself. I could look into Oxford Street, Bond Street was not far off. Within a minute's walk lay Grosvenor Square, the Embassy, and the American Express.

I talked with the clerk while bellboys, housekeeper, and maid formed their skirmish line and attacked the rooms. Suitcases here, coat there, towels and linen checked, fruitbowl emplaced, suits taken out for pressing, shoes for shining, all bags unpacked and contents stowed in drawers.

They were efficient, quick, and sure; they wasted no motion. The show was impressive. The suite waiter stepped up on cue with menu and winelist and I ordered dinner for Potter and myself.

"Would you like to be served in your drawing room, sir? Or would you care to come downstairs?"

"Downstairs, I think."

"No need to dress, of course, sir," the clerk said smoothly. "We have a number of American guests; a business suit is quite acceptable. Besides, hardly anyone bothers to dress for dinner any more."

I tipped the maid and bellboys, thanked the clerk and house-keeper, locked the door behind them and threw off my clothes. One of that mechanized brigade had drawn my bathwater. I bathed, shaved, and felt totally restored.

In a few minutes the suite valet brought my dark blue suit from the tailor's shop, neatly pressed. I watched him laying out the rest of what he thought the well-dressed American should wear for dinner in London. After he left, I smoked a cigarette beside the window, then began to dress.

Outside, daylight had ended.

The broad mouth of Oxford Street barely intruded with its scarlet neon, but Park Row shone mistily in the rain like a page out of a history book.

The muted sounds of traffic died in this dinner hour; I felt removed from time, taken back a hundred years into an era of quiet dignity, unfrenzied and predictable, as if the floodlit Arch, that gate into nowhere, were indeed a magic portal of some kind. Hyde Park was black behind it.

I went downstairs, feeling very good about everything.

The dinner wasn't very English: Cinzano and Chestnuts Joaquin, duck broth, red mullet with a good, chilled Montrachet, a ripe, soft Bel Paese with toasted salt biscuits and coffee (Turkish, demitasse).

The duck broth brought to mind another dinner eaten long ago in Italy, when I had still thought that I could interest a certain girl in myself, and entertained some hopes, and had been younger, thinner, wearing thicker hair, less armored, more exposed, and still not having signed my own personal cease-fire with the inevitable.

It had been a dinner redolent of the Adriatic, urgency and youth when nothing was unattainable and there was time for everything in the innumerable years ahead. London and the Adriatic dinner had nothing in common. But that time had also been the start of an adventure, hopeful expectation and a quick-beating heart. I wanted to feel the old, forgotten certainties.

I enjoyed the dinner, thinking with wry amusement about the other time made distant, foolish (but still worth remembering) by the perspective of years and fewer illusions.

Potter also enjoyed it, although he seemed surprised. Polite though they may sometimes be about it, the English seldom credit an American with taste.

When he was well into the mullet, he smiled. He said: "I think I'd better make a small apology. I thought the Culloden would suit you quite well. Now that I've met you I think you would have preferred something less chrome-plated. I think I'd better learn to differentiate between my Americans."

"Do you get that many?"

"A few. Hubertus Pohl likes it here. So do his clients."

"I would have thought Pohl would have more baroque tastes in hotels."

Potter grew pensive.

"Not entirely. Mister Pohl . . ."

But he didn't finish. He would not discuss Pohl with a stranger. Still, having brought Pohl into the conversation, we could start talking about the assignment.

Potter was sure that the glass-encased sample had been the true inscription. Fraud was out of the question in this case. He had applied all the standard tests except fiber analysis and chemical composition for which he would have had to strip the protecting glass, and that could have been disastrous without a vacuum chamber or controlled temperatures. The loss of even the most microscopic fragment would have been sacrilege. But Potter had additional proof; more personal and totally unscientific and thus, he said, incomparably more convincing than any ultrasonic analyzer.

He said: "About two years ago I met a man named Danilow. I met him through a friend, an old school chum who had gone into the Army. My friend is now something rather exotic at the War Office, does the sort of work you can't talk about, if you know what I mean."

"Intelligence?"

"Something along those lines. At any rate, this friend introduced me to Danilow. London is full of former generals but there was something about Danilow that raised him head and shoulders above the others. He was abrupt, but courteous, somewhat aloof in an old-fashioned way, energetic but extremely patient, satisfied with few words unless he knew you well. At first I put his silence to a poor grasp of English. I was wrong about that. The man was trained in languages from childhood. He also had an extraordinary grasp of power politics and a particularly fine, analytical mind. I suppose I should tell you that I'm very interested in political theory and everything connected with the practice. I've made a little study, very limited of course, of the behind-the-scenes influences in European power politics in the last twenty or thirty years. It's a sad indictment: assassinations, treason, bribery, and blackmail all pointing to . . . several connected sources. Have you ever heard of a man called The Magician?"

"No."

"I suppose you wouldn't. It's one of those strange names that seems to appear every time there is trouble behind the scenes, but hardly anyone knows anything about the man for certain. Danilow had been doing that kind of research for many years before the last war. We became friends, met often, talked often. Through him I met a whole gallery of people; excellent minds, absorbing ideas. They introduced me to another world: the uneasy, quicksand world of the emigrées with its intramural strife, plots and counterplots, political maneuverings, changing allegiances and intrigues. This world of emigrée activity is like a beehive with every bee working for itself, often at cross-purposes with every other bee, jealous of its prerogatives, its own special corner. Danilow kept above the factions. He alone seemed untouched by the squabbling but in contact with all. I used to wonder how he did it. Then gradually, and accidentally, I discovered that he and his special circle were the leaders of anti-Communist resistance in Eastern Europe. Danilow was the military leader. I had no idea that such resistance existed or that it was directed by a single source.

I imagine the Communist regimes knew it well enough. They must have had large prices on the leaders' heads."

The secret war, he said, was bitter. Men Potter met one week, would be gone the next. Their friends would say that they had *gone to the provinces.* If they never came back, their friends said that they had *emigrated* or *gone to Canada.*

"Four months ago, Danilow also *emigrated.* Via hit-and-run taxi outside this hotel. His death shocked me. I began to see secret threads. These led to others. I began to understand what had been happening so long under my eyes. I talked with my school chum, the one through whom I had met Danilow. Now that the man was dead, my chum could tell me a bit more about him. His part in the secret war became clear. His executioners were, of course, either Soviet or satellite secret service agents working through the Communist underground in London. And the name of The Magician appeared again. All this is background. I wanted you to know the man who brought us our sample. You might be working with or against men of that kind."

"Then Danilow was the man who tried to contact Pohl's *distinguished* client?"

"Yes. In this hotel."

"Why didn't he come to you?"

"I was abroad. I hadn't seen him for a month. He had *gone to the provinces,* the only such trip I ever knew him to make. He was too important to the resistance to take such risks. I remember thinking, then, that whatever reason he had for the trip had to be terribly important; something no one else could do. I had a card from him at about that time, saying he would be away but that, when he came back, he would need my professional advice. I was in Switzerland when he was killed. He came back from his trip with the inscription. He couldn't find me and he could not have been expected to trust my assistants. But he must have known that he had little time left. Something must have happened in *the provinces;* the Communist agents must have been breathing down his neck. He went straight to a visiting American who, by his record, could have been expected to listen to his story.

The American didn't listen. He had Danilow thrown out into the street. Danilow was killed as he crossed the street to the underground entrance—the subway, you call it. The taxi had been waiting outside the hotel door. So you see why I had no doubts about the inscription. It couldn't be a fraud if Danilow was involved."

I suggested, as gently as I could, that General Danilow himself could have been the victim of a forger.

"No, that's just my point. If he, himself, had to go behind the Iron Curtain to meet the people who claim to have the Romanowski Library, it must have been because he knew them and could trust them, and could identify them. His people wouldn't have let him take the risk if anybody else could have done the job."

But one question still remained conspicuously unanswered. Why should the military leader of a resistance movement get involved in the antiquities business? Because that's what it boiled down to in the end: a multimillion dollar deal between private parties.

"I don't know," Potter said. "Perhaps because the loss of the Pontic Tribunals by the Communist government would have a political effect in Danilow's country, something the resistance could exploit. Perhaps because Danilow was a patriot. Perhaps because he was a Christian. Perhaps there are more practical reasons. All these things are interrelated, anyway. I can only guess and guesses won't help you."

"But you think that we can expect to find the Pontic Tribunals intact? And perhaps the rest of the Romanowski Library?"

"I think so. I trust Danilow. Whatever is waiting for you over there, it won't be fraud."

We went on with our dinner, talking trivialities while the waiters served the golden Bel Paese and the toasted biscuits. After the waiters withdrew I speculated on whom the general had gone to see at such risk and what could have gone wrong. I would be following in his footsteps in a week. Potter couldn't help me.

"I don't know," he said. "I tried to find out after he was killed. But all his friends closed ranks and mouths extremely tight."

"I would have thought that as their dead leader's friend . . ."

"But that's just it! Somebody betrayed him. Somebody identified him for the other side. His people here know it; none of them have reason to trust an Englishman or an American, anyway. They blame us for betraying Eastern Europe to the Soviets after World War II. A man like Danilow has a broader vision but I can't blame the others for being suspicious. And that's one reason why we have to hurry."

"I don't follow."

"The people who killed Danilow must know he was after something very special. If they have managed to get a spy into the resistance, someone so trusted that he would know about Danilow, they're in good position to find out what he was after. Once they know what it is, it won't be long before they know who has it. They'll have a starting point for their search, and we will lose our only advantage. That's why the quicker you get there, the better."

The worry and uneaseness in his voice urged sudden caution. I knew he was going to ask me to do something unpleasant and unplanned, and that this would upset me as much as it was upsetting him.

I asked: "How quick is that?"

He said apologetically: "I thought you might consider starting out tomorrow."

I thought, at first, I had misunderstood him. It hadn't occurred to me that the basic plan, with its comforting solidity, businesslike efficiency of timetables and schedules, could be changed so easily. I had begun to depend on the precision of Pohl's plan as a shield against the thought of the possible dangers. The murder of Danilow hadn't really registered in my mind until now. My first impulse was to say *Impossible,* or *You can't be serious,* but I could see just how serious Potter was.

"Don't you think there are enough risks involved without last minute changes?" I said weakly. "Nothing but confusion can come out of changes."

The evening had suddenly lost most of its charm.

Potter said quietly: "I'm sorry. I know how you must feel;

I'd feel the same in your place, I imagine. But things are moving so much faster than we thought they would and each day's delay increases the dangers. Of course, it's up to you; I'm only making a suggestion."

"But the arrangements," I said. "The briefing . . ."

Potter looked at his watch and said: "I took the liberty of making a telephone call while you were upstairs. I asked a man I know to join us after dinner. His name is Karpovitch. He has a lot to say about your next port of call."

"He's been there?"

"He comes from there, as a matter of fact."

"You took a lot for granted," I said bitterly. "Does Pohl know about this?"

Potter nodded.

"He didn't tell me anything about this in New York. Don't you suppose I should have been told?"

Potter inclined his head with no great conviction. Obviously he wouldn't criticize his employer but I was in no mood to appreciate this show of loyalty.

I couldn't imagine why Pohl hadn't said a word about the possibility of a speed-up. Did he think that I'd back out as easily as that? And why wait until I got to London before springing this surprise on me? I could back out in London just as easily as I could in New York; a plane could take me home first thing in the morning.

What angered me most was the lack of trust implied in this deception, this duplicity. Pohl couldn't play straight if he wanted to. I wondered if I'd ever be able to understand his devious mind and learn to anticipate his treachery.

Potter was obviously not to blame for this dirty trick and there was no point in showing him my anger. But I promised myself the luxury of very bad language next time I saw Pohl.

And something else occurred to me suddenly—a thought I would never have entertained in New York where it would have seemed crudely melodramatic. Here, it neither surprised nor amused me.

"Once I get over there," I said, "always supposing that I'm still interested in going, I'm to wait until someone comes and makes contact with me. Is that still on?"

"Yes."

"What if someone does come . . . but to trap me? How will I know the contact isn't a plant? I wouldn't know a police spy if I stepped on one."

Potter sighed, nodded.

"Karpovitch can answer that question better than I could. But there is something else I must warn you about."

"Oh, wonderful," I said. "What is it? Another change of plans?"

"No. As a matter of fact it's nothing to do with our business at all. It's just something about the general atmosphere you'll be stepping into. All the satellite leaders are meeting over there and as you can imagine things will be a bit strained. Their disunity is far more serious than they've let us see."

"They seem pretty united on the basic matters."

"The only reason most of them came to the meeting is because it's a Warsaw Pact Affair; that's their defense alliance, like NATO is ours. They're very careful to keep it in good shape, especially these days. They might ignore a direct summons to Moscow but they would never dare miss a meeting of the Warsaw Pact. And so the Soviets can try to organize support against China, sure that every satellite will be represented. And China is, of course, not a member so there won't be any interference."

"Yes, I understand all that. But why should that make anybody nervous?"

"They don't know what the Soviets are going to propose and they won't know until the Chairman makes his speech. It could be important."

"More saber-rattling, d'you suppose?"

"Actually, it could be a proposal for some sort of *détente* with the West. It seems logical since the Russians and the Chinese have already started shooting at each other. If that's the case, the Chinese will do everything to stop it. And they may find some very odd new European allies."

"Who in Europe could be interested in prolonging the Cold War? That just doesn't make sense. Everybody is sick of this eternal tension."

Potter looked at me curiously, then made a troubled gesture. "Have you paid much attention to Germany lately?"

I confessed that I paid as little attention to Germany as I could.

"The Nazis are back again," he said thoughtfully. "They expect to win control of West Germany in the next elections but nobody on this side of the Iron Curtain seems to want to say anything about them. If the Cold War were to end tomorrow their dreams of rearranging Europe once again would dissipate a bit. I don't think they could thrive without an East-West split. I think they'd seize on any chance to foment bad relations."

I asked if Potter didn't think he was painting a disproportionally grim picture of what could only be a minor matter at the moment. Vietnam was still keeping the Americans and Soviets apart. After all, the Cold War had existed long before the Nazis reappeared.

"Fear of a resurgent Germany is the only thing that keeps Eastern Europe clinging to the Russians," Potter said. "Those people know that only the Soviets will be strong enough to help them when the Germans come. They know that the West wouldn't be interested in helping since the Germans are, after all, our anti-Communist allies. It's that sort of a silly circle now, and it's ironic that Britain and America are helping to maintain this fear."

"And you think the Soviets are going to propose a sort of Cold War cease-fire to deal with the Nazis?"

"To deal with the Chinese. But East-West agreement would be a blow for the neo-Nazis all the same."

"Well, I suppose it's possible," I said. "But not very likely."

"Sooner or later someone will have to propose a *détente*. And if the Soviets feel they need it now, for whatever reason, they could very well propose one. Still, that's not dealing with your problem, is it? I only mentioned all that to show you the atmosphere where you're going. With everybody so nervous, I'd advise you to be very careful."

"I've had some thoughts about that in the last hour or so. Frankly, I'm not sure at the moment that I want to go through with this business."

"Can't say that I blame you."

"I hope you understand how I mean that."

Thought didn't come easily, yet I knew that I would have to make up my mind quite soon about the assignment. I had never before considered myself as either a coward or any kind of hero and, to tell the truth, I still found it difficult to visualize myself in physical danger. And nothing I had heard made the importance of recovering the Pontic Tribunals lesser than it had been. But the conversation had introduced an element of menace and I knew that I would shortly find myself far out of my depth. The dangers which had seemed so unimaginable in New York were very real here. The talk of Communists and Nazis was depressing because in Europe, even in London which seemed so much like an elderly New York, they possessed a presence and a substance, not just the nightmare quality of an intangible, not-quite-believable threat.

I thought it likely that Potter oversimplified the European condition but I didn't know enough about it to prove him wrong and reassure myself. As a European, even though not a Continental European, and closer to the realities of Europe than I could ever be, he could offer persuasive arguments.

To change the subject I asked about the man who was to join us later; Potter smiled as if pleased to have his gloomy trend of thought interrupted.

"I'd much rather have you jump to your own conclusions about Karpovitch," he said.

"Why? What's the matter with him? Is he odd or something?"

"Well, let's just say he's unusual, even by London emigrée standards. You can't label him; he simply doesn't expose himself to any speculation. And yet, in many ways, he's the most improbable of them all."

"You could begin with a physical description. What makes him so odd?"

"Good God, it's lack of oddness more than anything. He has absolutely no distinguishing characteristics; nothing stands out. You could spend an hour with him and you wouldn't be able to describe him afterward. There is never anything you can remember. You just get a powerful impression of characteristics that may or may not have been there."

"He sounds like a ghost."

"That's exactly right! Everybody dresses him in the kind of flesh they think he should wear. I've heard a number of people describe him; you'd have thought they were talking about entirely different men."

"What is he? Another general?"

"No. He's a retired professor of moral philosophy. He also heads what is probably the best private espionage network in Europe. Danilow thought him the most professional spy he had ever worked with. I'm sure you wouldn't think so to look at the man."

I laughed because the idea seemed preposterous.

"A Master Spy? I thought they only had those in English mystery novels."

Potter smiled gently. He signaled to the waiter.

"There are several organizations of that sort; about two dozen in Germany alone. Groups like the German Lawyers' Union, for example; they cover East Germany like a blanket. Or the Hungarian Academic League. Or the Association of Baltic University Professors . . . Each has its information network, but they're mostly regional. They seldom cover more than one country. Karpovitch's agents are spread all over Europe, on both sides of the Iron Curtain."

"Who do all these people work for?"

"Mostly for the West. But they're not an official part of the allied spy systems. And sometimes, as with Karpovitch's people, their work is for sale."

I must have looked surprised because Potter paused for a moment, then went on:

"Don't see why it should astonish you, old man. It's very

Western, very democratic . . . a typical bit of capitalist free enterprise, wouldn't you say? The chap sells a commodity to whoever wants it. Except, of course, that he's never been known to sell anything to the Communists."

"Well, that's a comfort."

"It's also sound business."

"Your friend Karpovitch sounds like a useful man."

"The best thing about him is that no matter where his people work all the accumulated information passes through his hands. And so sooner or later he knows absolutely everything."

I started laughing, then. I didn't know if this was in relief that, at last, I would be getting professional advice, or because of the collapse of the day's tensions, or the warmth and comfort of good wine and an excellent dinner. I had a sudden picture of a Master Spy: False beard and opera cloak, the smoked green glasses of Hubertus Pohl, and a fistful of tickets for the Orient Express.

I felt ease returning. The room behind me became noisier as more late-dining people came in from the theaters. I found that I was enjoying myself and said so.

"I'm very glad," Potter said. "I'm only sorry I can't tell you more about Karpovitch."

"What more could there be?"

"Something about the man himself. That's the important part. What I've told you is largely guesswork, speculation, hints dropped by friends, an odd word or two picked up here and there. The man himself remains an unknown quantity."

I watched the friendliness, warmth, and humor leave the Englishman's face, the shoulders stiffen, and the kind eyes become disdainful and cold. He stared with a particular intensity across my shoulder towards the dining-room doors. I turned to see what had distrubed him so. The surprise was perfect. Coming in, bowed-in by the maître d'hôtel and trailed by waiters, was a mountainous, bronzed, beetle-browed man in his seventies, his heavy face corroded by deep lines, stamped with stubbornness and pride. His wild shock of pure-white hair swept back to his shoulders like the poetic mane of an ancient lion. He walked as if each footstep was a declaration of personal possession.

Potter said harshly: "There's your Senator Lindstrom." But I didn't need the identification. I had seen that raging, imperious face on too many covers of newsmagazines, in too many newspapers, on too many television screens on national holidays. And it was not the sight of the reactionary fanatic that brought my sudden sense of shock and unreality. Walking beside him was the man in brown I had last seen in Pohl's anteroom.

I didn't think they saw me. It would have made no difference if Per Lindstrom saw me; he wouldn't have known me from Adam. But Brown would have known me. And suddenly the last thing I wanted was to let this strange man, with his aura of menace and his prison pallor, know that I had seen him, and recognized him and would know him again.

Confusion came next. Surprise and shock gave way to disbelief or rather a refusal to believe. Brown's presence here linked Lindstrom with Pohl and with the Romanowski Library. I couldn't understand why I hadn't guessed that Lindstrom, who possessed all the necessary money, hatred, and ruthlessness, was Pohl's "distinguished client." It was obvious now.

I turned to Potter to ask him about it and make sure, but I changed my mind. The Englishman looked upset. He was no longer looking at the newcomers but stared bitterly at his brandy glass, searching his pockets for a cigarette. I offered him mine.

The Englishman shook his head as if to clear it of unexpected cobwebs. His smile was a brave attempt to restore the earlier warm and sympathetic mood.

"Sorry if I got a bit boorish just then. The sight of your Senator Lindstrom tends to do that to me."

"He has that effect on a lot of people. Is that the man to whom Danilow took the inscription the night he was killed?"

"Yes. Foolish of him, wasn't it? The good ex-senator had him thrown out on his ear."

"Is that why you dislike him so much?"

"Dislike is a rather mild way to describe it."

I tried to think quickly. There was no point in pushing the subject and showing Potter, and Pohl Galleries through Potter, that I had guessed Lindstrom's role in the conspiracy.

I needed a little time to come to terms with this new development and I wanted to give Potter a chance to compose himself. My hand shook a little and some wine spilled on my lap. I excused myself and left the dining room.

five

THE IDEA of working for Per Lindstrom didn't make me happy. Politics didn't interest me; they seldom had any direct bearing on either my private or professional life; but vulgarity, crudeness, stupidity, and violence were another matter, and these seemed a hallmark of Lindstrom's followers. I had no wish to play even a walk-on role in Lindstrom's private wars against anything or to become a Loyal Rifleman even by a trick of circumstances.

But did there have to be any connection, despite the circumstances? My aim was to restore and preserve the Romanowski Library . . . if, indeed, it really still existed. Per Lindstrom and his politics were no part of that. I supposed that this had always been the way to rationalize an unpalatable alliance but it seemed as good as any other—always provided, of course, that I did make up my mind about the assignment.

This is what really worried me, the heart of the matter. Should I or should I not fly east tomorrow as Potter suggested? I had no doubt that I was getting into something dangerous; some complex scheme that lay outside the conspiracy to acquire the Pontic Tribunals. The presence of Lindstrom guaranteed complexities, the appearance and reappearance of the man in brown fueled my suspicions. I couldn't believe that anything was a coincidence since the moment I had found Sempinski's letter on my mail tray. Everything that had occurred since then, or that I had heard about, seemed to form some kind of a pattern. I had no ready answers, only questions. One thing I did know: if my intuition was correct, there was no place in whatever was happening for an antiquities consultant whose most ferocious skirmishes to date had been morning battles with his housekeeper about scarves and overshoes.

I needed answers, but who could advise me? Potter was obviously more in touch with a variety of European madnesses but I had only met him a few hours earlier and I was no longer ready to trust anyone completely. Besides, he was a client representative and I had learned long ago not to involve clients in personal problems. And could I trust his friend, Karpovitch, a man I had never met? Too many strangers were becoming involved in the conspiracy; I had the uneasy feeling that everyone I met knew more about it than I did.

Tommy would know what to do. He was in government service, something quite as devious as what was happening here. I could trust his advice. Perhaps he even knew someone in London with whom I could talk.

I went to the telephone. It was ten o'clock in London, four in the afternoon in New York. Tommy would be getting home in another two hours. I placed a call to New York for that time. I was very much relieved. But I found that I was still on edge and nervous when I went back to the dining room, the wine stains forgotten and apprehension mounting.

Potter was no longer alone, another man was with him. They didn't see me enter the dining room; I had time to study the new man on my way to the table. He sat with his back to the door but with his head strangely tilted and face in quarter profile, showing an undefined assembly of darkly blurred features.

It was the sort of face you'd see anywhere, the man who wore it might be anything. There was no impression of either homeliness or beauty, cruelty or kindness, or weakness or strength. It was a face made remarkable by lack of definition, a crisscross mass of fluid wrinkles that would not hold still.

The man heard me and looked around and watched me with a

blend of caution and politeness—neither a welcoming smile nor a rebuff. He was a large man, heavy, and stooped by age. His eyes were hooded. I imagined an air of suppressed violence about him. He had the delicate, long hands of a concert pianist that seemed out of place in a violent man. His eyes were watchful but the gaze had a quality that bothered me; it seemed to slant right through me.

Karpovitch went straight to the point once I had sat down.

"I've known about the Romanowski Library for some time, but don't let that either worry you or surprise you. It is the nature of a secret to become known, particularly if those who hold the secret wish to make contact with another party. In the case of something as important as the Romanowski Library, it was inevitable that the word should spread."

"Exactly how far has it spread?"

"Your secret is reasonably safe. Specialists may collect and trade information but they never gossip. It isn't economical for them to do so."

He spoke without a trace of any kind of accent, so softly as to be almost inaudible, but with a note of such cold patronage that I found myself disliking him intensely.

"And you, I understand, are the foremost specialist," I said, matching his coldness. He laughed with genuine amusement.

"I don't know what Mister Potter told you about me but some of my friends, my former academic colleagues, have made a habit of collecting bits of information. By themselves, these fragments are meaningless. Pieced with other fragments they become interesting. When you have enough of these interesting pieces they may even make up a fascinating whole. Call it a sort of hobby with us, intellectual gymnastics. We are no longer in a position to exercise our brains; our academic careers are very much over. So, we play guessing games. We make up jigsaw puzzles."

"And one day you just happened to guess that there was a plot to smuggle the Romanowski Library to the United States? That's hard to believe."

Karpovitch looked at me with irritating patience, his eyebrows moved enough to indicate a mental shrug.

"Well . . . Perhaps there was a little more than that."

"I imagine there was. I'd like to know just how you became so very well informed about the Romanowski Library. It might suggest who else would know about it."

This time, Karpovitch's face indicated a mild speculation.

"These things are never very clear," he said finally. "There is no way to pin down the beginning of knowledge. But references to the Romanowski Library have come up several times in the past year or so. The most important reference came a year ago. There was an economic sabotage trial . . . a man named Novotny . . . a small government official who had lined his pockets at public expense. He made a special plea for leniency and offered to expose a far greater conspiracy than his. He mentioned the Library."

"And now it's a matter of official record?"

"Not necessarily. Records are bulky, particularly in totalitarian states. Papers become lost. Sometimes they are mysteriously removed. Official memories are short without papers. Whatever Novotny might have said is now quite forgotten."

"Can't he say it again?"

"I hardly think so. He died in prison. Or, to be precise, in transit between prisons. This, I might add, interested us even more than what he had to say; it showed that someone else was interested in Mister Novotny."

My mind registered in passing the appearance of another corpse. I thought again about Sempinski's disquietening letter, the hidden message it seemed to contain. Danger was evident but its source no clearer than before. I sensed Karpovitch's continuing speculation and decided to press for an answer.

"Do the authorities in your country suspect anything? I don't mind saying that your answer will decide whether I fly there tomorrow or not."

Karpovitch spread his fingers on the tablecloth and studied them for a long, silent moment. When he spoke again, his voice was ridiculously bland.

"You're cautious. Caution is admirable. But aren't you rather close to excess of caution? You demand an answer. I am not obliged to give you any answer. It is of no concern to me where you fly tomorrow."

If he had called me a coward and a weakling he couldn't have been clearer. The insult was so calculated that even Potter made a gesture of tentative protest. Karpovitch's mild tone and suddenly understanding smile merely compounded the offense. But I had been trained by Hubertus Pohl to withstand calculated insults. Karpovitch's reason for insulting me wasn't clear unless he wished to push me into a decision about the assignment and that seemed unlikely; what would he gain one way or the other? But I had no doubt that he had a reason; he simply wasn't the kind of man who did anything without one.

I repeated the question.

Karpovitch bowed, then; a strange, outmoded gesture: half courteous, half derisive. His voice became again the dry lecturing tone of a teacher dealing with an obtuse student.

"By the *authorities,* I imagine you mean the Secret Police. They're called the NKD where you are going, or the *Nakomda.* They are unaware of your business at the moment, but this may change quickly. You must remember that it is their nature to suspect. They are superbly trained, efficient, and their leaders are intelligent. If you share the popular American belief that all secret policemen, other than your own, are mindless thugs, you might as well return to New York tomorrow."

"I'm willing to respect the Nakomda," I said carefully. Karpovitch's quick frown was no compensation for my rising anger. The interruption had annoyed him but he decided to ignore both the interruption and its source.

"We came across your secret at the Novotny trial only because we were looking for something else that might come out of the trial. The Nakomda had no reason to give it more than routine interest. Pleas such as Novotny's are common; the Nakomda ignored it. Then, later, there were other mentions. Nothing specific, of course. Such things are never definite or specific. But a hint here . . . a suggestion there . . . an inquiry somewhere else . . . In time these formed a pattern, do you follow me?"

This time I only nodded.

"We became interested because everything that keeps recurring with no apparent reason interests us. We watched and listened and began to put together another jigsaw puzzle, and as it grew we became *very* interested. We found some interesting ramifications. I am not going to tell you about them; they can neither threaten you nor help you if you confine your activities only to your business. I suggest you do precisely that. Furthermore, the less you know of what doesn't concern you, the less you can tell if anyone should ever question you. Do you still follow me?"

"You mean the Nakomda?"

"Not only the Nakomda." And then, with heavy sarcasm: "But, I suggest, your part in this affair is quite challenging enough. The various ramifications would only confuse you."

"I'd like to be the judge of that."

"That's out of the question. I see no need to burden you with specialized knowledge. Our interests coincide to a certain point and to that point I'm willing to help you. Beyond that we have nothing to say to each other."

I had his measure now and, again, nodded briefly. The pained embarrassment on Potter's face made me sorry for him.

"The sum total of this puzzle of yours became so interesting," Karpovitch continued, "that we decided to take an active hand. There are still many pieces missing but we know enough. The question now is this: Are you going on with your assignment, or are you returning to New York? If I may paraphrase your earlier point: whether I tell you anything more depends on your answer."

I was not reassured by Karpovitch's sudden smile, a dispassionate grimace lost among fluid lines. Nothing I had heard had been reassuring. But the man's professorial tone, his sarcasms and his contemptuous air made further hesitation impossible for me.

I said I would not be returning to New York.

Later, I would think of that night as something that only might have happened, that was never real; and that if any of it had the solidity and substance of factual experience it could have been no firmer than a dream.

There was Karpovitch's dry, disembodied voice without a clearly defined face behind it, and so it had a shadowed quality like something merely imagined. The words themselves were unreal and measured like the monotonous beat of a giant clock.

Do this and don't do that (Karpovitch was saying) and go here and there, and (under certain circumstances) do the following and (under other circumstances) this is what you must do. Later, when it was so important for me to remember exactly what I had been told, with all the accents and inflections and possible shades of meaning, I couldn't pin down one word that carried more weight or color than any other word. Each had the same uninflected grayness that blurred whatever individual meaning it might have had and made them all, remembered only in their combination, as featureless as the particles of atoms in a smooth steel rail.

I was to fly aboard a Soviet turbojet next afternoon. There was a reason for this, other than the fact that it was the first nonstop flight available from Croydon . . . a subtle shade of difference that would help to establish my neutrality . . . an imperceptible advantage. It would make it far less difficult for NKD agents to keep an eye on me, or make contact if they wanted to, than it would have been aboard a British transport. Thus it suggested innocence and that was important. Police *dossiers* were compounded from innumerable small fragments, impressions and particles of impressions, and this would be one. If it made no impression whatsoever that would still constitute an advantage. And it would introduce me, no matter how slightly, to that indescribable feeling that comes from the knowledge of constant surveillance, the inner hollowness that must be so rigidly controlled (the wondering about *who* and *where,* with eyes that can never be allowed to search, with the gestures that can never suggest tension nor be too studiously at ease); something as alien to a Western mind as deserts are to oceans; a rule of life that never becomes natural unless a man is born to it, and not always then. It would be a quarter-day acclimatization—as gentle a transition as I could expect under the new ground rules. And there were certain other rules to follow, a whole vocabulary of innocent expressions to be learned, so that additional small fragments could find their way into my dossier.

"Does everyone have a police dossier? Is everyone watched?"

"Assume so. In your case, be certain of it."

"Are they always watched?"

"You can be sure you will be."

"Can anyone be trusted?"

"Never. Suspect everyone."

"Don't people ever relax? Can't they ever drop their guard?"

"They must be always careful but never show that they are being careful. Assume that even your most private moments are being observed and never let it show."

"Does anyone ever make an honest statement that means what it says?"

"You can't afford to think so. But never show that you are taking it as anything else. You may hear pro-Western comments, you may even hear criticism of the local system. Assume that it is all police-inspired no matter how drawn you may feel toward the critic."

"How do I handle that?"

"How would you naturally be inclined to handle it?"

"I wouldn't say much of anything. Can't very well disagree with a pro-Western viewpoint, and couldn't very well criticize my hosts."

"Admirable and exactly right. Take refuge in polite embarrassment. Never agree or disagree or encourage controversial comment or invite a confidence. But never fail to defend your own system if it should be attacked."

"Sometimes that's hard to do . . ."

"So much the better. Never be vehement in your defense or make comparisons between the various failings of the American system and the Communist sins. Forget that evil is only a matter of degree."

"I never thought so."

"So much the better, then."

And there were other rules and a timetable to follow; they were designed to give the impression of an amiable, apolitical scholar who was combining scholarship with an unorthodox vacation.

Thus there were to be three days of sightseeing, guided and alone; nonwork days devoted to the Baedeker, guidebook and city map with my supposedly vestigial American feet protesting the cruelty of cobblestones. *PABUT,* the government tourist bureau, supplied interpreter-guides to show this and that but never the other, only the clean and shining or historically celebrated; the approved New and the noncontroversial Old.

There was a standard pattern of tourist behavior, and this included violation of the regulation that forbad sightseeing without the PABUT guide, because three days of Soviet Gothic architecture, concrete-and-plateglass housing projects, dayschools and nurseries, the odd Filtration Plant and the State Opera were usually enough. Only German tourists marched in step under supervision throughout their stay; everyone else was expected to try a diversion on his own; it would make me conspicuous if I didn't try one.

"Absolute compliance with all regulations is immediately open to suspicion. It is unreasonable to suppose that absolute respect for all laws can exist unless there exists a parallel desire to conceal a crime. That is something every policeman is taught to believe."

"I'll remember."

"Be aimless in your wandering. Establish a pattern of unpredictable decisions. Let your guardian angels get accustomed to it."

"Guardian angels?"

"Plainclothesmen. The Nakomda, if you give them any reason to wonder about you."

"Won't unpredictable decisions give them cause to wonder?"

"Not if they are always unpredictable. When the unexpected is the norm, it is accepted as eccentricity. Scholars are expected to act without logic."

The colorless, cold words flowed like the metal of a ghostly right-of-way, a toneless superhighway lost in monotonous country.

Later, when it was so important to examine the shape and sound and coloration of each word, I wished I hadn't let excitement and anticipation strip me of analytical objectivity. But this was High Adventure, after all; I couldn't be analytical about anything like that.

"Establish a pattern of patternless thinking," Karpovitch was saying. "Be indecisive and make lightning-swift, spur of the moment decisions, start sidetrips only to change your mind at midpoint and go off on tangents. No one will be surprised when, later, you start in one direction and disappear in another."

"How will I get away from my guardian angels?"

"You will be told. Just make sure that you've laid the necessary groundwork."

"Tangents and lack of systematic methods. I understand. Incidentally, how should I go about contacting Sempinski? That's my official purpose, after all."

"Send him a note from your hotel. It will take a few days for his reply to reach you; that will give you time for all we've discussed. Then, make whatever arrangements you want with Sempinski."

"And my contact with the Library people?"

"Act as if there were to be none. Don't even think about them. Someone will get in touch with you at the right time."

"How will I know him?"

"His name will be Zimstern. No, don't write it down! Ferdynand Zimstern, dealer in antiques. He's a good dealer, too, with some handsome East European pieces, so it's logical that he'd get in touch with you after he reads of your arrival in the papers."

I had to admit that Karpovitch seemed to have anticipated almost everything. I wondered if he, himself, had any connection with the Romanowski Library.

"Remember: Zimstern, dealer in antiques. He has a store somewhere in the Old City. The name is easy to remember. What does it mean in English? A star of spice?"

"Cinnamon Star, I think."

And was that all?

"That is everything."

I would see the sights and inadvertently-on-purpose lose a guide and set out on some impulsive trip to one place and wind up in another, and I would set up an irrational pattern of behavior and lay the groundwork for a journey to wherever the Romanowski Library was supposedly hidden, and I would go about the business that was my excuse for being in the country and meet Julian Sempinski, and then a Cinnamon Star would appear and lead me to my journey's end.

I laughed, because it was so simple; I couldn't believe it.

"It doesn't look as if I'll have much trouble."

Karpovitch bowed his head; an abrupt gesture of assent that threw his face momentarily into shadow. And then the innumerable, mobile wrinkles and undefined angles and liquid planes that made up that extraordinary face, congealed in hard textured lines and features sculpted in granite. I was suddenly aware of diamond-hard eyes secretly amused.

The transformation lasted only a fraction of a second. Then substance melted and the rigidly defined mask flowed apart again and the quick light went out of the eyes. They had, again, the hooded transparency of windows opening on shadow.

It was well after midnight when Potter and Karpovitch left. I went up to my suite and tried to make up my mind about the call to Tommy . . . and about going East. Potter had made the reservations, but I could still change my mind and cancel everything.

Should I or shouldn't I? It seemed that I was starting to practice indecision a little too early.

Truth was, I didn't want to talk to Tommy then; I didn't want to be dissuaded from making the trip. I was too full of Master Spies, Nakomda agents and everything I had heard about that evening; my eyes were full of Cinnamon Stars, I supposed. I would go on, as planned, because I wanted to. It was my adventure. I had just enough time to get to the telephone to cancel the call before the transatlantic operator made the connection.

PART TWO:

The Pontic Tribunals

six

I STOOD at the top of the portable stairway they had pulled up with tractors through the snow, feeling the sharp bite of the wind, the bitterly cold air. The world was gray, filled with falling snow as thick as the invisible clouds; enormous snowflakes slanted past my face.

I had been the last passenger to step out of the warm cabin of the aircraft into the icy wind. The soft, luxurious warmth of the huge TU was fast disappearing, and with it the memory of soundless flight high above the billowing white blanket of the two Germanys and the other borders; the forests had looked like dwarfed clumps of steel wool pressed into the whiteness; everything else—roads, rivers, villages, and towns—crouched under the snow.

It had all looked pretty much the same, no matter what the country, once we had lifted off the gray-brown mass of England and dropped the washed-out ribbon of the Channel behind us. France showed blue water and stretches of vestigial green; Holland and the forest-screened approaches of North Germany were, perhaps, less consistently white, crisscrossed with more black lines of roads and rivers than the others; but once the Elbe had drifted westward under us all land took refuge under the neutral uniform of snow. There were no borders then; no artificial lines penciled into the clean white sheet of north-central Europe; it unfolded like a fresh roll of textured Bristol block, soft and unsegmented, until we flew across the ultimate demarcation line. There the West ended and the East began.

But even this was more a matter of the senses than plain sight. I had begun to feel the approach of this most unnatural of all borders long before the aircraft commander made his trilingual announcement. The metal walls had seemed to compress. I was aware of silence and a sudden stillness; the abrupt end of forty conversations. There was no more weight-shifting from one uncomfortable buttock to another, and no papers rustled. My fellow passengers were suddenly absorbed in mindless contemplation of their own dull thoughts, and eyes grew vacant with the blank gaze of the inward stare. It was as if everyone had become locked in a drugged, hypnotic trance and had stepped far into himself, diminishing in his own, warm darkness as the line drew near.

The plane had banked gently into the southward curve that led into the air corridor above Berlin, and at once the plane commander's voice crackled on the intercom. Passengers were reminded in Russian, German, and another language that the Government of the People's Democratic East German Republic forbade air-observation of the border.

I had retreated obediently into the deep soft nap of the artificial velvet upholstery, wanting to look out, to see Berlin before it disappeared. This was the last outpost, after all. We had been flying over East Germany for some time but I hadn't felt myself carried through alien air because Berlin, with its Western Zones, had still been ahead . . . I had not yet been irrevocably carried beyond the last border. And then, there it was: Berlin, slanting toward me under the white blade of the wing, spinning away on invisible rollers and soon gone. With it went everything familiar; everything I could take for granted. From that point to the far shores of the Bering Straits lay the foreign East; barbarism began where the familiar ended.

The dull roar of the turbojets, loud in the frozen silence of this border crossing, had receded. I had become aware of new, foreign sounds as the other passengers stirred and the illustrated pages of their magazines had begun to rustle and they resumed their crackling conversations. They were no longer the wholly human fellow passengers who had come aboard with me in London; now they were trolls and ogres carried by black magic to their ice mountains in the East.

I didn't think that I had ever felt more alone. A pink-cheeked stewardess offered me trays of canapés that would have tempted St. Anthony into gluttony, but I shook my head. I listened for one word of English . . . even German . . . in the forty conversations going on around me but there was only the singsong cadence of the Slavs. They were as alien to me as the man in the moon.

I had felt as if I flew in a private chamber, the glass capsule of the absolute outsider, across the vast sweep of a brilliant sky above snowclouds. The glittering white land that flashed ice signals in the cloud breaks had no relation to anything I knew.

The crystal capsule was still around me when I stepped out of the plane into the shock of an Eastern European winter. The blue-gray light of a January afternoon was a diffused glow that seemed to give everything an extra dimension. I saw great rectangles and squares splashed with luminescent orange; dark concrete cliffs wrapped in concentric wheels of light. It took a moment to realize that these were only airport terminal buildings bathed in their own window light reflected by snow.

My crystalline shield blew up in the cold and I was once again in a time-place context, with the wind slashing through my New York overcoat as if it were paper. I hadn't got the message from the fur hats and hairy overcoats that the disembarking trolls had broken out of their luggage aboard the TU. Someone called from the foot of the mobile stairway but the wind blew the sound away. I shook my head at a snowcapped man, understanding nothing, and trudged across the surprisingly hard snow toward the orange lights. Behind me came a spattering of sound like pistol fire; icicles snapped off the tubular steel framework of the stair tower.

Inside was warmth, lights, marble, tile, potted plants, brilliant decorator colors, astonishing graphics and twisted ornamental iron shapes: a hall the size of a football field with incomprehensible signs.

A man spoke to me, his face questioning and kind, his words a senseless cacophony. I showed him my passport. He held it in both hands, looking curiously at its golden emblem, then with equal curiosity at me, then passed us both—curiosities from another planet —to a platoon of men in uniforms of gradually increasing elegance who wrote on forms and pounded them with ink stamps.

In time, my brain thawed out. I began to see the men and women I was dealing with, their various uniforms. I didn't know one uniform from another, of course, and wondered which, if any, were the Nakomda men. The faces looking up at me from the desks were uniformly square, with high cheekbones and widespaced eyes like intelligent marbles. I wondered which of these pleasant faces concealed a policeman.

One man made a more distinct impression. He did no stamping or writing on forms, but paralleled my progress from desk to desk behind the officials, occasionally looking over the functionaries' shoulders, one hand tucked neatly behind his back, the other supporting a little cigarette in an amber holder. He wore a round-crowned military cap with a dark blue band, a long double-breasted overcoat buttoned across his chest, polished riding boots, leather belt and a small pistol holster.

I was curious about everything, but careful not to stare. Everything still seemed as if it was happening to somebody else but my airtight, isolation capsule had melted away; I had a feeling of double participation, the odd detachment of an interested observer.

It was all right to stare; they would expect me to be interested. Americans were rare in their country and we didn't know anything about them. And it was all right to look nervous which was convenient because I was nervous. I found it difficult to meet anybody's eyes; Karpovitch's lecture had not included a recommended response to friendly officials.

Then I was at the end of the line of desks, a ream of forms

clutched under one arm, Pohl's elegant briefcase under the other, and my valises dangling from both hands. A herd of porters and taxicab drivers formed for their stampede and, suddenly, as I got ready for the rush, I saw them thrown into confusion: first milling like startled animals, then drifting away with increasing speed. The officer in the blue-banded cap had come up beside me.

"Please come with me," he said.

His voice didn't give anything away.

"Where?" I said. "Why? Is anything wrong?"

The officer looked at me with no more than polite attention. His widely spaced gray eyes communicated neither friendliness nor hostility, his wide thin mouth neither smiled nor scowled, but I felt coldness creeping past my knees and my anxiety broke out of control.

"Because if anything is wrong," I said, "I mean about my papers, I'd like to call the American Legation."

He asked politely: "Why would you want to do anything like that?"

I was floundering and furious about it. Arouse no special interest, Karpovitch had said. My question had been thrown out by instinct, but if I had wanted to advertise that I expected trouble, I wouldn't have been able to do better.

I said, confused and groping, "Well . . . it's customary, isn't it?"

The officer laughed abruptly.

"Nervous, Dr. Shippe?"

I started on an indignant *What would I have to be nervous about?* but thought better of it, sure that the officer would immediately tell me.

He nodded pleasantly and pointed with his cigarette holder down the brightly lighted, tiled corridor, and I set out behind him, trying to match my nervous porter's stagger to his long military stride.

Afterward there was no way to judge whether the interview had gone well or badly.

There was a small office with bright travel posters: mountains and ruined castles and craggy-faced highlanders in flat hats and capes; girls in red boots, flying braids. The office had been borrowed for the interview. A soldier with a futuristic-looking weapon strapped across his chest, and with the same blue hatband as his officer, stood outside the door. Passers-by went out of their way not to approach him or the door he guarded. I assumed that I was in the presence of the NKD.

I couldn't understand what they wanted from me. The questioning gave no clue.

The questions came, flat and disinterested, as if it didn't matter what I answered. Each answer led into another question. Sooner or later the questions came back to Sempinski.

Yes, I had come to see Professor Sempinski. I had an invitation. No, we were not regular correspondents. Each of us had written one letter and one cable. Yes, I admired Sempinski as a writer. No, I didn't know anything about Sempinski's present projects and activities, supposing them literary. Yes, I realized the writer had published nothing since 1938, but books were not produced like vacuum cleaners. No, I didn't *send* Mrs. Napoji to Sempinski; I had merely suggested that she visit him. (I gave the reasons for suggesting it.) Oh, all right, I did ask her to visit Sempinski; a personal matter. What was it? I wanted the famous writer to autograph a book. No, I didn't think there was anything unusual about that. No, it did not seem odd. No, I had written nothing in the book I sent. No, I didn't know Mrs. Napoji well; in fact I hadn't heard about her accident until Sempinski mentioned it in his letter. But now, yes, I knew about it from a friend. What friend? Would I name him? Well, all right; I named him. I was sure I could tell the NKD nothing about the accident that they didn't know. What did I mean by that? Why, nothing! I merely supposed . . . Yes, I knew she was related to Senator Lindstrom, but I had no connecton with him. None. In fact I wouldn't welcome such connections. Why? I didn't agree with the former senator's outlook, viewpoint and, well, everything; they were too extreme. Yes I was opposed to extremism in any form. No, not *violently* opposed, that's why I disliked the Lindstrom solutions.

Would I say that my philosophy was liberal? Not in the active political sense. Yes, there were other senses. Yes, I was a liberal in the humanitarian sense, I supposed; at least I hoped I was . . . No! I was not a member of the Liberal Party. Yes, I supposed Julian Sempinski was a liberal. A militant liberal? Yes, I supposed that was true. And was Mrs. Napoji also a liberal? I supposed she was; I really didn't know. But wasn't that a little academic now? *I mean after the accident* . . . No, I never got an autographed book from Julian Sempinski. No, I had never met him; I looked forward to it. Yes, I thought him a very great man. No, this was not the general opinion in the United States; few of my countrymen had heard of Sempinski . . . And No! Nobody I knew kept contact with Sempinski. Nobody had sent me.

"When is your meeting with Sempinski? Where?"

"I don't have an appointment. I plan to write him a letter in a day or two. You see, this is a holiday for me, as well as an opportunity to meet Sempinski . . . I plan to see a bit of your country while I'm here."

"What do you wish to see?"

"Well . . . I don't know exactly. I'm an antiquarian. Eastern antiquities . . ."

I stopped, beginning to feel more than just a little alarmed and confused. The security officer was looking at me as if I were already standing in the dock with the Pontic Tribunals spread in evidence on the prosecution table.

"And one of our principal antiquities is Julian Sempinski," he finished soberly.

The NKD man asked to see Sempinski's letter and my invitation. I felt the time had come for a mild protest.

"But that's a private letter."

He laughed then and looked at me with something like pity.

"That's all right," he said. "We're used to it. Like doctors, you know."

I knew that protests would be useless, in fact more than useless; they would be dangerous. Only my own pride was involved here, my right to keep my mail to myself. But he had said so gently that he was used to reading other people's mail . . . *Like doctors,* he said. And it was better for the Nakomda to go through my mail than to mark me as uncooperative and, therefore, suspicious. The quicker the interview was over the better for me. I took the letter from the briefcase and handed it over.

He read it quickly but with deep attention, as if he had already an idea about the letter's contents. He smiled a little to himself and put the letter aside. He looked at me for a long quiet moment, as if making up his mind, then nodded briefly, returned the letter to me and lit a cigarette. And it was then that I knew why the half-mocking hooded eyes had seemed so familiar. They had the same quality of secret amusement and private knowledge I had last read in Karpovitch's face.

Five minutes more of expert questioning would have finished me but, curiously, the Nakomda officer changed tack as soon as it had become obvious that I was getting rattled.

This time there was no mockery in the smile. The cigarette he offered and I took was harsh and just what I needed to pull my wits together. But for all this sudden cordiality there was still a strain. I hoped he didn't know how close I had been to panic. So much depended on keeping clear of suspicion, avoiding attention. Everything would be infinitely harder if the Nakomda kept its eyes on me; Zimstern might even find it too dangerous to attempt a contact.

The interview had been anything but routine. I didn't expect the Nakomda to offer explanations; that would be hardly according to custom. They didn't seem to suspect my real reasons for coming to their country—the Pontic Tribunals had not been mentioned— but I knew that I had failed an important test. I had not convinced the Nakomda that I had come only to see the sights and meet an old man whose work I admired. I had upset Karpovitch's foremost principle by having failed to avoid notice. Ironically, it was the cover story that was supposed to make me inconspicuous —my own smug contribution to Pohl's plans—that had earned me my Nakomda interview and interest. Who could have imagined that the Nobel Prize winner was up to something other than writing a book? Knowing that it was too late for self-recrimination didn't help me feel less foolish than I did.

The officer smiled, as if to indicate that the interview was over. "You must be tired, Dr. Shippe."

But I had learned the first lesson in dealing with security policemen: you either told them everything or nothing; there was no middle ground.

"It must be quite a strain," he went on when I didn't answer. "All this excitement. First time in the country. New language, customs. It doesn't do to overexcite oneself. You should rest for a day or two; take it easy, as your people say. We'd want your first visit to our country to be memorable. And now I'll get somebody to get you a taxi."

seven

I DIDN'T think that I would be able to sleep, but I slept like a bear. I woke on my first morning behind the Iron Curtain feeling a high sense of excitement, determined to make no new errors or repeat the old. The airport interview didn't seem so bad after ten hours of dreamless oblivion in a feather bed. I remembered everything Karpovitch had told me and went about the morning as if everything—from brushing my teeth to eating a rich and satisfying breakfast, and from an interested reading of a day-old Paris edition of *L'Humanite* to writing my note to Julian Sempinski—was done on the clear end of a two-way mirror. I was conscious of an audience in everything I did and found myself enjoying my unfamiliar role. It was exciting trying to spot possible guardian angels.

Waiters were immediately suspect, but they were disappointing; more like cabinet ministers of deposed regimes than undercover agents. The PABUT guide turned out to be a well-mannered young woman who immediately warned me not to change American currency anywhere but in official centers; it seemed that half the capital traded black market dollars, but half the traders were Nakomda agents. But there was a definitely sinister bald, fat man, who sat in the lobby behind a newspaper, and a beetle-browed, thin man who bumped into me in the elevator and passed me a note.

The note turned out to be an advertisement for a night club with unusual floor shows.

I wrote a post card to Tommy and, after a moment of hesitation, to Hubertus Pohl. It seemed a natural thing to do and it allowed me to share some of my excitement, the feeling of participation in foreign intrigue.

I had allowed Miss Jablonska of the PABUT to take me on the expected tour of the city. We rode well-bundled in rugs in a horse-drawn carriage with sleigh runners instead of wheels, while the air crackled with the cold around us. She had suggested a late-model Russian Volga with a uniformed chauffeur, but I had spotted the other vehicle plodding through traffic, with a red-nosed driver perched high on the box, oilskin cap pulled down over his ears and frost on his whiskers. She urged the warmer means of transportation but I was adamant; I had begun to think of a plan that would set me free of PABUT supervision.

She shivered like a wet kitten in her threadbare cloth coat and inadequate boots. I was toast-warm in a magnificent overcoat (lined from neck to ankles with beaver, and with a collar of solid otter fur standing up around my ears like an electric fire) and in a silver-gray Karakul fur hat. I had bought both immediately after breakfast.

The capital proved to be more than I had hoped it would be. I had read all I could about it in New York but it had been old material. Ninety percent of this city had been turned to rubble by Russians and Germans. Now, everything was new. Whatever had been picturesque or meaningful had been carefully restored, gargoyle by gargoyle and cornice by cornice. Spires and cupolas, neo-classic palaces, Italianate galleries, and urban perspectives straight out of Leonardo.

I noticed many uniforms; squads of the military stood outside the hotels. The PABUT girl explained that the Warsaw Pact conference was responsible for the security measures.

"Where is the Chairman of the Soviet Union staying?"

"The Russians haven't come yet."

"When will they come?"

"Who knows about the Russians? They come and go as they please."

She didn't seem particularly enthusiastic about the Chairman and his delegation.

And then we were in the Old City, and it seemed impossible that none of that sixteenth-century magic of tall, narrow buildings had been there after 1945, except as rubble. Some of the bitterest house-to-house fighting in Europe had taken place here. But now it was exactly as it had been before the war. Communist or not, the country seemed to like its history within reach.

I was delighted with it all; from the worn thresholds, hollowed into basins, to the coats of arms carved among the gargoyles. The ancient cornices and the steep-roofed buildings that seemed to spread and settle on the cobbled streets like old dowagers, the huge gates studded with enormous nails, hung on ornamental hinges, the narrow alleys with opposite roofs practically rubbing lead rain gutters and copper spouts overhead, steep limestone stairs no wider than a fireman's ladder plunging between houses from the ancient market square to the riverbanks: all these appealed to my sense of history, the continuity of the human serial. Even the ancient city walls had been reconstructed, complete with holes that had been pounded into the defenses by Swedish cannon in the sixteenth century. These were streets made for the heroes of Sempinski's novels, fashioned for swordsmen and plot and intrigue. Time seemed to stand still here; yet it was moving softly in the dark doorways, through the winding alleys. It would be here that I would be taken by the conspirators, at least in spirit, no matter where they actually led me.

"Magnificent," I said.

The guide said something inaudible and sad.

She had begun to sniff among the plate-glass and concrete boxes of modern avenues; she sneezed and coughed among the cupolas and spires. In the Old City she was hoarse and fevered. I took pity on her. I suggested coffee. She led me to a cellar restaurant under the traditional wreath of a sixteenth-century tavern where, in the steam of Turkish coffee, she had to lean on my arm going down the stairs.

I couldn't face her accusing eyes and felt my resolve melting like the Napoleon pastries on my plate, but it was too late to turn back from my plan. I suggested that if she was ill she should go home; I would find my own way back to the hotel. The poor girl shook her head.

I looked around and saw the fat, bald man whom I had last seen in the hotel lobby. He had his back to us but I was sure that there was no mistake. His polished head caught the light like a billiard ball and seemed to flash signals. He sat like a gleaming idol, his beefy back encased in shining serge that made me think of stuffed sausages.

Back in the sleigh, I peered about with all the eagerness of a sightseeing tourist, but if the beefy guardian angel was on the job he kept out of sight. He would be in a taxi, of course; there were many taxis. Streetcars clanged and grated. There were horse-drawn drays. Quick crowds moved on the sidewalks hampered by the snow. We went on, the coughing girl and I; she pointed, whispered, and I looked obediently but I could no longer hear the explanations. I almost forgot to ask about the famous ghetto, but finally I did, and she made an odd, resigned gesture as if that wind-swept, icy wilderness was too much to bear. She stood beside me, huddled in her light coat, while I looked at the ruins that had been left untouched to serve as a memorial. I hadn't thought they'd have any effect on me; I was not a Jew, and without some bloodlink one battlefield is much like another. These foreign acres of uncleared, snowsheeted rubble should have meant nothing to me. But somehow, as a human being, I found myself awed and incredibly moved. There was a gaunt magnificence about the pyramids of broken masonry; the wind, shrill in this wasteland, boom-ing in the canyons of a hollow town, wrapped this monument in a Gregorian chant and peopled it with shadows. I felt no pain, no personal involvement. But the desolation sheeted my mind with lead. I was glad when the ghostly battlefield vanished in the snow that had begun to fall.

By midday, my guide had a burning temperature. Another hour of the icy tour would send her to bed. She would be too ill in the morning to take charge of me, but I counted on her Communist sense of duty to keep her off the sick list until the last possible moment. By the time PABUT could send reinforcements I would be on my own.

The alien city no longer worried me. I had it in perspective. If anything, it was this totally foreign air, the lack of anything familiar, that sharpened my pleasure.

The sleigh glided through narrow backstreets behind the Market Square, across pale pools of yellow lamplight between banks of snow. It was a silent, shuttered quarter, unpeopled and empty; its tall, narrow windows had the hooded look of sentries guarding secret meeting places.

I looked up and out and sat up with a start, caution forgotten and recovered too late. Above a dark window and a gaunt doorway hidden in the shadow of a narrow passage hung a wooden sign. It spelled the name of FERDYNAND ZIMSTERN, DEALER IN ANTIQUES.

Coincidence? I wished I could afford to think so. There could have been no mistake about the PABUT guide's sudden movement against me, the quick pressure that had made me look up at the sign.

I forced back an exclamation only just in time, but my surprised start had been exclamatory enough. How could she know that Zimstern's name would mean anything to me? Who was she? How much did she know?

I forced myself not to think of answers. That way lay danger. I would do my thinking when I was alone. There were implications here that made me suddenly feel as if my furs had turned into paper in the fierce cold of the darkening afternoon.

Occasionally I glanced at the girl. She kept her face averted, her head down; she seemed hardly conscious. I thought that she had kept her head down even as she had made that quick, insistent movement. What had it been, anyway? I was confused and shaken.

The icy afternoon swept without warning into evening and then into night. Snow fell in silent masses; soon the streets were a flickering dark haze of indistinct shapes smeared with pale splashes of yellow light and multicolored neon. I was alone, shut off in a private cubicle of darkness and snow, carried on hissing runners through a cacophony of Klaxons, streetcar bells and the whine of motors straining in first gear. Danger seemed very near in the spotted darkness.

I got rid of my furs in the downstairs cloakroom, not wanting to go up to the false privacy of my room. I would have given anything to be at home: dry and warm with apple logs burning in the fireplace and Mahler filling my study with a hurricane of sound. Thought would be calm and orderly with the sherry a mahogany red in the cutglass decanter, and the day safely locked outside. I ordered dinner, thinking that eating would be an ordeal, and enjoyed a sort of combination cabbage-roll and carpetbag steak: an envelope of delicately cured veal stuffed with brown rice boiled in red wine, mushrooms, a shellfish of some kind and herbs in a white-flour sauce. Tension gradually left me as I ate.

Why had the PABUT girl drawn my attention to Zimstern's sign? If the Nakomda suspected me of dealings with Zimstern they wouldn't need to confirm their suspicions by staging an elaborate confrontation. And how could they have linked me with Karpovitch's man? Only Potter and the Master Spy himself knew of my connection with the antique dealer.

It would be good to know just what the Nakomda had on Zimstern. A hookup with Karpovitch was one thing; the Pontic Tribunals were another matter. The Nakomda could link me with Zimstern only if they had got wind of the conspiracy. But, if so, why warn me by tipping their hand?

I wondered what to do. The easiest thing was to do nothing, and wait. If the police were setting a trap my best course was to play the tourist and take no chances; sooner or later someone would contact me and tell me what to do. If Zimstern was in trouble, he could be replaced. If he was not in trouble, he would show up when it was safe to do so.

But this simple course wasn't good enough. Perhaps it was too reasonable at a time when not much made sense. Zimstern had to be warned. He was my only sure contact in the capital; I couldn't afford to lose him. But I knew, even then, that the real reason for what I had decided to do lay in my own curiosity. I was drawn by the magnet of the dark night, the mysterious doorways and the shrouded windows of the Old City backstreets.

I took my time about leaving the hotel. I got my briefcase so as to have all my identification, then read the *Continental Daily Mail* in the dining room until it started emptying. No one followed me into the lobby cloakroom where I picked up my furs. My spirits rose as my excitement mounted. My fat bald guardian, his back to the lobby and the revolving doors, was in a heated conversation with a desk clerk. A crowd of young people pushing in, loudly and suddenly, out of the windswept street, provided a diversion. I was through the revolving doors in moments, struggling into furs.

"Taxi!"

The wind caught my voice and carried it away. But a familiar dark shadow broke through the curtain of falling snow and plodded toward me. The swaybacked horse staggered up to the curb. Behind him gleamed the oilskin cap and the frozen whiskers.

I gave the address by shouting *Old City,* the only words in the language that I could pronounce. The driver looked behind me, as if expecting another passenger, then grinned and slapped the reins and made a kissing sound with his lips and the old horse looked up, sadly but resigned. I climbed into the sleigh and spread the wraps about me. It was bitterly cold. The sleigh swung away from the curb and then we were weaving in and out of traffic, still heavy despite the snowfall and late evening. I thought I could hear the old driver chuckling above the tinny sound of the small bell on the horse's harness, the whine of motors, blare of horns and clang of streetcar bells. The sleigh moved nimbly through a fleet of similar vehicles and taxis. Anyone trying to follow us would have an awkward time; it was obvious the old man on the driver's box had done that kind of thing before.

Streets followed streets, and then the ancient, steep roofs began to crowd together, and the modern streetlights gave way to ornamental iron redolent of age, and windows narrowed and alleys became darker, and then we were in the Old City and it was time to stop.

The driver looked down at me, grinning, and winked conspiratorially and nodded toward the street behind us where whoever might have been trying to follow us would now be lost and cursing.

I was at once surrounded by small boys begging for foreign currency. The few odd dimes and nickels I had in my pockets quickly disappeared and the sight of a quarter quickly provided me with a voluble small guide and shortly afterward I was knocking on the antique dealer's door.

There was no answer, no sign that anyone inside had heard me or would hear me. I listened for footsteps. I imagined a small, stooped, myopic man coming through the store, silent in felt slippers, an unassuming man in bottle-bottom glasses who would blink in the sudden brightness of the streetlamp. And now I was anxious to get out from under the bright glare of the lamp, into the darkened store. I knocked again, louder. I listened. I heard nothing. There was only the soft hiss of snow falling around me and the distant sounds of disembodied traffic far beyond the dark mouth of the street.

The windows were dark. I supposed I might have imagined the gleam of light I thought I had seen moving between the shutters. I knocked once more, then tried the door. It swung inward with a slow, painful creak and a small bell sounded overhead. I stepped inside.

There was a smell of dust and dryness. Dark shapes retreated from the sudden light, resolved themselves into counters and tall cases, ancient metal, the dusty sweep of hangings stirred by the icy wind blowing from the street. Light from the lamp outside lay in shallow pools among small coffers, stacked canvasses and frames, disfigured plaster busts, bronze heads. Darkness clung to the corners among squat suits of armor bowed like crippled robots.

I heard a rustling movement on my left and thought of rats

and mice and then I thought I saw a larger shadow. I asked: "Is anybody there? Hullo . . ."

At once a powerful white light struck me in the face, blinded me. I fell back from the door as a foot came from the darkness and kicked it shut, and the tall shadow behind the white glare began to move swiftly backward through the store.

"Herr Zimstern," I began . . .

A harsh, cold voice said: "Don't move. Stand still." Then added, unnecessarily: "Close your eyes."

The man was an American. He backed away toward the rear of the store, shielded by the high intensity flashlight that made him invisible. He kept the light trained squarely on my eyes. Then a door opened in a corner and both the light and the man were gone. I heard light footsteps leaping over stairs.

eight

I WAITED in the darkness minute after minute, trying to recover my night vision and to make some sense of what had just happened. The startling presence of my vanished countryman had been the last thing I had expected to find in Zimstern's store. Who was he? His voice had been too coarse, too nasal and violent for an antiquities consultant and, anyway, I knew all my colleagues very well. I had never heard that unpleasant voice before.

But the man had seemed to know me. He hadn't asked who I was, or why I had come. He hadn't asked my name. I had spoken in fluent, unaccented German but he had known that I would understand his commands in English. And he had made sure that I wouldn't be able to see him behind his blinding light.

I heard footsteps behind the back door, on the same stairs that the unexpected American had mounted so quickly. I supposed that the stairs led to living quarters above the store.

Someone was coming down, carrying a lantern; I saw a wavering light frame the rectangle of the door, grow brighter, steadier, and then the door was flung open and a man came in carrying a hissing carbide lamp high over his head. He was a small, round man in a glittering pince-nez, black alpaca jacket and a wool scarf that masked the absence of a collar. His wispy hair stood on end

as if he had just been roused out of bed; it gave him the appearance of unreasoning fear.

I took a step forward, said: "Herr Zimstern? I . . ."

He uttered a peculiar strangling sound and fell into the room
as if propelled by a catapult. The lamp was shaking in his hand;
it threw drunken shadows down his yellow face, past the thin lips
of a petulant child to an angry chin. He peered at me with sharp
little eyes.

His voice was shrill with anger and alarm.

"What are you doing here? Why did you come?"

I said: "I'm Dr. Shippe. I came . . ."

"I know who you are! Why did you come? Weren't you told
to wait in your hotel? Oh, this is madness, madness!"

This wasn't the reception I had been expecting. The angry round
man wasn't the unassuming dusty little figure I had imagined as
the antique dealer. He placed the lamp shakily on a bookcase
and ran to the window.

"I'm sorry," I began, but he cut me short.

"Madness! Insanity! Are you trying to get us all shot?"

I said that No, on the contrary, I hadn't wanted to get anyone
in trouble. I had come to warn him about a development that
seemed significant. I had thought I would be rendering him a
service. And, I said: "I wasn't followed, if that's what's worrying
you."

He turned on me quivering with anger.

"How would you know if you were followed or not? Are you
such an expert?"

"No," I said, "but it had seemed to me that the cab driver,
a man of experience, had known what he was doing."

"A cab driver? You came here by cab?"

"How else was I to come? Look," I said, hoping to reassure
him so that he would listen, "I made sure that no one followed
me out of the hotel. No one saw me get into the cab. The cab
took me to the Market Square. A little boy brought me the rest of
the way."

"And why should anyone follow you when the man most likely to be your guardian angel brought you here in his cab?"

He had me there. It hadn't occurred to me that the picturesque cab driver could have been a spy. Why not? He hadn't looked the part. What do police spies look like? I didn't know that either. It seemed that there was a great deal that I didn't know and that I was making too many dangerous assumptions. Once again, like some sort of undercover Icarus, I had tried my wings and the wax had melted.

I said that I was sorry; I had not meant to endanger anyone. My apology seemed to mollify the angry round man. I told him why I had taken such a foolish chance to see him.

He listened with attention and, gradually, his humor improved. He chuckled when I told him how I had disabled poor Miss Jablonska of the PABUT. He found my fears about the guide especially amusing but, when I pressed him for an explanation, he merely shook his head.

He was less amused when I asked him about the mysterious American who had given me such a blinding welcome.

"That's nothing to do with our business," he muttered uneasily. "An unexpected guest. Another matter. But it is not good that he saw you here."

"He seemed to know me."

Zimstern became suddenly evasive. "Did he? You are a well-known man, Dr. Shippe"—he pronounced it Sheep. "Perhaps that's the answer. But now that you have given me the unexpected pleasure of meeting you, perhaps we can do business. I had hoped to arrange a different meeting, elsewhere, in a day or two, but your precipitation of the matter would make that difficult. So, perhaps, we can proceed from here, eh?"

"You mean you'll take me to the Romanowski Library tonight?"

He cocked his head, as if listening for a sound upstairs, then treated me to a yellow-toothed smile.

"Why not? Sooner or later I would have to take you. The Library will not come to you, so you must go to the Library, eh, Doctor? Isn't that why you have honored our country with your presence? If you have not been followed here, and I believe now that you have not been followed, at least not by anyone who means to do us harm, we could go. You like the idea?"

Events had begun to move far too fast for me. I didn't understand Zimstern's certainty that I had not been followed, but something in my story must have reassured him. I wished he would explain his unexpected American guest. I thought he had dismissed my concern about the PABUT guide with excessive swiftness. But all these matters lost significance beside the prospect of seeing the Library.

"Yes," I said. "Of course!"

He took me to a little office at the back of the store: a dusty room lit by a pale desklamp, heaped from floor to ceiling with crates, boxes, and bursting bales out of which protruded stone limbs of statues; racks of rusty halberds; furniture piled with long abandoned objects; none of it worth the cost of salvage from a rubbish dump. A row of bronzed, cast-iron heads of Napoleon Bonaparte lined a waist-high shelf like criminal remains above the gates of a medieval city.

I sat at Zimstern's open rolltop desk while he left me to, as he put it, make necessary arrangements. The Library wasn't in the city. We would go by car.

Now that I had come so close to the end of my mission, it seemed impossible to believe that I had been part of a conspiracy. Considering my blunders, errors in judgment (if *judgment* was the word for my impulsive descent upon Zimstern), and the near-panic that had gripped me during my Nakomda interview, I knew that foreign intrigue was out of my depth.

If all went well I could be back in the capital in a day or two and on my way to Sweden by the end of the week. It would be enough for me to satisfy myself that only a few pieces of the lost collection had an authentic look; one item, proved authentic, would repay Pohl his hundred thousand dollars several times over, even supposing the rest of the material was a downright fraud. And even if my tests in Sweden showed the whole thing to be a gigantic hoax, my client could still make a substantial profit on an academic curiosity.

I didn't really think that I would find the Romanowski Library where Zimstern would take me. The odds against authenticity were astronomical. I had accepted the assignment because no odds were too impossible to dismiss a chance; a mere suspicion that the Library could, possibly, exist would be enough to call for an investigation.

I had every reason to feel satisfied. I had done what had been professionally expected of me; no matter what the outcome of my research, my client could make a reasonable profit; neither I nor he would lose anything, and . . . I had a savored moment of the kind of life that had eluded me.

I had met a Master Spy and had been questioned by the NKD, and something could always be made out of poor, frozen Miss Jablonska, the picturesque cab driver, the fat man in the blue serge suit, Zimstern, Brown, Lindstrom and the mysterious American upstairs. Before I left for Sweden I would meet Sempinski, and that was quite enough to repay me for any frights I might have had along the way. Perhaps I would find out a little more about Kristin Napoji's accident.

There was nothing that I could regret. I was glad the adventure was coming to an end; I'd had the best of it—and just enough to know that any more would have been too much. When Zimstern, bundled up in furs like a diminutive fat bear, brought his car to the front of the store, I was in the best spirits that I could remember.

We drove through the silent streets of the sleeping capital, then crossed the river over a collonaded bridge and headed east. The night was still black when we left the city, but graying before us, so that the hushed streets and deeply buried country roads acquired the sudden look of water under ice. We flowed along this icy river without talking, each of us thinking his own thoughts. The sky was full of brilliant, pale stars that promised a clear day.

White fields gave way to black woods; silent walls of trees, diminishing in distance, bowed under their heavy winter canopies. Icy shrubs formed glittering cages among tree roots. Long, lonely lines of pug-marks trailed into the trees; I wondered what animals lived there. I supposed that there had been strayed cattle trapped in the snowy wilderness, perhaps even people. There would be timber wolves. Possibly wild boar and black bear in spring. There would be deer, lynx, wildcat, and the red fox. The prewar tourist guides I had read in New York had much to say about the bisons of the Eastern forests. I wondered if any of them had survived the war. At one time the bearded aurochs had crashed through these woods, but not any longer. So, maybe no more bisons either. Besides, this wasn't the forest that the guidebooks had been talking about; this was another country. During the war, fighting had been heavy in this neighborhood; I looked for war scars in the deep, unbroken wall of trees, some indication that the land remembered, as people always seem to remember, that there had been a war. But if there were scars, they were hidden under the white bandages of snow. And, anyway, scars had a way of healing, the land never failed to renew itself.

I looked at my watch as the white, icy miles sped away under us. It was 5:30, time for the sun to rise. The sun broke out of the mists and fog beyond the wooded dunes that made the open country like a frozen sea; it flooded the black forest with a scarlet light. The sun climbed, unhurried, as if unwilling to speed the new day and hung, without warmth, like a dull red bulb in the copper sky.

The lodge stood in a deep, dimlit clearing where an outcrop of limestone marked the convulsive heave of the ridge.

The biggest oak of all clamped its roots around a snowsheeted ruin at the far end of this undulating space, the white boughs swooping over the massive, wooden structure, foursquare and solid, built to resist time, spreading at the base, and now buttressed by ice. The lodge and oak were both elephant-gray in the indefinite light that threaded its way down from the snow canopy overhead. The air itself seemed frozen here; it shimmered with fine particles of light, suspended like a shield between the earth and the sun. It was a false light, distorting and dwarfing, as was the stillness on the forest floor.

An animal screamed deep in the forest, resenting the human invasion, and the forest wall answered with a belling chord: a violent protest stabbing the false silence. It made my vision shake. It rolled down from the depth of the retreating forest, splintered and dissipated seeking echoes.

We left the car at the mouth of the track which ran like a tunnel under the heavy-laden canopies of trees, and plunged into the deep snow billows in the clearing. Zimstern had brought a strange assortment of tools: hacksaws and chisels and a hammer as well as his lantern. We burrowed through the snow dunes crashing through the icy crust up to the waist and, occasionally, chest-deep, our progress marked by frantic heavings and thrashing as if the snow were quicksand. The lodge resisted our attempts to enter. We had to shovel aside the snow with our hands, tramping it down so that the door could open, and then the solid oaken door had to be freed from its seals of ice one chiseled inch at a time. The tinny hammering, the click of the chisels, were unnaturally loud in the breathless stillness, and when the chisel slipped, or the hammer missed, the house itself boomed a hollow echo that reminded me of violated crypts.

Inside was a powdery dry darkness and a quick illusion of impenetrable mass that seemed to fill the ancient dining hall from one invisible end to the other. The oak walls, bleached dead-white by time, tinder dry, caught up the hissing glare of our lamp and threw it into massed layers of cobwebs, turning the cobwebs into a furry whiteness that seemed as solid as cotton packed around a gem.

By midmorning, we had cleared a working space around the refectory table and the stone steps that, Zimstern said, led to the cellars where the treasure was stored. I was cold and hungry but Zimstern wouldn't allow a fire laid in the fireplace that looked big enough to accommodate a bear on a spit. We ate the black bread and goat cheese that Zimstern had brought and washed it down with the sweet wine of the country, and I looked up at the parchment skulls of long-slain animals that hung from the lintel the length of the hall, wondering how many rough and boisterous hunters' suppers they had witnessed with their hollow eyes. The lodge was older by several centuries than the country from which I had come. The heraldic device carved into the mantle had lost its identity years before the little fleet of Christopher Columbus had sailed from Cádiz.

But there were newer relics buried in the dust dunes: a rust-brown bayonet, a gaping leather ammunition pouch; during the war this island of antiquity hidden in the forest had been used by the partisans. It had been a band of partisans which had attacked the German column that was carrying the Romanowski Library away from its home a hundred miles to the east, or so Zimstern told me, but the treasure had not brought them luck. Each of the men who had helped to turn the lodge into a treasure house died violently in the ensuing years: in ambush, accident, betrayal to the Germans, mysterious illness, postwar anti-Communist resistance, show trial and purge. Ill fortune seemed to follow even the few members of the band who had been driven into exile.

The stairway was a narrow well spiraling deep into the rock on which the lodge had been built, with a small iron door, no wider than a coffin-lid, barring the way beyond the bottom step. We broke the padlocks and pried the heavy door open and entered the cellar.

The impression was one of a burial vault: long wooden cases branded with the Nazi swastika and eagle, stacked in dim rows the length of the cellar, frayed leather handles, rotted rope. The martial hieroglyphics of the Wehrmacht were still legible on the dusty wood: caliber designations. I had expected dampness but the air was dry.

We broke open the first of the cases. Nestled inside were five lead cylinders too heavy for one man to carry, hermetically sealed like time capsules. I thought that if I had ever wanted to store perishable materials, I couldn't have done better than this dry cave tunneled into solid rock and the lead containers. Whatever lay inside would survive anything. We carried the cylinders upstairs one at a time, and then took turns sawing off their ends, but the lead filament clogged up the hacksaw blades and I broke several before I got the hang of it. It was slow work; we had to be careful. Zimstern assured me that the contents were further protected but I took no chances.

Despite my skepticism my excitement grew, and when the first cylinder was finally open, and we had picked out the powdery wood shavings, and carefully lifted out one of the sealed glass display cases, I was certain that its contents would be genuine. If the dark brown fragment of papyrus between the fused panes of glass were a forgery then I had just inspected the most elaborate and believable stage setting in the history of antiquarian fraud. I was sure that if anyone measured the depth of the dust on the ammunition cases, and analyzed the age of the wood, lead, shavings, glass and even the crumpled dry newspapers wadded up for padding, he would discover nothing to contradict the story of when and how the Romanowski Library had come to be stored in the lodge. Zimstern had brought a jeweler's eyepiece and a magnifying glass and I went over every millimeter of the papyrus in the bright glare of the carbide lamp. The inscription was in ancient Aramaic, with that peculiar juxtaposition of clauses that went out of the language about a hundred years after the crucifixion. Much of it was no longer legible but enough remained so that I could follow this police report about a meeting of a group of Galileans at which wine had been drunk and bread had been eaten and strange words had been said about the Blood and the Body. I had no doubt that my microscope would confirm what my eyes accepted.

I wanted to open at least another cylinder—not to inspect the contents but merely to see them, read them, feel the medieval glass around them—but I had ruined all the hacksaw blades in my first attempt and, besides, the day was coming to an end. Still, having waited for so long to see the almost-legendary manuscripts and still unable to make myself believe the truth of what I saw, I didn't want to be parted from them. I wished that I could risk taking the spy's report on the Last Supper with me, just to have it near. But I knew that I would have to wait until it was delivered to me at the Royal Institute in Stockholm. I repacked the case and plugged up the cylinder with a part of Zimstern's car blanket, and then we carried all the cylinders downstairs, replaced them in the case and nailed it up again.

Simply to delay departure, and to have something to poke around with while I waited for the manuscripts to arrive in Stockholm, I had scraped some filaments off the cylinder, broke a splinter off the packing case, swept up a few of the dehydrated shavings and chipped the glass panes. I would leave no part of the story unchecked. Zimstern asked if Dr. Sheep was satisfied; I told him he was. He acted as if he hadn't expected any other answer.

We drove back to the capital while a desultory snowfall drifted down and covered our tracks. The skies were heavy with dark clouds that promised a snowstorm.

nine

I BOUGHT a stack of brightly colored postcards in the hotel lobby: castles and monuments and urban perspectives; and wrote my message to Hamish Potter over a dish of wild strawberries, whipped sourcream and powdered sugar. I wondered where they got the strawberries in the middle of winter.

The dining room was empty so early in the morning, but the fat, bald man had come bustling in close on my heels; he didn't look as if he had slept well. I knew I might have some explaining to do to the PABUT people but a sheepish story about girls and cabarets would take care of that.

I wished Pohl had concocted a more imaginative message but I supposed he knew what he was doing and wrote *Having a Wonderful Time, Wish You Were Here,* on the back of the restored throne room in the Royal Castle where, at that moment, the heads of the various Peoples' governments were probably meeting. Just for the hell of it I sent the same message to Pohl and to Tommy Mackin, adding to Tommy's postcard: *Hark, my postilion has been struck by lightning,* out of my book of useful conversational phrases.

But I didn't mail the postcards right away. To do so would be to acknowledge the end of the adventure and I wanted to savor it a little longer. I felt foolishly like a small boy walking on a fence, daring himself to do something he wanted to do anyway, knowing that he could jump down to safety anytime he wished. My fat, bald guardian angel was an adequate audience.

I went upstairs to file my postcards for use later in the week, and couldn't find my briefcase, and suddenly remembered that I had left it in Zimstern's office before the trip to the lodge. He had brought me back straight to the hotel, dropping me off with correct conspiratorial procedure some distance away. My mind had been on the Romanowski Library, I hadn't missed my briefcase until I needed it; it was too new to have become a habit. But all my documents were in it, including my passport and my traveler's cheques, and while I had enough currency on hand to last for several days the passport was another matter. This was another urgent reason for contacting Zimstern.

I had seen an old-fashioned telephone on his desk, the kind with the mouthpiece on a post and the earpiece on a tangled cord. But I couldn't identify the dealer on the page of Zimsterns, a dozen of them Ferdynands, in the telephone directory, and I didn't think the cautious conspirator would appreciate a call. That meant another trip to the Old City after dark.

This time I didn't want to go. There didn't seem to be any sound reason for reluctance. Perhaps it was a premonition of some unspecified danger, or the rising awareness that I was beginning to push my luck too far, or the anticipation of fresh blunders, or a combination of the three. My reluctance mounted throughout the day, matching the gloomy gathering of snowclouds, so that when night fell I left the hotel with all the enthusiasm of a convict ascending the scaffold.

No one followed me into the icy wind and snow that had begun to obliterate the city during the afternoon and now acquired the swirling dimensions of a minor storm. The city had a white, abandoned look. I walked three blocks before waving down a passing taxi, suddenly warmed by the checkered stripe painted around its side; it made me think of home. The taxi took me to the Old City. I paid and got out. I looked around to get my bearings and spotted the cafe where I had taken the frozen PABUT girl, and wondered why Zimstern had been so amused by that part of my story. The taxi driver made an impassioned speech, pointing to himself, to me, to his watchless wrist and to the street, but I shook my head. I would walk from here. I entered the cafe setting myself a fifteen-minute limit for comfort and warmth, to give the taxi time to disappear and to see if I had picked up a guardian angel somewhere along the way. Several people looked at me and one or two smiled. I knew I looked foreign. Sooner or later someone would talk to me. I started looking forward to the conversation, then remembered that I had not come here to attract attention or enjoy myself. I had a job to do. I waited for my fifteen minutes to go by, looking, in the meantime, about the low-ceilinged smoky room, intimate as an oak-paneled hunting club, with animated faces bent toward each other through the blue haze of tobacco smoke and the steam of coffee, and the sweet, almost tangible smell of confections wheeled among the tables.

No one looked like a police spy, not even the waiters. The customers were either young (late teens and early twenties; the boys in turtleneck sweaters, with too much hair falling across their foreheads, gesticulating, laughing; the girls scrubbed clean of makeup except around the eyes, long-haired and wholesome) or in their mid-forties, with that used look of Central European faces, sharp-featured and intelligent. They made me think of Hubertus Pohl who was nothing like them. Students and intellectuals, I concluded. I wondered if the animated young people were talking about me, if they had taken part in the recent student demonstrations in the capital, and if I'd have an opportunity to talk to them. It would have been pleasant to sit here and talk.

But my fifteen minutes were soon up. I went outside. The snow fell more thickly. The wind cut like ice. They made me wish I could have spent the night in the cafe. Still, it was not far to Zimstern's from here, I remembered. I began to walk. The taxi was gone. I walked, looking into windows, at snow-covered coats-of-arms carved into door lintels, at the traditional signs hanging over doorways. I wondered if the fat, bald man was anywhere about. It would do no harm to confuse the trail. I turned as quickly as the icy sidewalk would allow into a dark alley, then cut into another. I thought that Zimstern's street lay around the corner. I chose a dark angle of ancient doorway and buttressed cornice to stop, and looked back along the empty street behind me, a ghostly thoroughfare spotted with pools of orange light that seeped through falling snow. No one was there. I rounded the corner. I didn't recognize the street at all. Well, if not that corner, then the next; I was sure of that. But the next corner and the next and the one after that were all unfamiliar, and I could see no trace of the secretive doorway, shuttered window and the peeling letters of the antique dealer's sign. Well, if I had made too many right turns, a few left turns would mend the situation. I went on in the face of thickening snow that piled ramparts and glittering white mounds against the silent walls, through empty alleys that looked like all the other alleys, and soon the street lights began to thin out and disappear, spreading long corridors of blackness before me. I stopped, then, knowing that I was hopelessly lost.

Well, what now? The cold cut through my furs. My feet were numb and my ears seemed on fire. So much for masking trails, confusing pursuers. I swore. I felt like an idiot. To hell with it! I would find my way into the light of a major avenue, flag down the first cab in sight and have myself taken back to the hotel. Whatever my talents as a foreign agent, finding my way about a foreign city—at night and in a snowstorm—wasn't one of them. I'd telephone all the Ferdynand Zimsterns in the morning until I found the right one, whether he liked it or not, and have him send my briefcase to the hotel. At least, I thought, disgusted, I couldn't lose my way in the dining room. I went on. But now the storm settled above the city and threw down mountain-loads of snow into the dark, empty canyons of the streets. The gaunt, lifeless houses suggested wartime ruin, left like the ghetto as a monument to terror. I had no idea in what direction I was going. I peered at tall, drab houses in what might have been a working class district, an abandoned slum. There'd be no workers living here now. Who would? As if in sudden answer, I realized that there were men about: singly and in small, silent groups in the black tunnels that led to the inner courts of the ancient tenements; unsmiling men wrapped in shabby cloth, switching their eyes away as I passed the doorways. I tried to hurry, feeling more and more flat stares centering on my back, cursing my damn stupidity; each alley grew darker, narrower and seemed to take me deeper into the menacing quarter. And then I knew that I was no longer alone among the silent buildings; a man in a shabby leather coat had detached himself from a black doorway behind me, and another man in what looked like a broken military cap fell into step with me across the street. Both men turned where I turned, stopped when I stopped, hurried when I hurried.

Sweat soaked through all my clothes. I had to get out of this maze of alleys into the light, among decent people. Now Leather Coat was closer, coming faster, and Military Cap was gone. Where was he? Had he taken a shortcut to head me off? Street followed street, all dark, all narrow, all alike. I peered into alleys for the bright, saving glare of an avenue at the other end, and heard the quickening pad of footsteps crunching behind me in the snow, and turned one more corner under a blown-out streetlamp into a street I seemed to know—still narrow, dark and silent, housing secrets, but incomparably broader than the others—and there like a beacon at a harbor mouth was the sign with the peeling letters. I stopped there and looked back. The dim forms of the two men halted at the border between light and darkness, then withdrew.

I laughed, enormously relieved, and waited to recover both my breath and composure. It had been a narrow escape but now I was safe. The bright light of a lamp directly in front of the antique dealer's door gave warmth to the unpopulated distance of the street. I saw a fleeting gleam of light between the wooden shutters. Zimstern was still up. I stepped up to the door and knocked.

When no one answered, I pushed the door open, wondering with mild annoyance why the conspiracy-minded dealer never locked his doors, and went inside, calling out for Zimstern.

This time no one blinded me with flashlights. But I saw the pencil-thin stream of another light along the bottom edge of the office door at the far side of the deepest shadows. I slammed the street door and shouted Zimstern's name in the sudden darkness. The light from the streetlamp was now locked outside. No one came in reply to my calls. Perhaps Zimstern was out. But then, I thought, suddenly uneasy, why was the door unlocked? I called again and this time the sound of my own voice disturbed me in that still and unresponsive darkness. I stepped carefully through the dark, object-littered store, feeling my way along dusty tables, brushing the cold shoulders of suits of armor, like empty husks of petrified dead men. Then I was at the door of Zimstern's little office. I pushed it open and stepped into light.

Afterward, it seemed to me that I saw everything at once: the old and the new, the discarded and the usefully familiar: a man's jacket and vest draped over a chair; a folding cot piled with tangled bedding; the suitcase and the flat brown hat; the open desk and books and ledgers and the small, oddly deflated figure sitting at the desk. The gray, balding head was cradled in its arms between the ancient inkwell and the miniature Copernican globe.

"Mr. Zimstern?"

There was no answer; I knew there wouldn't be one. I felt curiously detached, as if the dead man had nothing to do with me, as if he were no more real and no more a man than the empty suits of armor in the store behind me.

I looked from him to the telephone receiver swinging on its cord, buzzing with the insistent hum of distant wires. The soft smoke of a cigarette curled out of the ashtray.

None of this seemed to mean anything to me; I couldn't believe it. I had never seen a corpse before, never bothered to imagine what a corpse might look like. The dead were ancient: potters who had shaped Byzantine amphorae, painters of parchment with papyrus reeds. I looked at this modern corpse, wondering why I didn't even feel curiosity; to feel curious seemed to be the least I could do. Obviously, the man had been alive only recently. There was the evidence of the cigarette laid only shortly before in the ashtray. How long ago? A minute? Two? How long does it take for a quarter of an inch of ash to form in an ashtray? There was the softly humming telephone still swinging off the hook. Whom had Zimstern been calling the moment he was killed? To whom had he been talking when he died? It didn't seem to matter. And who had killed him? Why? That seemed to matter even less. The wispy hair that had given Zimstern a look of perpetual panic lay across the black, polished rectangle of familiar leather.

Time passed. The drone of the hanging telephone receiver sounded like a far-off hive full of aggravated bees. My brain came gradually alive and accepted the unacceptable evidence of the corpse and briefcase that the dead man clutched with such desperate affection. It was my new briefcase, that unexpected gesture from Hubertus Pohl. With this thought came awareness; dispassionate coldness vanished. I had to get away at once before someone found me with the corpse; I would never be able to explain what I was doing here.

I felt a violent aversion against touching the dead man. But, damn it, why not? He was dead, he wouldn't mind. I took a cautious grip on the edge of the briefcase and began to pull it from under the dead man's head. The balding head moved with the case. The dead hands clung to it. They wouldn't let go. I got out a handkerchief and wiped my face with it. I stared at the dead man. The deflated face had turned toward me while I tugged gently at the briefcase and now one wide, strangely bulging eye regarded me with astonished outrage. The mouth was ajar, showing yellow teeth. The dead wrists showed the pinpoint scabs of fleabites. Small black specks like animated, frantic punctuation marks leaped among the papers scattered on the desk.

Fleas, I thought, astonished.

I had never seen a flea. I found myself frantically wiping my hands with my handkerchief, then threw it on the floor, then backed away from the frenzied asterisks as far as I could, then jumped as a spearpoint pricked me in the back. A rack of halberds tilted like a hedge of spears against one of those cavalry charges Sempinski wrote about, brought me up short.

I caught sight of my face in a mocking mirror: a shocked, disgusted grimace in an ornate frame.

I turned once more toward the desk and, suddenly, stood still. There had been no sound in the cavernous store, nothing to suggest that anyone else was there, but I was sure that I was not alone. I felt the cold certainty of danger, the inexplicable knowledge. Later, I could never tell how I knew or even what I felt; there were the frozen senses and the racing brain, the urge to shout, the crawling scalp and all the other signs. Someone was watching me. Who? It made no difference. Thieves, spies, police spies . . . they were all the same. Danger was the same. The watching man was the murderer. It was so obvious that I didn't know how I could have missed it. The murder was so fresh that the murderer wouldn't have had the time to get away. The murderer was still here.

Well, all right, I thought. The murderer's still here. What will he do? If I just tried to leave, would he let me go? Why not? I hadn't seen him, wouldn't be able to identify him. But supposing he didn't want to leave? He might think I'd bring the police down on him.

I forced myself to move toward the desk. I looked in the mirror. The mirror faced the open office door and reflected darkness. Nothing moved in the mirror or in the store but I thought I could hear a man's heavy breathing. Imagination, of course. Where would he be hiding? Back by the street door would be the best place. Out of those dark corners he'd be able to see most of the back room: a narrow aisle formed by the crates, bales, junk, spears and halberds that penned me between the desk and the cot. Like shooting carp in a pool. Well, there's no help for it, I thought. Must get the light out. How? Knock the lamp over and duck, and hope the fellow hadn't brought a flashlight. Maybe he wouldn't want to use a flashlight anyway; it would give him away. Once the light's gone he'll know I'm on to him. Then he'll come after me. He'd come after me anyway, with or without a light, so might as well make it difficult for him . . . even things up a bit. He knows where I am, I can only guess where he might be. But he can't move through that junkpile without making noise. He must be made to move. Meanwhile, I'll keep still. He'll have to do some guessing himself. That makes it almost fair.

I sighed, as if resigned to a long session with the scattered papers on the dead man's desk. I took off my furs, glad of the dark suit that would help to hide me once the light was out. Now, how to play my hand? It didn't seem likely that I would be able to outmaneuver the murderer and get to the street. And had I guessed the killer's intentions? I had to assume that I had. Very well. I thought over what my tactics were going to be. The agility learned in fencing lessons, silence and a cool head were all that I could pit against the other man. I wouldn't have a dog's chance unless I worked out a plan and stuck to it.

I had the advantage of the first move, provided I moved soon, but that advantage would be gone as soon as the move was made. I didn't worry about weapons for the moment. My best chance lay in outthinking the killer, forcing him to play into my hands and disarming him by making him strike only second blows. He had to come to me when I was ready for him. I had the tactical advantage of interior lines. I could reckon on the man to feel out if he was up against firearms, then to work his way carefully through the dark maze of the littered store and then to try to force me into breaking cover. He was somewhere between me and the outside door and he'd be careful to stay on that line. One way or another, he had to be kept moving. Unless he was the man who slept on the cot, he wouldn't know the geography of the store any better than I. All that seemed sound enough. I'd play the rest according to the way the game developed.

I stooped over the desk, measuring the distance to the cot; I'd dive for that as soon as the light went out. I was no longer concerned about fleas and dead men. All my attention was on the hidden man. And then I heard two slow, careful sounds of metal scraping metal: the bolts on the door. I hadn't reckoned on the door being bolted. Well, anyway, so much for the murderer's intentions. The contest would take place inside the store.

And now I heard the soft sigh of a sleeve brushed against furniture. The killer was coming. The game had started. Let's get on with it. I seized the lamp and threw it on the floor.

The bulb exploded. In that narrow space it sounded like a cannon. I dived. I heard the hiss of air rushing over my head, the sharp crack of the exploding mirror and ringing of glass shards. I inched across the floor on my belly, as a last shard of glass slipped out of the mirror and shattered behind me. At once there came a soft *ping,* like a hushed guitar string, and a projectile flew past me, low enough to hit me but wide of the mark, and struck against metal. Metal on metal, I was sure of that. Thrown with incredible power. Then from the darkness of the store came another ping and the whisper of the hurled projectile was loud in my ear.

What the devil was it? A mild ping and a gentle whisper. But the crash of the projectile against the brick wall settled all doubts about velocity. Some sort of catapult? A crossbow? Something automatic. Judging by the havoc the whispering missiles were causing behind me, they struck with the force of an elephant gun. And they came low! The killer had clearly anticipated my position; he was down on the floor, shooting at shin level. And that changed everything. I had to move fast. I hadn't thought of anything like this. At a cost of an initial slow-up, the killer had won the interior lines. His misses were so close that I felt them rushing past like miniature express trains. They smashed stone statuary, clanged into a cast iron head of Napoleon Bonaparte and sent it thundering down, heavy as an anvil, to the floor.

I started getting ready to jump up. I had already got my hands flat against the floor and drawn a leg under me, when a soft, slipping sound came from the direction of the desk. I didn't know what it was; perhaps the dead man had sagged against the briefcase. But the killer's response was immediate: two shots pinged and hissed and struck flesh with the nightmare sound of wet clay hit with a croquet mallet, and the dead man spilled out of his chair with a wooden clatter. And then the dead man sighed. I had heard about this kind of thing: air trapped in the inner cavitites, leaving a corpse long after death. The sigh became a gurgle, then expired.

The silence went on for what seemed all of a half hour. I didn't dare to stir. I prayed that the killer would think he had hit me and would come in to see if I needed finishing off. He made no move. He watched and listened, as I watched and listened. I couldn't understand what was holding him up. The sound of pierced flesh, the sigh and the gurgle, had been unmistakable but the killer's waiting indicated a doubt in his mind. This was clearly an old hand at the ambush game.

And then a floorboard creaked just outside the door. I had become accustomed to the darkness enough to spot the shadow of the man against the infinitesimally lighter background of the store. He came on cautiously. Something was puzzling him. He seemed to sniff the air. Then, all at once, he made up his mind. He stepped into the room and I charged him from the ground with a speed and force I wouldn't have believed, feeling my shoulder smash into the small of a lean, muscular back, hearing the sharp, short cry as the man was thrown into the desk and as he fell over the chair in a cascade of papers.

I was out of the door and running through the store in moments with plaster busts and furniture scattering behind me. I had to reach the street door before the killer recovered his senses. I didn't think I'd have time to get into the street. Getting the door unbolted would be enough for now. Everything depended on how quickly the murderer could get himself disentangled. I found the bolts and drew them, hearing furniture clattering in the back room, and something smashed against the door with a force that numbed me. I scurried among crates, trying to keep quiet. Then I stretched out behind a bale of carpets and struggled to control my breath.

Resting, I took stock. The honors seemed even. Perhaps I even had a bit of an edge. At some risk to himself, the killer had found out that I was unarmed and still very much alive. He'd also watch out for surprises from now on. On the other hand, I was out of the box, with better cover and space for maneuver, I had got between the killer and the outside door, and I had drawn the bolts.

But, for the first time, I realized that there would be no quick end to the duel. I had gained stalking-space, true, and I had turned the tables on the murderer and I had got back my interior lines, but the door was still as good as barred as long as that pinging, whispering cannon could be brought to bear. The weapon gave the killer a permanent advantage. He could keep me pinned down until daylight came and robbed me of my only shield.

I needed time to put together a new plan of action. It was no longer enough to keep the other man on the move, wasting ammunition. It was pointless to try guessing how many more deadly pings-and-whispers he was good for. The weapon was a mystery. The duel had to be forced to conclusion before daylight. That meant that the killer had to be enticed within reach of whatever weapon I could devise. Evasion and delay were no longer the point.

I wondered if I could be cold-blooded enough in the final moment to go through with murder. There was no way to tell. The idea was so alien that I couldn't fit it into any conception I had of myself. But I wasted no time questioning the morality of what I had to do. I knew that I should be frightened and fought against resignation and an acceptance of defeat. That way lay disaster. I prayed that my nerves would serve me just a little longer. The killer had me, unless I kept a tight grip on myself.

How did the killer see it? What would be the last thing he'd expect? He didn't know that I was changing the rules of the game.

I had to bait an irresistible trap. I had to make him think that my nerves had gone and I no longer knew what I was doing. It wasn't that far from the truth, anyway. He had to think that he had me boxed again, and there had to be only one way for him to reach me. Knowing the axis of attack would be my one advantage. I wouldn't get more than one chance to strike. That meant the back room again, the only site for ambush where the killer wouldn't be able to come in from any angle he chose.

I took off my shoes and lined them up with pointless care behind my bale of carpets. Time seemed to slide into a new order. Everything slowed down. Each of my movements unfolded with dreamlike precision. My hands and knees had begun to tremble. I couldn't control them. A deep breath would help but I couldn't risk it. I heard a sound in the street but I didn't bother to identify it; it seemed to have no relation to time and myself.

I stepped away from my protecting rampart of carpets and crates. I wasn't sure of my bearings in the darkness. I had the uneasy feeling that the killer knew what I was up to. Nervous laughter threatened to shake me apart. Shippe the Antiquities Consultant and Shippe the Hunter found each other hysterically foolish. I had to stop and recover control over myself. My eyelids seemed to weigh a pound apiece. My nerves were finally going, there wasn't much time left. Sound reached me through a filter.

The killer was on the move to my right, about midway between the office and the outside door. He made no attempt to keep quiet, advertising confidence. But there was something not quite right about the way the killer was acting. His movements made no sense but they had a pattern. He seemed to be circling in the middle of the room. The closer he got to the back room the less noise he made.

This could have been an attempt to lure me out of whatever ambush I might have prepared. I thought that was likely. The killer was playing right into my hands.

I went on, step by step with agonizing caution, until my hands found the hard edge of the office door. My knees sagged then, and the killer charged me.

I knew in one shocked moment of paralyzing truth that I had walked into the perfect trap. The murderer was on me in three leaps, coming straight down the path he had cleared while I had been wondering how to draw him out. Everything else he had done had been a diversion.

He came in with a shout. One hand crushed my throat, the other swept up. And then the street door flew open and a black shape launched itself into the store in a flood of light, and I had time to see the long colorless face a foot from my own jerking around in astonishment and rage, the upraised hand with its black, metal cylinder suspended over my head. The charging shape struck us both and I flew backward into the back room. I hit the wall with the top of my skull.

I struggled back to consciousness in a bitterly cold wind that swept through the store. The street door was open. My head was full of anvils. The light from the streetlamp hurt my eyes.

I got up and focused my eyes. The office was a shambles of scattered junk and papers. Broken glass and plaster crunched underfoot when I pushed myself away from the wall. Zimstern was stuffed into a narrow crevice between his desk and the rack of halberds. The killer was gone.

It had been Brown, the man whom I had seen in Pohl's anteroom and later with Lindstrom, and whose plainsman's hat I had failed to identify on the cot in the office. I could still see that dead-white face and reptilian eyes, and feel the fingers tightening on my throat.

I began to cough. The effort sent me staggering into the cold wind sweeping through the store. Snow had begun to form mounds inside the open door. I closed the door and bolted it, then went back to the little office, righted the lamp and tried to turn it on. It took me some time to remember that I had smashed the bulb. But I had a lighter. By its light I found a candle end. I lit the candle and sat back on a moldering pile of old books and closed my eyes. I began to tremble.

And then I heard the groan.

At first I couldn't understand what it was; then I saw a dark form on the floor. It was a man, the fat, bald man, my guardian angel, the polished skull no longer a symmetrical pink egg but a crushed red shell. The eyes were open. The eyelids trembled in the light of the candle. A drunken, bubbling voice brought out a word in English.

"What did you say?"

"Tell . . ."

"What?"

"Tell . . ."

And then a name.

"What was that? Chafield? Was that it?"

"Tell . . ." And then with dreadful clarity: "Dr. Shippe . . ."

"Who are you?"

But the bulging eyes were no longer blinking. The fat man was dead.

I took my candle end back into the small room. The first of my two corpses regarded me indifferently from the narrow cavity where Brown's missiles had thrown him. I righted the chair and sat down in it, and put my elbows on the desktop and my hands around my head. Afterward, I supposed that I had sat there as long as an hour. It took me at least that long to pull myself more or less together. The drowned voice of the fat man bubbled in my ears.

I went through the rest of it in a mindless dream, retrieving the briefcase, brushing it absentmindedly, unable to remember what it was that I wanted to brush off.

Light caught a gleaming object on the floor. I picked up a small dart, no bigger than a woman's ball-point pen, the kind sold chained to matchbox-sized address books. I wondered what it was. One like it had gone right through Napoleon's iron skull. Then I found the pistol. I supposed that Brown must have dropped it in his struggle with the fat man. It was the strangest pistol I had ever seen: a dull, black cylinder about eighteen inches long, with the muzzle narrowed by concentric black rings to the diameter of the dart. Two bright tubes ran under the barrel into the oval handle. Unthinking, I pulled the trigger. At once there came the familiar ping, the weapon jerked a fraction of an inch, and across the store a suit of armor clanged, toppled and fell over.

I threw the gun and dart into the briefcase. I was too tired to know what I was doing. I knew that I should try to identify the fat man but that meant going through his pockets, and that was too much. I wanted nothing more to do with corpses. The last thing I remembered was to find my shoes. Eventually, I got into my furs and went into the street, carrying the briefcase.

The snow still fell as thick as frozen oatmeal, but the storm had subsided. I headed up the street toward the Market Square. In no time I began to lose momentum and strength; each step became an individual engineering project. The inner slowing down, that had begun while I was circling my invisible adversary in the store, became complete. I had to stop and rest in the icy wind after each dozen steps. The snowdrifts became insurmountable. And then, as I was at the point of final resignation, the thin sound of the sleigh bell approached me from behind, and there was the familiar sleigh, the ubiquitous sad horse and the old man with the oilskin cap and frosted whiskers. A small voice at the back of my exhausted brain began to question the coincidence of the sleigh, always magically appearing when I needed it, but I refused to give it any thought. I had none left to give.

I didn't know then, or ever afterward, how and when I had got to my room that night. The elevators had shut down at midnight. The night-clerk handed me a key and a letter and told me something about visitors. Somebody was waiting. All I could think of with any clarity was bed and oblivion.

ten

THE MAN who waited for me in my room, and rose politely
as I entered, was the Nakomda officer who had questioned me
at the airport.

I didn't recognize him at first in civilian clothes. The surprise
was perfect. But I hadn't the energy to make a response.

I struggled out of my furs, wondering if he'd give me time
to get them on again when he arrested me. Arrest would bring
the night and the whole impossible adventure to a logical conclusion. But he did nothing threatening. He sat back comfortably
in my sole armchair and lit a cigarette.

He said: "You're quite the night-owl, Doctor, aren't you?"

I didn't reply. He smiled and began to inspect the glowing
coal of his cigarette.

He said: "I've come to have a talk. No, don't look alarmed.
You're not on trial and I didn't come to trap you into anything.
But I don't have much time so don't waste it with protestations of
innocence. Believe me, if you were a candidate for an NKD cell
no protestations would help you."

I started brushing the sleeves of my coat. My hands were
still trembling but I thought that I might have them soon under
control. The Nakomda man was careful not to look at me, a nicety

I didn't understand. He spoke in a relaxed, amused voice as if to give me time to pull myself together.

"When my department wants someone behind bars, it doesn't send its district deputy commander to spend half the night in the victim's room. Let me tell you how it's done; a tip for the future. There are four men. Don't ask me why; the reasoning behind this mystic figure is too complicated. But we, the Soviet MVD and the East German Abteilung always send four men. Your FBI uses two, with two in reserve. The Gestapo used three. Each country has its own pet theory on how many men it takes to put one frightened man in jail. In Mexico, I understand, it's ten to a victim. The favorite time is two hours before dawn. A man isn't likely to kick up a fuss when he is tangled up in bedclothes. And the last two hours of the night are supposed to be the time of the deepest sleep. Psychologists call it the nadir of oblivion. A man is helpless then. It takes most men twenty minutes to reach full consciousness if they are awakened at that point. Believe me, it's all been statistically computed. Thus you would have four visitors two hours before dawn. You would be given exactly three minutes to dress. That means no more than shoes, overcoat and hat; there is a psychological advantage to questioning a man dressed in a nightshirt. You would be taken to a small black car. It's always a small, black car. You would be in the interrogation room long before your twenty minutes of confusion were up. No one would chat with you in your room, as I am doing. Talk gives a suspect time to get his wits together. And it's an international principle with security policemen to have their victims as witless as possible. Silence suggests that the arresting agency knows everything. The victim feels helpless. Helplessness means terror. And without terror, Doctor, even your FBI would be no more than a society of muscular young lawyers. So, you see, you're not going to be whisked off to Siberia. I'm here to talk business without witnesses, stenographers or electronic gadgets. And I made sure this room isn't wired. I know what to look for."

I was done then with my hat and coat. I turned from the

closet. But the Nakomda man still kept his eyes off me. He was staring out of the window with quiet concentration, his fingers drumming a military march on the arm of the chair.

Very well, I thought. So the surprises of the night are not over yet. The stalking game goes on. My hands still trembled slightly. I put them in my pockets and sat down on the bed.

The officer nodded, whistling soundlessly. His face was turned, as if to invite a study of the sharply carved profile, the thick black hair with a touch of gray, the small-pored, dusky skin. It was a lean, ascetic face but the eyes were cynical and the line of the lip suggested consciousness of power. I thought that he was, probably, the most dangerous man I had ever seen. Despite all efforts I felt my pulse quicken.

He said quietly, softly: "Where were you tonight? At Zimstern's? There is hardly anywhere else that you could have been. He told me you had left your papers at his place so I suppose you went to get them, since you have your briefcase. I wish you'd stay put and follow instructions. You really make it difficult to keep you out of jail."

I blessed my slow reflexes, my exhausted brain. But even so, I started to mumble an incoherent protest. The officer cut me short.

"Please, Dr. Shippe; I have no time for amateur dramatics. I appreciate your conventional terror, but I must really get on with our business. Zimstern was my man, although I had recently begun to suspect he had other employers. He was connected with Karpovitch, which is how Karpovitch comes into this business."

I said: "What business? I . . . don't know what you're talking about."

The Nakomda man made an impatient gesture.

"I am the man who is selling you the Romanowski Library."

This time all I could do was to shake my head. I was lost and I knew it, but the knowledge seemed far less terrible than its anticipation. The main thing was to make no admissions, no matter what the Nakomda man said to reassure me.

"I had hoped to stay in the background," he continued. "But Zimstern's death makes that impossible."

I said: "Who is Zimstern?"

The Nakomda man gave me a look which was frankly bored.

"Still clowning, eh? I know he is dead because he was talking to me on the telephone at the precise moment that he was killed. He had told me all about your visit to the lodge."

It was my turn to shrug. The less I said the better. The Nakomda officer went on:

"You've heard of General Danilow?"

"Never," I said.

"You're a rotten liar. The general was my uncle. During the war, under the German occupation, he was a leader of our resistance movement."

I shrugged again as if to imply that none of this had anything to do with me.

"I led a small and highly irregular group of partisans," my visitor continued. "In one of my more successful actions I inherited the Romanowski Library."

"A handsome inheritance," I said. He laughed.

"Since there were no legal heirs left alive an accidental heir seemed as good as any."

Carefully, I asked: "What did your uncle think about all that?"

He grinned with sudden candor.

"My dear uncle, whose motives were always noble and impractical, didn't know anything about my inheritance. Needless to say I didn't advertise my windfall. I admit I had some patriotic notions about restoring the Library to the nation but fortunately common sense prevailed."

I said cautiously: "How fortunate for you."

"Yes," he said. "Wasn't it? The war soon took a course which meant the end of the old order in this part of Europe. Men like my uncle chose exile. I chose a connection with the source of power. But life at the source of power tends to be unstable; the competition is rather intense."

"And now it's getting a bit too much for you?"

"Not yet, dear Doctor. But from the beginning I could foresee a time when warmer climates would be more appealing. I took steps, some of them quite painful, to ensure that I became the only man who knew that my inheritance had survived the war."

"Are you telling me that you're planning to defect to the West?"

He was hugely amused.

"Wouldn't that be silly?"

I said: "I don't know what you'd consider silly."

"Defection is silly. You merely trade one hopeless situation for another. No, I have better plans. About a year ago I realized that the time for my retirement was approaching quicker than I had expected. Something quite critical was beginning to happen. My instinct for survival has always been remarkable. I decided to part with my inheritance and put out the necessary feelers."

"And is this one of them?"

He laughed, elaborately at ease.

"Well, you ought to know. I used Zimstern whom I knew in my official capacity as a fairly harmless Western agent. I also used my uncle."

I said, feeling danger near: "I thought you said his motives were noble."

"Nothing but the noblest. I convinced him that our national treasure should be sold on patriotic grounds."

It was my turn to laugh but the Nakomda man didn't take offence.

"You don't see it, do you. The Library has been more than just a treasure to the people here. It has been a symbol, and we tend to set high value on symbols in this part of the world. For many people it has a deeply religious meaning. For others it's a relic of this country's history. I convinced my uncle that the Library wasn't meant to be hidden from the world. The relic, if you like, had to find a setting in a country where it could continue its symbolic role."

I said: "And so America? A strange choice for you."

His yawn was ostentatious but his voice remained bland.

"Did I sound as if I didn't care for America? My error. I

wouldn't like to live there but I enjoy my visits. And anyway it was my uncle's reaction that mattered."

"So it was he who wanted the Library sent to America," I said.

He nodded. "Look at it this way. The presence of this symbol in a country is enough for many of our people to look upon that country as a kind of shrine: the home of faith, courage, decency and justice. D'you get the idea? Men like my uncle want America to have that kind of image."

"Why would they?"

"In order to maintain a spirit of resistance. If there were no difference between the moralities of the West and of the East why should anyone struggle over here? It wasn't difficult to show my uncle that the installation of our symbol in America would turn that country into a sort of Holy place. A Mecca where the faithful could address their prayers."

"And he fell for that?"

The Nakomda man shrugged contemptuously.

"He was an idealist."

I thought that my adversary's purpose was quite clear then: to goad me into a damaging admission. I struggled to show no sign of my awareness. If this were some extraordinary, devious trap, as it seemed to be, it was being laid with a master's cunning. Even the tone of the revelations was right for the job: cynics are always more convincing than moral enthusiasts.

Sooner or later the angle of attack would suggest itself. Until it did there was little I could do.

I said: "What happened to your uncle?"

The Nakomda man didn't reply immediately. He stared out of the window with intense ferocity, drumming a military march on the arm of his chair, then said coldly:

"He was killed. He came to see me here last autumn to verify that the Library existed. Somehow . . . I don't know how . . . he was betrayed and killed."

"Who killed him?"

"It wasn't my colleagues, if that's what you're thinking. If the NKD had uncovered his identity I would have been able to protect him. Have you ever heard of The Magician? No? Somehow The Magician is involved in my uncle's death but I haven't been able to get to the bottom of it."

I thought then that the time had come to strike back a little. I wanted my disquietening visitor to know that I, too, had resources for resistance.

I said: "You tell a good story. But I'm not interested in your stories. I want to go to bed."

He said, grinning fiercely: "Your innocence is almost convincing. If I didn't know better I might think that I had made a mistake."

"You did," I said.

He said, amused: "And you've really never heard about The Magician?"

"What's all this nonsense about magicians?"

"It isn't nonsense. The Magician is a very real person. Every intelligence officer in the world has been looking for him . . . at one time or another. He's a sort of private consultant in disaster. I don't like the idea of his connection with any part of our business. It's quite dangerous enough without him."

I said, as calmly as I could: "You're quite an expert on fairy tales, aren't you. Well, what's the rest of your fable?"

"You know the rest. My uncle went back to London, found Lindstrom and died. And here you are."

"And here I am," I said. "And now if you're all done, I'm going to call the embassy. I hope you don't mind?"

He shrugged.

"I don't have much time, Dr. Shippe. Don't waste it with bluffing. Nothing is going to happen to you anyway, if I've a say in it. So just let me finish what I came to say and wait a few days before you shout for help. If Zimstern hadn't been murdered and if I hadn't been obliged to handle the negotiations myself, you would have had no reason for panic. As a realist I can't expect you to trust me. Unfortunately I must make you trust me. Certain events are taking a very dangerous turn and there is no time for gentle parlor games. Tell me this, what in the world made you choose Sempinski for your cover story?"

I said: "Why don't you go home and let me get some sleep?"

"All right, consider that a rhetorical question. Because of your connection with Sempinski, you are under surveillance. I don't know who is watching you. The agents are NKD men from the personal entourage of our General Rauss. Rauss is the head of State Security and a most unpleasant man. God only knows how he survived the de-Stalinization circus we all went through here, but his survival instincts are as good as mine. In fact, they're better. Only Rauss knows what the Sempinski Affair is about; I have no idea."

The Nakomda man crushed his cigarette in the ashtray and immediately lit another, working it into his short, amber holder. He leaned back heavily in the armchair and crossed his legs, and closed his eyes, letting his arm dangle dramatically over the side as if to demonstrate how weary and vulnerable he was. I thought him about as vulnerable as a locomotive.

Despite myself, I had begun to like him. He would have been a personable, utterly believable rogue if there had been one word of truth in what he had said. I couldn't afford to think that he was anything but a clever liar; still, I found myself enjoying his cynical frankness.

Obviously he knew everything about my business in his country. I had to assume, for safety's sake, that this astonishing meeting was part of some Nakomda machinations too complex for me to understand; to trust the man would have been insane.

Oddly enough I didn't feel afraid. My earlier shock and feeling of entrapment had given way to a peculiar calmness that made me almost eager to accept the challenge of the situation. I had made some blustering noises, transparent denials, largely to bolster my own collapsing resolution, but now I thought I could fight back a little. Not that fighting would do me any good if the Nakomda officer was simply amusing himself at my expense. But both my fencing and chess had taught me that a wholly defensive game had little chance of success in the long run. As far as I was concerned, the time had come to invoke the emergency clauses of Pohl's plan; the assignment was too dangerous to continue. Morally, I was free to cut and run. Every instinct dictated a precipitous retreat. There was no hope of help from any quarter here or at home; but a meek surrender was out of the question. Sooner or later some opportunity would present itself.

I began to concentrate on my opponent's moves and, for the first time, quietly advanced a piece of my own.

I said: "You mean this business about Julian Sempinski is too much for you?"

He gave me a curiously appreciative look.

"When Rauss goes to the trouble of throwing a full security screen around something, it's a superb performance. A flea can't squeeze through. I know just enough about the Sempinski Affair to stay as far away from it as I can. In fact it only took one faint whiff of it to convince me that it was time that I became a wealthy coffee planter in Brazil."

"What could a man like Julian Sempinski have done? It doesn't make sense."

"Any conspiracy is the art of the improbable married to the unexpected."

"Maybe you're letting nervous imagination run away with you."

The Nakomda man laughed openly.

"Imagination is my stock in trade. How do you suppose one survives in my kind of jungle? Instinct and good reflexes are the first requirements of an intelligence officer. But in this case I do have a little more to go on. What counts, though, is to make sure you keep your nose out of Rauss's sticky little business. I have no intention of missing out on three million dollars simply because you blunder into something that's too much for even the best professionals. We have to move quickly on our deal. The time's just about up. Unfortunately, your involvement with Sempinski, and Rauss's interest in you, make quick moves sheer suicide. You would lead Rauss straight to me . . . and that is something I wouldn't enjoy."

"Then why did you take the chance of coming to see me?"

"It's not as big a chance as you think. Give me the credit for some expertise. But I don't intend to come near you again. Your next contact will be through that poor, unfortunate little girl you refrigerated. She is something of a friend of mine, though not as dear a friend as she might suppose. Still, she can be trusted for the moment."

I said: "You forget that I don't know what you are talking about."

He smiled. "And you forget that your life depends on my interest in you. I can't afford to lose you until you send a certain telegram from Stockholm. I will protect you as long as I can, provided you do exactly what you're told. But if you put me in the position of choosing between the life of a Brazilian millionaire and a penniless exile, I will be the most high-minded exile you have ever heard of. The only reason I'm still trying to shovel some sense into your head is that I would rather write checks than manifestos. Is that clear so far?"

I nodded and said that his words were clear.

"And just in case you have doubts about our General Rauss, let me say that he had his training in the good old days, in Russia and in China . . . when they threw people into locomotive boilers. Don't ever fall into his hands. If you do, I will have to kill you before you can talk. So I have this advice for you: Make no effort to contact Sempinski. Don't visit him, don't receive him if he visits you, don't write to him and don't accept his letters. Have nothing to do with him or with anyone who is sent by him. Don't underestimate Rauss since he is totally beyond your comprehension. And don't underestimate me."

I said that a threat of murder was hardly the basis for trust.

"Nonsense," he said. "I have nothing against you, and every interest in keeping you alive. I am even willing to respect you as an intelligent and courageous man. I know your type. I've known Americans like you. I also know that you are probably stubborn; once you start something, you want to finish it. You'll take my warning for a Nakomda trick; in your position I would

do the same. But don't stir from the capital where I can protect
you. If you go near Sempinski you are a dead man."

Then he got up, yawned, stretched, rubbed his graying temples
with a slow, gentle circular motion of long fingers, looked at the
graying light outside the window, picked up his hat and coat,
and left.

I collapsed on the bed.

Escape was the answer.

Zimstern was dead. Brown was the murderer. He had come
within a fraction of a second of murdering me too. With two
murders to conceal he'd probably try to get at me again. And the
Nakomda knew about the Library.

In formal spy language, I was burned—finished. The various
hounds were in full cry. All that was left was to run for my
life. I had never been on the run before; I hadn't the first
idea of how to go about it. And where was I to run?

The first thought was: the airport and home. But if the Nakomda were after me, and I had every reason to suppose they were,
I'd never get past Passport Control. All legal ways out of the
country would be closed to me.

I could hardly expect gentle treatment at the embassy if the
criminal police demanded my surrender for questioning in a sordid,
back-alley murder case. The Nakomda would see to it that I
was implicated.

That left Sempinski, an old revolutionary who knew all about
illegal border crossing, who had the necessary wisdom and experience and the rare humanitarian impulse of his disappearing kind.
Maybe Sempinski was my only answer.

This much I knew: I could no longer stay in the capital
where either Brown or the secret police could get to me at leisure.

I tore open the envelope that the clerk had handed me downstairs and read the hastily typed invitation to come at once to
Sempinski's home near the southern mountains. Sempinski even
suggested the train I might take: the crack Prague Express that left
the capital at seven in the morning.

I didn't hesitate. I put one suit, a pair of slacks, a sweater and three shirts into my smallest suitcase. I threw in the darts and the pistol. I thought I would be able to find an opportunity to get rid of this evidence in the country.

Money and documents went into the briefcase. Everything else would keep where it was. I wasn't abandoning anything that couldn't be replaced once I was safely back on my side of the Iron Curtain.

PART THREE:

The Sempinski Affair

eleven

SEMPINSKI'S MAN was to meet me at the Corn Exchange, an easy landmark in the heart of the ancient border city where I had left the train. I bought a picture postcard of this relic of the Middle Ages to show to my cab driver and, eventually, found myself outside a cafe that fronted the cloisters—an old place with bulging windows covered by steam. I would have liked to go in, out of the cold, but I was afraid of upsetting Sempinski's arrangements. I waited on the cobbled sidewalk, looking at passing cars. The wind was like a blade of ice laid along my neck. Time passed but I wasn't worried; I had followed my host's typed instructions to the letter; sooner or later someone would pick me up. And if we should miss connections I would always be able to hire some kind of transportation to Sempinski's famous estate near the mountains which, even on this gloomy afternoon, I could see towering in clouds to the south. In a few hours I'd be with Sempinski.

As far as I was concerned, the Library conspiracy was over. To go on with it, even if I had known how to pick up the broken threads, was suicide with the Nakomda in full possession of the facts. Even Pohl would understand this, after a suitable period of mourning for his lost commission. Besides, I wasn't sure that the whole affair hadn't been some intricate Communist attempt to capture world headlines. I remembered Potter's warnings about the satellites' restlessness and need for some unifying incident. I wondered if the Library affair would have been enough to cause the necessary indignation. It seemed a little weak but then I wasn't a Communist theoretician.

Anyway, faked or on the level, I was through with it. The deal was off and I was going home: to apple logs in my fireplace, Mahler, the chess and the sherry, and Zungfest's goulash. That was enough to make me feel content.

The chill awoke my hunger. I remembered that I had eaten nothing since the night before. So much had happened since that first dinner in the capital: treasures and corpses and secret policemen and my escape from it all . . . I couldn't quite believe that all that had been crowded into only two nights and a day. I wondered about the connection between Brown and Zimstern. What was Lindstrom's henchman doing with Karpovitch's agent? What was the link? And who was the bald, fat man (if not a Nakomda man) whom Brown had murdered instead of myself? And what was all that business about The Magician?

Then I remembered that I wasn't going to worry any more about spies, plots, counterplots or secret policemen. That was all in the past; I meant to keep it there. I started looking about eagerly for my transportation to Sempinski's home.

I saw the horses first, probably because I had always liked to see good-looking horses. This was a gray dappled pair pulling a boat-shaped sleigh. Two men were in the sleigh; neither looked particularly reassuring. The driver was a broad, scowling peasant in a tall fur hat, hugging himself against the sharp bite of the wind in a long sheepskin coat with the wool turned out. Straw spilled out of his sleeves like the stuffing from a ruptured scarecrow. The other was a big young man in heavy furs, half buried in the rugs and traveling robes in the back of the sleigh.

They drove past me, staring, and then the young man spoke sharply, gesturing toward me, and the peasant nodded. He brought the sleigh to the curb, stopped and got out, stamping his greased, untanned boots for warmth. The young man shouted and the peasant shrugged and came heavily toward me. He looked me up and down with dull hostility, picked up my suitcase and jerked his head in the direction of the sleigh.

My cheerful optimism slipped a little as I stared at the unfriendly pair. This wasn't a reception that I had expected. I hesitated at the curb. The peasant grew impatient.

"Kommen sie," he said. He spat into the snow.

"Are you from Professor Sempinski?"

"Ja. Ja."

He threw my suitcase into the front of the sleigh. The big young man stirred just enough to make some room for me under the fur robes in the back. His face communicated nothing except arrogance. The sullen peasant and the arrogant young man seemed an odd pair to send after a houseguest.

I asked how far we were going.

The young man's head turned with the deliberate slowness of a clockwork mannequin.

"Far," he said.

"But how far?"

"Four hours. Perhaps five."

"That far? I thought Professor Sempinski lived closer to the city."

The man ignored me. The cold face turned away. He ordered the peasant to start, shouting his quick command in contemptuous German. The peasant flicked his reins, the sleigh moved away from the curb. It was an astonishing reception.

The town slid out from under us, street by street, and soon it fell away altogether. We were in open country, flying down the white highway fenced in by telephone poles and snow-thickened lines of cable, past frozen fields that disappeared in the low gray clouds on either horizon. Small towns and villages went by, woods rose and sank in the unlimited white space.

At first we met other sleighs, wagons and some motor traffic staggering through the snowdrifts, but in an hour the highway was empty. There was no sound then beyond the whistling of the wind, the soft hiss of iron runners on fresh snow and the hard drumming of galloping hoofs.

The white miles went on. But by midafternoon the horizons narrowed into broken country: sudden black walls of rock, ghostly eruptions of old burial mounds, snowsheeted ruins, deep gorges floored by frozen streams, and thickening woods. The road rose and fell. Soon there were no more telephone poles or cables to show that there was a road.

I felt frozen to the bone despite the traveling robes and furs. I watched the black walls of a forest advancing toward the sleigh from either flank. Darkness came with it. The plain constricted. Soon the trees would be upon us, bringing their shadows with them. I watched the shadows, suddenly convinced that my eyes were playing tricks on me. The shadows were moving. They seemed to have a motion and direction independent of the marching treewalls. The shrubs and bushes and black, ragged vegetation had pulled up their roots; they ran in a swift, silent mass under the trees, parallel to the road.

I rubbed my eyes and shielded them from the wind, but they kept lying to me; the loping undergrowth came near with increasing swiftness as the white belt of snow narrowed between the closing walls of the forest.

And then the trees ended, brutally cut off. We were among fields. The dark, running forms spilled out of the forest and into the fields. I heard the long, baying howl.

Wolves!

I didn't believe it.

I turned to the others with astonished eyes but they paid no attention to me. The peasant driver was on his feet in the narrow neck of the sleigh, slashing the air with his braided whip. The young man was methodically loading an automatic shotgun. One of the horses stumbled then, and the driver laid into both of them with cracking leather. They ran with their ears pressed flat against their heads, stretched out like greyhounds in a terrified gallop.

"Uh-ha!" the driver shouted. "Uh-ha!"

The sleigh seemed to lift in the wind. The dark, howling mass came on behind us like black water rushing through a broken dam. White space shrunk before it as if devoured on the run. The deep baying was resonant and clear.

Then both horses stumbled.

The driver caught them up with the reins and his whip cracked like a flurry of rapid pistol shots. The horses recovered. But the white space between the wolves and the flying sleigh had narrowed by a dozen yards. The wolfpack was gaining. Its howl belled with triumph. I could see individual animals forge ahead of the tight, ragged mass: long gray beasts with maniacal eyes, taller than a calf.

Space vanished under us.

Acres fled. The wolves came on swiftly.

"How much farther?"

I had to shout in the big man's ear, my voice torn by the wind. He did not answer, but stretched out in the back of the sleigh and leveled the shotgun and, for a wild moment, I remembered that I too was armed and looked desperately about for my suitcase trying to remember where I had put the pistol and steel dart. But it was too dark to find anything in the wild-swaying sleigh. We were now deep in shadow, among trees.

"Are they gaining on us?"

I could see that the wolves were gaining. They were enormous.

One more stumble from the horses, I thought: That's all it'll take. And what if either horse ploughs into the ground? The rhythm of the hoofbeats had become ragged; I could hear the horses' whistling breath. They were beginning to falter.

Oh God, I thought: this didn't make sense! Sleighs . . . wolves . . . what century was this, anyway? Such things didn't happen any more!

"How much farther?"

The shotgun roared twice in quick succession. A dark shape leaped and tumbled and the pack boiled across it like a convulsed wave. The shrinking white space suddenly expanded. The booming shotgun beat out a steady rhythm. The wolfpack split, milled, and lost ground, then came together again in pursuit. But with each shotgun blast it hesitated long enough to lose a little ground.

Now the big young man laughed.

"You like this? Is that enough for you?"

At first I didn't know if the man was shouting at me or to the wolves. Now I could see what the wolves were up to each time the shotgun knocked one of them over.

And now the horses staggered. The sleigh snapped back and forth across the road like a loaded whip.

"Here they come!"

What happened then was so fast that I couldn't grasp it until it was all over. First there was the narrow white road rising among trees, the driver's heavy back and nodding heads of horses up ahead and the horrible dark mass coming up behind, the rattling breath of horses, the crack of the whip and the booming shotgun. That was all one picture, seen and heard in parts but possessing all the unities; making its own mad sense. And then a dozen individual dramas were being played out at lightning speed with no relation to each other but each possessed a terrible clarity.

A horse screamed and the two madly pumping heads disappeared. The driver shouted in a frantic voice. Trees spun, the lowering black sky revolved. The sleigh swung around so that for one, insane moment it looked as if we were about to charge into the wolfpack. I was down in the bottom of the sleigh, entangled in robes, then up, then down again as the sleigh ran broadside into a kilometer marker buried in the snow. I heard the desperate grating of the iron runners dragged across the stone, a crack of parting boards. Then the sky tilted. It was no longer spinning but hung crazily askew with the shaggy tops of trees spilling across the lower half of it, while the sleigh slid with agonizing slowness back to the road, off the embankment it had climbed after the kilometer stone.

God damn it all to hell, was all I could think of. One horse was down. The other was up on his hind legs, front hooves flaying, throwing himself violently against the leather traces. A broken chain described a lazy arc overhead.

The driver was out of the sleigh, up beside the horses. His whip rose and fell too swiftly to follow in one whistling motion, so that there was no interval between the hiss and the crack of rawhide exploding on horseflesh.

Then the fallen horse was back on his feet and the weight of the sleigh dragged both the horses back onto their haunches. The young man was up in the narrow neck of the sleigh, in the blunted prow, shooting across the horses. The horses were streaked with blood where the shotgun pellets scored their necks and flanks. The shotgun blasts tore long gaps in the dark mass of the milling wolfpack.

And then, as quickly as it had begun, it was all over. The sleigh was on the road, slanting through the snow. The peasant driver was half in, half out of the sleigh, pulling himself up over the side like a swimmer clambering into a lifeboat. The young man was beside me again, in the back of the sleigh, fumbling with shotgun shells. The wolves came behind.

"Can you shoot?"

"What?"

"A pistol, fool! Can you shoot a pistol?"

"Yes!"

Could I? I had never tried it.

"Here!"

And the man threw me a dark, heavy object, and I held it, wondering if I had lost my mind, understanding nothing. There it was, in my hands, with the blue-black metal cylinder tapering in concentric circles at the business end, the oval handle—much too long for pistols—and the silvery rods under the barrel.

"Compressed air!" the young man shouted. "Makes no noise, no recoil. Just aim and squeeze, aim and squeeze. You have thirty rounds."

Aim and squeeze.

Ping! Only there was no ping or whisper this time; the wind picked up those delicate sounds and carried them away. Without the sounds I couldn't tell if the damn thing was working. Aim and squeeze. So Brown had had thirty chances to nail me in the store. How many had he taken? *Ping!* That was two down, twenty-eight to go. Each one good enough to down an elephant. Tore hell out of armor, pierced cast iron heads. *Ping!* Twenty-seven. Brown hit the mirror with his first one; he drilled his cowhide suitcase, that was two; two into poor dead Zimstern, dealer in antiques, junk dealer and Karpovitch's agent, also double agent. Who said he was a double agent? My Nakomda tempter who had also talked about a Sempinski Affair. Aim and squeeze. Twenty-six. What was the story about Brown and Zimstern? *Ping!* Twenty-five to go. I don't believe in coincidences any more. Brown was the man who slept on the cot behind Zimstern's store. He was the man with the blinding flashlight, Zimstern's *unexpected guest.* Nothing to do with our business, Zimstern had said. But what about Karpovitch's business? That meant that Zimstern, Brown, Per Lindstrom and Karpovitch were together in something, and whatever that is I don't want any part of it. Except that (*Ping!* Twenty-four) I'm already in it. And Brown is after me. He would have got me if the fat man hadn't rushed into the store. Poor man, bald head caved-in like an eggshell. He knew my name . . . a dreadful voice but American. Good God, the man had been an American. I've got the accent now, why didn't I catch on then? Who was he? I could have found out if I had searched his pockets. Damn squeamishness, anyway. What the devil had he been doing there? I had thought he was a Nakomda spy but he wasn't, was he? Aim and squeeze, and there goes one of them; I've got the hang of it now. Aim and squeeze. Twenty-two to go. And now the shotgun's going again. *Ping!* Brown had put one into the cast iron, vacant head of the first emperor of the French, a boon to historians. He sent two to my left at shin-level (or what had been my head-level) on the floor, and two to my right, and then three into the outside door while I had been fiddling with the bolts. One, two, then two again, including Napoleon's. Four on the floor and three into the street door. I let one fly when I picked up the thing from beside the dead man. Five, seven and one make thirteen. An omen? Thirteen gone; seventeen still left. I picked up one of the darts in the store. How do you load these things? I've never heard of them; they can't be as common as all that. How did Brown get one? Why did this man have one? Why did they both have one? This man is a German. You don't hurl commands with such an accent unless you're born to it. The peasant's not a German. He hated the German. Hates me too. Probably thinks I'm another German. What's all that about? What's Sempinski doing with a German servant? And if the man's a servant I'll eat my fur hat. A serving German is the most servile servant in the world; ersatz butter wouldn't melt in his mouth. Servant, my suffering aunt! And armed to the teeth. The shotgun is for wolves; very well. But the crazy, futuristic pistol? The silent, secret, armor-piercing pistol is nothing that anybody can pickup in a pawnshop. It's an assassin's weapon. It is a firm connection between Brown and Sempinski's arrogant German servant . . . who is not a servant. It doesn't matter at the moment what he is. As with the splintered drama on the road, everything here was a part of everything else.

Now, everybody that I had come across since that day in Pohl's anteroom was linked and locked solidly together in some mystery that, I knew, had nothing to do with the Romanowski Library. Perhaps there was a Sempinski Affair after all; and perhaps it was as desperately serious as the Nakomda officer had warned me that it was; and perhaps he had been warning me, not laying some complicated trap.

Well, it was too late to think that way now. Wise or not, for good or for evil, I had come . . . I was here. A half hour's talk with Sempinski could clear up everything. Sempinski had asked me to come to his house. He wanted me there. I had come . . . or rather, I was on my way. It was up to the old writer to set his guest at ease. Aim and squeeze.

And that was twenty.

And suddenly it was over.

The narrow white neck of the road sprang open, the trees fell away. The forest vanished. We were on a hill, coming down. Ahead was a plain, the infinite white miles flattened out by distance. Below us lay the black ribbon of a river, glittering with the jagged scales of icefloes like the armored spine of a prehistoric monster. A narrow, wooden bridge pilloried the river. Beyond it were houses: twelve wooden cottages thatched with snow, lined up behind fences, with cartwheels nailed flat on top of wagon tongues set into the gound where storks could come to build their nests in spring, with chimney smoke spreading among the eves; and there were men in the village street. Trees made a black horizon.

We drove across the bridge with the hollow rattle of an express train. The wolves didn't follow.

I lay back against the cloth-and-leather seat in the back of the sleigh, an awkward, ill-designed bench with wrought-iron curlicues for armrests, feeling fatigue settle about me with the danger gone. I didn't really believe that there could have been danger. Relief had made me lightheaded, I supposed. I lay as still as the sleigh would let me, laughing to myself.

Even the German didn't bother me. It was too silly to worry about odd-looking people with odd pistols; road company mysteries. Sooner or later everything would have a logical explanation.

The German took his pistol back. I watched him snap open a tubular magazine in the oval handle and load half a dozen steel darts. His exaltation seemed to have left him as rapidly as it had come. But I thought I had better start someone talking as soon as possible so that some fragment of the truth might suggest itself. I made a comment about the gun being interesting, but he only grunted. Then, with an inspired bit of flattery, I asked: "Is that a German invention?"

He said, with unconcealed pride: "It was designed by Otto Skorzenny himself."

I had, of course, heard of Skorzenny but pretended vagueness. "Let's see . . . wasn't he the German commando leader who rescued Mussolini from an allied prison about the time the war ended?"

The young German treated me to a look that was half pity, half contempt.

"That was nothing for Otto Skorzeny. The allies had the fat Italian hidden on top of the Alps, with twenty thousand men around the mountain. With no way up except by cable car. We crashlanded two dozen men in a glider on top of the mountain. Do you know what a *Fiesler-Storch* is? A small plane. Artillery spotter. Like your Piper Cubs, only better. We put Mussolini in a Storch and dived it off the edge of the mountain. He was shaking hands with Adolf Hitler before the amis knew what had happened. But that kind of thing was just routine for Otto Skorzenny."

"Tell me more about him."

"Why, he invented a whole concept of warfare! He terrorized the whole Anglo-American army with four hundred men! He showed the world what a handful of men can accomplish if they have the audacity and imagination. Nothing is impossible if the coup seems impossible enough!"

"He sounds like quite a man."

"He is a man! Do you know what he did when the Hungarians started getting nervous in 1944? He kidnapped their Regent right out of his own castle in the middle of his own capital! He had the Hungarians back in line before they knew they were supposed to change sides. And what about the Ardennes? You know about that?"

"You mean the Battle of the Bulge?"

"The Rundstedt offensive. If the traitors around Adolf Hitler had only let him do what he wanted he would have won the war! It would have been just like that!"

He snapped his fingers to show how easy it would have been.

"We had the amis running like dogs after their own tails. Four hundred men in ami uniforms changing road signs, spreading rumors, starting panics. Ah, if only we could have got as far as Paris!"

"Paris? What could you have done there?"

"Killed Eisenhower, of course! What else?"

"Ah, of course. What else . . ."

"Listen, you think this is funny? You think that killing Eisenhower wouldn't have stood the Anglo-Americans on their heads? You think the other ami generals wouldn't have started shaking in their boots? They would have been so busy looking under their beds they would have had no time to think about the war. All you need is the audacity for the one great stroke. Cut off your enemy's head, tear out his heart, and what does he have left?"

The German slapped the cylindrical magazine into the pistol butt. It made a quick, conclusive sound.

"One man can change the course of history," he said. "You kill a president or a country's leader and you are telling everybody in the country that nobody is safe. With one shot you have wounded everybody. There is Hysteria. That gives you the necessary Terror. Terrified people don't think. They bite like frightened animals. They bite anything you tell them to bite no matter what happens afterward. For the price of one bullet you have won the world."

"Were you with Skorzenny?"

He hesitated, as if tempted to tell me that he had been, but he could not have been much more than a child when the war had ended.

"I was too young," he said, as if ashamed.

twelve

NIGHT CAME before we stopped outside the iron gates of a walled estate. I was too tired, cold and hungry to pay much attention to surroundings; I wanted to get up to the house, in and out of a bath, into clean clothes and to a dinner table as swiftly as I could. I was uncomfortably aware of my crumpled clothes and wilted linen. Sleep would be good. I hoped Sempinski could spare me some time early in the morning. But I had a moment of uncertainty at the gate; that undefined uneasiness that had served me often in suggesting danger.

A wild moon galloped through ragged black clouds in a spectral sky. It threw its dead white light on turrets and towers, a precipitous moat floored with glaring ice, and the insanity of the flaying tree crowns.

I heard the savage anger of big dogs, then saw them: three coal-black mastiffs hurling themselves against chains.

The horses backed away from the gate, their ears flat. They made mewling sounds. The German laughed. Then two men armed with rifles appeared on the parapet of the crenellated wall. The wall had fallen, in places, into the moat, giving the gray mass of ragged granite the look of a stormed castle after a massacre . . . a kind of haunted starkness. The gate was a giant grille hung on heavy hinges from two flanking towers that were clearly several centuries older than the gate itself. The two men came off the wall to open the gate and pull back the mastiffs, and the peasant driver guided the sleigh and horses across a heavy-timbered bridge.

We entered the park: The dogs were down, green-eyed and menacing in the angled shadows between the wall and a crumbling buttress. They made the horses mince as cautiously as if the ground before us was covered with eggshells.

We went up to the house—a monumental stone pile with a square tower like a Norman keep, round towers and turrets reminiscent of the fairy-tale castles of the Rhineland, and an irregular pattern of exaggeratedly pointed roofs radiating from the massive granite centerpiece. It was a blend of many centuries but neither incongruous nor disturbing; a historical document in granite, stained glass and what would surely be copper-sheet roofs under the covering of snow and mirror-bright ice. Light blazed through mullioned windows at all levels, gilding the snow on archers' galleries and the icicle beards of gargoyles brooding over rainspouts. A cluster of enormous chimneys was stark against the sky.

I knew just enough about Sempinski's picturebook retreat to understand the mixture of centuries. This was *Hetmanska Gora,* the Hill of the Chief, presented to Sempinski by his nation on the twentieth anniversary of the publication of his first book, a proof of affection, but sinister on first sight under a spectral moon.

It had been a small castle in the twelfth century—the keep, the moat and the crumbling outer walls testified to that—raised at the foot of the mountains to watch over the passes. It had played many roles in its country's history. When given to Sempinski, the castle was restored and more or less modernized by public subscription.

Judging by the number of lighted windows I guessed that the old writer had other visitors.

I asked the young man about my fellow guests. He didn't even pretend to listen but yawned and stretched and got out of the sleigh as soon as it had stopped, and another man, who could have been his surly replica, led me through an ecclesiastically gloomy refectory hall with a groined, painted ceiling of blue and gold diapers made dim by the centuries, supported by granite columns with carved capitals. A hammered iron torch-ring, grim and heavy as a millstone, hung overhead with Damoclean menace.

We went up a baronial staircase, down another, through innumerable corridors and vaulted passages—some dark, others dim-lighted with electrified gasoliers—in cavernous chill. This was the coldest house I had ever been in. I thought it strangely silent for a country house presumably filled with guests. And yet the silence wasn't absolute; it was a modulated hush composed of many sounds. Stony-eyed servants stood motionless as statues in the corridors. All seemed more or less of an age that could have been anything from twenty to thirty. All seemed to be of a size, as if they had been stamped out on the same press. In the rectangular shadows cast by granite pillars, under stained glass and the Gothic gloom of vaulted ceilings, their uniformity seemed almost monastic. But they had none of the patient serenity of monks; indeed, they seemed to suck serenity out of the air and to replace it with a current of violence.

None of them looked at me, as if they knew everything about me and didn't think me worth another glance. Servants? Not on your life, I thought, irritated. Anything but servants. And there were other men (glimpsed through open doors and through the arches of a gallery that turned the library into a shadowed cloister): with books and newspapers in armchairs, studying the lay of a billiard table, talking. Quiet voices, perfectly assured. Cold faces, austere and professional. My fellow guests? They could be nothing else; they bore an air of authority that raised them above the servants like insignia of rank.

I looked at them with curiosity. They were Sempinski's guests, presumably his friends; a clue to the man and to whatever was taking place in his extraordinary house. I wanted some idea of who and what they were; I needed reassurance after my reception. These men would be, in effect, my allies against rising uneasiness. But what I saw puzzled me; I wasn't reassured. I couldn't fit these men into a familiar category any more than I could explain the improbable servants.

Priests? Surgeons? They could have been either but, obviously, they were eminent. They looked as if it had been a long time since anyone had questioned their authority. Power made natural by exercise, no more remarkable than breathing; the habit of command . . . and there was something more that defied identification. What? I didn't know. Whatever the quality had been, it was something in keeping with the ageless quality of the house.

Some were Orientals. Most were European. But there was an underlying similarity about them, more subtle than the graven uniformity of the servants. It was as if in their case the blueprints had been more complex, the mechanisms more delicately geared and the workmanship infinitely superior. Even their austere calmness—the detachment of the Grand Inquisitor they all seemed to wear—had been refined to the needle sharpness of the icicles glittering outside.

There were perhaps a dozen of them in the library, each one distinguished enough to focus all attention on himself, lifted above ordinary people by an absolute assurance, a sense of belonging and a peculiarly inflexible quality of face: polished, with the high gloss of metal filmed over imperceptibly by a pale dust. I thought that if I were to put my hand on one of those faces I'd feel an unyielding surface.

And then I saw the man who sat apart from the others in a deep armchair placed in the brooding darkness of an alcove formed by the angle of the monumental fireplace where no light intruded.

He was a huge man, hunched forward between the sweeping wings of the tall-backed armchair. His massive head was covered with thick, close-cropped hair like a helmet fashioned out of steel wire. Enormous shoulders and a packed, shaven neck leaned out of the leathery gloom. He stroked the air with incongruous fingers, like rubber truncheons glittering with polish. His face had a hard, gray hue with vertical lines, sharp furrows; he might have been a soldier. He smoked a cigarette in a long ivory holder. The delicate holder, cocked across his knee, looked as if he might have borrowed it for the evening.

He looked up as I passed the open arch and I felt frozen needles sliding over me, as if I were being stripped and dissected.

I hurried past the arch, heart pounding.

Perhaps it was the damp chill of the ancient walls inadequately heated; or the platoons of hostile servants; or the sum-total of my bleak impressions that made my stomach lurch suddenly with a certainty of danger. It wasn't anything that could be grasped at once; nothing was that obvious. But I knew the danger in the watchful sharpening of my senses.

I thought I would do well to find out what I was up against. I asked again how many other guests there were in the house.

"Guests?"

"Yes. Like me."

Suddenly the young man laughed.

"Like you? There is one like you and one something like you."

"I asked you a question."

I heard in my voice the odd, faulty note of an angry man.

"So? You asked and I answered."

"Answer me properly. What about the others? The men in the library?"

"Oh, they're nothing like you."

"What kind of servant are you, anyway? What's your job in this house?"

"It isn't answering questions."

It had taken me many years to learn how to control my explosive temper. I supposed that few of my associates had ever suspected me of a capacity for anger and, to tell the truth, I seldom allowed myself to lose self-control. But if there was one thing that could demolish all my carefully constructed barriers of restraint—the barriers that allowed me to make just about limitless allowances for other points of view—it was gratuitous rudeness.

I wanted to attack the arrogant young man. I had always been able to control the impulse and clamp a tight lid on my indignation, remembering who and what I was and what was involved. But that was *then and there:* home—where you could understand the motives, where you could weigh your personal dignity, your civilized essence, against these motives and, inevitably, find that even verbal violence on your part was an affront to you as a human being. I eschewed violence in any form because it was an indignity, the last resort of an animal. For the same reason I had avoided involvement in Causes; because all causes sank into violence of some kind sooner or later. And no cause seemed sufficiently personal or important to risk the humiliation of being violent.

But that was then and there; this was here and now. I felt myself close to the boiling point, following the German.

The corridors narrowed, the ceilings drew perceptively closer to the granite flagstones. The vaulted passages had become progressively colder with the damp, truly penetrating chill of old tombs. I had been in enough crypts to be familiar with their curious duality: dry enough for the undisturbed dust of centuries to form its miniature Saharas, damp enough to cut through any clothing deep into the bone. The echoes were hollow, now. Clearly we had come to the old part of the house: the original fortress.

My room was a granite chamber as long and tall as an indoor squash court. Daylight would make small headway here against the heavy gloom, seeping through the armorial stained glass of three lancet windows, little more than loopholes. A man could hardly thrust his arm through them. Now, the solitary light of a dim bulb threw shadows out of a cast-iron trefoil bracket chained like a prisoner to the naked wall. Stone walls, stone floor; I had expected them. They were as much a part of this tower chamber as the battlements outside. The fireplace was like a thirteenth-century tomb—big enough to roast an ox and a pair of sheep—and equally expected. It looked as if it hadn't felt the heat of a fire in a hundred years. What heat there was, came from a porcelain stove in a corner; this century's addition. There was a huge, carved bedstead on a dais, under a canopy, some old chests studded with oxidized black iron, and heavy furniture. But the ceiling was fifteenth-century coffered wood, painted in white and red chevrons, with heraldic lions (rampant in goldfoil on sky blue) and crimson griffins (on canary yellow) in alternate squares. Elsewhere and at another time I would have been delighted with this rare find.

I put my bag and briefcase on a banded chest at the foot of the bedstead. I felt immensely chilled. The German youth leaned against the fireplace with quiet insolence.

"Does the gentleman find everything satisfactory?"

I nodded. "It will do."

He laughed. "That makes me very happy. We wouldn't want the gentleman not to enjoy his stay."

I turned my back on him. The granite walls were without ornament. The lancet windows were black with the night behind them; I supposed that they would offer a fine view of mountains that could be no further than twenty miles away. Beyond the mountains lay another country; I couldn't immediately remember which country it was.

The German asked if I wanted anything to eat but hunger was the last of my problems, even though my last meal had been an excellent dinner eaten on the train. When I refused a tray, he shrugged with indifference, heading for the door.

I said: "When can I see Professor Sempinski?"

He didn't answer as he left the room.

thirteen

I SAT DOWN in the nearest chair, grateful that my stomach was empty, hoping that no one would bring me dinner after all. I didn't think that anybody would.

After a while, I got up. I had a violent headache. I didn't care any more about seeing Sempinski; I wasn't interested in any explanations. I knew that I had to leave Hetmanska Gora as fast as I could. I started walking up and down the chamber, counting flagstones. There were two hundred flagstones in ten rows of twenty. The clatter of my leather heels thundered in my head.

I thought I heard a faint noise outside and went to the door and found the door locked. Locked? I pumped the ancient iron handle up and down and pushed against the black oak boards and bruised my shoulder on one of the rose-shaped iron bosses that studded the door. But the door *was* locked. The keyhole was empty. I put my ear to the keyhole and heard a man's breathing; the door was not only locked but also guarded: I was a prisoner.

Whose? Why?

I had no idea.

But I knew now that I had been brought to Hetmanska Gora by design. Nothing about this visit had been accidental—from the first letter from Julian Sempinski. But what the devil did they want from me?

I wandered about the room with no clear idea what to do. But gradually thought began to crystallize into a decision to escape.

How? Where? It didn't matter where. What mattered was to end the nightmare. I had been stalked, shot at, tricked, threatened, insulted and imprisoned. I had had enough.

I had read somewhere that condemned men experienced moments of terrible elation; as if (like moths heading for open flame) their destruction was coincidental with attainment. Having decided on escape, with no illusions about either the dangers or my chances, I was aware of a comparable sensation; relief—short-lived but consoling—sustained me for a time.

I had a perfect right to be afraid. What I proposed was little short of madness: a desperate journey through a hostile country, alone in the dead of winter, and definitely pursued. I had had several samples of what to expect; the wolves and the conspirators were only a part of it. I didn't know the language of the country which seemed paranoid about the only other language I could use here. I didn't have much money. I couldn't ask the simplest directions without making myself conspicuous. And my pursuers would probably know exactly where I was heading, and every step of the road I had to take. It wasn't a bright picture.

And to start this journey I had to escape from a castle in a snowy wilderness, past guards who wouldn't think twice about killing me, and killer dogs who'd do their best to tear me to pieces.

That had the sound of a damn poor start but there was nothing I could do about it. Daylight escape was out of the question. Only night offered any kind of chance. There would be fewer men about the corridors, none in the park if the dogs were loose. I might get out of the house undetected. Once out of the castle, I would have to make my way quickly across the park . . . by no means a gentle stroll by moonlight. Moonlight meant danger. I would have to keep carefully to the shadows. I didn't know the geography of the wooded acres, and darkness would be sure to add to my confusion. And there would be no time for any confusion. I would have to keep away from the well-used paths to get to the wall, then get across the wall and the moat (sure to be patrolled), and make my way as surely as a homing pigeon across the snowy wilderness of open country to the village road. In that cold, with those mountains of snow, in that bitter wind, I wouldn't last a half hour away from the road. Keeping away from the drive and the well-used paths was taking a chance on losing my bearings. But the mastiffs would be on me in a minute, otherwise. I had to take my chances with them anyway; it was a large park and there were only the three mastiffs . . . they couldn't cover it all. If they did sniff me out, there was always the compressed-air pistol. I hoped I would be steady enough to use it if I had to. I had been steady enough in the sleigh but I had no illusions about my prowess there; it was one thing to ping away at a dark, indivisible mass of wolves—who seemed utterly unreal anyway—with the shotgun booming and frantic horses hauling me to safety, and other men involved who knew what to do; it would be something else for me alone, nerves taut, jumping at every shadow, with silent killer dogs padding invisibly behind. The mastiffs were a deadly danger but the men were worse. It was the men I had to worry about. They would pursue me far beyond the walls.

But if I got away early enough—say, around midnight, with the household sleeping—I could have as much as six hours before anyone realized that I was gone. They would find me missing when they brought my breakfast. Add another hour for a search of the castle and the grounds. Perhaps another hour while they got a pursuit party together and on its way in the right direction. That was eight hours. In eight hours I could be well on my way to the ancient city where the sleigh had met me. With luck I could be getting on a train for the border before the hunters started after me. It wasn't very likely but there was a chance . . . if, I concluded bitterly, I ever managed to get out of my room.

It was at this point that the pretty tapestry of my little dream filled with gaping holes. The *ifs* and *mights* collapsed. Because escape from the castle was about as likely as a rescue party of United States Marines landing on the roof. The door was locked and guarded. The windows would defy a fugitive cat. The walls and floor were solid. That left the fireplace. The fireplace could give me access to the roof—*if* the chimney wasn't blocked by a hundred years' accumulation of debris or even other optimistic fugitives. Once on the roof, I could presumably flap my arms and fly.

I leaned against the wall, wondering how I could have been stupid enough to hope for some way out. My addiction to mystery novels and historical romances was to blame.

My headache came back, magnified. The stone floor was cold under my feet. I sneezed. I sat on the bed and tried not to think.

But thought persisted. I couldn't give up quite this easily; I had to try something. The fireplace wasn't much of an escape route but it was a start. Perhaps it would take me past other fireplaces and, thus, into rooms with unguarded doors. And if the chimney only took me to the roof, I might be able to find a way down the precipitous walls, or spot an entrance into another part of the house where no one would expect me. I wouldn't know until I had explored it.

I put on slacks and sweaters and took off my shoes and put on all the spare socks I had. I remembered gloves. Before I entered the fireplace and began the climb, I wedged a heavy chair under the door handle. I draped a towel over the door handle and the keyhole.

Later, I would think of that moment and what came after it as a monument to the incredible, a not-quite-possible experience that I could view with clinical detachment—a form of amnesia in which I had a vivid recollection of a variety of terrors but could not remember the terror itself.

The fireplace looked more than ever like the mouth of a crypt. I didn't know what I would find in the icy darkness, hearing the soft rustling and scurrying high up in the tunnel, seeing red pinpoint lights glittering in pairs like clusters of splintered glass. It was all something I recalled afterwards as a nightmare of darkness and dryness that went far beyond infinitely powdered dust, as though I had been drawn into the gullet of a science-fiction monster or the airless mouth of space itself. I rose hand over hand, peering into absolute blackness and now and then I looked down between my feet at the shrinking rectangle of light: my fireplace and granite prison chamber that seemed an embodiment of safety. And all too soon the light shrunk into nothing. I went up through pillow-thick cobwebs made solid with powdered brick and mortar, with the squeal and rush of rats like a loud river around me, lifting myself from ledge to ledge, feeling ahead with fingers that were gloved with dust. I couldn't see my hands against my face. The tunnel walls seemed to contract and expand about me like a living throat; I felt as if I was crawling into the earth itself with mountains settling over me, enormous weights shifting, pressing down. I fought panic. Blinded, I began to doubt my sense of direction. I couldn't tell if I was climbing or moving headfirst into a bottomless pit. I clung to the brick ledges, fighting vertigo and the certainty that the walls were moving down on me. I passed the open mouths of other tunnels, like caves in the subterranean passages, but I couldn't tell if these led up or down or even if they were horizontal. It was soon apparent that I was in the shaft of the main chimney, like the interior of an ancient, fossilized tree trunk, with an infinity of branches leading out of it to other parts of the house. The gaping mouths breathed with the torrential sounds of rats rushing from my approach. Or . . . were they rushing at me? My body tried to shrink into itself; I fought to keep from screaming. I had an overwhelming desire to let myself drop down the shaft. It would be so easy . . . Just let the fingers open on the ledge above . . . keep eyes closed . . . Drop. Straight down and away from your own contaminated skin . . .

A rush of cold air brought me to my senses. My hands were numb; I no longer felt the woven mat of cobwebs parting about me. The river-sound of rats fell away. No power on earth or beyond it could have induced me to open my eyes; I sniffed the ice-cold air, hoping for direction, then went on up (or was it down, or sideways?) hand over hand.

It went on like that for a time that had no relation to minutes or hours. Each moment was a small eternity. My body seemed to alternately shrink and balloon between walls, within the endless core and gut of a time without boundaries, the essence of darkness. But time did pass. Each of its subdivisions became progressively colder. Eventually I felt ice on my face and opened my eyes and saw the roundness of the night framed in the mouth of the chimney, and the incredible glitter of a star.

I lay above a world of ice: sharp-angled cliffs of roof, precipice of walls. Turrets and towers like the fluted columns of glaciers high above the treeline, festooned in icicles like frozen waterfalls . . . the furry rolls of gutter and drainpipe and spire and lightning rod grown heavy with snow.

Getting here seemed to have been an end in itself; I couldn't immediately remember why I had come.

But the coldness helped. The icy wind stroked me into motion. I raised myself out of the mushroom-shaft of the huge chimney, and slipped over the edge to the ridge of the roof. I went down on my hands and knees, feeling myself fill up with the cold. I knew I would be frozen solid in minutes. I had to move. But where? Anywhere. There were the turrets and the sharp slope of dormers soaring toward the torn and raging sky. Anyone of them would do if it had a window.

I edged away from the supporting mass of the chimney, inch by inch astride the icy ridge of the roof. The couloir of the ridge was a yard wide with ice and perfectly rounded, with polished sheets falling as smooth as water to the dark edges of the precipice, high-angled like the glazed roof of a house of cards. The wild sea of the tree crowns boiled in the wind far below. There were no handholds anywhere on the sheets of ice; one slip and I would rocket to the frozen ground. Ice burned my legs like fire. I crept out into the middle of the roof, making for the white wall that rose across my path: the central mass of the ancient fortress with a high archers' gallery above turrets. If I could climb up there . . . But I couldn't. The wind kept me pinned to my icy saddle. I began to freeze. I had to go back.

Again time slipped into its own private subdivisions with no regard for man-made labels of seconds and minutes. There was a sort of rhythm to the backward progress I made on the roof, the push-and-slide motion of retreat; I supposed this could have been a way to measure the seconds. But, toward the end, each of these seconds felt like a quarter of an hour. I had no recollection of reaching the shelter of the chimney, or getting up and over the high lip or sliding inside. But suddenly the wind no longer cut into me, the rocking buffet had stopped and, in the odor of ascending dryness, I dropped down inside.

I felt no disappointment then. That would come later. Sinking into the tight throat of the tunnel I felt and thought nothing.

I started making my way down and saw at once that the descent would be much harder than the climb had been. My feet were numb; they registered no contact. My hands were not much better but, at least, they could still signal the difference between handholds and empty, black air. I had to turn around and try it headdown. The shaft was slanted at sharp angles, I remembered; vertical drops were infrequent. And, going down headfirst, I would have my face farther away from the rats gathering behind me.

I eased myself into a side-tunnel and crawled out headfirst. I moved out cautiously across the crumbling edges.

The descent was also something that I remembered later in incomprehensible fragments as an exercise in horror; not my horror but an impersonal case history.

It was the same nightmare of ancient dust and darkness, giant rats and spiders, the dry smell of pulverized mortar, blindness and hallucination; but, going up, I had had hope and purpose. The roof had been a magnet, escape was the spur. Coming down, I had only the knowledge of defeat.

In no time I was sure that I had taken a wrong tunnel and lost the main shaft of the chimney. I had no idea where I was in reference to the shaft. The tunnels narrowed. They branched off in innumerable passages, each narrower than the one before. Soon I was moving with the crumbling stone brushing against my back, and there were bricked-up exits and holes that opened up suddenly between my hands, and there were blocked tunnels and masses of rubble that forced me to back off. I entered new tunnels, took new directions and eventually knew that I was hopelessly lost. Breathing became difficult. Small white stars began to revolve under my closed eyelids. I was starved for air. I scrambled forward, face-down against scampering soft bodies, trapped in the claustrophobic labyrinth.

My fears ballooned; doubts overwhelmed reason. I found that I was biting my own hands. A furry river of animals ran over my legs; my nostrils filled with their fetid smell. I thought I was drowning.

I didn't know how I got myself back under control. I was a bit mad then, I supposed. But the cold pushed me forward. Nothing else around me had any relation to anything I knew; but the chill summoned instinctive reactions.

And suddenly my eyes were open and saw what obviously couldn't be there for me to see: a white light knifing through the blackness, a pencil-thin beam of incredible brightness.

I heard human voices.

I didn't believe what I saw or heard.

And then the walls seemed to lift and fall away. There was space around me. There was a seeping rivulet of warmer air and the intoxicating smell of tobacco smoke. Threads of light dressed the walls in cobwebs. I lay on the floor, on my back, breathing the warm air.

fourteen

I WAS IN a small, vaulted chamber behind a fireplace, a stone closet angled away from the wall, tucked behind bricks. The brick curtain between my hiding place and the room on the other side was nominal at best. The bricks were crumbling, old. Most of them had fallen away on the inside, leaving one layer in the fireplace. Their mortar was fine dust; I could pick any of the bricks away with two fingers. The light and voices came from the room through this porous curtain. At first I didn't listen to the voices; it was enough to hear them. Hearing them, I knew that I was not going to die in the tunnels.

After a while, I rolled over on my stomach. There was plenty of room in my hideout for moving any way I wanted. I got to my knees and put my eyes against the broadest of the innumerable cracks between the bricks and looked into the room. I saw perhaps a dozen of the so-called servants but many more seemed to disappear in the shadows where the light of the lanterns didn't reach.

The room was enormous. Light from a half dozen lanterns fell on a long trestle table and the glass partitions of a conservatory beyond it. There were chairs, armchairs, chests, carved pilasters, partially dismantled suits of armor; these looked bloodily dismembered in the reddish glare of the lanterns. Debris of food littering the table, spilled papers and outdoor clothing piled without care, turned the hall into a stage setting for a guardhouse and the ready-room of a military task force. Pistols and rifles on and against the table among gnawed chicken bones. Fur robes and uniforms. Coarse voices. Odd packing cases spilling straw and metal. A greenish mound of ammunition boxes. Liquor bottles, red in the violent light. Light thrust with difficulty through the shifting streams of blue tobacco smoke.

I heard words and, at first, that was all I could hear: words without meaning. I could sense the jubilation of the laughing men, their soon-to-come moment of fulfillment. I didn't grasp much more than that. But gradually the words acquired meaning; I recognized their general direction. I heard my own name. Mention of The Magician also made me sit up and pay attention. It took me some time to understand how my name could possibly fit-in with what the so-called servants were so darkly pleased with.

Two of the nearest voices, a young one and an older one, were discussing murder; a political assassination. The men sat near the fireplace, out of my line of vision, but I thought that the younger voice belonged to the man who had met me with the sleigh. A note of respect and a kind of anticipatory, boyish excitement made his voice difficult to identify; I had heard only his arrogance and berserk exaltation.

The murder under discussion was not (as I had first supposed it to be) a gruesome fact of medieval history, but something still to come—a forthcoming event.

And then I understood that this assassination was to be more than an ordinary murder (thinking, even as I became aware of this, that I had surely come far if I could think of any murder as being ordinary): somehow the United States were to be implicated.

And I heard that I too had had an assigned role in the assassination plot. I had helped, apparently, to provide a vital ingredient: the undeniable evidence of American involvement.

I thought then that the terrors of the journey through the chimney tunnels must have scrambled my senses.

But this much was clear: the plot was the brainchild of The

Magician who was on his way to Hetmanska Gora to supervise the final detail of the operation—a detail of which I formed an important part.

"Tell me about The Magician," said the younger man. "Is he as good as they say?"

"He is the best, he's always been the best. Who else could organize an operation like this? Who else could bring together such a mass of detail? The man is a genius."

"Have you ever met him?"

"No. Nobody knows who he is. I don't believe his own men know who they're working for. Even to us, who have watched him operate for years, and who used his services in the days of the Reich, he never seemed to be more than a legend. But we'll both meet him in a day or two."

"You used to be with Skorzenny. Did you ever work on an operation as big as this one?"

"No. Oh, there were some fine times, some great operations. But our Otto was all dash and fire, a great man with the hand grenade and the submachine gun . . . This kind of subtlety would be beyond him. Look how long and how carefully The Magician spun his web around the amis. Look at the proof we have lined up against them. Each thread is strong enough to enmesh the amis, but spliced together, these threads make a hangman's rope. There is the old man upstairs, the girl, the letters, and now this new American has brought us the money. Who else but The Magician could have netted our big fish in America and even got us an American assassin for a scapegoat? We have everything tied up as neatly as you please and right on schedule."

"Are you sure that the American brought the money?"

"If The Magician said he was bringing it, then he brought it. We'll know where it is when The Magician gets here."

I couldn't understand what money they were talking about. I had brought very little cash to Hetmanska Gora, and only about a thousand dollars in travelers' checks. I didn't know what other role I had played or was supposed to play in this new conspiracy but there was *some* role and that was enough.

The scope of the affair put me in a mild state of shock, I supposed. This was a matter for professionals. Nothing like this was ever supposed to happen to an ordinary man, a private citizen who paid his bills and taxes, crossed streets on a green light and fed parking meters, met his responsibilities as best he could and tried to make a reasonable living for himself.

I didn't want to have anything to do with this affair, but I had little choice. Some kind of a conspiracy was being aimed at the United States; I couldn't just stand by and watch it unfold, although I had no idea what to do about it.

Was this the awakening of a latent patriotism? That word had always had a rowdy, dull-witted sound for me; it smelled of beer and sweaty auditoriums and the comic-opera uniforms of paunchy old men. I had my own, quieter definitions of America. But what it all boiled down to now was that I'd be damned if I'd let a bunch of reconditioned and pubescent Nazis get away with some propaganda stroke against my own kind without, at least, trying to upset their plans.

This put the whole affair in a new perspective. Escaping from Hetmanska Gora just because I resented being pushed around was no longer the point. My feelings weren't important. I had to unravel at least a few of the threads the two Nazis had been talking about so that the embassy in the capital could be told about the Sempinski Affair.

To start, I had to find Sempinski. I didn't believe that Sempinski could be a party to the plot. He had been used by the conspirators as I had been used. He might be able to provide the necessary details that would illuminate the entire plot. Once I knew exactly what I was up against, I would find a way to reach the capital.

I started looking about the room with greater care, noting details. A plan began to take shape in my mind. The Germans had now found a new subject for discussion—the girl they had mentioned earlier, some other dupe. They made coarse jokes. I didn't have to listen to Teutonic humor. I took the opportunity to fix the layout of the huge hall firmly in my mind. The glass doors of the conservatory captured my attention. They were incongruous in that medieval chamber, an Edwardian addition. But beyond them would lie the greenhouse and it would abut on the park and, since glass was a lot easier to break through than granite, it could be the way out of the house that I was looking for.

Almost at once, another piece of luck presented itself. A new man entered. Someone asked him what he was doing away from his post.

"I got hungry," he said. He found a piece of cold chicken and began to eat.

"Who's on the old man's door?"

"Nobody. What's the matter? You think Sempinski can get to the door? Besides, Grossmayer can see it from where he is sitting."

"Grossmayer has his own job."

"Then you better get up there and wake him, before his American crawls out through the keyhole."

An hour seemed to pass before the men started to leave the hall, taking their lanterns with them. In the sudden darkness, the echoing click of the closing door had a grim finality.

I felt a return of panic; the black walls seemed to close on me again; I was once more entombed underneath the mountain. I struck against the bricks, feeling them shift and grate under my knuckles, hearing their clattering fall in the room on the other side.

I heard the thin, melodious chimes of a musical clock striking the opening measures of Mozart's Little Music of the Night, then beating out the hour.

I sat back on my heels, breathing deeply. I brought my body and mind back under control; I couldn't afford panic. I counted the ringing strokes of the chimes: there were eleven of them. I had been in Hetmanska Gora exactly four hours.

Soon all sound ceased; the household was asleep. I forced myself to wait in the darkness, adjusting my vision to the moonlight.

The terrors of the journey through the chimney tunnels were

still very much with me but they were no longer a matter of the moment. My thoughts were orderly. From the exchange I had over-heard, Sempinski's room was off the same corridor as my own in the central fortress, close enough for one guard to watch both the doors. The guard on my door had fallen asleep. By the time I got there, Sempinski's guard could also be sleeping, having stuffed himself with chicken before my eyes. And even if I didn't get to Sempinski tonight, I would manage to pinpoint his door for a try at some other time. Sooner or later I would have to see him.

I was cold and hungry; my muscles were cramped. But I began to pry out the bricks until the hole that I had punched in the wall in my earlier panic was big enough to crawl through. The various darknesses of the moonlit hall did not confuse me; I had the room's geography fixed firmly in mind; and so I moved quickly among the litter of supplies, making no sound on the cold stone floor in my stockinged feet. I had one bad moment when a black, formless shadow leaped at me out of glass: but it was only my own soot-smeared reflection.

The double doors to the conservatory were bolted and locked but the key was in the keyhole and the bolts were oiled. I was inside the abandoned glass house in a moment, taking care to leave no telltale footprints between the doors and the exit to the park.

The outer door was locked and keyless but the ancient lock was rusted and ready to crumble at a touch. One good kick would send the door flying off its hinges. Beyond it lay the black wilder-ness of the park, threatening in moonlight.

I came back to the hall hardly able to believe my luck. I had found the way out of the castle. The chimney tunnels would be the escape route; the greenhouse would be the final exit. I'd have to blaze some kind of trail in the chimneys, and that meant going back into the catacombs, but there was no way to avoid that chore. Besides, I knew what to expect in the tunnels; once faced, a terror lost much of its bite.

This new excitement had wakened my hunger.

There was enough leftover food on the table to feed a small

army. I attacked the sour black bread and garlic sausage as if I had never eaten anything better, and washed down this explosive dinner with a fair wine. The wine sent warmth into my numbed arms and legs. I lit a cigarette. My spirits rose. My vision sharpened. Everything became marvelously clear and defined. Nothing seemed impossible.

I searched through the piles of the conspirators' equipment until I had found a powerful flashlight and some lengths of thin but strong nylon line. These were just what I needed for exploring and marking the tunnels off the main chimney shaft. I didn't bother with any of the weapons; they looked too complicated for me. Clothing was more to the point: short sheepskin jackets, fur-lined boots and hats, quilted gloves . . . I noted what I would need but left it alone. It would be right here when I needed it.

I was tired then. The wine began to make inroads on my senses. My arms were suddenly extraordinarily heavy. My head filled with a gentle, soporific humming.

It had been a long, brutal day and it wasn't over; there was a great deal more that I had to do. I set about repairing the breech in the fireplace, sure that I was doing it all wrong. Whatever my manual skills might be, they didn't include masonry. I got the bricks together more or less the way they might have been before I had disturbed them, hoping it was a good enough job to hide all traces of my break-in. I swept up the dust and pocketed the small debris and risked a flash of light along the fireplace. The wall looked all right. A bricklayer would laugh himself sick at the sight of it but I didn't think the conspirators would spot my mistakes. I took the nylon cord and the flashlight and went to the door.

The corridor was silent, dark, empty and unguarded. There was no threatening sound inside the house; only the creaks and groans of old timber, the unremitting ticking of large clocks and the sad echoes of the wind speeding down the ancient corridors. Out of the heavy shadows rose the familiar granite pillars of the refectory hall, so that I knew where I was and which way to go.

The clocks were striking midnight by the time I felt the dank walls of the granite fortress closing about me, and saw the dim lantern of the sleeping guard outside my door. There was another light farther up the corridor, where a second guard slept, head-down, at the head of a stone stairway that curved into the black arch of a tower entrance.

This would be Sempinski's door, the one I was seeking. It was partly hidden in a deep, black recess not much wider than the lancet windows and less than half their height. It would be a tight squeeze past the guard who sat under the arch of the doorway, growling and muttering in his sleep. His chair took up more than half the space on the landing.

The guards seemed sound asleep but getting past them was an alarming proposition. Each had his lantern. These made twin lakes of light. Once I was out of shadow I would be totally unprotected. If either guard should wake while I was in the light, the game would be over before it had properly begun.

It took all my sagging resolution to get going. Each step within the pools of light was a minor miracle. With each I listened for the yell of an awakened guard. But the men slept. My good luck seemed to be continuing. I crossed the trembling pools of light that seemed like crimson quicksand and reached the new shadow on the other side of the curving stairway. There I could rest, taking time to pull myself together, hearing Sempinski's guard yawn and stir on the stone platform above me; his hobnailed boots hung over my head like a pair of clubs. But the man settled back to sleep and I started the soft, slow climb toward him. The steps were worn and hollowed into basins. The wall was cold and dry against my back. My hands left wet marks there. I took one step at a time, eyes fixed on the cretinous face crumpled in sleep above me. A dozen times I thought he would awake and see me. I couldn't understand why he didn't sense my approach. I thought that the air around was filled with so much tension that some of it was bound to penetrate the guard's stupor. He muttered restlessly but did not awake. I edged past him, brushing the thick oxlike back and pressed myself into the alcove of the door. The key was in the lock and the lock was shining with oil. I unlocked the door, pushed it open one millimeter at a time, and entered the room. I closed the door behind me with infinite care.

fifteen

THE NEAR half of the room was bright with multicolored moon-light that slanted through the leaded stained-glass windows in cha-otic beams, but the far corners were in opaque shadow. The tower-ing catafalque of a fourposter bed advanced out of darkness as the torn clouds struggled with the moon outside; the sudden flat gleam of gold curlicues around gloomy portraits, dark wood and colorless iron shapes, retreated into unexpected distance. The meas-ured breathing of the man in the bed seemed to come from every-where at once.

I looked down at the gray, ravaged face and knew it at once; I would have known it anywhere. Even in its terrible disguise of time and disease it was the same face that used to stare at me from the frontispiece portraits of my favorite historical romances, different only in texture like a bad translation. The savage wing of white hair had become a deathly gray in the uncertain light, the mouth had fallen into stricken hollows, and two weary trenches had been driven into the gaunt escarpments of the cheeks. But there the difference ended; the thin nose still leaped like a violent beak out of its ambush of innumerable wrinkles and the famous eyebrows spilled across imperious eyes like chalky tree roots over-hanging the banks of a river.

I started explaining who I was, how I had got into his room

and why I had come. There was no way of proving to the silent, watchful old man that I was anything more than part of a bad dream. I felt like giving way to tired hysteria; everything seemed so absolutely senseless; I had been a fool. My experiences had acquired the unreal quality of a nightmare from which there is no way to awake.

"There is a chair behind you, Dr. Shippe."

Sempinski's soft voice would have gone unheard if there had been another sound. But after my hoarse whispering, the sound seemed explosive. I threw a wild glance at the door, expecting the bleak mass of wood and ornamental iron to erupt into pounding boots and violent light, but it remained closed. Sempinski's eyes had followed mine.

"There is no need to whisper."

"Can't the guard hear us?"

"The door is oak, ten centimeters thick. Nothing that happens in these rooms can be heard outside."

"I'm a bit jumpy, I'm afraid. This is all very new to me."

Sempinski smiled. His head remained rigid, pressed back into the pillows. Only his eyes and lips moved.

I asked: "What about you? Are they keeping you a prisoner in your own house?"

He nodded, said softly: "I'm paralyzed. My prison is this bed."

"I had begun to think that you didn't believe who I was. I know I don't look very reassuring."

"Why shouldn't I believe you? I knew you had come to Hetmanska Gora. As for thinking that you might be part of some kind of a trap . . . well, my keepers don't need to set any more for me."

"How did you know I had been brought here?"

"They had shown me your letter from the capital and the answer that they had written in my name. They take good care to keep me informed about their successes. It's one of their most popular amusements."

"Who are they, sir?"

"An ironic combination of young Nazis and the original breed that had found refuge in the East German police in the Stalin era. There are also important local Stalinists among them, men who had lost power in recent years and want it back. I'll tell you all about them in a moment. What is important is that they underestimated you. Our only chance lies in the mistakes they may make. They would never have thought you capable of doing what you did tonight."

I said: "Neither did I."

"You are planning an escape, of course? You have to warn your embassy about this as soon as you can."

"I'm going to try it, as soon as I know what this is all about."

"The quicker the better. These people are professionals. Have you found a way out of the house? You seem to get around quite freely."

I explained about the chimney passages and the conservatory. Sempinski laughed then: a clear, almost youthful sound.

"I can help a little. There are some blueprints and architects' drawings of the house in my desk. The National Historical Society took measurements before the world war. We can go over that. And I can help you plan your route across the park. But what about the other side of the wall? Do you know anybody who can help you?"

"I had hoped you would know someone."

"No," Sempinski said. "I can't trust anyone any longer. The old friends are dead. The new men are largely . . . reconstructed; I can't vouch for the way they think."

I was too upset by this revelation to say anything; I had counted on Sempinski to arrange my entire escape out of Eastern Europe. Now that the situation had become so very much more dangerous, and my plans so much more involved, he could barely help me get out of his house.

I told him what I thought I might do if I managed to reach open country beyond the park walls. Light seemed to leave his face as he listened to me.

"That has damn little chance," he said finally.

"What else can I do?"

"Nothing. That's the trouble. Damn, but I wish I hadn't brought you into this."

I said quietly: "I wondered why you had me come."

"I didn't want you to come at all. I wanted to send you an autographed book, and in that book to include a message which you could take to your government. I had no idea you were coming here until you sent your telegram from New York. Our keepers cabled you the invitation. They wanted you here."

"But why choose me?" I asked. "I don't know anything about this kind of thing."

"You were the only man, anywhere, to whom I could write. I had to make some contact with the West . . . any contact. These murderous animals would never allow any other letters. They had their own reasons for wanting you here, so they permitted a letter to you."

I couldn't keep the bitterness out of my voice.

"And I walked right into their trap."

Sempinski said: "If it's any comfort, you're only one of many to have done so."

"But what the devil could these people want from me?"

"You sent Kristin Napoji here. You knew where she had gone. You could have directed possible searchers to this house and that would have exposed the whole conspiracy."

"But why should anybody search for her? She is dead, killed in an accident. Her case is closed. Even the American Embassy has gone along with that."

Sempinski sighed, smiled. He said: "There never was a real accident. Kristin is in this house. She has never left it since she brought me your letter and my book."

I couldn't believe that I had understood properly. Sempinski laughed a little.

"No accident?"

"Oh, there was an accident, yes; but she wasn't in it. Don't look so stunned, Doctor, so bewildered. If these mad animals could conceive their incredible conspiracy, it would be child's play for them to hoodwink a bored embassy official. Kristin's so-called accident was undoubtedly a magnificent production."

"But she wasn't in it, thank God!"

"That was one detail they couldn't supply. It must have hurt their professional pride; they glory in detail. Which, incidentally, is another reason why they wanted you here."

"I don't understand."

"You had become an unexpected detail, an unraveled thread. You had brushed against their conspiracy and so you had to be tidied up. These people leave nothing to chance."

"Couldn't they have dealt with me in New York? Why have me come here?"

"That I don't know. Perhaps you are to be an exhibit . . . as I am to be. I only know that you're important to them."

He had begun to look very tired then.

"Are you finding all this too hard to believe?"

I didn't know what to believe. My all-too-brief sense of well-being had evaporated. I was too tired to think clearly, anyway. Too much had happened: the night, its terrors, disappointments, revelations and astonishments pressed down upon me like a suffocating cloth.

I urged the old man to go on but it seemed as if Sempinski wasn't listening to me. He had stepped deep inside himself, out of range of voices. Clearly, he was approaching a moment which would be both painful and difficult for him.

I said, as gently as I could: "Well sir, what is this all about?"

His voice had become low and uncertain.

"Forgive me if I don't come to the point at once. This can't be done quickly. There is only one sequence in the telling that makes any sense. And there is also the matter of my own pride—because, you see, I am responsible for much of this."

"I can't imagine how you could be to blame."

"I have been a gullible old fool. The bitter truth is that you will be risking your life to undo the damage that I helped to cause. Perhaps that is why I find it so difficult to start telling you about it."

I said: "I can't believe that you could ever be involved in something like this."

"Why not? I can be fooled as easily as anyone. And probably easier."

The multicolored beams of light swept away then, as the clouds covered the moon, and left him in darkness. His face was suddenly luminous against the banked pillows.

"You overheard a fragment of a plot and this fragment shocked you. No, perhaps not shock. Anger and indignation would fit you better than shock. You were indignant. Shocked too, of course, but in a different way . . . It's a preposterous plot, you said . . . These people must be absolutely mad . . . Isn't that right?"

"Yes. More or less. How could anybody be made to believe that the United States could be involved in an assassination?"

"A few years ago it would have been impossible for anyone to believe it," Sempinski said gently. "But now there are precedents. Political assassination isn't so far removed from the American scene, is it?"

I wanted to protest that the assassinations he was talking about had been the work of deranged men. The conspiracy aimed at implying an official American involvement. But the difference seemed morally uncertain . . . only a matter of degree. I waited for Sempinski to go on but it was some time before he could continue.

He said, simply: "I call myself a patriot . . . In this country patriotism is still considered a virtue. In many ways we're old-fashioned, with old-fashioned values. Some of us love our country more foolishly than others, I more foolishly than most. The system under which my country lives today is an insult to me as a human being, an alien imposition. You have to know what *we* mean by freedom to understand how far we would go to secure it and why I became involved in this conspiracy."

I nodded in the pause that followed, growing aware of what had apparently been happening for some time: a gradual cooling of the atmosphere in the room, a change in the air, as if the physical balance and chemistry of atoms had been carefully altered. An inarticulate warning began to form like a shadow in my mind.

"Freedom to us is individual freedom," Sempinski continued. "We think that the individual is the ultimate defense against tyranny. Individual freedom creates; everything else destroys. Everything that creates the dignity of the individual is freedom, but its particles are fragile . . . perishable. They can be made to disappear quicker than a dream. Even in your America, that fragile prop for our hopes, this freedom is gradually eroding. It is a gentle killing . . . you neither see nor feel this terrible erosion . . . in fact it can be made to seem pleasant and desirable. We are more fortunate than you. No one bothers to make our loss seem painless. We have neither dignity nor importance as individuals, but no one pretends seriously that we do. Time is against you because you still have freedoms you can lose. But it can't erode a particle of what we don't possess. And so we have a special kind of patience, like a kettle kept carefully on the boil. We nurse the fire and wait. Do you understand me?"

I said I did and watched the old man anxiously; his face had assumed a waxlike quality that made him seem depleted. He lay with eyes fixed rigidly on the shifting shadows as if they were assembling judges and he the accused.

"I also waited," he began again, his voice growing harsh. "What was I waiting for? A signal, a sign that the West had not forgotten us . . . that is what we wait for. There have been many signals through the years but never the right one . . . First the Hungarians, then the Czechs . . . And then, suddenly, I thought that the years of waiting were over. Foolish? Perhaps, in view of experience . . . But when you want something very badly, Doctor, when you have prayed for it and waited for it for a generation, you do not examine it as carefully as you might when it it finally handed to you . . . Can you understand?"

"I think so," I said. Then seeing the other's pain, I added quickly: "Of course, sir. Yes."

The sign, Sempinski said, had been more than he had ever hoped for: an American plan to overthrow Communism in Eastern Europe at one blow: the signal for a general uprising of all countries east of the Iron Curtain.

"But that's impossible," I said.

"To seize the Soviet leaders," Sempinski continued as though no longer believing he was saying anything. "And with this act to signal the beginning of the slaves' revolt . . . No longer just one country making its hopeless protest, but all our countries simultaneously in arms. The Soviets shocked and stunned . . . confusion and chaos . . . and in this chaos the whole might of the West coming to our rescue. Do you think this an idle dream? Nothing could be more practical and realistic . . . This is exactly what causes nightmares in the Kremlin. Think of the unrest in the Red Empire . . . the whole, vast structure shaking . . . the time had seemed perfect. It was easy to believe that the time had come. I had no reason to doubt that the people who brought me this signal were CIA agents."

"How could you?" I said despite myself.

Sempinski stared at me with something like pity. I felt foolish, like a bluffing schoolboy with his hand raised and no answers ready.

"I only mean that we've never done anything like that," I finished lamely. "That isn't our way . . ."

Sempinski nodded gravely.

"Forgive me," he said. "I've made this too abrupt. Certainly, every man believes his country innocent of spying, treachery, broken promises . . . That is the way your enemies go about survival . . . Your hands are always supposed to be clean; you are—how do you say it—St. George in silver armor . . . No, please don't interrupt; I am not mocking you. In fact I envy you this innocence. But only Americans see themselves with American eyes. In Europe, we don't listen to your clergy and your politicians, we do not read the reassurances in your daily press . . . We know that a man does not need absolute purity to stand for a just cause; we have all recognized rust on our own armors. And, in this corner of the world, we know better than most how well your country plays the game of practical politics. Believe me, I had no reason to doubt the source of the plot. And I allowed my patriotism to trap me into organizing violence that, even if it had been inspired by our friends, could only have brought disaster for everyone here. It was an honest act of patriotism, but a form of patriotism that does not belong in the twentieth century."

"But the conspiracy was not American-inspired?"

"No. My first contact was one of our people, a member of an underground organization which works for the West."

I said, feeling a sudden certainty: "Was his name Zimstern?"

"Yes. How did you know?"

"I was sent here to see him by a man called Karpovitch."

"Professor Karpovitch is the famous Magician. A brilliant man. I've known him since he was a child. A truly evil man. But that's a recent discovery of mine. When Zimstern came to see me I had no reason to doubt either him or his master."

"And you began to organize the conspiracy on their word, sir?"

"I received letters from prominent Americans. And, of course, British and American agents began to arrive."

"What agents?"

"It isn't easy to confess that I was a fool . . . My Western agents are our present jailers. But they had been well schooled, their credentials faultless, and those who came as Germans, not as Americans, were vouched for by the others as West German agents of the CIA."

A fit of coughing silenced the old man. When he resumed, his voice was practically inaudible. I leaned forward to hear him, sure that he must soon reach the end of his strength.

"Behind that portrait of the man in armor is a safe. It is open. There's no need for my keepers to lock it from me. The letters are in there for the proper aging and the required dust. That's where they're supposed to be found after the assassination. Get them and read them, Doctor."

I took out a thick package of letters, feeling the familiar opulence of good American bond. I thought that, surely, this white handful of expensive stationery should enjoy extraterritorial rights like embassies; it seemed incongruous in the black tomb of the little vault behind the portrait, with the dungeon coldness of the room laid on its glossy surface.

I took the letters to the window, where the light was better. My tired eyes and the pale conspiratorial moon combined to defeat me; the typescript blurred, words advanced and retreated on the textured pages, but I had no trouble deciphering the sprawling signature of Per Lindstrom.

The letters told the whole story: the conspirators' version. In one letter, Lindstrom wrote "for the President"—as his friend and unofficial agent. Even those typical cautious White House platitudes about freedom took on a sinister ring. In another letter Lindstrom underwrote the coup with half a million dollars. He implied that behind him stood all the American treasure and resources. In yet another letter he urged the execution of the Soviet leaders as the signal for revolt. He undertook to provide the assassin, and promised to advance fifty thousand dollars as the killer's fee. And there were copies of memoranda to and from directors of various United States and allied agencies and the supposed nerve-center of the conspiracy in London—each circumspect enough, as they should be, no single paper deadly in itself, but in sum-total an unanswerable indictment.

Even I, knowing what I did, and sure that these papers could only be forgeries, thought for one nauseating moment that they were authentic. I could imagine how this "proof" would sound and how it would look in the hysterical pages of the world's newspapers.

"The bastards," I said. "Oh, the miserable cunning bastards . . . They really think they can get away with this, don't they?"

"They do."

"The dirty little forgers," I said and threw down the papers, and Sempinski said: "They are not forgers. These are not forgeries."

And I said in a wobbling voice: "They couldn't be anything but forgeries!"

"Perhaps the memoranda. Lindstrom's letters to me are genuine enough."

"Nonsense! Of course they forged the letters! Without the letters they wouldn't have anything, would they? But with the letters, and with you, and with these other forgeries to be found with you after the murder . . . ! Well, they'd have everything, right? Do they have the money?"

"I don't know about the money," Sempinski said gently. "If they have it, it's something very recent. All I know is what they have told me. They have laughed about it. They've said that the money is coming by carrier pigeon."

"I am the carrier pigeon but I certainly didn't bring them any money. Oh, well, I suppose they could always say the money had been spent, although cold American cash, shown as the intercepted payment to the killer, or found on the killer, would really give them an airtight case. And, of course, they'd have the actual assassin."

"I understand they have one," Sempinski said.

"It's Brown, of course, a man who tried to kill me with an air pistol, the same kind of pistol that one of your Germans was carrying. I don't know why he tried to kill me unless he didn't know that I'm also supposed to play some role in this plot. Perhaps the plotters are keeping the two conspiracies apart: their own and Lindstrom's. And Brown is Lindstrom's man . . . But if Brown who is Lindstrom's man is also their assassin, then Lindstrom must also be in this thing . . . And if he is in it, then the forgeries . . . are not forgeries, are they?"

"No. They are not."

I said, cried or thought I did: "How could he do it?"

Sempinski said: "Perhaps he couldn't help it."

"Couldn't help it?"

"Perhaps he thought that he was using *them*. Later they could bring pressure he couldn't resist."

"What pressure? How? What kind of pressure could they bring?"

"They have Kristin here."

"Oh," I said, no longer doubting but still unwilling to believe. "That would do it, wouldn't it? Would that be enough?"

"I think so," the old man said. "If Senator Lindstrom is that kind of man."

"He is that kind of man. Oh, they don't miss much, do they!"

"They are professionals."

But wait a minute, I said, still pleading because there had to be some way out of this. "Wait a minute. This is too complicated, too involved for what they'll get out of it. They aren't going to get that much out of it! It's only a cold war gambit, isn't it? It's only propaganda. Why should they go to such infinite trouble for such trivial gain? That's what I don't understand about this whole business. And whom are they going to kill?"

Outside, the wind picked up and the ragged clouds fled before the storm and a vast chill came from the stone walls of the chamber, and this, and the unspoken fear of what was coming next, make me shake inside.

Sempinski said, quietly: "The intended victim is the Chairman of the Soviet Union. He is to be murdered as he speaks this week in the capital."

I was silent, overcome I suppose.

"My good friend, I wish these letters were a forgery. But they are not. They are what convinced me. But in the end it wouldn't have mattered who had written them. What matters is the authorship of the plot itself."

"Old Stalinists . . . new Nazis . . . it doesn't make sense."

"Why not? They were partners once before. Nothing is impossible in practical politics. They're both after the same thing, the continuation of East-West hostility. But there's more to this conspiracy than that."

"What more could there be?"

"This is China's attempt to destroy Soviet authority among the satellite countries and to win control over them. America is the target of the plot only as part of this Grand Design. She must be dishonored, her alliances shattered, her leadership rejected by the

Western world so that she can not interfere with Chinese ambitions. But the main purpose of this murder is to show the Eastern world that a *détente* with America and the West is impossible. Every Communist government will feel as mortally threatened as the Soviets themselves. At one stroke, the Chinese will sweep us all into their camp, and destroy you as a moral force in world politics. What more could they want for now?"

"But surely," I said, arguing as if I could force reason into madness, knowing that what I was attempting was hopeless but doing it anyway because, as long as I could resist belief, the truth seemed unproven. "Surely the Chinese involvement will become apparent? The Russians are no fools."

"The Chinese used fools like me, dupes like Lindstrom, Nazis, Stalinists masquerading as CIA agents, and a professional terrorist from London to organize it all. Every thread of the conspiracy leads to the West."

"But what about the Soviets? Surely they'll know who is attacking them."

"If they attempt to ignore or explain away this ultimate blow, no Communist will ever feel safe in their hands again. Besides, no one will want to listen to any explanations."

sixteen

THERE WAS little more that I and Sempinski could tell each other after the novelist's final explanation: the killer's target named and the conspiracy fleshed-out. Now that I knew who was to be murdered, there was even a kind of natural logic to everything that had happened to me, as though by identifying the eye of the hurricane I could see its whole dimension and follow its entire course. Even Lindstrom's involvement on behalf of China made a kind of nightmare sense that needed no particular explanation.

We studied architects' drawings and blueprints made during the reconstruction of Hetmanska Gora and looked at photographs and watercolor sketches of the park and the surrounding country—done in the lost days, Sempinski observed, by long-lost friends. I gave up wondering where the old novelist stored his reserves of strength.

"Once you have left the house," he said. "Cross into the woods here at this point, by the giant oak. You can not miss it even in the snow. It is magnificent . . . I wish you could have seen it in the autumn . . . Then follow the path to a grove of pine . . . there used to be a wooden summerhouse beyond it. Then leave the path. Go west. It will be difficult . . . snow, vegetation, fallen timber . . . Can you read the stars? Good. I hope the night is clear. The park is thickly overgrown at this point but it's the best part of the park for you. It is the closest part to the village. The wall is about a kilometer away. It's far but, again, it's the best wall for you. It's the oldest, in the worst repair. The ditch should be filled with rubble and easy to cross. Once you're across the wall, turn north. Walk across the fields. Don't stop no matter how tired you are; you would freeze in moments. In half an hour you will reach the village road."

I wanted to destroy the letters but Sempinski stopped me. I would need them at the embassy; without them, no one would even bother to believe my story. I put them back in the safe with misgivings.

"Take them when you come to say goodbye to me," Sempinski said quietly.

We took particular care to avoid the subject of Sempinski left alone to face the conspirators' vengeance. He was calm, seemingly untroubled. His face was marked with a kind of exaltation as if whatever lay in store for him had been preordained. I did not pity him; he would have disdained pity. Also, I sensed his need for expiation.

Then, because this was another matter that was very much with us, I asked Sempinski about Kristin Napoji. Abandoning the ill old man to the plotters' anger was unavoidable; leaving her behind would be inconceivable.

Sempinski was adamant about that.

"You can't seriously think about taking her with you? That is out of the question."

I said: "I'm not so sure."

"You have no right to jeopardize your chances. They are miserable enough as it is. Surely you can see that? Nothing can be allowed to burden you or distract you or load you down with additional responsibility. She'd tell you that herself."

"Perhaps she would. But I'm still responsible for her being here."

"So it's a matter of your conscience, is it? Is that more important than what you have to do?"

"I have to live with it."

"Be wary of it. A conscience is the hobble of the intellectual man. If she were my own daughter I wouldn't allow her to jeopardize your chances."

"Would she really do that?"

"You'd never reach the capital if she were along."

I didn't want to offend the old man or to have him disappointed in me. It seemed a good idea to distract him.

I asked: "What kind of girl is she?"

"I see her often. It amuses my keepers to let her visit me. We've talked a great deal. She is the kind of young woman that young men can dream of. But no matter how fine she may be you can't take her with you. A man can lose himself in crowds if he is lucky and if he knows how to go about it. But anyone who had ever seen her would remember her."

"I don't remember her too well," I said.

"Then leave it at that."

I left Sempinski's room soon afterward through the huge hearth and chimney, armed with plans and blueprints, and found my own chamber without any trouble. I marked my several secret roads through the labyrinth and moved my furs, pistol and briefcase to the bricked-up hideout. I thought that I would transfer my passport, papers and money to my pockets later, and abandon the briefcase but, for the moment, the briefcase was an adequate container. I burrowed with the stolid assurance of a mole, a resident of long standing, through the black tunnels that had meant such horror. They were still a foul, infested maze of web and glittering eye and softly undulating ceilings and hungry, pulsing walls. But once mapped and measured they were no longer menacing with the dark promise of the utterly unknown. I made work for myself despite my exhaustion: folding the furs, counting money. But I was conscious of fraud as I did it and, in the end, after I had run out of hairs to split, I had to get on with what I had been trying to put off. I studied the mapped maze where, at the end of yet another tunnel, there was a granite chamber similar to my own: the young woman's room, one floor below.

It would be up to me whether I took her along or not but I

didn't want to make any decisions just then. Everything that Sempinski had said about jeopardy was probably true; our trail would be marked as clearly as a highway for the pursuers to follow. And the girl, no matter how fine or brave would call for special care and compromise with hardships. But everything that I had thought about my responsibility for her predicament had also been true.

I half hoped that I wouldn't be able to find her room but Sempinski's drawings had been accurate. Her room, like mine, lay off a main shaft easy to find and follow. I hoped I'd find her fireplace bricked-up and thus have no need to make any decision. But the granite cave was open, clean and dry. She had an iron lantern splashing light off her bedside table. I could see the glow long before I got close to her room, crawling much slower than I had to and making more noise. I dropped into the fireplace and the light, rising slowly, aware of a particularly soft smell and a whispering sound to my right and above me, the motion of swiftly parting air, an object descending. And then my head blew up and the light withdrew into a pinpoint rainbow nucleus turning like a wheel with multicolored spokes.

Cold water revived me. I saw her face above me: whiter and thinner than I remembered or thought I remembered, not quite sure what there was to remember. My head was pounding like a copper kettle.

She had spread a cold wet facecloth on my forehead, and put a pillow under my neck, and all too soon I had no more excuse for lolling about in semiconsciousness. She helped me to sit up and to lean against the carved brackets of the hearth. I took my time about speaking, not sure I could do it. I looked about the room, focusing my eyes experimentally on the delicately fluted columns of her bed, the dark hangings, the maroon richness of an inlaid hardwood dais, iron-studded coffers, benches heaped with a barbaric profusion of cushions, and the blue and gold checkerboard of the painted ceiling. I had expected to see a barricade in front of her door: chairs, chests, tin basins and that sort of thing; it was the kind of thing I thought a woman would construct under the circumstances. But she had piled nothing against her door. Well, I thought, no wonder. My head felt as if the girl (now so quietly attentive, waiting so patiently for me to start talking, neither anxious nor afraid) had pulled the ceiling down on it; paint, molding, coffered squares and all.

"What did you hit me with?" I asked. I groped with cautious fingers around my aching head. I didn't care about her choice of bludgeon but an acknowledgment was due.

"A shoe."

"A football boot?"

"A sensible English shoe. Is your head all right?"

"I can't say."

"It looks all right. A little sooty, and there's a small spider walking on it, but it looks all right."

"I can feel the spider. He's wearing the boots."

She brushed the spider gently into the fireplace.

"He's really very small."

"Large feet, though," I said. "What size shoes do you wear, anyway?"

"Six and a half," she said smiling.

I looked at her then, feeling as if my face and head were covered with feathers.

She was fine drawn; her face seemed smaller than I remembered and terribly young: the richly textured, smooth face of a beautiful young woman that, I thought, should be worn in lockets. There was the start of a troubled line above her left eye; an astonishing brown eye like a brightly lit intelligent almond that was suddenly no longer brown but deep gold; a very large, thoughtful eye seated calmly over a delicately angled cheekbone, reaching out toward the dark frame of hair with a small starburst of humorous wrinkles. Small shadows under the cheeks, small but firm chin. Her hair was brown but, I thought, there had to be a better way to describe it because it was a great deal more than simply brown hair. She had worn it like a red-gold cap in New York but now it was combed out and brushed past her shoulders: two even wings of chestnut made bright by the yellow-red light of the lantern. I wondered why I should have thought of her as having been blond. I suppose that I had been too full of Sempinski during my lunch with her to get more than a general impression of summer-light hair, the deep gold tan that comes from tennis and the foredeck of a catamaran in the Sound, thoughtful eyes and an odd tranquillity. The lunch had been business and she an interviewing editor. I had thought her particularly well-read and interested, and her questions had been not only pertinent but intelligent and that, in itself, was such a revolutionary change for an editorial lunch that it would have crowded the other impressions aside.

Beautiful, yes; she was that, I could see. But there was no one feature or set of features that made her beautiful. Nothing intruded, nothing said: Here, this is beauty, this couldn't be improved upon, take note and pay attention and never mind the rest. Perhaps her hair and the delicately arched nose and finely turned nostrils could have made some such statement. They seemed independent enough to say anything, but I had the feeling they would say nothing of the kind.

Nothing was truly perfect anyway, anywhere. And beauty is a joint internal and external production. Her mouth might have been too broad, too generous, but I thought it splendid. Her face was possibly too small and young and unmarked; the laughing star-burst and the gentle lines so hard to credit on her forehead were more ornaments than blemish. I would not argue with a beauty expert about her, I supposed, but I would demand proof of expertise if there was an argument. As for the rest, she wasn't gaunt, bony, concave or cadaverous enough to model for high-fashion magazines. She had a fullness quite as generous as her mouth but it was not intrusive, so that, at first glance, I would have thought her more delicately constructed than she was.

In total of face, features, body, bearing, the lessons she had learned and those she had rejected, her manner and the sense of quiet awareness that she seemed to wear as naturally as her hair, I thought her extraordinary.

There was no longer any question in my mind that she would

come with me from Hetmanska Gora. All that mattered was to have her out of the madman's dream of plots and castles, back where nothing could do her any harm. It was as if I had come to that country for no other purpose.

And, in the meantime, I was in her room, and the bottle-bottom panes of mullioned windows had become dull and ill-defined, and there was a pale blue edge along the hem of the sky.

She asked, again, if I was all right.

I said that I was.

"I didn't know who or what you were," she explained. She gestured toward a serviceable, low-heeled walking shoe. Then she laughed. "You sounded like a bear in that chimney. I didn't know who you were until I washed your face. Does your head still hurt?"

"Yes," I said, feeling stuffed with sawdust. I coughed to clear my throat. "I suppose it does."

I watched her push the shoe out of sight behind her. She sat back on her heels and put her hands carefully in her lap and waited. And I was suddenly aware of the deep, unnerving V of her robe where it had become disarranged a little: a tawny, tailored garment of cashmere or camel hair or Shetland wool trimmed in small dark flowers, making her look both coolly competent and vulnerable: a young girl home for the holidays. (To be what after school? An actress? A writer? Something that required both dedication and illusions.)

Listen, I'm not a dull, witless clod, I wanted to say. Instead I said: "We haven't much time."

"Yes," she said.

I stared. "Yes what?"

"The time," she said. "I was just agreeing that it's getting light outside. You have to get back to your room before morning."

I nodded and at once my head threatened to roll off my shoulders. My eyes slid out of focus.

"Your head is really bad, isn't it."

She looked at me steadily and with particular care as if aware of a new and unexpected quality. Then she smiled, the eyes warmer, bigger. She said that sunrise was at six. The pale light outside meant that there was not more than an hour before breakfast. I should be starting back to my own room.

"You've had a bad bump. Probably a mild concussion. I'm sorry about that. I put my heart and soul behind that shoe. Next time I'll make sure I have the right victim. You obviously don't feel like talking very much and, besides, you must be asleep in your bed before they bring your breakfast. You mustn't let them suspect anything."

"Yes," I said. "Of course."

"Will you be able to sleep? I mean, really sleep. They are so terribly clever, you see . . . I'm just afraid they'd catch you if you were pretending."

"Are they that good?"

"Quite first rate. They've caught me every time I tried anything. You will try to sleep?"

"I'll try."

"They mustn't catch on to what you're going to do."

"We," I said. "We are going to do it. I'm taking you with me."

She didn't comment. Instead she said: "Do you know what this is all about?"

I told her about my visit to Sempinski.

"Oh, of course," she said. "That's how you knew where to find me. God, I am sorry about that damn shoe."

"It's all right," I said.

"The devil it is. You don't know how glad I was when I recognized you. A bit late, I admit. We waited for you as if you were some kind of a Messiah, and the first thing I do is bop you with a boot."

"Shoe," I said, dull.

She laughed then; a clear, open sound that was remarkably good to hear. It didn't bother my headache at all. The dull pounding roar in my head began to subside.

"You're too forgiving. But I'm glad. When can you come back so that we can talk?"

I said: "Let's talk now. There might not be another opportunity."

She looked doubtful but agreed that we could try to talk now if we kept one eye on the graying windows and one on a watch. She had a lot to tell me. Was there anything about the plot that I didn't know?

"Two things," I said. "The Zero Hour for the assassination and the money. Did they ever get that half million dollars?"

She said that she didn't know but didn't think so. She and Sempinski had wondered about that. None of the guards had boasted about it, which they would have done if this last necessary piece of evidence had been acquired on schedule. As for the date of the assassination, that would depend on when the Soviet Chairman was to speak.

"Has he already arrived in this country?" she wanted to know.

"I think he was expected this week. I wish I knew how much time we have."

"How much do we need?"

"Three or four days to reach the capital. That much again for the embassy to check our story, contact Washington and get their instructions. Or perhaps Washington will take over the job from then on. Then a few hours to get the security people in this country going. I've no idea what the embassy is going to do to get the officials in the capital to believe them. Frankly I don't care. I just want to get all this into competent American hands and forget about it. Ten days wouldn't be too much for everything that has to be done."

"I am sure there is at least that much time. Do you know anything about the American assassin they are supposed to have?"

"Yes," I said, suddenly uncomfortable. I told her about Brown and the episode in Zimstern's store, then about the wolves and the air pistol.

"I don't think there can be any doubt that that's our man." Then, because her pallor was extraordinary and her eyes bleak: "Do you know him? He works for your uncle?"

She nodded.

"I'm sorry," I said. "I wish your uncle wasn't mixed up in this.

Perhaps there's still some explanation for his part in it. The letter could still be a forgery."

She shook her head. She said she knew her uncle's signature too well; and she knew her uncle. He could have written such letters, knowing what they meant.

"Because you are a hostage?"

"Yes. But the first letters were written long before I came here. You see, Uncle Per wants a war with Russia. To his way of thinking it would be a sort of Holy War . . . provided America got the chance to strike first. He could have been blackmailed into writing some of the later letters and reports. But his offer of money was made almost a year ago."

"I see."

"Do you really? I wonder. You probably think him either mad or evil."

I didn't want to cause her any pain. I said: "Perhaps he is less evil than misguided."

"He's not misguided. To be misguided a man must be led. Uncle Per has never followed anyone; he would always do anything to have his own way. And since he thinks that his way is the only right way you can't call him evil. He is a dedicated man. Terribly wrong but not evil."

I nodded to change the subject and watched her warm, impassioned face, the intense eyes, and shoulders straight and rigid under the soft robe. I saw the fragmentary tremor on her lips. I thought that I would give a lot to see her come to my defense as readily as she had come to that of Per Lindstrom.

But time was passing all too rapidly and there were still arrangements to be made for the escape. I told her quickly when we would escape, and how. And she said quietly: "You know that you don't have to take me with you, don't you?"

"That's what Sempinski tried to tell me."

"He's right, you know. You don't owe me anything. The plotters would have got me into their hands one way or another. They know Uncle Per's weaknesses and I am one of them. They would hardly have missed the best possible pawn for their blackmail games. That's why you shouldn't blame yourself for sending me here. And besides, I planned an escape of my own. Now that I know a way out of the house I have a chance to try it. Don't worry, I'll do very well."

I laughed then, feeling better than I had felt all night. Her face flushed quickly, her eyes alight and wide to meet this challenge that I had not meant as a challenge at all. Her breast rose, the shoulders lifted, the round chin came up. She stabbed the cold, dank air with small fists.

"You don't believe I've thought about escaping?" she demanded. "Who do you think would have had to do this job if you hadn't come? I really don't need any help from you."

I said: "Maybe I need your help."

She was immediately silent. Then her shoulders bowed and her hands moved once more into her lap and folded there. Her angry flush receded. I watched her thinking how beautiful she was in or out of anger. I wished that I could make my voice less hard and impersonal but everything I said sounded abrupt and cold.

"I'll come for you early. Perhaps in the meantime we can find out about the money and the timing. We'll start a little after nine tonight. We'll go down into that bricked-up fireplace and wait until the guards have cleared off. Then we'll try the greenhouse and the park."

I laughed then because there was a question that I had to ask and it made everything seem ridiculous: the night, myself, my plans and even the girl.

"Any questions?"

"No," she said. "No questions. Except one: Are you sure that you want me along? If you have any doubts about it, I'd rather not go."

"No doubts," I said aware of several. "The problem will be to get to the village and to hire a sleigh. From then on . . . well, it will be up to luck and to whatever gods look after fugitives."

"I'll have to make a special sacrifice," she said, then laughed.

"Sacrifice?"

"This is an old house and there are all sorts of very ancient gods to get on our side. I'm an expert on them, thanks to Professor Sempinski."

"I hope they're not reconstructed gods."

But she was no longer laughing. I supposed that she might have been thinking about the old man who would not go with us. I listened to the silence of the house.

The corners of the room had become light blue and the lantern dimmed. There was a particular coldness in the room, the chill of the morning. Outside, black clouds fled before the wind. I thought that there might be heavy snowfall later in the day. I heard the sound of my own breathing and the low humming of the wind high up in the chimney.

"Well, I'll go now," I said.

She nodded, quiet.

"And about tonight . . . Don't pack anything. Wear everything warm that you have. And listen" (I went on, leaning forward, suddenly anxious to see her smile or to hear her laugh, and troubled about it): "Do your best with the *Lares* and *Penates,* will you? I have a feeling we'll need everything they've got."

Back in my room I washed myself from head to foot in the cold water basin that, along with an enameled white jug, a towel and a chamberpot (a porcelain cauldron bordered with hand-painted forget-me-nots) was my medieval bathroom. Scrubbed clean, the black water carefully poured into the deep cracks between flagstones, dressed in fresh pajamas (the grimy debris of my clothes stuffed high onto the first ledge of the chimney) I lay in bed under the reassuring canopy and watched the gray day stalk across the tree-tops.

I waited for sleep, sure that it wouldn't come. My hunger returned and with it an extraordinary thirst. But I didn't waste time thinking about discomforts. I reviewed the night, not quite able to believe anything about it. I was, at best, a mildly interested observer watching myself go through the mental motions that would have puzzled me if I had understood them.

seventeen

GUARDS WOKE ME with breakfast: one slice of black-brown bread crusted with yellow flour, a peeled cucumber, coffee stiff with sugar. I was instantly awake.

Outside my window, the clouds were thick and black, an oily mass twisting bitterly overhead. Under them, the day was crisp and clean. I could see a long way toward the purpling towers of the southern range.

The house stood on a mound. The park fell steeply away from under my window into an ironed flatness. Tree crowns were globular with packed snow and ice. Beyond them was the plain. The land was still, and desolate and dreaming.

I drank my coffee while I shaved and dressed, taking my time. I took my time about everything that morning. The snow began to fall; soon I could see nothing through the window in the new, gray light.

I didn't think about the coming night. I supposed that I hadn't had enough sleep: no more than an hour. My head felt heavy but there seemed to be surprisingly little in it beyond a gray dullness. I didn't think that I would be able to come up with anything new to do with the escape; it seemed less real with each passing minute.

The sour black bread tasted like damp putty. I was about to

start on the cucumber when locks ground and grated behind me, the door opened and struck against granite, and there was the harsh clatter of heavy boots more or less in step. The doorway filled with men: my escort of last afternoon, my inefficient guardian —looking well-rested after a good night's sleep, and a dozen others. I noticed that my guide of last night, the insolent young man who had so annoyed me, wasn't there. The men wore the holiday faces of Roman circus-goers. Behind them was Karpovitch.

He wore a faultless suit of English country tweeds and a pale mustache. His hair had been cut short; it was no longer non-descript as it had been in London. He looked younger, fresher and infinitely dangerous.

"Good morning," he said. He sat on my bed and lit a cigarette. "Don't let me interrupt your breakfast."

He waved a careless but imperious hand toward the others. My former escort snapped to attention behind me. The others began searching the room. They wasted no motion. My suitcase was emptied on a sheet, the clothes and toiletries were fingered and probed. I thanked whatever providence looks after secret agents for my foresight that had allowed me to save and hide my briefcase and its contents in the bricked-up fireplace downstairs; escape would have become impossible without my passport, papers and the little money that I had. The searchers worked in disciplined silence that was broken only by the soft tapping of Karpovitch's elegantly shod foot on the granite floor.

"Continue with your breakfast," Karpovitch said easily. "I'm sorry we can't compete with gourmet fare, but it's good, nourishing food. Peasants thrive on it in this country."

I said: "It's hardly first-class service."

Karpovitch laughed.

"But that's the way of the world, isn't it? The world is a cucumber, like the one you're eating. Just as you think you have it in your hand, you find it has been rudely pushed up another portion of your anatomy. But, I must say, you don't seem surprised to see me?"

"Surprised? Yes, I'm surprised."

Karpovitch studied me with quiet curiosity and I felt my heart beating up a little. I knew that this was the principal adversary, the enemy-in-chief; I found myself shaken despite my best efforts.

I tried to look into the cynical cold eyes, and the sharp fox-mask, without showing fear. Everything about Karpovitch made me think of foxes: the angular thin face with protruding cheekbones, the thin mouth and the yellow mustache streaked with white and stained with nicotine, the narrow forehead receding under the tight cap of close-cropped pale hair, and the sleek impression of a winter pelt in his russet clothes. But if this was a fox, it would have to be a particularly cynical and cruel animal, with a touch of the wolf.

The trick was not to panic. I thought that Karpovitch would expect me to act both surprised and angry but I had little faith in my histrionic abilities. I had no wish to underestimate him; more than anything, I needed time to arrange my tactics. I stared at Karpovitch with worried indignation.

"Yes, I'm surprised," I said again. "Although nothing should surprise me about this damn place."

"You don't care for it? I find it picturesque."

"This is a madhouse. I don't know what's going on here but someone had better be ready to explain my locked door and these incredible housemen. What are you doing here, anyway? What's your connection with this?"

"One question at a time, Dr. Shippe. Let's just say that I am here to taste a moment of triumph."

"You're mad," I said. I hoped my anger sounded and looked convincing. "I don't know what you're talking about but you're stark raving mad."

"You've made your point, Shippe. Now do be quiet. This is necessary. A faithful servant expects his little moment of strutting and crowing. I find it quite amusing not to disappoint my critical employer: he must be made to realize in full the importance of my contribution. Also, I expect an interesting reaction from you. But go on with your cucumber. I'm sorry we could not get you an egg for your breakfast but there is a temporary shortage of dairy products."

"A necessary sacrifice, I'm sure."

The wooden platter was too far away to reach with the cucumber, and I didn't think that I would be able to walk the necessary three or four feet without betraying how frightened I was. I started eating the watery vegetable; it tasted clean and cool.

"Good of you to take this attitude," Karpovitch said coldly. "I agree that the servants here are incredible. But they are only temporarily in domestic service. The older men, in fact, are really high-ranking officers of certain government departments in East Germany and here. Once a colonel, always a colonel, you know—whether the fellow is driving a taxi or polishing silver. You must have met several types like that in London."

When I said nothing, Karpovitch nodded to himself, smiling a little.

"You never met the good General Danilow, did you? No, he was already an *emigrant* when you came to London. Gone to Canada, as they say. His own fault, you know. He had stumbled on a clue to my identity during his visit to the capital last year; our friend Zimstern slipped up. I think you might have liked Danilow. Whom else did you meet? Let's see, there was Potter, an unimportant cog. There was Brown. You'll have an opportunity to meet him again. That really answers most of your questions. As for your locked door, that's easy to explain. You are a very special guest."

"You mean I am a prisoner."

My voice, I noted, was quavering a little, which was the correct sound for the impression I was trying to convey. Something was going to happen and I realized that I was too tired to cope with it; I felt as if my mind was falling off a hillside.

"Well, yes, if you insist on a specific definition. A little patience, and you'll know everything that might interest you."

One of the searchers said something then in a voice that promised nothing good, in a language that I didn't understand. Karpovitch listened carefully. His knowing eyes were amused and curious but also watchful now, as if he had sensed a distant possibility of danger. His thin lips formed a speculative circle.

"Where are your papers?"

"In my briefcase," I blurted out, trying to play for time.

"And where is your briefcase?" Karpovitch asked softly.

"Downstairs," I said. My stomach turned slowly over and over. I tasted the muddy coffee and the sour black bread. It had been sheer afterthought that had prompted me to take the briefcase to the bricked-up hideout.

"Where downstairs?"

"I don't know," I lied. "The man who brought me here took it away with him. Something to do with reporting my arrival to the authorities. At least that's what he said. I don't know anything about it."

"I think you're lying."

"Why should I be lying?"

"There's something wrong here," Karpovitch said slowly. "No one reported taking your briefcase from you. I don't like coming up on unreported facts . . . they have a way of proving quite significant. I think we had best send for the man who brought you to this room."

He said something quickly to his men. One of them answered with a prolonged shaking of his head and a gesture indicating both his watch and the white distances stretching outside the windows. Karpovitch became very still. He barked an order and my former escort left the room at once.

"The man who brought you here has already left for the capital," Karpovitch said quietly. "Another surprise? But you couldn't have known that he wouldn't be here. Are you bluffing, Shippe? I truly hope I haven't underestimated you. That could prove dangerous to us both. You are, quite frankly, not what I expected."

I felt a tremor start along my upper thighs. I couldn't control it. I was terribly afraid that I had given myself away. I tried to calm myself, counting numbers and keeping my breath shallow.

I was afraid of Karpovitch's brain more than of any possible violence or pain. It was a brain that had survived decades of international plotting and maneuvering; I was no match for a man like that. Be calm, I told myself. Make your mind blank. Communicate nothing. Karpovitch will sense it.

Two more men left the room on Karpovitch's order. He had lit a fresh cigarette and I suddenly realized that he was under extraordinary tension. His calmness was a fraud. I couldn't help admiring his iron self-control even though I didn't understand the reasons for his tension. I was aware of my own heightened perceptions and my growing calmness as I weighed and evaluated Karpovitch's inner turmoil.

"Something about you puzzles me," Karpovitch said. "You're not as stupid as you should have been. There is a feeling of, what shall I call it, awareness? about you . . . a cold emanation . . . I wonder just how much you've guessed and what you're up to. I have a feeling that you're trying to fool me. You had better not try. I'll have you flayed alive if I should think that you represent the slightest danger to me. Make no mistake about that. You are among men who kill people as easily as you might kill a fly. I am beginning to regret that I had you brought here."

He got up and began to walk about the room. He looked at his watch and ordered two more men to go downstairs and to join in the search for my briefcase. I couldn't understand his interest in my luggage.

"It's all gone so well," Karpovitch said more to himself than to me and his remaining two men. "Everything is ready. The Chairman landed in the capital this morning. He'll speak in three days. The press of the entire world will be there to hear him and see him. I've worked too hard to have anything go wrong now; there's too much at stake. And something has already slipped a little. The CIA has come into the picture. How? What could have happened?"

He turned suddenly toward me.

"I have an idea that you know something about that. I had

Brown hidden at Zimstern's store, exactly where he should have been hiding if he had been a Western assassin. But something went wrong, he had to run for it. He left two dead men behind him and one of them was a CIA agent. What was he doing there?"

I said: "I don't know what you are talking about."

"Oh, you don't, eh? Well, I'll tell you, since we have a little time. In three days we are going to kill a man in the capital. We've gone to great lengths to make sure that this murder is blamed on your CIA. Brown was to be the weapon found at the scene of the crime, along with his host Zimstern, a known Western agent. Why did Brown suddenly kill Zimstern and a CIA agent who had no business knowing about Zimstern? The puzzle is beginning to assume dangerous proportions."

I said: "As I remember, you are fond of puzzles."

"You didn't have anything to do with Zimstern's murder, did you? You wouldn't be, by any chance, an agent yourself? But no, that's impossible. If you had been an agent, suspecting anything, you wouldn't have walked into this trap. And you wouldn't have sent me Lindstrom's girl. I'm grateful for that. I had that megalomaniac well in line but she made all the difference. With her in my hands I could give the orders . . . You should have seen Lindstrom's face when he finally knew who was the tool and who was the master. How quickly he collapsed . . . We could move rapidly after that. There was no question, then, of getting all the necessary papers and, of course, the money. And that is something else for which I must thank you."

"Money? What money? What in hell are you talking about?"

"Whether you know it or not, you've brought me half a million dollars. It's in your briefcase, in large denomination notes easily traceable to Lindstrom. It's the last evidence that I needed to hang your precious United States."

"What do you have against the United States, Karpovitch?"

"Absolutely nothing. I don't like Americans but that is merely a matter of taste. Hardly anyone likes Americans except the Americans themselves and that, of course, is useful to my plans.

But, unlike everybody else in my conspiracy, I have no ideological involvement. Nevertheless there'll be a certain satisfaction in knowing that I shall be instrumental in the overthrow of one of the greatest powers on earth."

"If you're so confident about that, why are you so nervous?"

"I don't know why I am uneasy. It must be the strain of this climactic moment. We'll find your briefcase and we'll find Brown in time to leave him dead, shot by security men, with the murder weapon in his hands and American money stuffed in all his pockets. And we have unanswerable documentary proof that Brown was sent and paid by Lindstrom to murder the Chairman and that Lindstrom was acting for the American government."

"You'll never get away with this. This proof can be repudiated."

"Who'll repudiate it? Lindstrom is committing suicide day after tomorrow, on the eve of the assassination. The horror of America's crime will have proved too much even for that fanatic. Do you think that I am such a fool, such an amateur, as to leave a single thread unraveled?"

"Somebody will stop you."

"Shut up. You bore me. If I didn't need you here as Lindstrom's courier and Brown's paymaster I'd have you killed right now. So don't, as your people say, push your luck, Shippe."

"But I didn't come here as Lindstrom's messenger. I've had no contact with him, have you forgotten that? Pohl sent me here to inspect the Pontic Tribunals. Or is he also working for you?"

"Peripherally, yes. He is quite adequately linked with Lindstrom, Brown and Zimstern as far as your being sent here is concerned. He doesn't even know that I exist. All he knows is that Lindstrom ordered him to give you a certain briefcase and to see to it that you took it with you. Besides, is your Mr. Pohl likely to kick up a fuss once he knows what kind of conspiracy he has been involved in?"

"You didn't miss a thing, did you?" I said. Karpovitch started laughing.

"You look so damn forlorn, like a child who finds out that Father Christmas is a fake, like Lindstrom looked when he saw himself as a witless tool . . . Of course I didn't miss a thing. And in your briefcase is the most spectacular proof of my efficiency. I want to present this proof to my employers and earn my place of power in the sun."

Karpovitch no longer paid any attention to me. He walked up and down the chamber, occasionally stopping to look at his watch. I supposed that nothing was important to him at that moment except the contents of my briefcase. But what contents? Where could they be hidden? I was sure that I had not brought a fortune in dollars in my briefcase.

I heard footsteps in the corridor, the quiet drone of voices. Karpovitch became still.

A dozen men came in, followed by the heavy, commanding individual whom I had observed in the library. I was aware of an air of menace, an almost tangible emanation of antagonism rigidly repressed.

The new arrival sat down in my only chair. He took a short black cigarette from a silver case and worked it carefully into his ivory holder. One of his men hurried forward at once with a burning lighter.

The man said: "Proceed."

Karpovitch said carefully: "Shouldn't we wait for the Chinese delegate, General? For the rest of the staff?"

"They aren't coming."

"I had hoped . . ."

"I know what you had hoped."

"It would be simple to take the briefcase to the conference rooms," Karpovitch said, his words unnaturally precise. "I am sure that the whole staff would be pleased to see what we have, General."

The heavy man's yellow and strangely flat eyes centered on Karpovitch. He blew a careful smoke ring and watched it drift, dissolving, across the agent's face.

He said, as if unaware that he was speaking: "What you are sure of and what you are unsure of can be of interest only to yourself. I caution you against putting undue strain on my patience.

You've done competent work, you are in fair standing. What is it that you want? Praise and salutes?"

The general raised his cigarette and holder slightly in the air, and inclined his huge head a fraction of an inch.

"Consider yourself saluted. Now proceed. I have come here despite an understandably busy schedule as a token of my appreciation for your work. I have no time to waste."

A nerve had begun to work spasmodically in Karpovitch's cheek.

He said: "We have to wait a moment, General."

"Wait?"

"We must find the briefcase. In this briefcase lies the last strand of the conspiracy . . . the absolute proof of American complicity . . . the money used to pay the assassin and back the revolt . . . in notes of $10,000 traceable to the emissary of the American government."

"We are quite aware of the importance of the money," the general said. "Please don't waste my time."

"Yes," Karpovitch said with deceptive mildness. He would not look at any of the others who now began to stare at him.

"Without this money," he said. "Without the documents . . . But yes, I know the general has no time to waste. I will not waste his time. The money, then. We shall shortly have it. I have sent men to get it."

"Where is it?"

"Downstairs, sir. It had been left downstairs. A man will shortly bring it."

"I will wait one minute," the general said.

"The briefcase will be here in a moment. It is a special case with a compartment built into the lid. Absolutely foolproof . . . a part of the case itself. There are no secret locks, no such amateur devices. The case was built for this specific mission. It is clearly labeled with this man's name and address. When it is ripped open before the correspondents . . ."

My former escort came into the room, his lips fixed in an idiotic smile.

"Herr Professor . . ."

"The briefcase," Karpovitch said sharply. "Well? Do you have it?"

"No sir. We've looked everywhere."

"Everywhere?" Karpovitch's voice was heavy with elaborate patience. "Obviously you haven't looked everywhere, idiot. Go back and find it at once."

The German said: "Maybe it's here somewhere."

"It isn't here! Go back downstairs and get it!"

"Where shall we look, professor?"

"What do you mean, fool? Look everywhere that you've already looked and everywhere you haven't!"

Karpovitch's voice and manner had lost some of their calmness.

The general leaned forward. One set of fingers whitened on a knee. The other grasped the carved lion's paw that ornamented the arm of his chair.

Karpovitch seemed to bend as if a heavy weight had settled on his shoulders. His silent lips moved with terrifying slowness. They had lost their color.

The general said icily: "You have lost the briefcase?"

Karpovitch said nothing.

"Five hundred thousand dollars is a substantial sum," the general said as though bemused. "Enough to tempt most men into treason. I am prepared to hear any reasonable explanation. You have one, of course?"

Karpovitch slowly shook his head.

"This wouldn't be another of your magic games, would it, Magician? I don't believe that even you would dare to jest with me."

"I am not joking, sir," Karpovitch said quietly.

"I see," the general said. His voice was soft and distant. "Then I assume that you have failed to procure the money. That is the most charitable assumption I am able to make. Is that what happened? You've failed? You blundered?"

Karpovitch said nothing. He stared with the mild expression of a disillusioned child over the general's head, past me and the others, at the soft mounds of snow transfiguring the windows.

"You were a famous man, Karpovitch," the general said slowly. "You were a legend that even I had been tempted to believe. That is why I recommended you to Pekin. And now you put me in a difficult position. I have never been known to fail at anything. I'm sure that you're familiar with my record. I can not, therefore, admit that I have failed. The only explanation I can offer to our Chinese allies is sabotage and treason. I hope I've made myself clear?"

"I've not betrayed you," Karpovitch said quietly.

The general gave a dry, unpleasant laugh.

"Astonishing how alike all you intellectuals are. How ready to swear undying loyalty as soon as a sword hangs over your heads. Your oath is hardly worth five hundred thousand dollars. Your head, at this moment, is worth about five cents."

"Then give me five cents' worth of opportunity to repair the damage."

"You mean you have an explanation after all? Perhaps you will produce a magic briefcase for me?"

"The briefcase was brought into this house, General. It can't have flown away."

"Reassuring. I think that you are merely playing for time, Karpovitch. But I will give you five cents' worth of mercy. If by tomorrow morning you can produce the money, you will keep your head. That's a fair exchange. As you know, I am leaving for the capital as soon as we conclude this ridiculous performance. I shall be in my office at seven in the morning. If you are there at seven-thirty with five hundred thousand American dollars, you will be alive at seven-thirty-five."

"That's only slightly more than twenty hours . . ."

"Damn you!" the general shouted. "Do you think you can bargain with *me*?"

He was out of his chair and on his feet with speed I would never have believed possible for such a heavy man, and gone from the room as if a hurricane had swept him through the door. His men backed out behind him.

Karpovitch uttered one sharp, violent exclamation. I tried to keep absolutely still so as to draw no attention to myself. Despite my fear and awareness of terrible danger I looked at him with a fascination that bordered on pity.

As far as the top echelons of the conspiracy were concerned, Karpovitch was finished. He had less than a day to find the missing money and he wouldn't even suspect where to look for it. And that meant that when I fled the castle with Kristin and Sempinski's letters, I would have the money. The plotters would lack their evidence. Even the spent old man up the corridor wouldn't be useful to them.

This wouldn't mean the end of the plot, I knew well enough. But it might slow it up a bit; it might gain time for Washington and local officials to move against the plotters. If nothing else, I would be able to upset the schedule.

My God, I thought, silly with relief. It might work, after all. They're not infallible. They can be defeated. I might just manage to get the job done.

eighteen

THE REST OF THE day passed in a blur of conflicting thought. I swung from wildest optimism—seeing myself and Kristin safe in the embassy, the Lindstrom papers and the money turned over, the plot exposed and the conspirators scattering for cover—to the deepest doubt. Karpovitch wasn't a man to give up that easily. And he was not a man ever to take for granted.

I couldn't help feeling a grudging admiration for the Master Spy. The Nazis and their middle-aged compatriots had fallen into bewildered pieces with their hopes demolished but Karpovitch had stood his ground before the menace of the general.

I wondered who the general was and where he fitted into the framework of the plot. I was sure that he was one of the highest leaders, in power in the capital where he had an office. The embassy would have to be told about his complicity. I hoped that I would never come across him again or have to face him.

I tried to put myself into Karpovitch's place to guess how he would go about recovering the money. The only reason he had not guessed my part in the disappearance of the briefcase was that no one knew that I had found a way out of my locked and guarded room. It wouldn't take him long to get on the right track; all he had to do was contact the man who, I had said, had taken the briefcase. I had no doubt about what would happen then: Karpovitch would find a way to persuade me to tell him where his money was.

I waited for the day to pass counting interminable hours. I expected Karpovitch to return at any moment. I couldn't keep my eyes away from the door; each second was an eternity of dread and waiting. I grew progressively more nervous about the escape; it was all right to think about as something that I would have to do in the unspecified future, but each of the terrible slow minutes brought that future closer. I was sure that I had forgotten something vitally important.

Guards brought me my midday meal: boiled meat and a boiled potato. I hadn't seen these men before, they didn't look German. I had heard several cars driving away from the house in the morning; there was an impression of great activity going on around me but the thick walls insulated me from anything that might have told me what was going on. I supposed that with the Chairman of the Soviet Union already in the capital, the conspirators were moving their forces into position for the coup. Loss of Lindstrom's money wouldn't change the plan. In my brief and now forgotten moment of relief, I had thought that they might hesitate or falter with the money gone, but there was no reason why they should. The money was Karpovitch's problem. Everything else must have been proceeding according to plan. And that would still call for the assassination to take place in three days—an impossibly short time for everything that I had to do. But there was one bright spot on the otherwise dismal and threatening horizon: Karpovitch had said something about the CIA. The fat bald man whom I had thought to be a Nakomda man had been, apparently, an American agent. But why had he been following me around the capital? And how had he been so miraculously at hand in Zimstern's store? There was no use even thinking about that, far less seeking answers. But if the CIA already had some inkling of the plot it would make my job at the embassy infinitely easier. All I had to do was to get there with Kristin, the letters and the money.

Night came eventually. I forced myself to eat my evening meal —thin soup, another boiled potato and another slice of the sour black bread. Outside, the clouds had covered up the sky. Desultory snow fell past my windows; there were no stars, no moon. I heard the mastiffs baying in the park. I sat still for a long time after eating. I did not think that I would be able to move.

The time had come. Now there was no more future to consider as far as the escape was concerned.

I supposed that if there had been some way to back out, I would have welcomed it. But Sempinski was expecting me in his room. Kristin was waiting for me. The thought of Karpovitch's vengeance on her was unendurable. Outside, the mastiffs and the guards were probably also waiting; but there was nothing I could do about them.

Nine o'clock came all too soon—the time I had assigned to myself for the start of the escape. I stared with painful concentration at my watch, counting off the seconds as if it mattered whether I began to move before this arbitrary deadline. But it seemed suddenly important to make the escape precise and defined as if some guarantee of security could be found in time tables. The sweep of the second hand wiped thought from my mind. It implied order and routine and normalcy in a situation where nothing was normal. It was the only lifeline that connected me with reality.

My heart beat heavily and my mouth was dry.

Very well. I had gone over every step so often in my mind that it became as automatic as the marching seconds. Cold. Must be ice cold about this, can't have any nonsense. No thinking or planning now more than a second or two ahead. I got up. I went to the door and listened at the keyhole. No sound of any kind. I nodded profoundly as if this silence were some kind of revelation. I pushed the heavy iron-studded coffer against the door and jammed it securely in the doorway. The armchair came next, on top of the coffer, the cruel lion's paw pushed under the door handle. I reinforced the barricade with the nightstand; it gradually acquired a comforting solidity that would defy the efforts of several men, more than the pair who would bring my breakfast. That would mean fifteen, possibly twenty extra minutes before the alarm. I had no reason to despise any extra minutes. My tactics were clear. I put on all my clothes: three shirts, a sweater and my suit. No shoes. They would be useless in the snow outside. I would replace them with the felt-lined winter boots in the guards' ready-room downstairs. Now there was nothing to keep me from leaving. I couldn't think of anything that I hadn't done that might delay discovery and pursuit. I looked at my watch. It had taken me seven minutes to build my barricade and to dress. The time was nine-oh-seven. It would take me eleven minutes to reach Sempinski's room. Allow five minutes there to collect the letters and to say goodbye. Formal and cold, of course. No emotional claptrap. Nerves were uncertain at the best of times and this was, certainly, not one of those times. Iron control of nerves, time, all the faculties was mandatory. Mandatory. I savored the word. It had a comforting and reassuring sound. So, five minutes for the old man. The trip to Kristin's room would take eighteen minutes. Eleven from the old man's room back to the level of my own, then seven more to drop down to hers. She would be ready for me, all ready to go. No need to waste time there. In forty minutes more we would be in the cave downstairs behind the guards' bricked-up fireplace. That made it seventy-four minutes. The time was now nine-oh-eight. We would be in the cave at 10:22. We wouldn't have to wait there more than half an hour if the guards closed up shop at eleven as they had last night. Germans are creatures of remorseless habit; no reason to suppose that their bedtime would be different this night. I thought it likely that Kristin and I would be out of the house by 11:15.

And suddenly the room, the cold granite chamber with its gray patina of age, violence and danger looked so warm and welcoming that my knees buckled under me with longing for safety. The fireplace and, by association, everything beyond it looked more than ever like the yawning mouth of a cavernous tomb.

I leaned against the cold marble and granite. I tried not to think. Then I began to climb.

I moved through the chimney shafts, following the knotted white nylon cord, with an impatience bred by familiarity. Rats, spiders, matted cobwebs no longer perturbed me. I smashed slow-moving spiders and hissed at the rats. Everything that could do it, ran away from me.

I wasted no time in Sempinski's room. I dropped into the old writer's fireplace with the agility of a paratrooper. I nodded to him, making for the safe.

"Everything all right?"

I meant the contents of the safe and the old man knew it.

"Yes," he said. "The papers are there."

I went quickly through the letters and other documents, wrapped them in a handkerchief and stuffed the bundle between my second and third shirt, away from my body. My fingers were like nervous sausages fumbling with the buttons.

I said: "I'm ready. And listen, professor: I've got the money. We have everything. After I'm gone the plotters won't have anything."

The old man looked up, questioning, then smiled, delighted. He nodded, asking nothing. He looked at me with a quick and quiet admiration that made me suddenly ashamed. Only I knew what a fraud and what a coward I was.

I said: "Goodbye, professor."

"Goodbye, Dr. Shippe. Good luck. Or as the Germans say: *Hals und Beinbruch.*"

"Actors say that in the United States."

"Well, there's a point in common."

The old man turned his face carefully away as if to study the violent shadows moving in the windows. The room was darker and more threatening than it had been the night before; the shadows were deeper. I thought I could detect a certain hopelessness in the novelist's collapsed body and turned-away face.

I got back into the fireplace and made my way rapidly back to my own roomlevel and then down to Kristin.

She was ready as I had thought she would be but I was too nervous to notice immediately how pale she had become. She was dressed perfectly for what she had to do: ski pants, wool socks, several bulky sweaters and heavy skiing boots. Her hair was stuffed into a knitted helmet that fell in folds like a medieval shirt of mail over her neck and shoulders. It left only a fraction of her face exposed.

"All right?" she asked, smiling.

"You mean your uniform? Couldn't be better. I wish I had thought to get outfitted for skiing before I came here."

"I came here on a holiday," she reminded me. I noticed that she packed a small bundle that looked like towels wrapped in a pillowcase.

"What's that?"

"My battledress," she said still smiling. I noticed her pallor then. Her hands seemed more nervous than they had been the night before. But her eyes were bright.

I said abruptly: "I told you not to pack anything."

She looked at me steadily, then shrugged. She undid the bundle and showed me flimsy underwear, stockings, fashionable shoes, a purse and cosmetics. There was a dress as well, something bright, full of greens and yellows. The sight of this pretty trivia angered me out of all proportion. I knew that I was too nervous to keep anything in perspective but this reminder of her femininity seemed suddenly too much.

Women. I knew that I didn't know anything about them but, at this point, with what lay ahead, what I knew seemed enough. Perhaps taking Kristin with me was an invitation to failure and disaster; I had been a fool to hope that it could have been anything else. The trouble was, of course, that I hadn't thought; I had refused to think after having seen her. Oh well, damn it, it was too late now to do anything about it. That's how it always is, I thought: you see a beautiful young woman, Dr. Shippe, and you send your brain on a permanent vacation.

I barricaded her door as I had my own. That, anyway, could be done according to plan. The similar barricades in the empty cells would be as good as an announcement of our joint escape but the conspirators would link the two disappearances together, anyway. The point was to delay discovery and, therefore, pursuit. She helped me with the barricade, saying nothing. When we were done with the fortifications I moved toward the fireplace and she followed me.

"Keep close behind me," I said, my voice harsh. Its harshness surprised me.

I didn't know how to go about being rude to women, and no one can be rude for long to a beautiful young woman for whom one begins to feel an idiotic longing and attachment. And, anyway, what would come next—the rats and the spiders—wouldn't be easy for her. I remembered the horror of my first encounter with the tunnels:

I smiled as best I could and said:

"How did you do with the household gods?"

"I did my best," she said.

"Then it should be all right, shouldn't it? They ought to be glad to do something for you."

"They are a nice bunch of old gentlemen."

Her voice, I noted, had steadied and so had her hands. Good nerves, I thought; perhaps I had been wrong to doubt her for a moment. I wished my own nerves were as good as hers. Either that or that my memory had been better. What the devil had I forgotten to do? I had been so letter perfect in my calculations, but I knew that there had been something that I hadn't taken into account.

Time was passing, more than I had allowed for this part of the attempt, but this didn't worry me. I had saved several minutes in Sempinski's room. I wanted to say something to her to prepare her for the chimney shafts and for what lived and scurried inside them, but I could think of nothing that might do.

"All right," I said. "We'd better get started. Now remember to keep close behind me. I'll have the flashlight but I won't use it much; it might shine through some crack in the wall and give us away. And don't allow yourself to get upset by anything. It's not a long trip."

She wanted to know how long it would take us to reach the bricked-up fireplace and looked unbelieving when I told her.

"Forty minutes?"

"They'll seem like forty hours. But don't think about it. Try not to think about anything. It's . . . well, it's not going to be pleasant but try not to mind it."

She nodded then, looking serious and vulnerable.

"Let's start," she said.

Later, when clear thought was possible again, I would think that this had been the easiest and the safest part of our attempt. I wondered why I had been tense and nervous and upset because, not in my grimmest calculations had I been able to include all the elements. How could I have calculated something that I could not imagine? I had made up schedules and time tables, and I had assured myself that I would not think more than a second or two ahead, so as to avoid panic, and I had hardened myself against emotional distractions. I crawled through the colonies of spiders and rats with a girl who was frightened and distressed by the horror but who crawled bravely in the shower of mortar and old stone, in the squeal and rush of rats, trusting me or perhaps only hoping that I knew what I was doing and that the dreadful journey would come to some end. I was tuned wholly outward like a cornered animal and so I could not help her. This was the first proof of my miscalculation but I pressed on because (I told myself, sententious with fear) I had no other choice. There was a brief confirmation of my calculations because we did reach the bricked-up cave behind the fireplace at 10:23 and by 11:45 we were in the empty, no longer festive hall of premature German celebrations, and there were all the boots and sheepskin jackets to spare for the next stage of the escape. I had my own furs and pistol and the precious briefcase. A hunting knife made quick work of the briefcase. I had a moment of blinding unreality as I looked at the long notes which amounted to more money than I had ever seen . . . the savings of lifetimes. Kristin was overjoyed, and hugged me enthusiastically at the sight of this last piece of vital evidence that we were stealing from the conspirators. I packed this fortune in a soiled napkin inside my shirt and after I had thrown all the scraps of briefcase into the fireplace, and repaired the breeched wall again to hide our escape route, I felt that I had accomplished everything that I had set out to do.

I couldn't understand why I wasn't able to congratulate myself on an accomplished mission. But the deathly pale, bright eyed, admiring and enthusiastic girl beside me served as a reminder. She urged me on into the cold outside where a storm was raging. And then, of course, I realized what I had forgotten to do while making brilliant calculations and composing schedules; I had not thought to look out of the window at the storm outside.

The night was unbelievable. I couldn't force myself to go out into it. My resolution, or whatever had carried me so far in the nightmare, suddenly ebbed away, and it was only when Kristin took the lead that I stumbled out into the frozen whirlwind.

I had not thought that there might be a storm. I had assumed there would be a moon and stars to guide us; I had studied landmarks. But as soon as the bleak castle disappeared behind us we were flung into the raging night and I was immediately and absolutely lost.

There wasn't one star in the mad black sky to show us the way. We had to shout to be heard above the wind. I felt the blinding snow freezing on my face.

What happens to your calculations then? The clouds which had brought twilight at noon show what they can do. The icy wind cuts and a thick cold mask spreads across your face. You haul the girl along, or perhaps she hauls you, it is impossible to tell;

and within minutes you can't tell whether or not you are still together. The only way to tell is by the weight dragging against your arm or by the stumbling collisions of two bodies. But the weight vanishes when your own body becomes too difficult to drag through the snowdrifts, and the collisions are with trees as often as not. There is no sense of direction. There isn't even any sense of motion. For all you know you may be standing still despite all that effort, pounding along on an icy treadmill. It goes like this hour after hour or, perhaps, minute after minute; there is no way to tell. There is the battering cold and blindness. There is no terror because for terror there must be understanding and you understand nothing. You suspect that you are going to freeze unless you find shelter. Indeed, you feel yourself beginning to freeze. The body refuses to respond and that is a signal. Everything slows down. Thought processes dissolve. There is a lack of air despite all that wind. You feel that you are drowning but there doesn't seem to be anything that you can do about it. You settle down to a mindless contemplation of your own destruction. Time dissolves. Well, well, you say and Oh well, and you fall and stumble and drag something along—something shapeless and unrecognizable—wondering what the whole business is about. There is a vague thought about guards and mastiffs; that makes you keep going. Legs like white logs sinking into snow, coming out and plunging. The snow grasps and holds like quicksand. It has formed walls and corridors among the trees and deflects the wind upward, and you are in a maze of wild toboggan runs carved out of ice mountains, and this too drives you on with the thought of the pursuing danger. You have to keep moving. The walls soar and fall; white buttresses and castles in the blue-gray light. Moats and pinnacles. Everything is white and frozen and unsympathetic; still more blue than white in the new blue light but beginning to glitter: diamond studded hills in the spreading whiteness. But the hills sink and flatten and begin to spread like melting confectionery, and soon you wonder what has happened to the trees, and you recall climbing over something that had the hardness of stone under the snow and the ice and that appears to have been a wall other than an ice wall, and since you have a vague idea that a wall and ditch contained the trees, you think that this phenomenon might account for their disappearance. You are out of the park and it is broad daylight. You see dunes of snow sweeping across fields. The park is far behind you; you experience an upsurge of thankfulness and gratitude that makes you want to fall onto your knees and rest. You want to give thanks for a storm that had kept the mastiffs skulking in their kennels but you remember that you must go on because to stop in that cold is not to move again. Daylight is no friend. You should have been in a village long before daylight. Time is suddenly important again, but there is no sign of any village in the windswept plain. There is a small black object moving rapidly at the extreme edge of your field of vision and you focus your inadequate eyes upon it, and it resolves itself into a sleigh, a horse and a man. The foreshortened sleigh looks like a lifeboat plowing through white waves, with snow spume sweeping up and sideways and falling behind. There is the white steam of a horse's breath and a man's red face. The man makes distant, incomprehensible sounds which seem sympathetic, as if finding you in the open fields after a storm explained everything. You croak the name of a town and the man nods, pointing with his whip, and you lose consciousness under the revolving gray sky.

Pain brought me back to consciousness. Warmth made a gradual return under the straw and sacking in the sleigh and as my body thawed out the pain strengthened its attack on me. I had never experienced anything like it.

My hands and face were particularly painful, being rubbed with snow that Kristin scooped up as the sleigh carried us along. I tried to focus my eyes on her to tell her to stop it but my eyes were tired. Their pain was white and sharp. Everything blurred when I looked at it. I'm snowblind, I told myself as though this was a remarkable discovery. I thought I felt the quick pulse in her icy hand even though I couldn't feel the hand itself. My voice sounded extraordinarily remote and I suspected that my ears were frozen.

I muttered the name of the ancient border city where we would have to board a train for the capital, and Kristin said: "It's all right. The driver knows. We're going there. Move your arms and legs. Can you move them yet?"

"Of course I can," I said but I couldn't do it. When my eyes had steadied I studied Kristin as she worked on my wooden fingers. She had taken over. I was astonished that she was in command.

"Where are we, anyway?" I asked. "How did we get here?"

She gave me a curious glance that I didn't understand.

"We're on the road to the city. You got us out of the house and through the park into open fields and the sleigh was there. I wouldn't have believed anyone could have got through a storm like last night's."

"We didn't get to the village, then," I said, beginning to remember.

"No. If we had we would probably have been caught by now. They must be searching all over for us by this time. The village is the first place they'd go to, don't you think?"

"After they've searched the house," I said. I struggled to sit up and to look behind us. "They must be coming after us."

"But that's just it," she said. "They are not behind us. You took us out of the park on the side away from the village. If they went to the village they will be on another road. When did you change your mind?"

"About what?"

"About not going to the village but trying the other side."

"I didn't," I said. "I got lost."

She laughed in an odd, disbelieving way.

The peasant driver cracked his whip and called out cheerfully to his horse and the sleigh rushed headlong over the icy road. Sooner or later, I knew, I would have to give some thought to how we were going to get aboard a train. I was sure that our pursuers would beat us to the city and watch at the turnstiles in

the railroad station. But there was still a little time before I had
to think. I lay back and tried to ignore the sharp pains in my
thawing body.

I looked at Kristin bending over me and found it difficult to
recognize her. The small circle of exposed cheek was crimson,
the deep eyes underlined in frostbitten white. I supposed that the
snow and wind had scrubbed us both clean of the black traces
of the chimney shafts but, even so, she looked a far cry from
the beautiful young woman who had so distracted me before our
escape. She must have understood my glance because her back
stiffened, her chin went up, and she attacked my face with a
particularly ungentle handful of snow.

"That hurts!" I said.

"It's meant to. Or would you rather have your nose and ears
fall off? You'd be a little less critical about other peoples' appearance."

"It feels as if you were tearing them off anyway."

"You have a lovely case of frostbite."

"Didn't you get frozen?"

"No. At least not as badly." (Then her voice softened.) "You
must have shielded me from the worst of the wind. I never
thought we'd get through."

"Neither did I. It's lucky this sleigh came along this morning.
Are you sure the man is taking us to the city?"

"I told him you would pay him if he got us there. He thinks
we are lost tourists."

"He's not far off. But can you speak the language?"

"Enough to make myself understood about meals, soap, money,
things like that. This is the country where my husband came from.
And Professor Sempinski taught me a few phrases when I was
planning my own escape. That poor man . . . what will they
do to him?"

"They'll kill him," I said. And then, to soften the impact of
brutality as much as I could: "But I think he knew that. It's
what he wants now, I think."

"Why should they want to kill him now that he's useless to them?"

"For revenge. Or perhaps just because he's useless. But we'll make them pay for it, won't we?"

"That won't bring Sempinski back to life," she observed.

"Perhaps not. But it will give me a great deal of pleasure to make these animals suffer."

She looked at me carefully and paused as if she wished to say something more. But then she changed her mind. The pin-pricks of returning feeling were stabbing my fingers.

"That's good now. I feel fine. Why don't you get your hands under this straw and sacking and get them warm? And get down out of the wind. The storm is almost over but you can still get frostbite."

The flat land slid past us in a hiss of snow under the runners of the sleigh and the steady pounding of the horse's hoofs. Our front horizon was blocked by the driver's patched sheepskin jacket. I was conscious of the girl beside me and her clean, snowy smell.

I said: "This could be something out of a Sempinski novel."

"This kind of thing?"

"The sleigh should have three horses and it should be driving through a forest. The hero and the heroine should be in love with each other. Other than that we just about have it."

Almost at once, as if by command, woods surrounded us. She laughed.

"There is your forest."

"Well, it's a start. But I'm afraid the hero is supposed to be a fiery young man, resourceful and brave. He has come back from the Tartar wars covered in all kinds of glory."

"And the heroine?"

"She is a beautiful, proud and high-minded young woman who knows her own mind. She hasn't seen the hero since he was a boy. They had been betrothed as children by their parents and she has been wondering what he would be like as a man."

"Does he disappoint her?"

"He does at first. He's a bit wild, I'm afraid; keeps rotten company. But in the end he recovers his reputation by magnificent, patriotic deeds."

"And she, of course, has loved him all along even though he had been a bit of a bastard."

"That's right. Have you read anything by Sempinski?"

"I never even heard about him until you sent me here. But I think I'd like to read him now. You have a lot of his things in your library, don't you?"

"Everything that he ever wrote."

"Good," she said. "Then I'll be able to read him."

She laughed then; a quick, pleased sound.

"What is it now? Changing your mind about Sempinski?"

"It's not that at all."

Then we were silent, conscious of each other. I thought about my books and about her reading them in the warm apple-glow of my library and Mahler's thundering music. New York had never seemed as far away as it was then. There were innumerable dangers and uncertainties between us and New York. I had no guarantee that there were no pursuers coming fast behind us although it seemed more likely that they would be on the village road. The snowstorm would have covered up our tracks but they would assume that we had headed for the village; anywhere else would have meant disaster. The hunters would be puzzled in the village where no one had seen us. I almost wished that I could be there to watch their confusion. It all depended on Karpovitch and what he was up to.

I told Kristin about Karpovitch and the scene with the general in my room. She said at once that she thought Karpovitch had left Hetmanska Gora before our escape.

"My windows overlooked the stables where they kept their cars. Most of the Germans left yesterday morning. The man you described left early in the afternoon. He seemed in a hurry."

"That means he might be waiting for us in the capital. And

if he figures out where we are heading, which he is sure to do, he'll block our every route."

She said, smiling: "You'll think of something."

"Damned if I know what. We've had a streak of luck so far but we need more than that. This is like playing chess in a blindfold; you can counter one move, perhaps two. But we must have some idea of our opponents' game to know what moves to make."

She smiled and pressed my hand; a warm reassurance.

"I think you've done beautifully so far."

"And anyway," she added after a while. "Didn't you say that the CIA was in this already?"

"That's something I can't understand at all. But I don't think that we had better count on anyone to help us until we get the letters and the money to the embassy."

"But you don't doubt that we'll manage, do you?"

"I'd feel a lot better about it if we had more time. The assassination is planned for the day after tomorrow; that doesn't leave us much space for maneuver."

"Something will happen," she said fervently. "I know something will."

I laughed, partially relieved. "That's a very Slavic way to look at it."

"How's that?"

"They're always looking for miracles to get them out of trouble, always waiting for some sign from heaven. I don't think we can afford to count on miracles although it'll take one to get us to the embassy in time. Still, maybe you made some points for us with those household gods?"

"I didn't try very hard," she confessed. "I'm afraid I've given up believing in miracles."

"That sounds a little bitter . . ."

"I don't mean to be bitter or cynical about it. It's just that I no longer believe that good things will happen simply because one wants them to."

"Did you ever think that?"

"I used to think that before I was married. I thought that if one really wanted something and believed in it and worked for it too, then it would come. But it never did come, not completely. And if it looked like what you really wanted, it didn't last."

I said: "Are you still talking about your marriage?"

And she said quickly, looking up: "What made you think that's what I was talking about?"

"Nothing," I said. "I had heard that you were married and that your husband was killed. I'm sorry if that sounds abrupt."

"That's how it should sound," she said quietly. "We were only married a year when my husband was killed."

"In Saigon, wasn't it?"

"Yes. He was sent there by his government as an election observer. He was hit by a speeding car, you know. The car never stopped. And no one seemed to care very much about it."

I said that I was sorry.

She said: "I couldn't understand why they had to have him killed."

"Had to? You mean it wasn't an accident?"

"Oh no. It was a political matter. The Vietnamese were very bland about it. It seems they're used to that kind of thing. Our own people wouldn't tell me anything. They were only interested in getting me out of Vietnam and back to New York."

"Then you had your own reasons for hating Communists."

"It wasn't the Vietcong who killed Jan. It was our own people. They thought that Jan was a Communist secret agent. He could have been. It doesn't really matter. They couldn't prove anything against him so they had him killed. It seems that's the way it's done all over the world."

"My God!" I said. "Are you sure? That's terrible . . ."

"I couldn't believe it for a long time. I never thought our side could do anything like that. But it all added up after a while when I remembered small incidents, little things that I hadn't paid any attention to before. It could have been as they said. But I didn't care. All I cared about was that it had been our side which had murdered Jan. After that it was hard to believe in miracles."

"My God," I said.

She smiled, squeezed my hand. "You're a nice man to listen to all this. I've never really told anyone about it. It isn't the kind of confidence that one can share easily. But you can see how I could accept Uncle Per's letters without a sense of shock, of how I could believe that poor Sempinski could have been fooled into thinking the CIA responsible for the conspiracy."

"No wonder you looked at me in an odd way when I talked about revenge on the plotters."

"They are everything you called them."

"But so are the people who murdered your husband. Don't you hate them for it?"

"No. I never did, I suppose. At first I was too shocked, too bewildered, and later it didn't seem to make much difference what I did. Hate doesn't help anybody. You can't hate something you can't even understand."

"My God," I said. "I had no idea."

"About me and Jan? No reason why you should have known anything about it. Things like that aren't supposed to happen to people like us."

"But they do happen, don't they? We get caught up in things like that whether we like it or not."

"Not often. Most people wouldn't believe any of this if it happened to them. People have a way of living their own lives and seeing only what they want to see no matter what happens to anybody else."

"So what does it all amount to then? A choice between two evils?"

"Oh no. The systems are on the surface and that's where people live. They have nothing to do with what goes on under the surface; it's not their concern. We make our choice from what is available where we can see it. The rest . . . well, that's for the murderers on both sides."

I sat quite still then, my thoughts awry. I had been badly shaken by her story but my sense of shock had little to do with her husband's death. I was quite willing to accept the fact that no one faction had a monopoly on evil. In fact, I agreed with Kristin's summary that under the surface of systems and slogans moved another world peopled by creatures who had no relation with the world of ordinary men. What made me pause was the realization of her knowledge. She seemed so young and vulnerable, so capable of naïve hopes and ideals. She couldn't have been older than her middle twenties but she already knew what I had only begun to learn at forty-two. I was ashamed that I had been so complacently naïve, and that I had misread her so completely. Her youth and beauty had dazzled me but now she had allowed me a brief glimpse of depths underneath the surface. I wanted to know more about her; it seemed suddenly important to find out everything that mattered to her. The only starting point for questions was her husband's death and I didn't want to talk about her husband. I supposed that I was jealous of the dead man. The odd, diffused feeling of disappointment that I had felt when I had first discovered that she had had a husband came back, magnified.

She took my silence for worry about the uncertainties ahead and went on to encourage me with quick words that showed confidence and trust in my judgment. I had no reason to share her trust in my abilities; on the contrary, I had every reason to think the opposite. I cautioned myself against being optimistic about anything. I had been lucky, certainly; a fool's blind luck, a beginner's luck. It wasn't anything to bank on in this league.

I was aware of quickened feelings toward Kristin and told myself at once not to be a fool.

The woods ended shortly afterward; trees gave way to the familiar windswept whiteness that seemed to slant upward into the gray sky, and then we drove into and along a highway thickening with traffic. The distant spires and towers of the ancient city rose clear and defined in the odd blueish light.

I looked down at Kristin to comment about that and saw that

she was sleeping. The night and the storm had been enough to drain anyone of strength. I felt the gentle rocking of the sleigh on the hardpacked snow and longed for sleep and rest, some mild oblivion. But that would have to wait until I had got Kristin and myself safely aboard a train.

The sleigh slowed down and then crept off the road onto the snow enbankment. Ahead of us, other sleighs and trucks began to lurch and spill into the highpiled drifts among the telegraph poles, and then I heard the furious bleating of a Klaxon horn and the roar of a powerful engine driven at top speed. A huge black car splattered with the grime of a desperate journey hurtled past in a spray of snow. I had a momentary glimpse of streaked windows and tense, glaring faces, and in the fraction of a second that it took for the mass of metal to fly past the sleigh I recognized my former escort, the insolent young man whom I had blamed for the disappearance of the briefcase, and Karpovitch.

All thoughts of rest and sleep went down the road with the car, driven at mad speed for Hetmanska Gora. I was seized with an icy chill far deeper than the cut of the wind. Whatever margins of safety I might have wrested from the situation earlier in the morning had now shrunk into practically nothing.

PART FOUR:

On the Run

nineteen

SNOW CAME IN from the south, from mountains, carried by the wind. It piled minarets and ice towers on the train sheds, and blotted out the pale light in the glassed-in concourse, and shifted restless dunes between the tracks, and drifted along platforms in the false heat of steam that froze when it touched stone. The wind smelled of mountain passes and wet granite.

Time, like the snow, hissed through cracks in the windows. I looked at my watch; my eyes were blurring with anxiety. I walked through the concourse peering through the crowds in search of the hunters.

My arms and shoulders, back and thighs ached as though I had walked long and far carrying a burden. My eyes stung; they were red-rimmed and the flesh under them was gray. I didn't recognize myself in the mirror of the ticket window, looking haggard and a little mad. I had lost my fur cap in the night and now my tangled, overlong hair stood stiff on my head like a frosted mane.

"Two first class tickets for the capital," I said to the clerk, a pig-eyed little man with a sharp pointed nose. He gave me a look of bored distaste, hearing me speak German.

"Returns?"

"No. No returns. One way."

The clerk pushed the ticket coupons through the grille, looked at the single banknote that I held out toward him.

"I've nothing smaller," I said. I wondered what the clerk would think if he knew that I had a fortune in dollars stuffed inside my shirt. I asked when the train was due to arrive.

"There will be an announcement," he informed me.

"What platform will the train be on?"

"It will be announced."

"Is the train on time?"

"It is winter."

"Does that mean that the train might be late?"

"All trains are late in winter."

I moved as quickly as I could into the crowd. Time had become an implacable enemy. It had been several hours since Karpovitch's car had passed our sleigh and that meant that we could expect the hunters at the terminal at practically any moment.

I stooped as I walked, knowing that without this cramped bearlike stagger I stood head and shoulders taller than most men who passed me. I had to make myself inconspicuous. My face astonished even me when I caught sight of it in glass. My furs were matted and dirty. I thought that I must have looked like a demented bear.

I passed a group of children, then some foreign tourists whose sudden bursts of English made me sick with longing for security, but whose name tags proclaimed them all to be a cultural congress of British workers. The children had red winter faces, bright pebble eyes and wool stockings and quilted coats with fur collars. They chattered, pointing at the trains, with a peculiar mock adult restraint. Everyone seemed unnaturally strained. A small boy looked at me, solemn as a fledgling owl, then hid his head behind the shoulder of another. Soon all the children were silent and watching. Their round eyes followed me across the concourse. I kept my eyes carefully away from the English tourists who wore the puffed uncertain look of jungle explorers: half anxious indignation and half dysentery.

"An hour late. Terrible. So inconsiderate."

"Terribly inconvenient. I suppose we'll have to wait *another* hour."

"Still, I suppose the snow . . ."

I edged past them, keeping my head averted as they stared at me, and made for the stairs. Outside, the wind smashed into me. I crossed the square into a narrow street, no more than an alley. The snow lay deep here, undisturbed by footprints. The wind rattled toward me. I searched for the workmen's canteen where I had left Kristin and knew sudden panic when I couldn't find it. Somewhere around here, surely? Where the devil was it? The narrow doors, thick walls, ill-smelling corridors were dreadfully familiar and all looked alike; bare, cheerless sheds with ancient furniture, gray windows, iron stoves and the smell of sour cabbage, dishwater and mushrooms. Dour men sat hunched over cooling bowls at tin-topped tables under naked bulbs. I wished that I could have taken Kristin elsewhere to wait for the train, a clean place where she wouldn't be the only woman. But everything that had seemed cheerful and pleasant was too far from the terminal. And so I had taken the instinctive course of the fugitive and looked for a dark place, a hideout among people who would pay no attention to anybody but themselves. They had seemed less men than ragged heaps of clothing, old rags and wornout furs held together with string. Bleak faces with sliding eyes and chins buried in cloth. There was a modicum of safety to be had among them. They wouldn't lift their eyes to watch a murder at a neighboring table.

I pushed old doors, peered into gray shadows, and finally found the place. I was too tired by then to feel relief. Kristin moved in her corner; I saw her at once. Even in her dark skisuit and bulky sheepskin coat she had a luster that made her vivid and impressive. I sat down beside her.

"All clear so far," I said. I put the ticket coupons on the table. She studied them as if a little puzzled, then smiled.

"They haven't got here yet?"

"I didn't see anyone I knew."

"When is the train due?"

"Nobody seems to know. They say the trains are always late in winter."

"But approximately?"

"I don't think there'll be anything for another hour. We've missed the morning express anyway. But there's a local train."

"Another hour," she said. "Do you think they'll be here in an hour?"

I hadn't told her about seeing Karpovitch and the others in the speeding car.

"It's possible," I said.

"Perhaps we should take the first train out, no matter where it goes."

"We have no time to go anywhere but straight to the capital."

"You're tired," she said. "Why not rest for an hour? Nobody will notice if you sleep right here."

"No, I can't sleep right now. Was everything all right here?"

"Nobody bothered me. Nobody went out or came in while you were gone. I don't believe that anybody even looked at me. I don't know if I'm too happy about that."

"What? Why?"

I was aware of a pounding headache. I had considerable trouble keeping my thoughts in order.

"I may be on the run and I may look like hell but I'm still a woman," she said. She laughed. "Or have you forgotten that too?"

I assured her that I had not forgotten, my voice cracked with fatigue. I was more conscious of her now than ever before.

"You ought to get some rest," she said. "You need it."

"I can't sleep here," I said. "There isn't time to sleep. We'll sleep on the train."

"At least we're not going to sleep together," she mocked. "That's a prim arrangement."

"What?"

"The tickets, coupons or whatever they are. One is for the

first class and one for the third. Isn't that carrying propriety a little too far? And which of us gets which?"

"What? Let me see . . . That goddamn clerk!" I was suddenly enraged. She stared at me astonished and, I thought, oddly pleased. What in hell would she have to be pleased about? "The son of a bitch did that because I spoke German."

"Go to it," she said, laughing.

"Are we quarreling? What are we quarreling about?"

"We are both tired," she said.

"That's right." I felt the anger crumble and a great weight seemed to collapse on me.

"You need some coffee," she said and waved her hand at the old woman who sat, mountainous and greasy behind the zinc-topped counter. She had a face like a bag of walnuts and hands like drowned hams.

"One other thing has occurred to me," I said. "I don't like to carry all this money in my shirt."

"Why not mail it to yourself in care of the embassy? Then we can pick it up as soon as we get there and hand it over."

"I'm not sure about that. I have a feeling embassy mail is watched, particularly if it comes from inside this country. I'd rather mail it to myself at my hotel. I still have my room there."

"Would that be safe?"

"I don't know. But that's what I'd like to do. Then if anything should happen to me at least the money will be out of reach of the Karpovitch gang."

She said quietly: "You still think that Karpovitch will catch up with us, don't you?"

I was sure of it but said evasively:

"It's not only that. This money is a fortune, more than anyone in this country can earn in a lifetime. It's an invitation to robbery and I'd rather not take any more chances than we have to."

"Then let's send it off. Although I still vote for the embassy rather than your hotel."

Then she added:

"I've been thinking about the train. Do we really have to go by train? Isn't there another way?"

"What way? Why?"

The train to the capital had been such an important part of my planning that I couldn't think of anything that might replace it. And why replace it? I clung to all my plans, futile as they seemed to be, with the unreasoning stubbornness of a child. Elimination of the train from my painfully worked-out equation of safety seemed as revolutionary as an elimination of the embassy itself. But she said reasonably:

"Karpovitch will expect us to take the train. His people will be watching at the terminal. They can't help seeing us. They'll follow us aboard. But what if we don't take the train? What if we rented a car? The PABUT people advertise car rentals."

"A car? Well, yes, a car. That solution wouldn't have occurred to me," I said.

"You've already blazed a trail at the terminal," Kristin went on. "You've bought the tickets. Karpovitch's men will be sure to board the train even if we did manage to slip past them somehow. Let them take their train ride by themselves and, in the meantime, we can drive. Well, what do you think?"

"But what if Karpovitch doesn't take the bait? A highway can be lonely if you need some help."

"Would anybody help us on the train?"

"All right. We'll do it. They've pretty well run us into a corner as it is; we've nothing to lose."

She laughed and clapped her hands, delighted.

"That's the spirit!"

I found myself laughing with her, too tired for control. Besides, I didn't feel like controlling laughter. She was so obviously delighted and so impressively right with her suggestion. It was the only sensible thing to do. She seemed particularly pleased when I told her how impressed I was and how lucky I felt to have her along.

I had an AAA International driving permit, thanks to Miss Gruber's efficiency, and the PABUT clerk provided both the AIT and FIA carnet and required insurance. I wondered what good it would do me if Karpovitch ever caught up with us. The car was a five-seat Volga. It would be ready in an hour. Was I sure that I didn't want a driver? Only a little bit more. Yes, I said I was sure. The clerk assured me that the journey would be much more comfortable with a driver but if I wished to drive that was up to me; a PABUT guide or driver were no longer mandatory equipment for tourists. In the meantime, while the car was being prepared, would Monsieur and Madame care to tour historic landmarks in the city? The clerk seemed offended when I declined the offer.

I used the time to buy a heavy manila envelope and to stuff the money into it, address it, and take it to the post office. I felt totally unreal mailing half a million dollars to myself at a foreign hotel. Kristin still opted for the embassy but she said nothing when she saw me scribble the address.

We drove north on an old Imperial highway, with the land suddenly desolate around us. Ahead rose the dark misty battlements of a minor range of wooded mountains.

The car rocked through the icy blue coldness with windows starred and webbed by frost. Outside the windows the world was hushed and white. Inside, there was warmth.

I drove stupefied, all my senses blunted. My body moved in odd spasmodic tremors as if no longer willing to obey my brain. I swayed in would-be sleep, conscious of Kristin's cowled head heavy on my shoulder. My brain sent down weak and garbled messages like a defective telegraph key. I had to keep myself going if our escape was to have its desired if illogical conclusion. The logical conclusion was disaster but that was not desired. What was desired more than anything was sleep and rest and an awakening in which the day and the preceding night were erased from memory so that the shocked brain and the weary body could come to terms again.

A village slid by, then another. A warning sign leaped out of gathering darkness. Steep road and narrow road, snowdrift and broken pavement. I worked the car down into second gear feeling the back wheels sliding under us.

Then the day vanished in surprising blackness. There was no moon. Snow started falling heavily again. The road was empty. No traffic. No sign of anything alive. The road began to climb in short, angry loops among sudden hillocks. Pinewoods descended on the road from towering escarpments. I was aware of a rhythmic drumming in my head. My feet were heavy, leaden; and it was only the wild slide of the wheels on sudden hill corners that brought me back to partial consciousness and reminded me of the weight of my numb foot on the accelerator.

A sudden lurch threw Kristin's head off its perch on my shoulder and she woke with a quick cry. It took her several moments to locate herself within the time-place continuum of car and night.

"I fell asleep," she said as if apologizing. Then she peered around. "Where are we?"

"Mountains," I said. "Road. I'm not sure, exactly."

"Have I been sleeping long?"

"About an hour. Maybe more. I don't know. I think we've been driving for more than two hours."

"You must be dead tired. Let me drive a little."

"No," I said. "I'll do it. I want to get through the pass. Then you can take over."

"You've got to rest."

"I'll rest later. Got to get on now, make time. Can't stop now. Road is terrible. If we stopped now we'd never get started again. Just keep talking to me."

"I wish there was a radio," she said. "Yes. Then we'd be able to put on some music. What kind of music do you enjoy the most?"

"Mahler," I said. "Oh I don't know . . . anything."

"So you're a Mahler enthusiast too? That's a revelation. There's something very special about Mahler people."

"How special?"

"Well, let's say distinctive. They seem to be a quiet, self-contained lot, rather introspective. The sort of people who keep to themselves a lot. Is that how you are?"

"Yes. I suppose so."

"You don't go out very much at home, do you? What do you like to do? Whom do you see? Do you have any friends I might know?"

"I like to play chess," I said, and suddenly the idea of chessboards seemed ridiculous. I didn't want her to think me ridiculous. But having started talking I couldn't stop myself. "I study fencing," I added. "I'm not very good."

"Jan was a fencing-master," she said, suddenly reflective. "And we both liked chess."

"Did he like Mahler too?"

Kristin sighed and reached out and pressed my shoulder.

"He didn't know anything about Mahler and I don't know enough. But I would like to know. And I'm a good chessplayer if you need a partner."

"Do you fence too?" My slow words surprised me. I could not make myself believe that the high, trembling voice was mine.

"No, I'd be rotten at it. I'm terrified of knives. People with swords awe me and mystify me. I'd be an awful flop in the seventeenth century. I'd be far too impressed with all the gentlemen."

"I would be too," I said. "Ah, it's a silly pastime in our time."

But she said no, it wasn't, on the contrary. It seemed somehow moving to study fencing in the twentieth century; it reaffirmed some kind of faith in the human future. Didn't I think so?

"I used to. I used to think a lot of things like that."

"And now you don't?"

"There is so little time for thinking outside the practical."

"But your work is more than merely practical, isn't it? You're a scholar. Don't tell me that takes no thought. I know how eminent you are in your field. Believe me, I had all sorts of qualms before I had that lunch with you in New York."

"And after the lunch?"

I wondered what she'd say. I thought it suddenly important that she would think very highly of me but couldn't see why she would.

She said: "After I met you I thought you were a very nice, very gentle man. I thought it would be nice to know you a lot better."

"Well," I said. "Your wishes certainly came true."

She sighed and laughed a little. "They certainly did."

She was quiet for a moment after that and I felt the weight of my fatigue pressing down on me again. My eyes, I thought, were playing tricks on me. The clouds seemed to have blown apart and threw a scattered mass of stars across the sky and the car seemed to be heading straight up into them as they leaped and turned, advanced and retreated. The stars were yellow-green and oddly paired in darkness. And then I heard the long chilling howl of wolves deeper in the darkness.

My foot hit the accelerator in quick, vicious panic and the car leaped crazily around a sudden bend and spun, flying straight for the ghostly suggestion of a wooden guardrail along the highway's edge, with the black cavern of the night beyond. It took all my strength and wits to hold the wheel steady and to leave the brake untouched. Instead, I geared down, hearing the unsynchronized mechanism howl, and Kristin's quick alarm. The car spun, slid; a fender crunched against splintering wood, and I sat frozen into sudden immobility watching the darkness rush toward me, waiting for the precipice to appear. But the car had bounced clear of the railing and stopped in deep snow at the foot of the escarpment, lights tilted crazily to bare naked branches. I sat there trembling. I put my head into my hands. I was too tired to go on any longer.

Kristin asked if we were stuck, too deep to get out.

I said: "You take the wheel and I'll get out and push."

I got out feeling as if I had been broken in half, legs and brain completely disconnected. I thought it took me an incredibly long time to gather up the fragments of the broken guardrail. I pushed them under the rear wheels.

I signaled and she put the car in gear. With infinite care and patience she put in the clutch, then let it out and engaged the motor. The wheels spun madly. Snow flew, the rear of the Volga sank into the snow. Stop it, I shouted, Easy! But she couldn't hear me above the roaring of the engine and the whining tires. Too late, too bad, no good. Again! The car sank deeper then, with a slow lurch; it slid like a tired prehistoric monster into the six foot snowbank. She tried again and again. I paid no attention. I sat in the cold wind feeling my sweat freezing. I couldn't feel the metal of the car with either hand. After a while I got back inside the car. I hunted for a cigarette with hands that felt nothing.

"I'm sorry," she said. "Are we dug in for good?"

"I'm afraid so. But it wasn't your fault. The back wheels were hub-down in snow before you even tried."

"So now we're stuck," she said, oddly reflective.

I sighed, swore quietly. "That we are. And we can't stay here. We're all right as long as the engine and the lights are on. Once the motor cuts out we're out of a heater and we'll freeze in minutes. What are we like on fuel?"

She checked the gauge, shook her head. "Nearly empty. Where are we exactly? We seem to have gone about a hundred kilometers. Aren't we close to some town? Somewhere we could walk to?"

I found a road map in the glove compartment but it defied my cold fingers for a moment. I couldn't feel the edges to open the map. I said: "There seems to be a sizeable town ahead of us. It could be five or six kilometers away."

"Couldn't we walk that?"

"Can't you hear our company?"

With the tires silent and the motor idling we heard the lonely calling close and very clear.

"What is that?" she whispered.

"Wolves." I saw her shudder.

"Oh God," she said. "What else will there be?"

"I don't think they'll come to the car so long as the lights are on and the engine's going."

An icy chill ascended through the floorboards. She tucked her feet under her on the seat and massaged her ankles. I tried to follow suit. It took me a long time to hoist my feet up and fold them on the seat. The effort left me breathing in white clouds and hunchbacked with effort. The cigarette fell out of my hand and I watched it stupidly burning on the floorboards. I was too tired and indifferent to bend after it.

Whether it was the horror of the plaintive howling, or the beginning of a strong feeling for me or plain rebellion against meek acceptance of disaster so early in our bid, Kristin refused to give up. I had a momentary pang of doubt, a sense of hopelessness and sorrow when I thought about her and all the odds that were still stacked against us. I cast about for some plan that would save her, if not myself, with further struggle useless. But she seemed to have no doubts. This was the strong, impassioned girl Tommy had talked about.

"We can't just quit! We can't just give up. We have to do something. Too much depends on us for us to quit now. Think of Sempinski. Think what he is going through now. Think of what will happen if we don't get to the capital before tomorrow. We have to go on. There has to be some way. Can't you think of something?"

I grunted, tired. I tried to shake off the torpor of cold and fatigue. I knew that I could not allow myself to fall asleep; and there was nothing that I wanted more than sleep.

"Something . . ." I said.

"Perhaps someone will come along," I thought I heard her saying. "Some other car. We can't be the only people traveling by this road tonight."

I mumbled something in reply, felt my head sinking, my chin on my chest. Felt nothing. I was immediately asleep.

twenty

SLEEP MUST have been a matter of no more than moments. I was numb throughout as I awoke but oddly aware of her voice, her hands and her excitement. She was pummeling my arms and shoulders to get me to awake and she was shouting at me. Words without sense. Sobbed out more than shouted. Chaotic words tumbling into the fog that had enveloped my brain.

"What . . ." I said, waking. "What happened?"

"It's a car! There's a car coming up behind us. Look! You can see the lights."

Perhaps a mile down the road, at the foot of the hill winding up toward us, a pair of headlights stabbed through the spangled darkness with flat orange beams. The wind brought the thin wail of the Klaxon horn, the drone of the motor.

"I think that's wonderful," I said also laughing. "It's a miracle. You must have done an A-One job on those household gods."

"Good old gods," she said. "Wonderful old gods! Oh, I knew they wouldn't let me down."

We got out of the car, stumbling in the snow, with the strange headlights suddenly vanished around a bend in the road far below us. The night was darker than before with the lights gone. But the black escarpment was bordered with silver. The snow had stopped falling. The clouds had blown away. The sky was dusted over with bright stars and there was a moon. In the white light of the moon the road had a peculiar cleanliness and smoothness, and I could see it clearly all the way to the bend where the light grew stronger. Come on, I urged it, laughing. Come on! I couldn't understand such a stroke of luck.

The lights came on, unsteady, at great speed on the treacherous surface of the snowpacked road, with the Klaxon blaring. There was an oddly chilling note to the Klaxon and the roar of the motor as if they meant to clear the road ahead of any obstacle, living or dead, or fling them aside in passing. Then the headlights burst into a white glare around the last bend, wavered in a wild skid, steadied and came on, and the great black car hung in uneasy profile for a moment at the edge of the road. Black lights danced madly along bespattered sides. The strident cry of Klaxon, widespread wheels churning up a silver spray of snow . . . It was an eight-passenger Opel Admiral, its shining bulk unmistakable in the moonlight. And I said No, numb beyond understanding, frozen in disbelieving shock.

"It isn't fair," I said, now blinded by the white, triumphant lights coming up the road, hearing the gears pushed down, the motor roaring.

"What," Kristin said. "What?"

I shook myself free of paralysis.

"Come on!" I shouted and jumped off the road, heading into trees. She ran after me, uncertain.

"What? What's the matter!"

"Karpovitch!" I shouted. "It's them! It's their car! Come on!"

We scrambled up the slope, plunging in and out of the snow like horses swimming across a river. Behind us on the road tires screamed, the horn blared, the motor protested.

"Karpovitch . . . But how could you know . . ."

"Come on!" I shouted.

There were shouts behind us.

I ran.

I fled. It was a leaping, soaring superhuman flight. Branches smashed into me but I didn't feel them. Kristin had caught up with me, still clutching her bundle, and had seized my hand and I pulled her along as if she were weightless. We topped the ridge and dived into darkness among trees and gigantic bushes, a tangled cage of vegetation made soft and doubly treacherous by snow. Trees closed about us, skeletal in the moonlight. Heavy black shapes boiled at the edge of vision. What now? Good Christ, what now? A blaze of light blackened the trees behind us as if the hunters meant to follow us up the steep escarpment in their car. Not fair hunting out of cars, I thought idiotically. I should have known. Those stabbing lights had come up so fast, they had been so urgent. They should have warned me, I thought, feeling the hot sweep of fear and self-pity. Instead I had jumped up and down in the road shouting like a child. And now Karpovitch's killers were coming up the slope using the tilted headlights for a path. How many are there? Two had gone with Karpovitch to Hetmanska Gora. How many had come back? I ran and then I fell into a sudden opening in the ground, a deep dry hole of leaves and rotten branches only slightly salted with snow under a heavy canopy of trees. Kristin rolled over me, gasping. Snow showered on both of us from the disturbed branches. My nostrils filled with a sharp acrid smell of fur and of wetness; a fetid animal stench that made me struggle for breath. And then I heard both the wolves and the hunters.

The wolves were near. They had withdrawn before my stampede and the shouts of the hunters. But their paired yellow-green lights blinked in the shifting shadows as they studied both the hunters and the hunted. They wouldn't wait long.

The hunters had stopped on the ridge, at the edge of the tree-line, and now peered into blackness. There were three of them: Karpovitch and two others whom I didn't know. I saw them clearly outlined by their headlights on the white sheet of snow. They were too far away from me to hear what they were saying but there was no mistaking Karpovitch's angry gestures and his men's reluctance. It would be only moments before they made up their minds and ventured into the darkness. Once they got some light on our tracks we would be as good as caught.

And suddenly I was cold in a manner that had nothing to do with temperature; thought became frozen and defined. There had been three men in the car as it sped toward Hetmanska Gora: Karpovitch, my former escort and the young man whom I had accused of taking my briefcase. Now there were two new ones. The Germans who knew me by sight would be on the train. I didn't think Karpovitch had brought further reinforcements. That meant that I was up against the trio and whoever had been left in the plotters' car.

I pressed my mouth against Kristin's ear and began to whisper.

"They've made a tactical mistake. They've split their forces. They don't know where we are but we know where they are. They've given us every possible advantage. We'll stalk them just as they think they are stalking us. We'll circle behind them. They'll come straight in along our tracks as soon as they've found them. Meanwhile, we'll go around them, get down to the road and steal their car."

"And leave them here?"

"Can you think of a better idea?"

"I was thinking about the wolves."

"So was I."

"They terrify me," she whispered.

I assured her that she was not alone in her fear of the wolves. But there was no time to wait precisely because of them.

"They'll move in any minute now. They're used to us now and they'll soon lose their fear of the lights. Ready to go?"

She nodded, her hand tight on mine.

"I love you," I said. My heart was hammering.

"I love you," she told me.

"Thank you," I said, not knowing what else to say.

We crawled to the lip of the hole, rolled over into snow and moved into the darkness of the bulbous shrubs, walking hunched over as if there was a guarantee of safety in making ourselves small. From one dark patch of safety to another. Hearing large forms moving. The creak of snow under our boots seemed as loud as unoiled hinges. Karpovitch shouted something from the edge of light, a question muffled by distance and scattered by the wind. One of the searchers replied from less than a hundred feet away. We were abreast of him then, moving toward the edge of the escarpment as he moved deeper among the trees. I hoped the German would have eyes only for the darkness and for the yellow eyes of the wolves that massed and stared in an unblinking wall behind us. With each step I thought that I could hear the start of their inevitable charge.

I stumbled and almost fell when a searcher's shout came suddenly from behind and I waited, every sense alert for the moment of discovery. Instead there came a sudden wave of terrible swift sound. The wolves were gathering for the rush. I heard the lone searcher shout again and then start running panic-stricken through the undergrowth, and then the savage baying. We ran across the naked ridge, sliding down the slope in a cloud of snow. No thought then of searchers. I heard a pistol shot behind me and then another and a furious howling, and then a terrible short scream drowned in growling sounds and snarls. Some black form was leaping down the slope beside us in its own cloud of snow. I struck the hardpacked snow and ice of the road on the run with both feet together, Kristin in my arms, and then we were running like madmen for the black Opel Admiral whose huge spotlights illuminated the ridge and the black waves of animals boiling over it. Then we were in the car, slamming doors, hearing another door slamming behind us and then a pistol shot blasting in my ear, and Kristin's muffled scream and Karpovitch's voice raging in white passion:

"Drive! Drive!"

I released the handbrake, flung the car into second, trod on the long accelerator pedal and the machine leaped across the ice. The night tilted, suddenly askew, trees spun out of sight. The white slopes revolved and the road itself twisted and bucked; white rails, telephone poles and milestones crisscrossed every window. My eyes saw nothing then, seeing everything. I was aware of the raging tide of animals crashing against the car and falling behind. The flat snap of Karpovitch's pistol was very loud. The hill-road rose and fell and suddenly the car was on a straight and level stretch of tolerable pavement, a dizzying transition with the hills behind it. The wolves came on. There was a rush of cold air and sudden loss of balance as Karpovitch flung a rear door open and emptied his pistol into the milling pack. The wolves stopped. The car went on. Karpovitch shut the door and the air stopped rushing in. The wolves and trees and towering escarpments had fallen away.

I drove headlong between huts and houses and the lighted windows of a little town. My face, when I caught sight of it in the rear-view mirror, wore the stricken look of slack-jawed idiocy. I began to tremble violently. I heard my own dry sobbing and Kristin's stillness and the labored breathing of Karpovitch behind me. Resigned and not at all surprised, I felt the cold muzzle of a pistol pressed against my neck.

Small towns passed in sad procession of black and gray buildings streaked with tearful moistures. Then there was a provincial administrative center jammed with horse-drawn drays, then the massif of the mountains, more gaunt and lonely than any mountains I had ever seen, and then, with sunrise, we had crossed the pass— a wild, disturbing place designed for inarticulate destructions.

I drove until I could no longer see or feel the wheel in my numb hands. I gave a hopeless sideways glance to Kristin and saw her huddled in the corner of our seat. She was terribly pale, despite the fresh bite of the morning air. I brought the car to a gentle halt at the side of the road and shut off the motor, not caring about Karpovitch's reaction. He seemed as tired as we were and as glad to rest. Too much had happened to us all, including Karpovitch; we were beyond mere tension. It would take several long moments of silence and lack of motion for anything to start making sense again, I thought.

I lit a cigarette and passed it to Kristin.

I wondered if she had meant what she had said about loving me. I knew that I had meant it. All my life, I supposed, I had looked for someone with whom I would be able to share whatever life provided. There was so much to get out of life, I knew now. It didn't have to be sterile and empty, uninteresting and gray. I had it in perspective now that the future looked as brief as the short barrel of Karpovitch's pistol, no longer than his interest in keeping us alive. Once he had got what he wanted from me, there would be no future to worry about.

But now, wondering if Kristin really loved me, if she could love me (and wondering why she should), I was desperately interested in having a future. And I wasn't going to give up what I had found so unexpectedly without at least putting up a fight. The gentle, amiable and unoffending consultant on antiquities seemed a shadowy figure whom I could no longer picture clearly to myself.

To start with, Karpovitch would be even more tired than I. His reflexes would have become blunted by tension and fatigue. He couldn't risk hurting us until I had told him about Lindstrom's money. Thus his hands were tied by the necessity of keeping me alive; I had no such problems in relation to his health.

I hoped to make good use of all the lessons the plotters had taught me; choosing the moment of attack was a more ticklish matter; I didn't think that Karpovitch would give me more than a solitary chance. I had to be careful not to force matters until I was ready.

It would be safer to start defensively and get the feel of the enemy's offensive, but I already knew the general line of Karpovitch's wishes. Defensive play would only delay the final violent conclusion and each minute worked to sap my strength faster than Karpovitch's.

I said: "All right, Karpovitch. It's your game; I know when I'm beaten."

Karpovitch's voice was harsh, broken with fatigue. "Wise of you. I've no time to waste. I want that briefcase. What did you do with it?"

"It isn't here."

"I know that, you fool! Do you think you'd still be breathing if you had it here? I want to know where the money is, not where it isn't! What have you done with it? Quick, or the girl gets it in the head."

"I'll give it to you if you let us go."

I thought that Karpovitch would expect only my immediate and unconditional surrender but he had clearly learned not to take me for granted.

He said: "I'll let you go when I have the money. Now, tell me: Where is it?"

"I'll take you there."

"Where? Where is it? Tell me now or I'll start hurting your young woman. This pistol fires an eight-millimeter bullet that spins at two thousand revolutions per second. At such close range the laceration is severe, the flesh tatooing is extremely vivid. It will have the same effect on this young woman's beautiful face as a high-speed drill combined with a blowtorch. Am I quite clear?"

"What guarantee do I have that you won't kill us as soon as I've told you what you want to know?"

"My word!"

"That," I said, calm, "is not good enough."

"All right," Karpovitch said, his voice difficult. "I know what you're up to. You're trying to drive me out of control. You think that if you enrage me I'll make a slip and give you a chance. A chance for what, you fool? Do you suppose there is anything I wouldn't do to get what I want? Killing you painfully has been a dream of mine for several hours and yet you're still alive. Obviously, I've decided to let you live but don't test my patience. I am tired and under considerable pressure. You should know by now that I must be taken seriously."

"I know it."

"Very good. Now perhaps we can understand each other. I want the money. You want yourself and the girl safely out of this country. Between the three of us each of us can get exactly what he or she wants."

"Aren't you working for the plotters any more?"

"What business is that of yours? Besides, you know what I'm

up against; you're the man responsible for the pressure. Oh, I would give anything to be able to kill you!"

"With that, how can you expect me to negotiate with you?"

"To hell with that! You have no right to expect anything!" Then he passed his hand wearily across his eyes. "All right. You push me too much. I am not used to this position of partnership by necessity."

I started laughing.

"You're on the run, aren't you, Karpovitch. You've broken with the plotters. They're after you as much as after us now, aren't they?"

Karpovitch swore and suddenly brought the sharp muzzle of the pistol hard on top of my head. It was an expert blow; the pain was astonishing.

The pistol slid, trembling, about my head. Karpovitch's breath was labored; he had clearly come to the end of his road. I fought to ignore the pain, the clouds of fatigue. I had to seize control of the situation. Karpovitch was helpless without Lindstrom's thousands if the conspirators were after him, but doubly dangerous with himself in danger. I had to disarm him.

"Let's talk," I said. "I've mailed the money to a place in the capital. I can't give it to you until we get there. So let's talk. We're in the same boat, more or less. Let's see if we can help each other a bit."

"I don't need your help," Karpovitch said slowly.

"I have the money you need to save your neck. You have the contacts to get us to Sweden. Let Kristin drive us to the capital and we can talk about it. Well, what d'you say? Or would you rather sit here until your former buddies catch up with us?"

"All right," Karpovitch said. "But no tricks. I still have a pistol."

"I'll keep that in mind."

I walked around the car and got in beside the Master Spy in the rear seat. Out of the car I felt suddenly alone and everything was clear; it was a moment that could be savored. The icy air felt clean in my lungs and my boots were springy on the hard-packed snow and, for a few seconds, I was vividly aware of the remote possibility of success. I asked if the plotters were on the road behind us. Karpovitch shook his head.

"They're looking for me in the capital."

"They'd kill you even if you did get them the Lindstrom money. What does loss of the money do to the conspiracy?"

"Nothing. It goes on as scheduled; three o'clock tomorrow afternoon in Napoleon Square. It is too big to stop just because a part of the plan went wrong. It's too late to stop it anyway; everything is in motion. You'd have as much chance stopping the Prague Express by standing on the track."

"Couldn't you stop it?"

"Why should I? It doesn't concern me any longer. I'll be in Sweden an hour after you hand me the money. Then South America. I have a few friends there."

"And what about Sempinski? What have you done with him?"

"Nothing. Why should I do anything to him? Let him be found where the conspirators want him to be found. He has a role to play in the conspiracy . . . some letters to back up."

I thought quietly for a moment, then I said: "I have those letters with me."

Then it was Karpovitch's turn to stare and to start laughing.

"You have the letters? You really wrecked everything for them, didn't you? I really misjudged you. I had no idea how dangerous you were."

"Do you still plan to kill us once you have the money?"

"What for? Revenge for wrecking the conspiracy? I am all done with that. Personal revenge? I have more pressing problems. To keep you quiet? The only people who might want my skin are the conspirators and you're not likely to go to them with news."

He relaxed then, and sat back in the seat for a moment and even closed his eyes. It was a fragmentary dropping of his guard; his eyes were immediately open again and fixed on me intently. But the movement had suggested the possibility of further relaxation. Clearly this was no time to alarm the Master Spy or to put him on his guard again.

I sighed, pretending to relax. I watched Kristin's rigid shoulders hunched over the wheel. I wondered if she knew how dangerous our situation had become. When the time came to attack Karpovitch in the speeding car, success would depend on her nerve as much as on mine.

I closed my eyes, yawned. I smiled at Karpovitch.

"I'd like a little of that money," I said conversationally. Karpovitch grimaced. His pistol hand relaxed.

"You are about to propose an American deal?"

"There's plenty to go around."

"Not for me, there isn't. I got that money out of Lindstrom, it belongs to me. If I leave the conspiracy, the money goes with me. You're getting enough as it is."

"I am? I didn't know that I was getting anything out of this."

"How much is your life worth? That's what you are getting."

Karpovitch laughed. He passed his hand across his eyes again. He seemed to have trouble with his shoulders; they appeared too heavy for his tired, thin frame. I knew that only moments separated me from the final act.

With infinite slowness I gathered myself together, too nervous to think. I got my legs under me, testing the suddenly slack muscles against the limousine's rich carpeting. I could throw myself sideways into the Master Spy. The problem was: how to make my body get on with the job. I could not clear my head of the image of the small black pistol.

I felt my resolution ebbing and forced it to stay. I felt my arms push off, my body going sideways and turning toward the staring spy; I heard a shout spiraling in a harsh blend of fear, and a wish to frighten; my left hand clutched and closed upon Karpovitch's wrist with a strength I didn't know I had; my right hand smashed bruised knuckles into Karpovitch's face.

I heard Kristin's shout, oddly thin in the chaos of other sounds around me. I twisted the wrist I was clutching and heard the dry snap of a bone, a wild yell, and the fall of the pistol. I felt another hand closing about my throat. Then the car rocked and swayed, thrown into a sudden swerve with the brakes pushed down hard, and I was hurled off the seat hauling Karpovitch with me. Karpovitch lost his grip on my throat. I drew back my fist and let it fly blindly, conscious of nothing beyond terror and despair, and felt the sharp pain of cracked knuckles. Then there was a struggling body under me and I was hitting it and kicking. The car swerved again and rode up on the bank. Kristin was shouting something that I couldn't understand. I beat the spy until I could no longer find the strength to hit him again. Then I sagged back. I sat on Karpovitch, jammed between the seats. Only then did I realize that my eyes had been tightly closed all the time.

Kristin was calling, laughing. I felt her hands around my painful face and then her arms around me. The car doors were open and I was bitterly cold.

"You did it! Oh, I love you, you wonderful, mad scholar. You've got him out cold. Could there be anybody like you?"

I tried to say something but my teeth were chattering. I couldn't stop shaking. Then a quick pain burned in my face where her hands were resting.

"You're hurt!"

I tried to tell her that it was not serious. Just cuts and bruises. But I was too spent to argue with Kristin. She shook her head and looked concerned.

"How does it look?"

"Awful. You're all bloody."

I was suddenly delighted.

"Stop grinning," she said. "This is serious."

I went on grinning. "I am in good hands."

She kissed me quickly. "We have to get you a doctor. Something might be broken."

"No, it's just cuts and bruises."

"I can clean you up with some of that useless stuff I bundled up in Hetmanska Gora but you must have proper treatment."

"I'm getting it," I said. I felt pleasantly luxurious and didn't want to miss a moment of it. "That was some pretty fancy driving, incidentally."

"I used to wreck a sports car a year," she said. "I'm an expert at it. It's one of those skills you never forget."

Then she began to rip up silk and linen. "Now hold still. Oh, sorry. Is it hurting now?"

I admitted that my face felt a bit tender, particularly the nose.

"I almost expected you to say that it hurt only when you laughed. You're an incredible man, do you know that?"

"I'm willing to have you tell me all about it."

"Oh, I will, I will. You can be sure of that. Now, is that comfortable? It's the best I can do. It doesn't look very professional I'm afraid."

I touched the white cocoon she had spun around my face and head. It was trimmed with lace. I knew better than to laugh although I had a devil of a time to keep my face straight.

"That's beautiful," I said. "You make a splendid nurse. And you're a scary driver. Do you think you could take us on to the capital? Where are we, anyway?"

"We have a little less than a hundred kilometers to go. We can be there in a couple of hours if you can stand the bumps."

Then we both looked at Karpovitch's bloodless face. His eyes were vacant. His nose was blue and swollen wide across his cheeks. His mouth was partly crushed. His wrist was obviously broken. Kristen looked at me without saying anything, but she shook her head. I felt uncomfortable then, as if suddenly ashamed.

I said: "A pretty murderous job. He looks as if he had tangled with a madman."

"A rather wonderful madman, I would say."

"I feel a bit sick about that. I'm afraid I'm not much good at this kind of thing. What are we going to do with him?"

She thought a moment, shook her head.

"We can't leave him here. He'd freeze in half an hour. Or maybe more wolves . . . no, we'll let him out nearer the capital. There isn't much harm that he can do us now. He'll be too busy saving his own hide to cause any problems."

We tied Karpovitch with his own belt, with my belt and with strips of Kristin's slip. We left him lying on the floorboards of the car. I got into the passenger seat beside Kristin and sat back on the cushions, my head suddenly heavy. I put Karpovitch's pistol in my pocket. Kristin got in behind the steering wheel. She got the car back on the road.

We drove a long time, with the white countryside broadening and opening into fields as the hills and slopes and violent escarpments fell away behind us. The day was brilliantly clear. We could see far toward the horizon. Small towns and villages went by at irregular intervals. I slept a little, lulled by the sound and motion of the car.

The day began to end at midafternoon. Darkness came quickly. The sun hung for long reluctant moments behind the thick clouds piling up on the horizon, turning them purple, then vanished. In the sudden darkness, the chill seemed particularly penetrating and the night unfriendly. The road flowed under us narrow as a stream tunneling through mountains; I longed for daylight and its broad horizons.

As we got closer to the capital, traffic became heavy; cars, trucks, antique excursion busses, horse-drawn drays moved out of snowy side-roads; and soon the highway filled with dark, unlighted shapes swaying dangerously out of gloomy blackness, and then began occasional long moments without motion. Far ahead of the lurching column, I saw waving lanterns and the long tongue of a barrier swung upward in the white beams of innumerable headlights.

"What do you think is going on up there?" Kristin wished to know. "An accident?"

"Looks like some kind of roadblock."

We heard distant whistles and shouts of command. Behind us, Karpovitch drew a long groaning breath and moved on the floorboards. I looked into his disfigured white face; his eyes were wide with pain and hatred, faintly luminous.

I said: "We'll have to dump him here. We'll never get through a roadblock with him in the car."

Kristin said quietly: "What about my papers? Isn't that the first thing they want at a roadblock?"

I had forgotten about Kristin's lack of papers. I said: "We'll just have to try to talk our way around that. Maybe they aren't as hard on foreign tourists as they're on their own people. After all, that's how they get hard currency."

"What do you think that roadblock's all about?"

"God knows. But I don't think it's anything to do with the plot. In this country, it could be routine."

She said: "Perhaps it's something to do with the Chairman's visit? Security precautions?"

I thought it was likely.

Kristin drove slowly and I climbed over the back of the seat to our prisoner and got him sitting upright on the floorboards. He said nothing to me but his eyes were eloquent. I covered him carefully with his own pistol while I tugged at the knots and buckles that had him trussed up. As an afterthought I went through his papers. Some looked imposing, with seals and heavy signatures. He didn't answer when I asked him what they were. I put them aside.

Then the column of traffic staggered again to a chaotic halt. Kristin pulled up behind a ladder-truck piled high with sacks out of which spilled dark mounds of winter potatoes, and I threw open the car door on The Magician's side and pushed him toward it. He shrugged off my hand with abrupt violence, got out and walked slowly to the walls of snow piled at the roadside. There he turned, cradling his injured arm, and looked toward us. Instinct told me that he would not try to reach the roadblock ahead of us. He was not yet ready for a public confrontation. For the moment he was in check. I closed the car door more hastily and locked it.

I sat back on the cold leather cushions, Karpovitch's papers on the seat beside me, wondering how to solve the problem of the roadblock. The traffic edged persistently toward the small group of soldiers and the striped pole they raised and lowered across the road, and then I saw trucks and cars stop before us, and dark forms started dragging bundles out of them and threw the bundles, packages and other odd objects far into the snow. Kristin began to laugh.

"What's the matter?"

"Looks like there are some others worried about the roadblock," she said. "I wonder what they're throwing away."

"Can't imagine. Could be black-market stuff. But that reminds me about something I'd better get rid of."

I threw Karpovitch's pistol across the roadside snow bank. I said: "Now all we have to worry about is passport control. Are you a good actress?"

"Not good enough to be paid for acting. How about you?"

"Oh, great. I used to play the Train in Shakespeare's historicals at school."

"What train?"

"You know where they say things like Enter Gloucester and Train? Well, I was the Train. It won't help us here."

"It might," she said. "Are those Karpovitch's papers you have there? Could you do anything with them? If the conspirators are as highly placed as we think they are, there ought to be some passes."

I looked through the papers. Karpovitch had a Swiss passport which was useful; I would be able to speak German at the road-block. His photograph was unrecognizable. With luck and in the wavering light of hurricane lanterns it could have represented anyone, possibly even me. I thought that if the signatures on the passes were important enough the guards might not scan the photograph too closely.

"Well," Kristin said. "What about the passes?"

"There are a couple of papers here that look authoritative. National emblems on the letterhead, big black signature and a red seal. Looks like the Nakomda."

"Well," she said, laughing. "That ought to do, don't you think?"

I said, uncertain: "It could be a traffic ticket, for all I can tell. Well, what else is there? We can't risk getting stopped for any questioning or a search for passports. I'll try it if you're game."

"I'll do it all," she said. "You just relax and look important in the back seat. It looks better that way. I'll be your secretary and driver. In this country that's a common combination."

"How the devil do I act important?"

She laughed. "That's very easy. You keep your head motionless, eyes fixed ahead except for a flicker when the soldier shows up at the window, and say nothing. Think yourself a millionaire driving past his plant guards."

"They look stuffed."

"Exactly. See how easy it is?"

Then there were only two vehicles, a truck and a small car, between us and the striped barrier, and a soldier began to move heavily toward us, bulky in furs, with the odd, futuristic submachine gun they all seemed to wear, strapped across his chest. He gave Kristin an appreciative look and saluted, smiling. She handed him Karpovitch's documents."

"How far is it to the capital?" she asked in German, her voice pleasant. "My employer is an important Swiss comrade on special business. You know who is visiting the capital, of course?"

"Oh," the soldier said, unconcerned. "That's why we are here, to have a look at whoever's coming into town. It's a cold night but it'll be worth it."

"You mean if you catch someone suspicious?"

"Hell no," he said. "Didn't you see the speculators tossing out black-market stuff a mile back? Who do you think is going to pick it up tomorrow?"

Kristin laughed. "No wonder you don't mind the cold."

The soldier went on grinning. "Best duty there is. You don't catch me missing roadblock duty." And then, about the papers: "These look fine, miss. Drive carefully, there's a lot of ice ahead."

He raised his arm and, ahead of us, the striped pole went up and Kristin trod on the accelerator and we were through the roadblock.

twenty-one

WE GOT to the capital in early evening, with the day long gone and the night grown dark. Snow started falling again heavily. The people hurried with heads down along gloomy streets, whipped by the wind and the snow, blurred and unreal.

We drove through a pleasant, nineteenth-century suburb with its parks and gardens now hidden under snow, old royal pleasure grounds sheeted over as if for temporary storage in the owners' absence. Then into the city proper: tall houses, steep roofs and ornamented balconies and then the broad expanse of a glazed boulevard bordered with palaces.

We passed the university gates and the Fine Arts Palace and eventually the opulent façade of my hotel. On a sudden impulse I told Kristin to pull over and stop.

"But shouldn't we hurry? The embassy will be closing up for the night soon. It's almost five o'clock."

"That's the trouble. Can you imagine anyone letting us in to see the ambassador? Looking the way we look? With our kind of story?"

"But we can't waste the time asking for appointments."

"I don't intend to ask for one. I want to call the embassy and get a name. Someone we can ask for. I have a friend in New York who works for the government. I've picked up enough from him to know how to make contact with his kind of people. Maybe I'm wrong, but I don't think we'd get anywhere just barging in with a wild story about murder plots."

"We have the letters."

"I can imagine the reaction to the letters. We'll have a better chance once we have the money. Nobody can dismiss half a million dollars without, at least, a second thought. Let's see if the money has come and call the embassy right now. And maybe you would like to freshen up a bit and put on your dress. That's if you have anything left to put on after playing nurse."

"I'd like that, thank you. But do you think it's safe?"

"I don't see why not. The plotters wouldn't be looking for us here. And we're not in trouble with the authorities. On the contrary, we are trying to do them a service."

"That's right," she said. "What could happen now? This whole nightmare is over!"

"Well, not quite over."

"Well, as good as over! I can't believe that we've finally done it. Or rather that *you've* done it. I don't believe I've ever known a man like you. I don't believe that there is anything that you wouldn't be able to handle. And don't start being modest. Don't tell me how lucky we've been. Luck's had damn precious little to do with it; it was all your doing. It was your courage and ingenuity that got us here safely, and I'll be the first to crown anybody who talks about luck."

"Then I'd best keep my mouth shut," I said, also laughing. "I still remember that shoe in your room."

"It might be wise to keep it in mind," she observed.

Coming into the marble lobby I was uncomfortably aware of my battered and unshaved face, tangled hair and dirty, rumpled clothes. Kristin's appearance seemed only a little better. The desk clerk looked hostile, then astonished and finally dubious until he saw my passport and checked his registers. Even then he looked unhappy about surrendering my key.

I sent Kristin upstairs so that she could bathe and change and went to the bar. A stiff brandy helped steady me a little. I asked for the telephone and, when it was brought, called the embassy.

I could imagine the cool, marble pillars, the efficient lobby with its burnished Marine sergeant and uniformed doormen, the crisp click of high heels, and the candy-striped flag with the golden eagle—so reassuring in the foreign city. That was, indeed, another world and for a moment I wondered if I had the right to intrude.

Certainly, my reception, so close to the end of office hours, indicated that I had no rights. But I managed to impress three Midwestern women in succession with the importance of my mission and, eventually, I was explaining my implausible tale to a Mr. Stevens—speaking guardedly, conscious of an audience. I was alone in the bar but God only knew who was listening in to the conversation.

Stevens cut me off as soon as the general drift of my story began to present itself. He took my number and said he'd call back after checking with someone in another department. I offered to come to the embassy to see him but he hastily assured me that my visit would be unnecessary. What made him pause was my announcement that Kristin was with me.

I heard the murmur of a conversation at the other end: soft American voices over the insufficiently shielded telephone, and then Mr. Stevens told me that someone would shortly come to see us at the hotel. In the meantime, I was to make no more telephone calls. Was that clear?

It was and I said so, grinning to myself. Tommy Mackin had taught me several valuable lessons.

I checked with the desk clerk to see if I had any mail and found, to my surprise, a letter from Tommy and a postcard from Hubertus Pohl.

Tommy wrote that he had heard that I was taking an Eastern European vacation and that he hoped I'd be careful not to drink the water. He had some friends in the capital, he wrote, whom he had asked to keep an eye on me. He hoped I wasn't taking any silly chances on the ski slopes. Hubertus Pohl wanted to know when he would hear from me.

The bulky envelope containing Lindstrom's money hadn't been delivered. I cursed myself for not having taken Kristin's advice to send this vital piece of evidence to the embassy. The clerk's assurance that one more postal delivery would be made this evening depressed me; I was sure that I would never see that money again. I hoped the letters would be enough to intrigue whoever was coming from the embassy. I had no faith in my ability to convince the man.

Kristin came downstairs shortly afterward, looking so little like my recent fugitive companion that, at first, I didn't know what to say to her. I delayed my own cleanup to enjoy her fresh, new brightness longer; it was as good for me as the Russian brandy. And before I could go up we were joined by the embassy man.

He was tall, thin and stooped like a questionmark, with thinning gray hair. His hands were deep in his pockets, his tie was askew. He shook my hand and smiled enthusiastically at Kristin. His name, he said, was Field and he sold vacuum cleaners. The vacuum cleaners confused me for a moment; now that the time had come to tell what I knew I didn't know where or how to start.

I blurted out: "Are you CIA?"

Field smiled quietly. "I've always been a salesman of one kind or another."

Then Kristin shrugged and closed her eyes. Her face was suddenly terribly drawn. Field nodded to her, at ease like an old friend, but I thought him watchful.

"Well, Doctor, supposing you tell me all about it. Start at the beginning and just run through the whole thing step by step. I gather that you have a pressing problem but we'll save more time than we'll lose by getting the whole story on the table before we decide what to do about it."

I said: "All right."

I heard my thin tired voice begin the story and wondered where the voice was coming from; it didn't seem mine. Pohl and Per Lindstrom and the Library deal, Karpovitch, Brown, Zimstern and the fat man who died in Zimstern's store, General Danilow's ruthless but endearing nephew, Sempinski and Hetmanska Gora, the Germans and the plot, and the brutal, powerful man who had so quickly destroyed The Magician . . . none of these people and places and events seemed to have anything to do with me. Telling the story I thought that I would never believe it if Field and I were suddenly to change places. I told it all from my lunch with Tommy Mackin and the arrival of Sempinski's letter to my escape with Kristin from Hetmanska Gora and our coming here. And out of the entire account only Kristin mattered; the Pontic Tribunals were only crumbling bits of parchment; the Sempinski Affair a matter for the professionals to handle. I was no longer concerned about anything except ending the nightmare so that Kristin would be safe.

Field listened intently, his face noncommittal, but I could sense his interest wax and wane with certain names and places. The Library affair didn't interest him except for the part apparently played in it by the Nakomda officer. But the awesome general who had condemned Karpovitch, and Karpovitch himself, brought instant reactions.

He didn't tell me anything about anyone involved in my narrative but, when I was finished, he watched me for a long moment with curiously appreciative silence. Then he read Lindstrom's papers and folded them and put them almost reverently into his inside pocket.

"That's quite a story," he said and laughed uneasily. "You don't happen to be a mystery writer on the side?"

I said that I wasn't.

"We would have problems trying to convince anyone important that all this could be true."

"Then you don't believe me?"

"It doesn't matter whether I believe you. Oh, I can pass the word to some friends and they could start checking, and, in enough time, they would check it all out. But if your story is true there is no time for that. How can we be immediately convincing?"

"I thought the letters and the money . . ."

Field shrugged. He tapped his breast pocket. "I can predict the reaction to the letters, Doctor: forgery. A clumsy attempt at blackmail. Possibly an attempt to discredit an important American citizen. The ambassador is a personal friend of Senator Lindstrom. He would never believe that these letters could be genuine."

"The CIA does not report to ambassadors," Kristin said coldly.

Field nodded, smiled. "Quite right. We have the privilege of going our own way. But we must pay our rent, you know; the ambassador would have to be the first to know what's going on in his bailiwick. And you don't get to be an ambassador without a few friends of your own. He could be obstructive."

"So now we have to play nursemaid to your ambassador?"

"Be reasonable, Dr. Shippe. If the ambassador's personal friend and political idol turns out to be a traitor and a fool, the ambassador must be given the opportunity to cover himself. Otherwise he'll stall us. We can't afford delays. He must be on our side from the start."

"Would the money help?"

"It might. Can you get it?"

"It hasn't come yet. I expect it after dinner."

"You must get it for us. But tell me a few things more. You say that Senator Lindstrom is about to commit unplanned suicide?"

"That's what Karpovitch told me. He has people in London. He had no trouble murdering General Danilow there."

"And this Karpovitch is here? He is The Magician?"

"He admits it. But let me ask you something. Why are you so willing to listen to my story? You don't even know me."

"Oh, I expected to hear from you sometime. Your friend, Mr. Mackin had mentioned you to some mutual acquaintances. He said you might need looking after. I think he'd be surprised to see how well you can look after yourself but, to oblige him, we kept an eye on you."

"You had me followed to Hetmanska Gora?"

"I wish we had. But you dodged us along with everybody else after the Zimstern murder. The fat man whom Brown killed was a friend of mine."

"I thought he was a Nakomda spy tailing me because of the Library affair."

"That's how it goes sometimes. Everything is pretty much a misunderstanding until it's too late."

"And what do you think about that Nakomda officer who told me he was the man with the Library for sale? Could that be true?"

"If your talking about Colonel Danilow, the Nakomda deputy commander for the capital, I wouldn't put it past him. But he is just about the last man in this country I would trust. Next to his boss, of course. Anyway, Doctor, will you get me that money as soon as you can?"

I said I would, but there was a condition. I wanted Kristin out of this whole business immediately. If Field would take her to the embassy and protect her there from the conspirators, Karpovitch or whatever other danger could still threaten us, I would wait at the hotel until the money came.

I said: "I don't suppose you want me to deliver it to the embassy?"

Field shook his head quickly.

"That's the last place I want to see you in until this affair is over. We don't want any link between you and the embassy until everyone has a chance of smelling like a rose."

"I thought embassies are supposed to protect American citizens in trouble," Kristin said bitterly.

Field smiled. "That's the theory of it. In practice that could prove a secondary matter. As you see, I'm being quite honest about it."

She said, contemptuously: "That's nice of you. Is there still some danger?"

"I wouldn't discount the possibility," Field said.

"Then why don't you wait here and get the money? Why must we get it for you?"

"Only Dr. Shippe can pick it up without arranging a burglary. That's hard to do in a country where the authorities don't share our point of view."

"It's not hard to do in Saigon, I imagine," she said bitterly.

Field inclined his head.

She said: "You can arrange all sorts of mischief in Saigon, can't you? I remember you now. What was it you were selling in Saigon? Earthmoving equipment? I'm not going with you to any embassy. I'm staying here until we get the money."

I said: "Go with him. As a favor to me."

"What makes you think I would be any safer with him than with the other killers?" And then, with quiet intensity to Field: "What difference is there between you and Brown and Karpovitch or the others out there?"

"None, really," Field said calmly. "We are all pretty much alike if that's how you see it. But I think you know what your husband was doing in Vietnam. You didn't know at the time, of course, but you must know now."

"It makes no difference what I know," Kristin said. "What you did is what matters."

"Jan Napoji was a very dangerous man," Field said.

"So are you," Kristin said. "I have no reason to think better of you than of any other murderer."

Field said: "I'm sorry, Mrs. Napoji. I can't say more than that. I would be glad to see to it that you are taken care of at the embassy tonight. You're not directly linked with the conspiracy, as Dr. Shippe is linked, and besides we owe you something for your accident. But I can't force you to come with me."

"No you can't," she said. "And where is Dr. Shippe going to spend his time until all the plotters are jailed? Sitting in the hotel lobby like a target?"

"I'll find him a place once we have the money."

I said urgently: "You must go with him."

"Oh God, I don't know," she said. "Will you be careful, though? You can't trust these people any more than you can trust the others."

"I'll be careful. But there isn't much to worry about now."

"You know better than that."

"I'll get the money as quickly as I can and hide somewhere

until everything is over. I'll join you at the embassy in a day or two and then we can go home. That isn't much to worry about."

She said: "I just don't like it. I have a feeling that if I lose sight of you something terrible will happen."

"Nothing will happen," I assured her, then said to Field: "Well, where am I to meet you? And how do I get there?"

"When you leave the hotel don't use the front entrance. By the time you have the money your Nakomda friend may have a tail on you. Get to the Old City. There is a wine shop on the south side of the square."

"I know it," I broke in.

"I'll wait there until midnight. When you come into the wine shop, come straight to my table, without any fuss, sit down and act as if we had a date for a drink and a talk about vacuum cleaners. From that point on I'll look after things. All clear?"

I nodded.

"Then we'll leave you now," Field said. "You've given me a lot of work to do between now and when I see you later. If you don't get the money tonight just don't show up and don't stir out of the hotel."

"Why not?"

"If what you say is going to take place tomorrow, all of us are going to be dodging lynch mobs. If you're not out in the street no-body can hurt you."

It didn't occur to me to wonder, then or later, why Field had seemed so anxious to leave the hotel. An hour's wait could have provided him with Lindstrom's money. I supposed that he had a lot to do and couldn't spare the time. Kristin went with him re-luctantly. I was glad to see her in safe hands; I couldn't quite convince myself that Karpovitch was now completely out of the picture.

I told the desk clerk that I expected mail and left him my sole remaining dollar bill—a week's wages for the clerk, according to the black-market exchange rate, an hour's wage by the official scale. He was to bring the envelope to my room as soon as the mail was delivered and sorted. I wondered if I would ever see either the clerk or the envelope if he had had any idea of what the envelope contained.

My room seemed just as I had left it. Nothing looked disturbed but I had an uneasy feeling that everything I touched would transmit a signal to a hidden listener. I thought of a hot bath and the warm feather bed and the thought came close to unnerving me completely. I chose the least comfortable chair in the room and sat down. I don't know how long I sat there. Perhaps I slept for a time. Finally there was the expected knock upon my door, and when I flung the door open there was the clerk and the bulging envelope. I didn't look inside it, afraid to open it before my imagined or real observers, and equally afraid that the contents would not be the money but some kind of fraud. I put the envelope on the dresser and backed away from it and watched the trembling lamplight give the envelope a semblance of life; it appeared to breathe. My tired brain was playing tricks on me. I hoped that I would be able to hang onto my wits long enough to get the money into Field's hands.

I threw off my clothes, feeling as if I was peeling off my skin and, with it, my old identity which spelled danger. I must stink, I thought. I stole the time to wash, shave and finger my bruises, explaining the time-waste to myself as a need for cleaning-up, changing my appearance, putting on disguise. I dressed in fresh underwear, a clean soft shirt and my warmest suit. I couldn't touch my filthy furs again and stuffed the envelope into my New York topcoat pocket, and put on the topcoat, feeling momentarily free of conspiracies and Iron Curtain winters.

There were room-service waiters in the corridor, wheeling a guest's dinner cart and champagne bucket from the service elevator, and I took the stairs to the floor below so as to have the service elevator to myself. I got out in the basement and left the hotel through the freight entrance without seeing anyone, as Field had wanted me to. The envelope felt incredibly heavy in my pocket. Each moving shadow increased my alarm.

The snow came down like an avalanche in the alley behind

the hotel; I could see nothing ten feet in front of my face. All lights were blurred and diffused into an unreal orange glare, forms were dim. People loomed through the thick white snow curtain like wavering ghosts.

I rounded the hotel building and came into the main boulevard without a thought of taxis, and headed north toward Castle Square, guided by the statue of an ancient king that rose high above the rooftops in that part of town. Floodlights made the lone bronze figure appear suspended in an inward flame, unsupported above the falling mass of snow. I was aware of many men moving near me but I couldn't see them. And then I was in the Old City again and the ancient houses closed about me with their welcome sense of permanence; a partial reassurance.

I supposed that I was quite completely frozen at this point, moving by instinct, numb; feeling nothing, quite sure that I was being followed. I wondered which of my many possible pursuers had picked up my trail and hurried, feeling time narrowing about me, into Market Square, then down the stone steps into the cellar wine shop where music was playing.

The place was crowded. I peered through the smoke until I saw Field waving from a corner table, and made my way toward him, hearing a cacophony of languages around me. I hung my topcoat on a hook behind Field and sat down across the table from him.

He said, with unexpected bonhommie: "Hi there, O.H."

I said: "Been waiting long?"

It seemed like the correct question for the role I thought we were playing.

"Oh, maybe an hour."

"Who are all these people?"

"The world's press in for the big show tomorrow."

"You mean the Chairman's speech?"

"That's the one. The speech is billed as a major Soviet policy announcement. It looks as if the whole world had been invited to a grandstand seat . . . I'm glad you gave us that call when you did."

"You mean that all your doubts about my story are resolved?"

"There's no doubt about it."

"What settled it for you?"

"We heard from the London office as soon as I got back to the shop. I had to give your fiancée some bad news about her uncle. It seems he just couldn't take the strain, just as you said he would not. Nobody could have made that up without prior knowledge."

"So you got things moving?"

"Right away. The word went out from head-office an hour ago; we're all busy as hell. But the competition's had a long time to dig in and it's hard to uproot them."

I said, thinking about Lindstrom but unable, even now, to drum up sympathy for him: "So they did it, did they? That makes it look as if they're going on with their plan despite everything."

Field said: "It looks that way. They must be pretty sure of themselves. But right now I have a couple of other small problems and finding you a place to stay is one of them."

I started laughing, too exhausted to resist hysteria.

"So you didn't need the money, after all? I had to play the part of a clay pigeon for nothing? And don't give me that bit about there being no danger to speak of. That was all right to set Kristin's mind at rest, but you and I both know how much danger I'm in. You people really are a ruthless lot."

"Of course we need the money. We can't have the competition get its hands on it, can we?"

"What are the chances of stopping the plot?"

"Too damn tight, but we'll do our best. The trouble is that our government and this one aren't on speaking terms, so we can't take our story to the local boys. We're trying to do the whole business ourselves and we're damn short-handed. Anyway, I hope this report cheers you up a bit?"

I said, tired: "It's a nice change to have everything in professional hands. How's Kristin?"

Field looked away, then, suddenly evasive. I waited, feeling suddenly sick with premonition. A waiter came up and Field quickly ordered two double Russian brandies, crackers and caviar.

After the waiter left, I said: "I asked about Kristin."

Field nodded: "I heard you."

"Well, what about her?"

"Fact is . . . the fact is she changed her mind about staying with us. We couldn't hold her. She said she was going back to the hotel to wait with you for the money."

"You let her do that, knowing the place might be watched? My God, she was right about you!"

"Stop shouting. You'll attract attention."

"The hell with attention! You and I are going right back to the hotel. I'm sure somebody got onto me there, and if she walked into any kind of trap there . . ."

Field said, his voice calm but firm: "Shut up and keep still. I tried to argue with her but she didn't listen."

"Oh, that's just fine," I said. "That makes everything perfectly all right. She was damn right that we couldn't trust you."

Field said: "Hey, listen, don't you have that twisted around a bit? Who walked out on whom? Stop worrying. If your colonel friend picks her up before we get to her it won't do her any harm. The Boss is her late uncle's friend, remember? We'll have somebody at the proper place the first thing in the morning."

"And what if it's somebody else who picks her up first? Like Karpovitch?"

"Listen," Field said, no longer cold, smiling, his eyes sad but friendly. "I know how you feel. But you mustn't complicate the situation. It could be a lot worse. She has her papers back, she's all in the clear. There is no reason for anybody to hold her after the Boss gets on the phone tomorrow. Now relax, sit back, listen to the music. Enjoy your canapés, they taste pretty good. You've more than earned a little relaxation."

"But dammit, Kristin . . ."

The brandy clouded whatever clear thoughts I had had, except a feeling of immeasurable fear, despair and an anxiety that exceeded any worry I had ever had.

"She'll be fine, I tell you," Field went on. "She may get a bit frightened if Danilow picks her up but that's all that'll happen. When an American citizen gets in trouble in a foreign country, even a country that is not as friendly as it might be, there's usually little to worry about if the embassy takes immediate action."

"I've had an example of the care that I could expect."

"You're not the niece of a Per Lindstrom, friend," Field said reasonably. "Besides, at the moment the ambassador is very anxious to make a good impression. As for Karpovitch, don't worry about him; he has to stay low until he has managed to get his demoralized Krauts together again."

"How long will that take?"

"At least a day, Doctor. By that time everything will be over. So for God's sake disconnect that fuse and relax. That's it, that's much better. Want another drink?"

I shook my head, too dispirited to care. Field looked casually around, sighed with satisfaction and signaled a waiter.

"Well, thank God the shouting is all over, anyway. I don't think anybody noticed . . . they're all too busy anticipating the Chairman's speech and reshaping the world. I'll make a phone call in a minute and see if our people have some news for you. Will that help?"

"Yes," I said. "Oh, I don't know. I'm too tired to think."

"That's good. Don't think. Let me do your thinking. I'm far more concerned about you than Kristin at the moment. Everybody seems to be looking for you tonight. Your friend, the colonel, is turning the capital upside down to get to you before anybody else. His people have barged into just about every place where I thought I could hide you. I'm embarrassed to admit that he must have known my business for a long, long time."

I didn't want to think about the Nakomda man or the Romanowski Library or anything else. Field went on, reflectively:

"Why should he be so interested in you? There are just too many unknowns in this case; it's the damnedest can of worms I've ever come across. Maybe we ought to let him find you. Maybe he had been on the level all along and you have an ally you don't know about. Danilow would be a good ally to have in this situation. We'd have no trouble stopping the conspiracy if he took a hand."

"Then why not tell him all about it?"

Field looked shocked. "You want *us* to cooperate wih *them?* I wouldn't trust Danilow if he gave me directions to the men's room. What an idea . . . the Nakomda and the CIA working together to save the Soviet Chairman! I almost think you might have something there; it's just ridiculous enough to be the best way."

I shrugged, weary beyond reason. "Do what you want."

"What I want is to have you on ice, out of the way, until this mess is over. I guess it'll have to be the embassy, after all. But I've got to have your word that you won't try to beat it out of there, like your girl friend."

I said: "Why don't you just leave me alone?"

He sighed. "It's a tempting thought. Except that you'd make things difficult for me if you disappeared. Well, Doctor, what about playing ball and going to the embassy with me? Do I have your word that you'll stay put?"

"I don't know," I said. "Give me time to think."

"There isn't any, friend. You know what's involved. I know it's easy to give advice but you're in no shape to make any decisions and I want you out of this business right now."

"All right," I said. I didn't want to think even if there had been something that I could have done about the chaos of disjointed images and confusion in my tired head. Whatever resolution I might have had throughout this whole affair had finally left me.

"Fine," Field said. "You just sit right here. I'm going to telephone the shop about your girl friend. That should cheer you up a bit."

But suddenly his grin dissolved and he said sharply, urgently: "Where's the money?"

"What?" I said.

"The money, Doctor. Give it to me now."

"It's in the coat," I said. "Behind you."

He got up and quickly put on my coat, pointing to his own. "We'll trade for now, if you don't mind," he said. "Just in case the roof caves in or something. And remember, whatever happens you have nothing to worry about from this point on."

I nodded and Field left at once. I watched him walk away among the crowded tables, and suddenly I knew that something was terribly wrong. The dancing couples who had been moving like ships in a fog to the plastic strains of *Winchester Cathedral* began to disappear. Talk died down rapidly and the music blared in the sudden silence. I saw Field's stooped figure vanish behind a group of waiters near the kitchen door.

And then I was aware that a group of men in leather trench coats had appeared at the main door, and that another group was moving quickly through the room toward me. I half-rose as they came around my table, looking desperately for Field, who would know what to do, and they grouped around me so that the room, the smoke, the people and the silence were obscured by the blackness of the polished leather. Someone took my right elbow and someone the left, and I was propelled swiftly across the room among the hushed tables and up the stone steps to the bitterly cold street where a small black passenger car without markings stood with open doors.

I was inside the car, crushed between two heavy men with impassive faces, and before I could gather a fragment of my wits about me, the doors were slammed shut and we were rushing through the streets. My silent captors did not look at me.

PART FIVE:

The End of the Affair

twenty-two

THE CITY WALLS were gone in this part of the bleak antiquity but the huge gates still stood astride their narrow streets, guarded by the barbican that Mongols had stormed in the eleventh century, and the gray walls and towers of a royal castle perched on a black rock, as they had hung suspended over the heart of the city for a thousand years. Twelve hundred years of human progress were on display here: from loopholed barbicans and bronze bells cast from Turkish cannon, to the roar of a turbojet slanting invisibly overhead, and the headlong rush of the black car which carried me, as so many terrified captives must have been carried through these ancient streets, to a threatening destination. The city was like an old family house, in the same hands for fifty-seven generations, built to defy time, furnished with what each generation thought best in its time; each adding something but subtracting nothing, finding room for its own fancies without disturbing whatever it inherited along with the house. It was a world far removed in concept from my own, and yet I was ironically aware of how hard I had tried to reproduce this world in my apartment with its books, scrolls, old maps rolled up in Morocco, my brass telescope and Dick Turpin pistol, the chandelier, Flemish tapestry, dark oak and beeswax candles, goulash and red wine. I had found so much to resent and avoid in my world and had sought the sense of permanence that history could give me, and here I was: enveloped by history and longing for the reassurance of my own time. I looked at my frightened face in the rear-view mirror, half-hoping that the rumpled image would give me a clue. But the face was a suddenly unfamiliar arrangement of mismatched oddities: gray eyes puffed with anxiety, broad mouth drooping at the corners, ears fattened by the glow of frostbite and my prize-fighter's nose—a souvenir of freshman intramural boxing. It was an incongruous element in an otherwise ordinary and undistinguished face, a kind of badge, like the names I had been given with more hope than aptness: Oliver Hazard Shippe. There had been an attempt at school to call me "Battle" Shippe but it hadn't lasted beyond freshman year. Now friends, and even strangers, called me O.H. as if the appropriation of the first and middle names of the defender of Lake Erie, a distant ancestor, were too broad a joke for politeness. I had accepted the abbreviation as a discretion; I had not earned the names and I had wished that I had really done something to earn the nose, something more than to walk into a boxing glove held up with more hope than skill by a fellow freshman. Since that time I had walked into few fists of any kind; each year there seemed to be fewer to walk into in my world.

The thought of secret tribunals was only a dim shadow in my mind. I felt an odd sense of exaltation mixed with my bewilderment and fear, as if my seizure had decided something, given me direction. Terror would come later, I knew, along with despair, but I didn't think about them in the speeding car. Wrapped in the icy darkness, rocked along the silent, secret streets, I could feel only a weary if anxious relief. The music of the interrupted dance moved sluggishly in my head.

I wondered if Field had noticed my arrest; he could have hardly been able to help seeing it, everyone had seen it. He had, in fact, made himself scarce with suspicious speed as soon as the Nakomda men had appeared in the restaurant. Perhaps this had been regular procedure for CIA agents, but I could not help thinking myself abandoned and betrayed.

I wondered where the Nakomda men were taking me, a gradually crystallizing curiosity, largely academic at the start. Prison? It could be prison but I didn't think so if, as I had begun to suppose, Colonel Danilow had had anything to do with my arrest. This was his district, after all, and he was in charge, and he had told me that he would be able to protect me in the capital, and there was more reason now than ever before why he should want to protect me. The Sempinski Affair would probably destroy him; its threat would make his defection urgent, and only I could get him the money he needed. The more I thought about it the more I believed that the cynical colonel could have been everything that he had said he was. He had known everything about the Romanowski Library. All his warnings about Sempinski and Hetmanska Gora had proved so terribly correct. Nothing would have happened to me if I had stayed in the capital, as Danilow had urged me to do, if I had not panicked after my early-morning interview with him and run to Sempinski.

Seen in this context, my present situation made a sort of sense. Danilow could have sent his men after me to get me safely hidden from the conspirators; I was his only key to money and defection. Thus, instead of being a catastrophe, my arrest could be a form of salvation.

That was the way to think of it. This thought meant hope. Hell, I thought, suddenly ebullient, it was more than hope; it could be the solution to everything if Danilow, with all his connections and manpower, could be enlisted to help against the plotters. He could be drafted to help in the crisis if for no other reason than to save himself and to keep secret the Library affair.

The Nakomda car slowed down, hissing like a rubber-tire hearse through the empty streets, wrapped in its own peculiar darkness that seemed to make it invisible. It stopped before a heavy gate of wrought iron reinforced by steel bars, and rolled between striped sentry boxes into a floodlit courtyard full of hurrying men. My captors pulled me out of the car and herded me up long stairs, through lobbies where typists and clerks were busy and along innumerable echoing corridors full of armed men in uniforms and civilian clothes. I felt as if I was in the middle of an armed camp on the eve of battle. The vast building which formed three sides of the courtyard seemed an amalgam of a corporation headquarters, medieval fortress, barracks and a communications center; a humming, clattering world of modern machinery and old stone. I supposed myself in the headquarters of the Secret Police, still not as worried as I might have been, although some of my earlier ebullience evaporated. The huge guards set a headlong pace and, tall as I was and used to striding out, I had a difficult time keeping up with them. The stairs rose and fell, long corridors unfolded becoming gradually more luxurious, and finally there was a kind of modern opulence about me that made me think of a Sultan's anterooms transported into the heart of an industrial empire. I was now in the executive section of the building and my hopes went up. Soon I would be face-to-face with Danilow, a possible ally. I didn't need the guards' impatient urging to hurry me along.

My escort halted before a heavy door of polished walnut gleaming with brass fittings, and here the sentries seemed to glitter more brightly than at any other door. The double doors swung open and I was quick-marched through a vast but delicately hushed office where uniformed men and women worked behind steel desks, and then there was another portal with sentries who cradled submachine guns in their arms. Behind them lay a richly paneled room hung with brocade draperies.

"Inside," one of my escort said in sibilant English. The sound of English was shockingly unpleasant in this place.

I stepped into the inner office, feeling the soft carpeting sink under my feet, confused by the oriental profusion of barbaric luxury, Chinese vases, Persian hangings, rich rows of books in leather, ornate furniture. I saw the battlement of the enormous desk at the far end of the room and the men grouped behind and beside it. They stared at me without curiosity or interest, as they had done when I had caught their eyes in Sempinski's Library. I searched for Danilow with suddenly anxious and impatient eyes but I did not find him. And then I saw the man who sat, dark in a brilliant uniform, apart from the others. I thought that he would always be apart, no matter where he sat, reducing all others; stained with darkness in the alcove formed by the angle of a massive fireplace, looking just as he had when I had first glimpsed him in the leathery gloom of an armchair at Hetmanska Gora. No one spoke within the undefined borders of his presence; even the air around him seemed cowed into stillness as if a deep mesh of a transluscent material, an impenetrable barrier of energized crystals, hung between him and the other men. He drew the others despite their apartness as though the barrier around him was their sustaining force. I thought of moths and fire, but that was wrong; fire had warmth, this man's presence provided an icy chemical incandescence. It seeped through the invisible wall into every corner.

I looked at the graven, gray-hued face with its vertical furrows and felt all my composure, strength, courage, or resolution abandon me at once.

I was lost and knew it, and I also knew that everything was lost. Nothing that Field or anyone else could do, could save me, or prevent tomorrow's public murder and its consequences, if the Nakomda itself was in on the plot. No miracle could take me out of the hands of this man who had destroyed Karpovitch with such ease; even Danilow had been afraid of him.

So it had all been for nothing, I thought. I would have fallen if two of my guards had not held me up.

Everything was finally in place and clear but the explanation would do no one any good. I would never be able to tell anyone what I now knew. I waited quietly for the conspirators to tell me what they wanted from me.

Someone was speaking to me. I listened with polite attention; it seemed suddenly important to be courteous now that all my other principles had failed me.

Yes, I said quietly. I was Oliver Hazard Shippe, aged forty-two, American, antiquities consultant. No, I was not an American intelligence officer; the idea would be quite preposterous. I had never been connected with any agency of the United States. No, I would not admit that I had violated the hospitality of the country or any of its laws, and I had not been officially involved in subversive activities anywhere. But yes, it could be said that I had been unofficially involved. I had come to the country to visit Sempinski and had, thus, come upon the conspiracy. Yes, I quite realized that I was on trial.

I didn't waste either my time or that of my judges by claiming the prerogatives of a visitor; the embassy had no value in these circumstances. Besides, I realized that the trial was a game with a specific goal. The goal had nothing to do with either law or justice.

The man who read my indictment in a language that I didn't understand wore the close-shaved, disciplined look of a Russian officer, his voice unmarred by either inflection or emotion, and the small, neat, murmuring civilian who droned a translation provided counterpoint so that their joint performance had the quality of a musical arrangement. They did not look at me and my eyes were drawn as remorselessly as theirs to the brooding figure of the general which loomed, impassive and motionless, out of the ecclesiastic shadows of his tall-backed armchair. He smoked a Russian cigarette in an ivory holder, as he had done in my room in Hetmansaka Gora, and the pale drifting of the smoke rings provided the sole movement in the air around him. This was the man who, Danilow had told me, used to throw people into locomotive boilers.

The voices of the military prosecutor and, I supposed, the civilian counsel for the defense, provided a bizarre background for my thoughts.

"This is a special tribunal of the National Security Commission of the People's Democratic Republic," my defender droned. "You are charged with conspiring with persons both known and unknown, to prevent the execution of a known deviationist from the original Marxist-Leninist revolutionary principles, with an attempt to halt the progress of the democratic peoples' revolution and with interference in the internal affairs of the People's Party. You are charged with having committed these crimes against the people with full foreknowledge and of your own free will, with the connivance of the capitalist espionage apparatus, and traitors both known and unknown, and with the assistance of, and in service of, foreign-based reactionary-terrorist organizations and, both directly and indirectly, in the service of the espionage and subversion agencies of the United States. You are hereby informed that witnesses have been examined and depositions taken and that you have been found guilty as charged on each count of each charge, and that the legally prescribed sentence of the tribunal on each count of each charge is death. You will be informed in due time as to any clemency provisions allowed to condemned criminals by regulations governing the tribunal. Do you wish to make a statement at this time?"

I said: "No, thank you. Are you my defender?"

The droning voice went on as if I hadn't interrupted.

"You are informed that the privilege of examining prosecution witnesses is not extended to criminals condemned on capital charges. But because of the extraordinary nature of this special tribunal and its attendant circumstances, by permission of the convening authority and president, General Karol Rauss, here present, you will be supplied at this time with the names of the witnesses who testified against you. These are: General Karol Rauss, here present; and Kristin Napoji, widow, not present."

"I don't believe that," I said.

The defense counsel frowned with obvious irritation.

"The tribunal is not concerned with what a condemned criminal believes. However, because of the extraordinary circumstances attendant on this case, you are permitted to confront the witnesses if you wish. Do you wish to confront General Karol Rauss?"

"I believe I am confronting him," I said quietly. I nodded toward the silent figure seated in the corner.

"That is correct. Do you wish to confront the witness Napoji?"

"Yes," I said. So they had her, too.

"You are warned that you are not permitted to speak to the witness who is, herself, a condemned criminal."

"What are the charges against her?"

"That is not your business. However, again due to the nature of this special tribunal, and by permission of the presiding officer, I am allowed to inform you that her crime is treason."

I said, disbelieving: "Ridiculous. Your country has no jurisdiction over her."

"Under the law she is a citizen of this country by marriage. She has committed crimes against her people."

"You are not her people!"

"The prisoner will be silent!" defense counsel shouted.

"Very well," I said.

The small civilian no longer translated whatever the military prosecutor was saying, as if the prosecutor's speech had nothing to do with either him or me, as if those harsh, clipped words addressed to the silent group behind the desk were unrelated to me. All semblance of reality slipped from the proceedings.

"The prisoner is warned to follow rules of conduct governing condemned criminals. He will speak only if directly addressed by an officer of the tribunal with the president's permission. I am now directed to inform you of clemency provisions allowed in your case. The sentence of death passed upon you by this special tribunal may be commuted to imprisonment at the discretion of the presiding officer. I point out that this is an extraordinary act of clemency in itself, under the circumstances."

I said: "You must want something very badly from me. Under the circumstances."

"You are impertinent," defense counsel said.

"Does this clemency extend to Mrs. Napoji?"

"Are you trying to bargain?"

"It seems that I'm in the position to do so," I said.

Neither the military prosecutor, nor the general, nor any of the others seemed to react or even notice this exchange between the civilian and myself. But the civilian became agitated.

"You have been warned about speaking only when addressed. Another such breach of prescribed conduct will be severely punished. But I may answer you, under the circumstances, that such clemency may be authorized at the discretion of the presiding officer. Such clemency is contingent on your conduct before this tribunal. You are obliged to make complete confession of your crimes, naming all persons, agencies and governments who have participated in your crimes. Such a confession has been prepared for your signature. Will you sign it now?"

"No," I said.

The military prosecutor finished his speech abruptly and now turned toward me, and I became aware of the newly charged atmosphere in the room. The general's huge head turned slowly in the shadows and I felt his icy eyes upon me.

"You!" he said.

The small civilian reacted as if he had been stabbed.

"Sir?"

"Make it clear to him."

"Yes, sir," the small man said. And to me: "You are warned that your refusal is tantamount to a dismissal of any possibility of clemency either for yourself or the criminal Napoji. Is that understood?"

I said nothing.

The small man said: "Silence is agreement."

I said: "I won't sign anything."

The general shrugged and made a brief gesture. A side door was opened and Kristin was led in between guards.

Her face was dead-white, and the shadows under her eyes had the dark stain of those who are bereft of hope. She looked up at me and her eyes narrowed as if she was unable to bear even the softly muted lights in the tribunal room.

It didn't matter any longer what would happen to the world tomorrow afternoon. The world was an enormous concept; too broad and impersonal for me to comprehend. And it was presumptuous of any man to think that anything he did or didn't do could have a permanent effect or bearing on the world. I could continue to resist the plotters as a kind of patriot, but I could not make decisions as a patriot, only as a man. Only Kristin truly mattered to me. I could not trust anything the conspirators might promise but I could not allow her to be killed without some effort on my part to save her, no matter how unreasonable and how hopeless.

I had robbed the plotters of all their evidence and now they wanted me to replace it by confession. There was the possibility that if I replaced it Kristin would not be killed. It was up to me whether I allowed her this shade of opportunity to live.

What would confessions matter anyway? What mattered was my own decision. I could not hide from making it. Nothing could intervene to save me from the need to make the decision, whether or not there really was a chance that the conspirators would not kill her.

Kristin was gone from the room as quickly as she had appeared in it, taken out by her guards. I was alone with the conspirators and with myself.

I heard the prosecuting officer, the little civilian and the somber men behind the desk continuing with the ritual but I paid no attention. I wondered why they had bothered to put on the show. Why did they need these vestiges of legality to blackmail and murder? Why not simply forge my signature and put a bullet in my head? Was it because men who are above the law always took care to shield themselves with law? Perhaps they never would put a bullet in my head but break me and keep me as a witness to my signature, their only evidence. That too was possible.

Time was no friend, no matter how much time they might give me for reflection and I knew that they wouldn't give me much. The ritual came to its conclusion. The prosecutor finished whatever he was saying. The officers conferred. The general rose and slowly left the room. The guards formed their moving wall around me and led me outside. Then it was the former ascent-to-luxury in reverse: the well-appointed rooms and corridors fell away, darkened, became colder. Passages narrowed, grayed. There was an elevator falling like a stone, and then an icy coldness and the dead white light of an unshaded bulb trapped in a wire cage and a steel cell without furniture or windows. The cell door boomed with hollow echoes, closing.

twenty-three

TIME PASSES. Night flows on. The muffled sounds of prison have sunk into silence, the anxious silence of unsleeping men staring into darkness.

My thoughts were calm and orderly like corpses in a morgue; I could examine them at leisure, almost without feeling. I thought, at times, that I could hear footsteps in the corridor and waited with quiet resignation for the conspirators to come with their confession for my signature and, perhaps, with their instruments of torture.

I had got away with it too easily so far; bluffing and luck were an unrealistic set of crutches in this league. I had expected that Karpovitch would have had me beaten to within a millimeter of my life at Hetmanska Gora—a realistic price to pay for my deception in the matter of the missing briefcase—but there had been no beating. Granted that Karpovitch may have had too much on his mind with his own life in danger, and also granted that it wouldn't have occurred to him that I could have outsmarted him even by accident, and further granted that my lie had been temporarily supported by the absence of the German whom I had accused of taking the briefcase, sheer frustration at being deprived of his moment of triumph, and his humiliation before the general, should have been enough for Karpovitch to vent his spleen on me. I had no reason to suppose that Karpovitch, despite his brilliant mind, was any less a vicious animal than his assorted Germans. My bluff had worked too easily. But now I could expect no bluff to succeed. I could expect all the punishment that I had escaped before.

I thought about Kristin, with whom life would have promised so much good. I didn't think that there was any hope to save her. I hated the conspirators; all plotters of all sides and factions. It had been their games that had got out of hand, and people who had had nothing to do with conspiracies would be paying for them. Well, perhaps the innocent non-participants could have done something to prevent the games; I didn't know. But I didn't want to feel the blame for what would happen the next afternoon; it was easier to hate the Rausses, the Karpovitchs, the Fieldses and even the Sempinskis for starting their games.

Midnight came and passed. There were no more footsteps or other illusions about sound. And then I did hear footsteps: a quick energetic echo that stopped outside my door. So they have come, I thought, and began to shiver.

I heard the bolts slide free on the other side and then the door opened. I saw the Nakomda uniform, the boots and the badges. The man's face was shadowed by the dark peak of his military cap. Then I recognized Danilow leaning toward me with an extended hand.

"Quick," he said. "On your feet. We have no time to waste."

What kind of trap was this going to be? I got to my feet. The colonel put both hands on my shoulders to steady me.

"Have you been questioned? Beaten? Have they given you an injection? Anything like that?"

"What? No . . ."

"Can you walk?"

I nodded.

"Come on, then. The guard will be away for only two minutes."

Danilow looked out into the corridor, then went through the door and motioned to me to follow.

We came out of the cell into a white-tiled antiseptic passage, and now I could hear the soft humming of an air ventilation system and the drone of hidden generators. So there had been sound all along; the silence had been an artificial lie. They would have tried to rob me of sound, of course; it was an old technique. You take away sound and a man's consciousness of time and, eventually, you dislocate a man's identity. Once you have undermined a man's identity you can make him do anything you wish. The corridor was cut by many black steel doors. There were no guards in sight but I thought that they were probably watching. I followed the quick-striding officer down the tiled tunnel; I didn't care where he was taking me. This, like everything else I could expect in this place, could only be some kind of trick. I didn't believe that this could be any kind of rescue. To believe that would mean starting to believe in the impossible again.

The corridors unfolded in surprising turns and loops and unexpected length. I tried counting cell doors just to keep some kind of a hold on reality but there were too many and any figure beyond ten seemed astronomical to me.

Then the condition of the corridor changed. It became drab and the cell doors gaped vacantly open. This must have been the old, abandoned section of the ancient prison: old brick and crumbling stone and stale air. We seemed to be falling, as if on a gently sloping ramp. The corridors narrowed. Soon we could barely walk abreast through the tight passage between glistening wet walls. And then there was a rusted iron door that groaned and grated as if a long time unused, and then our footsteps were echoing under the vaulted ceiling of an ancient sewer. The air was cold here, but redolent of antique stenches, and the pavement under our feet was slippery with old slime. Rats moved in cautious masses at the edge of vision, running before us like a shadow. I almost laughed with pleasure, seeing the familiar red pinpoint lights staring at me again, unblinking, in the dark.

"Stop here a moment," the colonel said.

He went on alone and I watched his shadow melt into the general darkness. I heard the officer's grating footsteps, then a clang of iron and the deep breathing of a silent struggle with a weight. Then came the clatter of cast iron rolling over cobblestones and a flood of suddenly icy air. Fresh air? I couldn't understand the meaning of this portent. The colonel's voice came to me from somewhere on the ceiling.

"How does that smell to you?"

"What . . ."

"The fresh air. Smell good? This is an old sewer, a road we used during the occupation. The Germans used to pour gasoline down on us through the gratings. Well, come on Shippe, climb up."

I stepped forward and walked into the bottom of an iron ladder. My shins burned from the sudden contact with the icy iron. I began to climb. Each rung was solid with a coat of ice. Each scorched my hands. I looked up and saw an impossible star winking at me from the roof of darkness. The colonel's impatient voice urged me on.

Then I was out of the manhole and standing in an open street among silent ruins, gaunt pyramids of brick, a snowswept wilderness where the wind made plaintive weeping sounds as if lost generations had come there to make their complaint. The obelisk of the Heroes of the Ghetto rose above the rubble.

"Are you all right?"

This was Danilow again. I felt the firm touch of his hand on my shoulder.

"I'm all right. Where are you taking me?"

Danilow pulled me toward a small car hidden under the arch of an ancient gateway. I moved toward the car as if that, too, was less an undeclared friend than an enemy. And suddenly the rear door of the car was flung open and Kristin was there . . . running toward me . . . putting her arms around me. She was laughing. The colonel's hand applied heavy pressure to my shoulder blades.

I said: "I don't understand this. What is going on?"

I thought I could detect a note of weary hysteria in Kristin's broken laughter.

"He got us out! He's on our side, darling."

"Don't trust him," I said. "We can't afford to trust anyone."

"Get in! Get in!" Danilow urged me impatiently and we got into the car. The car lurched across rubble.

"Where are you taking us?" I said to Danilow.

The colonel laughed softly. Kristin said:

"We're on our way to a hideout where we'll be safe while the colonel tries to do something about the plot. I've told him everything I knew about it."

"You told him . . ."

Danilow went on laughing, then said:

"Dr. Shippe has learned to be cautious. He thinks that Rauss is going to pop out of the trunk at any moment. And he still doesn't know what to make of me."

I said: "You can't blame me for that."

He said with deceptive lightness: "I found out where they had you locked up only about an hour ago. Mrs. Napoji is more spectacular, she was easier to track down. There was no time to organize anything properly but sometimes an *ad hoc* action is as good as a plot of a year. I ought to beat you to a pulp for causing me this trouble."

"I thought someone would get around to that by this time."

Danilow laughed.

"Do you feel deprived? If you had stayed in your cell four hours longer you would have had all the beatings you could wish for. I told you when the Nakomda does its questioning. The nadir of oblivion, remember? The hour before dawn."

"I can hardly remember anything you've told me."

"That's obvious. Don't you Americans ever do what you're told?"

"We're not conditioned to instant obedience."

"That's also obvious. But, I suppose, if you had done what I told you and stayed in the capital, I would never have had the pleasure of meeting Mrs. Napoji."

"Or finding out about the Sempinski Affair," Kristin reminded him.

"Yes, there is that. I'm damned if I know what to do about it."

I said quietly: "Why should you want to do anything about it?"

Danilow made a rude, impatient gesture. "The situation must

be restored to normal. Rauss must be muzzled. We still have some unfinished business, Dr. Shippe, remember?"

"Good God, are you still thinking about smuggling out the Library?"

"Do you have anything more pleasant to think about? I've survived a great many plots and conspiracies but this Sempinski business is too much. I've told you, it's time to retire. I don't want any post-assassination hysteria to interfere with that."

I said: "I didn't think you were helping us for any high-flown motives."

He laughed. "I haven't had one of those since my sixteenth birthday. Well, is our deal still on?"

It was my turn to laugh. "How on earth would I know? Lindstrom is dead."

"But his money is waiting in Sweden. Your Mr. Pohl has the authority to spend it. So let's clean up this Sempinski mess and get on with something profitable, eh? I've been doing a lot of reading lately about growing coffee."

I shrugged, said: "Have it your own way. I haven't thought much about the Library lately."

"I can well believe it. But you can take another look at it, that'll revive your interest. We're going to the lodge where you went with Zimstern. And, for God's sake, stay there, will you? You've given me quite enough to do without searching the country for you again."

I nodded.

"How are you going to move against the plotters?"

"That's a good question. Rauss is well entrenched even though most of the Nakomda is unaware of the conspiracy. But that's neither a help nor a hindrance to us. I must go to the Premier about this and I can't go empty handed; my word simply wouldn't be good enough to overthrow Rauss."

"Can you get to see the Premier?"

Danilow laughed without amusement.

"In this uniform I can get in bed with him if I wish. The trouble is to convince him that I am not out of my mind."

"There are some papers that might help," I said.

"Well, I don't have them. But you had better tell me the whole story. Something new might occur to me. Your young woman was very impressive but she was so concerned about you that her account of your adventures was more a paean of praise for your ingenuity and courage than an intelligence report."

"All right," I said.

Danilow listened carefully and, when I had finished, I knew what troubled him. My story, even if it could be believed without evidence, was simply hearsay. It would not be enough for him to take to his government.

I hesitated for only a moment.

"There is a man called Field at the Embassy. Do you know him?"

"Counterespionage happens to be my business."

"He has the letters and the money."

"It'll be nice to see five hundred thousand dollars. So you propose that Mr. Field and I join forces to save the Soviet Chairman? The novelty itself should be enough to get us to the Premier."

"But will Field work with you?"

"He won't have a choice. You can leave that part of it to me."

"There's one other thing," I said. "I know who killed your uncle. It was The Magician. Your uncle found out his identity. His name is Karpovitch. He's somewhere in the capital. He's after us because he wants the money."

"Good God," the colonel said. He laughed. "Is there anything that you haven't found out? If I ever come out of retirement and back into the business I'll only employ amateurs."

Then he said softly: "Yes, it must have been Karpovitch."

I said: "What now?"

"I found your Mr. Brown in the capital at about the time you were being arrested," Danilow said. "It was a routine matter of an unreported alien, with routine surveillance. But we lost Brown almost as soon as we had found him. He disappeared with another man. It must have been Karpovitch."

"Then Brown is also out of the conspiracy. What do you think he and Karpovitch will do?"

"Search for you and the money, I suppose. It might not take them long to pick up your trail."

"How could they do that?"

"Have you forgotten that Karpovitch knows about the Library? Zimstern might have told him where the Library is hidden. It won't take The Magician long to add two and two once he knows about your escape. And, don't forget, he might still have friends on Rauss's staff. We must take care of him, permanently, as soon as we can."

The sun rose shortly afterward. The morning was cold. We entered the forest. Danilow stopped the car at the edge of the clearing where the narrow trail sunk under the snow. I could see no track on the crisp, unmarred surface of the snow to show that Zimstern and I had ever been here. We walked the rest of the way to the hunting lodge, carrying the provisions and equipment that Danilow had brought in the trunk of the car. There was a rifle wrapped in an army blanket, canned food, a kerosene lamp and a transistor radio.

"It's not for entertainment," Danilow explained. "It's to tell you what is happening in the capital. If I fail to stop Rauss and the conspiracy you'll have to make some rapid decisions on your own. I won't be able to warn you."

I thanked Danilow for this thoughtfulness but he only gave me an amused glance and shrugged.

"Thoughtfulness has nothing to do with it," he said.

Inside the lodge, the dry chill of the crypt enveloped us at once.

"Quick," Kristin said, shivering but smiling. "Light the fire."

"No fire," Danilow said. "The sight of smoke might bring someone here. And this place is as dry as a tinderbox. It would go up like a bomb at the first misplaced spark."

"The Library would be quite safe in the cellar," I observed.

"What good is the Library to me unless you are safe?"

"You have a point there," I said.

"You have to do the best that you can with blankets to keep warm. There are more in the car."

I laughed. "Is there anything that you forgot?"

He said, suddenly annoyed: "Lots of things. But the less I tell you about that the better for your peace of mind."

"All right, no fires," I conceded. "What else should I know?"

"I'm going to leave you this rifle and my pistol. Do you know how to use them?"

"I've never seen as many guns as I've had thrust at me, one way or another, in the past few days. What will I need guns for?"

Danilow said, impatiently abrupt: "For . . . emergencies. Protection. Rauss knows by now about your escape. In the next few hours he'll turn this country upside down looking for you and Kristin."

"Didn't you say that only a small circle within the Nakomda is in on the plot?"

"What difference does that make? Rauss can call out the entire army for a manhunt, and keep his reasons to himself. He doesn't depend on just his fellow plotters. What a fool you are, Shippe! Did you really think that you were out of trouble?"

I said nothing because I had begun to think so. Danilow went on:

"And then there's The Magician. Would you like to fall alive into his hands?"

"No," I said. "I wouldn't."

I was enormously tired. I tried to focus my unsteady eyes on the dark, intense face bent impatiently toward me.

I asked: "When will we hear from you?"

"The only thing you'll hear is the radio. That will tell you whether the plot has succeeded or not. If it succeeds, you will know that my career as a Brazilian millionaire has been indefinitely postponed, and that you had better start running as fast as you can."

"Where should we run?"

"Toss up a coin. You have five hundred miles to go before you reach a border. Any border. You could try the coast, that's the way most of our defectors take. It doesn't really matter where you go if Rauss is after you."

"You don't sound very confident about stopping him."

"I happen to know him."

There was no longer anything appealing in his saturnine face. The gloss of cynical amusement had long worn away and the sardonic eyes were clouded over with a reflection of my own depression.

I followed him up the dusty stairs to the second floor where massed cobwebs and a litter of wartime debris blocked off the entrances to three yawning rooms. It was ice cold there, a ghostly emanation of forgotten years inhabited by God-only-knew what memories for the Nakomda man. He brooded in the doorways, touching dusty lintels, as if recalling faces and hearing voices and reliving unspeakable events.

I remembered what both Danilow and Zimstern had mentioned about the bad luck that had seemed to follow the partisans who had rescued the Library from the Germans; all had died violently except Danilow, the ruthless inheritor of the treasure. I seemed to feel their presence in the icy coldness of the empty rooms. Danilow also seemed to sense it; he shuddered suddenly and passed a slow hand across his eyes. I wondered what he saw in the lowering dark rooms, beyond the curtain of cobwebs and dust, what memories had thrust themselves upon him. What had he been like as a young leader of partisans? What had been his hopes and how had his men died?

We went back downstairs and into the cellar where he stood for a long time staring at the cases, touching the near edges with lingering fingers, nodding to himself.

He said remotely: "This should all be safe, no matter what happens here . . ."

After Danilow had left us, I stood for a time at the window— staring but not seeing. I felt remarkably alone.

Morning passed in silence. Kristin and I sat side-by-side on a wooden bench, huddled under two blankets. I had set and wound the ornate clock that occupied one whole corner of the downstairs hall and now the clock haunted me with its persistent ticking. I wished that there had been some way to halt the passing minutes and extend the deadline of the afternoon.

For all I knew, Danilow might be heading straight for a waiting firing squad in a Nakomda cellar. It wouldn't have taken Rauss long to discover how we had escaped and, even if Danilow did manage to avoid immediate arrest, the escape had been so hastily arranged that innumerable telltale threads must have been left unraveled for the conspirators to follow. Also, I couldn't put aside the thought of Karpovitch making one last attempt to secure the money which he so desperately needed to survive the plot. It would be unlike him to give up either the loot or the revenge. It was, I was sure, only a matter of time—time counted in hours—before one manhunt or the other swept us up again and, this time, there would be no miraculous deliverance from prison, only a savage enmity to be faced in a lonely forest. Time, that implacable enemy, threatened us everywhere I looked.

I was too exhausted to eat any of Danilow's provisions. Kristin nibbled on some bread and cheese. Later she held my hand as we listened to the radio hoping for a sign of change in the Chairman's program, some indication that the plotters' plans were going awry, but we heard nothing that could have suggested a change in anybody's plans. Even the weather, threatening in the night, had cleared up into a brilliant morning at the capital and, early as it was, a quarter of a million people had already started massing in the square where the Chairman would speak.

As noon drew near I could no longer doubt that the plotters were still in control and in full command. There was an interview with Rauss about the security arrangements for the Chairman's visit. His voice reflected only satisfaction and icy confidence. How could I have supposed otherwise? How could I have been so stupid as to hope? I stared at the white clock face as if to will the hands into immobility but the remorseless minutes ground on with a soft scraping of unoiled gears.

I was no longer willing to believe in miracles. I forced myself to walk away from the radio. The crackling bulletins followed me the length of the hall. My slurred footsteps frightened me a little; I knew that I was close to nervous exhaustion, the near limits of endurance. I smiled at Kristin, feeling as if my face were carved out of soapstone.

"Let's light a fire," I said. I didn't think it mattered any longer what happened to the lodge. We would soon be on the run again. I thought that a cheerful fire in the fireplace would take the chill off the way we felt, the chill that had nothing to do with temperature. Kristin did not object. So she has also ceased to hope, I thought; a fire could no longer threaten us since everything appeared to be over. I built the fire and lit it. The dry tinder blazed high into the chimney.

"Won't that make lots of smoke?" Kristin asked carefully and looked at me as if to make sure that she had read my mind correctly as to why I was disobeying Danilow's instructions.

"I don't suppose it matters any more. Do you?"

"It would be nice to think it did. Are you sure that it's now too late to hope for success?"

I pointed to the clock.

"Well," she said. "A lot could happen in three hours. Haven't we been through too much to give up now? Isn't there still something that we could do?"

"I don't know what. I think that we had better start planning how to get away. We have no transportation and nowhere to go. It's not a very encouraging beginning."

"We didn't have much more at Hetmanska Gora," she reminded me.

"We had a purpose and we had direction. The embassy was a goal. Now we'll be simply running for our lives."

"It would be silly to start running until we knew that we had no other choice."

I agreed that we would wait and listen to the Chairman's speech. Besides, I had no idea how to set about our second escape. We could, presumably, walk out of the forest along the buried trail, but that would only take us to the capital highway, the one location where the manhunt would be sure to begin. True, we were armed but, the thought of weapons seemed repellent and unrealistic; we could not allow our plans to depend on weapons. Fast transportation, warm clothing and a guide were what we had to have; these I could neither hire nor provide. I had no more money and, anyway, where would I find a guide and horses in the forest?

Kristin was right about the smoke, of course; it would soar high in the still and snowless air and attract attention. Our future visitors would be sure to spot it. But did the smoke need to draw only enemies? Why couldn't it do the same for a curious woodsman, woodcutter or peasant who might come to see what was going on in the abandoned lodge? They would have sleighs and horses since no one would be able to walk far in this snow, in such cold. Sleighs meant transportation. The peasants could provide sheepskin coats and hats, felt-lined boots and warm straw. They could be persuaded to guide us to the coast.

I felt excitement begin. Here was a chance, weak as it might be, but I had had no more than that at Hetmanska Gora. What would I use for money? Unsurprised, I found myself looking at Danilow's pistol, a clumsy-looking revolver of shining black steel.

I picked up the pistol, weighing it experimentally first in one in one hand then in the other; it felt awkward, heavy but not out of place. A month ago the thought of hijacking a sleigh would have been impossible for me. Now I found it logical and simple. If we were lucky, we could force someone to take us to the coast. There we could look for a sturdy fishing boat, one large enough to take us across the Baltic Sea to Sweden in the teeth of winter and the fierce winds that swept out of the north at this time of the year. We could obtain the boat the way we would obtain the sleigh; the thought of piracy was now no more foreign to me than that of hijacking and robbery on the highways.

For the time being I decided to keep my new excitement to

myself. There was no point in raising Kristin's hopes if my solution proved unrealistic. And, just in case our smoking chimney drew the wrong, unwelcome kind of visitors, I went outside to look at our defenses.

twenty-four

OUTSIDE, I was immediately frozen; colder than I had ever imagined possible, even colder than during our escape from Hetmanska Gora. After the mild warmth of the fire in the lodge, the dry coldness of a winter noon seemed to scrape my face. My breath hung motionless behind me as I moved. The corners of my mouth began to ache at once.

I walked around the house, inspecting the windows. They glowed a pale pink with the fire behind them. Snow and ice had begun to shift their patterns on the window panes, offering fresh shapes and textures: frosted branches, thistles: a miniature white forest.

I fingered the heavy shutters: three-inch planking seasoned to the hardness of iron, with a small heraldic device carved into the center. I peered down to read the motto under the device but it had been obliterated by years and weather. I thought it possible that the heavy shutters might stop a rifle bullet. I didn't think the conspirators would bring anything heavier than rifles. The door was even thicker, blacker with age and weather, and reinforced with brass studs and thick iron bosses. All this seemed satisfactory. I worried about the flammability of our would-be fortress, remembering what Danilow had told me and Zimstern had implied, but I decided that the danger of fire would be worse inside where the walls and flooring were bone dry. Outside, the snow and ice could foil arsonists.

All in all, I was satisfied. If Kristin and I were forced to fight for our lives in this place, I thought we could do it. I wouldn't let myself think beyond that.

I looked at the smoke, pieces of flying white ash and burned wood no bigger than snowflakes, and the myriad whirling sparks high in the branches of the giant oak. I thought that the smoke should be blacker and thicker to attract attention as far as the highway. The wind smeared it brownly under the vast-spread canopy of icicles and snow packed among the branches. Well, there was wet wood in plenty to throw on the fire.

I walked around the house and noted the ravine which tumbled precipitously to a frozen stream behind the house. The back wall was blank, without windows, nothing that invaders could use for an entrance. The ridge and the gulley would defy them if they tried to approach the lodge from this sheltered direction. There were two windows facing from the wings, one on each side of the building: small, narrow, glassless, solidly iced loopholes in the upper floor: too high for anyone to reach, too narrow to enter. Only the front of the lodge offered a way in with three shuttered windows on the upper floor and one each flanking the door downstairs. I decided that I would shutter both the downstairs windows and shoot through the door. The upper floor may have offered certain advantages for defense but I felt oddly ill at ease about it, as if a human presence in the empty rooms were an intrusion. I could see no obstacles, other than rolling dunes of snow, to mar my field of fire as far as the trees. My new vocabulary amused me: fields of fire, indeed. Very military. I felt an odd sense of elation, dismissed it as foolish, but didn't particularly mind when it returned at once.

The sound of birds startled me; I paused for a moment. A huge black flock had risen cawing in the forest, raucously indignant. At once the tree-wall answered with its cough and snarl; the silence was over. The harsh, riverlike murmur of the forest began again. In fact, I realized that there had been no silence at all;

the thick winter air had been full of dry, remorseless sound: grinding and whirring and so penetrating that it seemed to come from within the blood, chipping the bone with an abrasive whisper. I had scarcely noticed it, but now the persuasive sound of this collective menace filled all the space under the vaulted canopy of the trees.

I stamped my feet to warm them, moved my arms inside their difficult cocoon of clothes and fatigue. The dark chill of the forest had penetrated my bones. I listened to the distant anger of the crows.

All the events since my breakfast with Tommy Mackin at the club appeared momentarily before me and were understood. Neither the people nor the plots surprised me or mystified me any longer. I didn't question my involvement in conspiracies. Neither Hubertus Pohl, nor my work nor my way of life—the comfortable routines of so many years—interested me any more. I viewed them coldly and dispassionately like objects behind glass. I didn't think that I would ever again choose such a simple, selfish, uncommitted way of living, not even if there was a future to consider. I realized that whatever I did from now on would be something that I had never done before. Life, as I had thought of it in New York, no longer made sense. I would never again go hunting after relics, let relics stay buried. That's where they belonged: in the past, in their own time. If Kristin and I survived what was coming, our time would be the future.

And so with the Pontic Tribunals and the Romanowski Library. Let them remain a scholars' Holy Grail that is never found. After the Chairman's speech, in less than an hour, the world would have a need for Holy Grails; faith could become important again.

I looked at the brooding solidity of the lodge with mild astonishment. I had come so far to find the treasure that was hidden here, and the start of the adventure seemed so very long ago, that I could hardly believe that the treasure waited for me in the dry old lodge. I knew that I would look at it again with Kristin, to share with her the experience of touching and seeing the source of faith and inspiration of so many centuries. But I would not allow the library to be moved from here.

Why should it travel to America? Why should any one place be picked out as a sanctuary for human aspirations? Who really deserved to possess this treasure? No one played the game of international power politics with clean hands, no one seemed to be beyond reproach. It was only the degree of dirt that mattered and even that was impossible to determine at first sight.

I had been commissioned to insure the Library's preservation; I was to make it available to scholars. Well, I was a scholar of a kind and I would always know where the Library was hidden. And if the world ever returned to sanity and there was time, again, for beauty, reverence and inspiration, I could produce the Library. It seemed unlikely that I would ever want to. Let it stay where it is. The Library, and what it represented, could wait for more appreciative times.

I turned toward the house, again aware of the crows and ravens which now rose from near trees and circled the forest. I was very cold. I found it difficult to breathe in the suddenly still air.

twenty-five

WE SAT before the radio. Kristin was pale. Her face was stony, a beautiful white mask with staring black eyes.

"When is the speech due to begin?" she asked.

"Any minute now."

We were listening to an American commentator, one of a Delphic pair heard throughout the Western world. His broadcast, like a hundred others, would be simultaneously translated into every language. Orbiting satellites would bring it into every instrument in the listening world.

The day is clear and cold here, at the foot of the giant building, the Palace of Culture and Communication, the gift to the people of this capital from the Soviet Union. Millions are flocking into the snowy square. There is an air of tense expectation. The Chairman of the Soviet Union is expected to make the most significant announcement of Soviet policy since the beginning of the Cold War, the end of World War II. The whole world has been invited to attend through the modern facilities of international radio and television . . . It is, in effect, as if the whole world had come to this city today . . . a momentous occasion.

Total press, radio and television coverage . . . (the commentator said) facilities never before offered to Western reporters east of the barrier which, up to this day, had so bitterly divided the East from the West.

It is believed here, in this city, that what we shall shortly see and hear may well affect the future course of human affairs. More than a million people stand within sight of the draped balcony from which the Chairman will speak. They stand in silence, heads raised, waiting. As all of us are waiting. They have come from far as we have all come today to see . . . whether this will be, indeed . . . a day to remember . . .

Nothing like this had ever happened before in the long, troubled history of the world and of East-West relations, the commentator said.

He was reminded of another historical moment . . . the return of Neville Chamberlain from Munich in 1938 . . . *the assurance of peace for our time* . . . even though that assurance preceded World War II by only a few months.

But there is a feeling here today that the time has come for all men to live together no matter what their systems and . . . perhaps . . . something of that feeling has gripped the world today. Peace has been too long absent.

I could imagine the tense, waiting crowds.

The preliminaries of the program were under way: minor speeches, welcomes and introductions, a concert by massed military bands, hopeful commentaries.

I got up and went to the window. Something about the scene (white glare of snow in the early afternoon sun, blue shadows sloping among roots and deadfall) brought a vague warning, an unspecified alarm. The wind had fallen away, and the suddenly unburdened air was particularly still. The silent tree-wall mocked me with its artificial stillness, the false and watchful lack of motion and sound. I had the feeling that each time I took my eyes off anything, inside the lodge as outside, intense activity broke out silently and that this stealthy frenzy, somehow touched with malice, ceased at once when I swung my eyes toward it.

I wished that I had closed the shutters while I had been outside.

I turned and saw that Kristin had come up to join me.

"Nervous?" she asked.

I could see how very frightened she was then. I put my arms around her. She did not tremble but she moved against me. She said that hers had been a stupid question: "I should disregard it."

"I wish I could answer it. But I don't know if I'm nervous or not. I can't really feel anything. Nothing makes sense now."

"I'm terrified," she said. "I can't believe that it's going to happen in just a few moments. And we'll just sit here and listen to it happening and won't be able to do anything about it."

"Oh," I said. "You mean the assassination?"

"Yes, of course. Wasn't that what you were thinking about?"

"My mind has slid away from that entire subject."

"It's all I can think of."

"That's why I can't imagine it. Who could?"

"How could it ever be allowed to happen?"

"It didn't happen overnight."

"That's just what I mean! How on earth did we all come to this? Why couldn't someone have done something to prevent this? Couldn't anyone see where we were all heading? Oh, I don't mean the Chinese . . . and this conspiracy. I mean all the conditions that make war possible, whether hot or cold. Where do these terrible things start, anyway? Why can't the starting point be clearly recognizable to all? There ought to be a warning sign somewhere, but there isn't, and we all march ourselves, over and over again, step by step, into this kind of horror. And now we've really done it, haven't we?"

I pulled her toward me.

"Oh God," she said. "I can't believe it. Step by step. Each one taking us a little nearer, a little closer to the precipice. All that talk about peace . . . all those politicians! Didn't any of them know what they were doing?"

Oh my dear love, I thought. I asked, gently:

"Couldn't you find an easier question?"

"But it's so stupid," she said. "So thoroughly stupid! Why do we elect stupid men?"

"They haven't all been stupid, have they?"

She said: "I don't want to get hysterical. If there was only something we could do!"

I kissed her.

And then the commentator's voice spiraled with excitement. We heard a quick, roaring flutter of anxiety from the gray masses marshaled in the square as the commentator reported an unexplained shooting in a neighboring area. Some kind of malcontent, rumored to be a possible assassin, had been trapped and shot.

What happened, Kristin wished to know.

"Somebody has been shot."

"It has to be Brown!"

"Well, no," I said gently. "It could have been Field just as easily . . . or Danilow, if he was still alive. This could be part of Rauss's preparations to set the stage for terror and hysteria."

I heard a wavering note of fear in the commentator's voice, a voice made famous by its bland assurance and kindly authoritativeness. Now it climbed an octave and fell uncertainly.

There have been rumors of a plot to embarrass the Chairman. Several persons were arrested last night and this morning, some prominent . . . One report implicated a high-ranking officer of the Security Police. Police activity has been heavy in the past few days . . . it was unusually heavy last night and this morning. In an interview three hours ago, General Rauss, the national security director, said that every precaution had been taken to protect the Chairman. But here in this historic square where a million persons have waited since daybreak the air is charged with tension. Rumors run from person to person . . . anxiety is mounting. Another such incident could be catastrophic.

The murmur of the crowds had now become a sustained roar.

And now the mood of the thousands gathered here has changed. It's an explosive, almost angry mood. The tension has reached an unbearable pitch. No matter whether these uneasy masses are Communist or not, they have come here to hear a message of hope. The rumors, the extraordinary security precautions, reports of arrests and even executions that have been circulating through the capital this morning, have set everyone on edge. And if an attempt were to be actually made on the Chairman's life, the consequences could be beyond comprehension. Everyone knows that no matter what measures are taken, there is always someone . . . somewhere . . . some deranged mind . . . which can . . .

I could imagine the assassin waiting among the cornices and ballustrades on one of the placid, neo-classic roofs that had so delighted me. I imagined him as Brown; the cold white face would be settling close to the stock of his rifle. I supposed that it would have to be a rifle rather than a pistol, and wondered if the conspirators had compressed-air rifles in their arsenal. I didn't see why they shouldn't have them.

The thin black cross of the telescopic sight would be moving now back and forth across the draped balcony that the commentator so meticulously described, as if to stroke the scarlet hangings, massed banners, golden wreaths of wheatsheaf, the hammers and sickles.

I listened to the nervous roar of the waiting crowds.

Kristin's eyes, her face, indeed her whole body, were turned to the radio. No part of her appeared to be moving; she did not seem to breathe. Only her eyes, fixed with absolute intensity, wide and unblinking, betrayed her with tears. She cried without a sound, motionless as if her narrow body had been marbled over.

And then an inward tremor passed over her. A scarcely noticeable shift in lighting and color showed that her lips had begun to tremble and the tremor spread to the stiff muscles of her face and the dilated eyes. The shadows underneath her cheekbones began to move, compressing and expanding. Her eyelids fluttered faster than eyesight could follow. Her body moved violently forward and she was suddenly out of her chair and on her feet.

"Is there one chance that Danilow . . . Field . . . could still . . ."

I shook my head.

"I don't see how they could. It was a wild chance at best. If they had succeeded we would have had some evidence by now."

"What about all these arrests the man just talked about? Couldn't that mean something?"

"Rauss was still in command when they interviewed him."

"But that was more than three hours ago. Everything could have changed in three hours."

"That's true, but I wouldn't hope."

"Why not?"

"I don't think we should build up any more illusions. I think hope would be unreasonable at this point. I think it's better to simply accept what is going to happen."

"Accept it! I can't even believe it!"

"Nobody ever will."

"I think I'm going mad," she said. "This is impossible."

"Yes. But it's true. Can you accept an impossible truth?"

"Oh God, I don't know."

I could imagine the festive balcony with its flags and ornaments and its dark interior that had begun to fill with the shapes of men.

The welcoming roar of the crowds and the nonprofessional excitement of the commentator told me that the Chairman and his entourage were beginning to emerge, pacing with easy majesty, like sated banquet guests leaving the midnight hall. The Chairman's position would be in the center, flanked by the national president and premier, with many others taking their places behind, filling every corner of the balcony. I could imagine the cold eyes, hard faces, stern shoulders in boxlike greatcoats, heavy furs. They would stand in smiling rows, eyes resting with the serenity of undisputed power on the crowd below, while the crowd welcomed them. There would be that angular polished sameness to their Eastern European faces under the hats and fur caps: faces made familiar by the public prints but, in mass, undistinguishable from each other. The announcer named them in order of appearance on the balcony; he also named Rauss.

I looked quickly at Kristin to see if she had noticed, but if she had she gave no sign of it.

I listened to the speculative roar of the crowd: tense party regiments brought from every secret corner of the world to hear the new standing orders for mankind and to witness what was going to happen. I heard their sudden silence and then the brilliant speech. I listened to the wasted rhetoric, the promised pacts of friendship that had come too late, the call for open borders (soon to be permanently closed), the call for destruction of all nuclear weapons. I strained to catch the moment when the Chairman would falter and choke on his words. There would be no gunfire with the compressed-air rifle. The mild *ping* would be lost beneath the roar of the stricken crowds; their cry of anguish would rock across the world.

The lifting of restrictions on freedom of expression . . . freedom of conscience everywhere . . . freedom to seek new social and political forms . . . Peace . . . end to the Cold War . . . coexistence brought to its only logical conclusion in cooperation . . . the wealth of the world to be thrown into service of all humanity . . .

I listened, waited. I could not look at Kristin.

And now, I thought, the assassin is taking aim. The thin black cross of his telescopic sights moves across the body of the stocky man who stands with upraised arms on the blood-red balcony.

The crowd had gone wild. Their roar drowned out the high, excited voice of the commentator. And then there was another sound.

As if unable to transmit the excitement of the moment, the radio blew up; all its multicolored components were momentarily visible: tubes, coils, wires, small bulbs, odd shapes disintegrating.

A breath of silence was followed by the rattle of machine-gun fire which burst in with an icy blast of air from outside. The windows splintered and the great skull of an ancient elk sailed off the wall which was suddenly pitted with rows of dusty explosions.

Glass showered down. I threw myself face-down on the floor with Kristin beside me. I couldn't see in the dust and smoke. Where had the smoke come from? I had not noticed it before.

But the fresh air rushing through smashed windows blew the smoke about in thick clouds.

"Are you all right?"

This time she heard me. "Yes."

The crash of falling furniture, the exploding mirror, and the remorseless hammering of bullets on the walls and door, had deafened us both.

I looked at Kristin's face under mine; her eyes were enormous. I pulled my upper body over her while shards of glass and splinters sharp as razors spattered the floor around us.

And suddenly the sound was over; the silence seemed explosive in my head. I felt the wind sweep over me through the broken door. It took me several moments to find my voice, to whisper:

"You're not hurt? You're sure?"

"Yes. Are you all right?"

"I think so." I looked up at the bullet-pocked walls, the ruin and debris and at myself. What blood there was had come from cuts, all minor.

"Who are they?"

"Rauss's men, Karpovitch, what's the difference?" Then I choked on smoke. "Goddamit! I wish I could have got you out of here."

I thought: If only breathing wasn't so difficult in the smoke. Where had the smoke come from? Perhaps a part of the house had been set on fire. Well, if that's the case, we're really in for it.

Kristin said: "What are we going to do?"

"I don't know. Can you use that pistol?"

"I used to fool about with a twenty-two on Uncle Per's ranch. It was a long time ago."

"This thing looks like it might work the same way. Could you . . . shoot somebody?"

She looked at me soberly and nodded.

"I think so."

"Then watch the left window. If anything shows in it, shoot at it. I've got to look outside. I'd like to know how many we are up against."

"Are we going to fight them?"

I looked at her, touched her face.

"If it's Karpovitch, there isn't any choice. He means to kill us. Maybe there is some kind of a chance with Rauss, maybe not . . ."

I crawled to the door which hung grotesquely askew on one hinge, and put my eye to the crack formed by the splintered black oak and its icy frame.

"What do you see?" Kristin asked. "Can you see anything?"

"Not much. The clearing. There's no one out in the open. I see a little smoke. It's almost like a mist rising around a few trees, about waist high for a normal man."

"Is that where they are?"

"I suppose so. There seem to be four positions, about ten yards apart. We couldn't hope to leave the house without being spotted."

"Can you see anyone?"

"No. Wait. Yes. There's one. He's looking up from behind a tree. Now he is standing up!"

"Be careful!"

At once machine-gun fire raked the lodge again, downstairs and upstairs. The bullets whined about us. I ducked down. When I looked up again, the man I had seen earlier had moved into the clearing. He disappeared suddenly behind the snowdrifts. Then the barrage lifted and a man shouted: "Shippe! I want to talk to you!"

It was Karpovitch's voice.

twenty-six

NIGHT CAME so swiftly that neither of us noticed it until it was there. The white plate of a crooked moon, and another light that we could not at first identify, lit up the glazed trunks of huge trees. An animal roared nearby and crashed through the thickets; the sound of its passing died fastidiously in the absorbent darkness of the forest roof.

Stray shots thundered against the forest wall from time to time. The riflemen were hidden. Their silhouettes showed occasionally near the fires they had lit at the edge of the clearing.

I sat on the floor under the right window, raising myself up on my haunches to peer into the moonlight. I had put out the kerosene lantern so that the pink glow would not betray us to snipers. I had hoped that, with nightfall, there might occur an opportunity for escape. But the moon had lighted the clearing and turned its snow surface into a white sheet on which every shadow stood out stark and black. The light grew rapidly as if an auxiliary red moon had been hung in the sky where I couldn't see it. I knew that a great fire was burning nearby. Sometimes I even thought that I could hear its hungry roaring in the wind. Smoke seeped into the lodge; it lay in acrid strips under the ceiling. And yet the lodge was nowhere on fire, I knew. I had gone over the house to make sure of that much shortly after nightfall.

I looked at Kristin. She was facing the window, the gun in her hand, her head and hair bright against the scarred walls and shattered furniture. I felt a deep resentment, knowing that I had finally found a reason for working and living. It struck me as particularly cruel to lose her so quickly: a spiteful and gratuitous piece of mockery. I was determined that she should survive.

And now a strong ground-wind swept up so that the fire, where ever it was, burned fiercely. It roared like an express train through the forest. I supposed that the besiegers must have built a bonfire in the ravine on the blind side of the lodge. They had tried arson earlier; a man had run up with what looked like a five-gallon gasoline container. I had shot at him and missed but he had dropped the can, which now lay blackly in the bright-lit snow, and dodged back under cover.

Snow swirled into the house through the glassless windows. I saw sparks spiraling in the clearing. I thought that ice and snow would probably protect the old building unless the fire was so close that it melted the snow and dried the old timbers. Then the lodge would become a furnace in moments. But the smoke was the more immediate problem.

I lay down on one elbow, closer to the floor. Here I could still find some unpolluted air. I could no longer feel Danilow's rifle in my freezing hands. Hunger, exhaustion and the ache of my small wounds had driven me close to my limits. My eyes felt as if they had been rubbed raw with sandpaper then sheeted with lead. I had no doubt that Karpovitch's next attack would be the last; all my resources had been expended.

I propped myself up by the window sill, peered out. Karpovitch was still in the hollow behind the nearest snowdrift. He had a cheerful fire going. He had been quiet for some time. Now he began to call again:

"Shippe! Are you still alive?"

I said nothing. Images without substance moved across my eyes.

"Shippe! I want to talk to you! Come out!"

My frozen hand on the rifle stock jerked in a sudden reflex. A single shot thundered into the sky.

Karpovitch laughed.

"What are you shooting at? Come out! I have news for you! How would you like to know what happened in the capital? Or don't you care about that any more?"

Care? No, I thought. I don't suppose I care; everything is over.

"An old friend of yours is here," Karpovitch went on. "Brown! He saw it all happen."

The image of the pale face and flat eyes filled with an unseeing malice shook me back into consciousness.

"How come Rauss didn't murder him?" I cried out in a cracked voice wobbly with hysteria.

"So! You can talk! Come out and stop being a fool! Nobody knows where you are, none of your friends can help you."

"What happened to Danilow?"

"He is dead. We met him on the road."

"How did you know where we were?"

"Easy! But I'm tired of shouting. Either you come out or I am going in. And don't try anything heroic!"

Then he began to laugh again. "Shippe! Your roof has just caught fire! I thought that old tree would never burn down. Well, you'll have to come out now, whether you like it or not."

I sank back to the floor. My eyes were watering with smoke and my throat was raw. Kristin crawled nearer to me.

I whispered: "Did you hear him?"

"Yes. What are you going to do?"

I stared at her, then shook my head. I didn't want to make any more decisions.

"Let him come in," she urged.

"In here? Karpovitch?"

"Yes. Have we really anything to lose?"

The smoke had blotted out the top of the stairs. I wondered if the fire had now broken through the roof to the upstairs rooms.

"Shippe!" Karpovitch shouted. "Your last chance!"

"What chance?" I asked. "What is he talking about?"

"Perhaps he wants something."

"And is that a chance? We've nothing to trade."

"Perhaps he thinks we have. Let him come in."

I shook my head, then nodded. I heard the swelling roar of the fire and thought that I could feel a gradual tremor starting through the house as if the old building was also suddenly awakening and seeking life aware of its danger.

"All right!" I called. "Come in!"

Karpovitch was laughing.

"None of your tricks now, Shippe! No more idiotic heroics! My men are coming around the house. They'll blow you all to hell if you don't behave. We have about ten minutes before your house caves in. You give me what I want and I'll let you go."

"He won't," I told Kristin, wondering where my odd voice was coming from. "He'll kill us."

"Perhaps he won't. Perhaps something will happen to give us a chance."

"What could happen now?"

"I don't know. But there is no chance at all unless we get him within reach."

I watched Karpovitch coming clumsily through the deep snow, thick in his coarse furs like a menacing animal, his head grown hugely in a bushy hat. One of his arms was in a black sling. I had forgotten that I had broken his wrist while we had been struggling in the car; I didn't think that he had forgotten. His other arm cradled a submachine gun. I wondered how he could fire it with only one hand. He kicked the shattered door and it fell apart.

"Smoke's getting thicker, eh? Your upper floor is well alight. I know these old houses. The ceiling will come down on you in about five minutes."

"On you too," I said.

Karpovitch shrugged, smiling maliciously.

"It was your fire, Shippe, that dried off that old oak. Then sparks got the tree burning. That got your roof nice and dry and now your house is burning. Well, it was time that one of your stupidities caught up with you."

I said nothing, unable to think.

"How do you do it?" Karpovitch went on. "You are a clumsy, incompetent amateur . . . you blunder into situations that would defy the most experienced agent, ruin the most painstakingly planned operations, and somehow you blunder out again. You survive everything. I am beginning to think that you are the real magician."

"What do you want?" I said.

"But it's all over now. There is no escape for you this time. It's all finished in the capital and my time is short. Rauss is shooting everyone who had anything to do with the conspiracy. I have no doubt that he'll remember about me."

"Rauss?" I said. "Rauss is shooting the conspirators?"

"Of course! What do you think? Washington warned the government here. As soon as Rauss saw that the game was up he started covering his tracks. He has an instinct for survival. Last night and this morning he rounded up, court-martialed and shot everyone connected with the plot except you and me."

"So there was no assassination?"

"Not even an attempt. Rauss will probably get a half dozen medals."

"Don't his superiors know about his part in the conspiracy?"

"What kind of fool are you? Who is alive to tell them? Perhaps you told someone in your embassy about Rauss but do you think the CIA would give away a blackmail plum like that? They probably have Rauss working for them already."

Karpovitch's laughter was laden with a dark intensity. He was wholly coiled within himself. He did not seem to hear the violent roar of the fire upstairs or see the scarlet lines which had begun to spread between the ceiling timbers. All his senses were totally focussed on the dark game he had come to play.

"And so by virtue of mutual allegiance, Rauss is now almost a countryman of yours. Doesn't that make you proud? You could have saved yourself, your woman, and even Danilow if you had simply stayed quiet in your embassy. But you're a stupid, virtuous, idealistic fool and so you had to go blundering about until you had accomplished what virtue and stupidity and ideals invariably accomplish and that's the destruction of everything that has meaning for you. Now do you see yourself, Shippe? Where did it all get you? What good did you do? Officially there never was any conspiracy. No one is ever going to admit how close they came, this time, to blowing up the world . . . not Washington, not Moscow and certainly not the Chinese. They'll simply try it somewhere else at a better time. Nothing has changed, the same old game goes on. Nothing you've done will make any difference."

"What do you want?"

"The money, fool. Did you think I'd let that get away from me?"

Karpovitch's face hung like a disembodied narrow fox mask in the smoke before me. I could no longer hear him through the roar of the fire and the deep groaning of the house as beams parted and gutted timbers shifted.

The house shook and quivered. Restless pools of light began to appear on the walls and along the stairs. The red lines overhead began to part and rivulets of flame spilled out of the ceiling.

I was aware of men running outside and calling and of Karpovitch shouting. Kristin's white face swam into view as she stared at the cascades of flame splashing the floor around us. My lungs seemed on fire. I heard as if from an immense distance the sharp explosion of disintegrating walls. The ceiling had vanished. A mass of flame hung overhead, suspended by its own whirling vacuum. I felt flames brush my face; my clothes would be burning in a moment. I had the unreal sensation of watching an interminable silent film running in slow motion. Karpovitch shouted and retreated into the doorway, his furs smoldering. His mouth moved but I heard no sound. The short barrel of the submachine gun came up. And suddenly I felt blind rage. I ran at Karpovitch pulling Kristin with me through a stinging red and yellow shower, and saw the barrel of the submachine gun twist upward in Karpovitch's one uninjured hand, and heard the crash of the bullets sprayed over my head. Then I was upon him, and the submachine gun was torn from his hand and he fell heavily into the fire. A man loomed in the doorway and I turned the weapon upon him and saw him blown out into the snow. Then a twisted, colorless face swung in front of me, the reptilian eyes no longer flat but oddly bulging in the firelight, and I went on shooting as I ran toward it and this face, too, vanished suddenly.

And then my lungs were full of icy air. Kristin was behind me. We ran through the fire-tinted snow. The submachine gun fell out of my hands. We heard a booming sound and looked back. The lodge had vanished. In its place stood a column of fire that rose beyond the glittering canopies of ice, snow and branches, shooting a whirling mass of stars into the sky.

I heard myself ask in a grave, stiff voice if Kristin was all right, if she could walk to the track where, undoubtedly, Karpovitch had left his transportation. She wished to know where we would go in Karpovitch's car.

"To the capital. Once we get to the embassy, Field will know what to do."

I got behind the steering wheel but Kristin pushed me gently to the passenger side. Neither she nor I had anything to say.

The sloping countryside around us was gray with the light of a new day; the night was over. I thought about the night. I saw again the swaying pillar of fire which had destroyed the lodge and which had been a funeral pyre for Karpovitch. I wondered how long the fire would burn before the new snow that had begun to fall would stifle the embers and bury the ruins.

Then the woods thinned out, the flat open country spread in front of us. I looked for the spires of the capital in the cold red light of the new day.